Marti Leimbach is the author of several novels, including the international bestseller, *Dying Young*, which was made into a major motion picture starring Julia Roberts, and the acclaimed *Daniel Isn't Talking* (2007), inspired by the story of her autistic child. Born in Washington DC, she moved to England in 1990; she lives in Berkshire with her husband and two children.

www.martileimbach.com

Also by Marti Leimbach

MARTI LEIMBACH

The Man from Saigon

FOURTH ESTATE • *London*

To Alastair, always

FT Pbk

First published in Great Britain in 2009 by Fourth Estate
An imprint of HarperCollins*Publishers*
77–85 Fulham Palace Road, London W6 8JB
www.4thestate.co.uk

Visit our authors' blog: www.fifthestate.co.uk
Love this book? www.bookarmy.com

A catalogue record for this book is available from the British Library

ISBN 978-0-00-730599-5

Typeset in Minion by Palimpsest Book Production Limited,
Grangemouth, Stirlingshire

Printed in Great Britain by Clays Ltd, St Ives plc

Mixed Sources
Product group from well-managed
forests and other controlled sources
www.fsc.org Cert no. SW-COC-1806
© 1996 Forest Stewardship Council
FSC

FSC is a non-profit international organization established to promote the
responsible management of the world's forests. Products carrying the FSC
label are independently certified to assure consumers that they come
from forests that are managed to meet the social, economic and
ecological needs of present and future generations.

Find out more about HarperCollins and the environment at
www.harpercollins.co.uk/green

I

The first shots came as they were flying northeast toward Danang. Over the terrific noise of the engine and rotors, she could hear a *pinging* sound, something like coins being lobbed against the metal where she was sitting. It wasn't particularly loud, and didn't sound remarkable or worrying. For many minutes she sat stiffly in the nylon seat of the helicopter, the wind rifling across her trouser legs, sending her field jacket back so that she could feel a button pushing against her neck, being aware of many things, but not the pinging sound, the bullets directed at her, at all of them, as they spun above a canopy of jungle.

She had much to distract her from the pinging: the roar of the engine as the chopper skimmed over the tops of trees, the throbbing of the rotors, the explosions of fire from the door gunners, the effort she made to keep from being sick. It was a while before she even thought about it. She only registered the gravity of the sound because she felt a force behind her, a sudden pushing in of metal as though a fist had pressed the fuselage of the chopper inward, feeling mildly uncomfortable and new. The place where the metal had bent was low on her back, just above her belt. Had the bullet passed through the side of the chopper, it would have found a home in her right kidney. When she reached back to check that it was not her imagination, that there really was a small, convex lump behind her, she felt the hot metal at the same time as a rising panic, a kind of insistence from inside her that she respond to the assault, as involuntary as a sneeze.

It may have been that her body knew even before she clocked it in her mind that they were being shot at; that they were being hit. When she realized the sound she'd been hearing was of bullets meeting the skin of the chopper she found she had to control herself as she might a bucking horse, staying focused, intent, sitting the ride as the chopper dipped and swerved, as the pinging sound seemed to dissolve all others, so that it felt to her that the volume had been turned down, that the whole of the earth was silent, except for this one noise. She felt a kind of last-minute, hopeless panic, her life opening before her. Not her life passing year to year in a flash as it is said to do at such moments, nothing like that. Only where she was, and that she'd had a choice some time back, not now, and that she'd made the wrong choice. It was a feeling of being trapped and desperate, of having been cornered by her own mistakes.

She did not look at her colleague, her friend, Son. She knew he did not like being so close to American marines, that he did not like this particular route into Danang, flying over the jungle. There were always VC there, cloaked by the jungle's thick canopy, willing to take a few quick shots in case they got lucky. Son had warned her, but she had not taken it in. Now, she could not bring herself to look at him. Nor did she watch the door gunners or turn to see the pilot. In fact, she could not see properly; every nerve seemed to focus inward at the terror brewing inside her.

If she'd had the presence of mind, she'd not have blamed the enemy, or the pilot, or command operations—not even the war, itself, for what was happening, for what more might happen—but would have cast the blame on her own poor judgment for getting on the chopper in the first place. For

4

every small, seemingly inconsequential decision that had led her here, to this place, right now. Under fire, she found it hard to breathe or swallow or make a noise. More than anything, she wanted to run, which was of course not possible, and the fact that she could not run, that she was caged and airborne and entirely at the mercy of whatever would happen next, was almost unbearable.

She wrapped her hands over her head, over her eyes. She stared down at the floor and watched as a bullet made a mark there, a little rise of hot aluminum not far from her foot and she wished she'd followed the advice she'd read about traveling by helicopter in Vietnam, which was not only to wear a flak jacket, but to sit on one as well.

And then the pinging stopped. She waited for it to begin again, but there was no sound. She heard the chaos of voices and gunfire, wind and rotors, loud and relentless, hammering at her skull, but the pinging was gone. She felt something inside her shift and she was able finally to look up, scanning the faces of the others. She looked at Son. His black hair stood straight up, a result of sweat and wind. He tried to smile but his mouth was dry and taut so that all he managed to do was squint and meet her eyes with his reassuring gaze. One of the gunners was intent on unjamming his gun, the other so pale she thought for a moment he would faint and fall out of the open door. The gunner's shirt was wet, as though someone had poured a bucket of water across his chest, and she watched as the wind dried it little by little, all signs of the terror of the last few minutes quietly disappearing.

Someone began to laugh. The pilot whooped and the gunner with the jammed M60 suddenly opened fire at no particular target. They had flown through it; they had won this moment. It wasn't long before they could see the sands stretching east-ward toward the South China Sea, the chopper landing safely in Danang. They trotted out, inspecting the fuselage for dings, for all those little holes that meant bullets. She walked around the helicopter, finding the area outside where she'd been sitting, looking up at the dented metal, the pocket where she'd felt the heat, the sharp splinters of metal beginning to fracture. The others were pointing to more serious breaks in the chopper, but she stared only at that one place where the bullet hadn't quite broken through. Nothing had come of it. She would tell herself this thin truth for many days: while in the shower at the press center, while standing in line at the USO for burgers, while drifting off in thought when she was supposed to be interviewing someone, she would insist that nothing happened. The bullet had fallen back through the sky; the chopper had touched down like a giant trembling bird; everything ended the way it ought to have, with them safely on the ground, the heat gathering round them as the rotors slowed. It was a July afternoon and the air was still.

Shall I take a photograph? Son asked her, nodding up at the chopper, at the scar in the metal that held her attention. It seemed so innocuous now, the bullet hole, like the head of a lion mounted on a wall.

She told him no, the words coming out quickly, perhaps a little too loudly, as though he'd asked for something inappropriate and personal. Then she said, *I didn't mean to sound like that. Take the picture. Go ahead.*

He brought the camera to his eye, framed the photograph, adjusted the focus, and released the shutter. They walked together across the airfield with their packs and cameras and she suddenly ran forward and was sick on the dirt by the fence-line. Son waited, then carried her pack for her.

You might one day want it, he said. *That picture.*

She was wrung out of emotions. She felt places in her body that were like bruises, the result of clenched muscles. She shook her head and wondered why anyone would want that photograph. Why would they keep such a thing? She did want

6

it, not then but many months later when she was packing for home. It was among the few mementos she took with her.

A month before, in Saigon, a guy had given her a mimeographed pamphlet written by another reporter, the pages stapled together, corners curled, the title stamped across the front in capital letters: HANDBOOK FOR NEWSMEN IN VIETNAM. It was written during the years when the war was still young, a small affair with none of the sense of increasing disaster that hung about it now. Its author mixed practical advice with his own, idiosyncratic observations about the locals, warning reporters never to travel without ID papers, for example, and that the Vietnamese will always tell you what they think you want to hear. Nobody spoke much about the *Handbook*; everybody read it and pretended they had not. In fact, the reporter she borrowed it from made a point of saying he did not want it returned.

They were in a bar, a group of other newsmen around them, enjoying the air conditioning and the darkness that contrasted with the extreme light outside. She had arrived exhausted into Tan Son Nhut airport sixteen hours earlier, the plane diving toward the landing strip as though it meant to bury itself there. She'd never been to Asia, or covered a war. Now she found herself in a bar that might as well have been in New York or Chicago. She didn't know what to expect. She felt a little disoriented. The chatter of the reporters confused her; she couldn't even figure out what they were talking about—this infantry, that unit. Drinking did not help, but she certainly was not going to sit in the bar surrounded by men drinking scotch and order a ginger ale. The reporter who had asked her to meet him said he had something for her, and that something turned out to be a copy of the *Handbook*. He gave it to her along with his business card, his home number handwritten on the reverse side.

Let me know when you get back, he said. *I'd like to hear how it went.* He was ten years older than her, maybe fifteen, the beginnings of gray in his hair making his head appear to shine. He looked as though he felt a little sorry for her. He regarded her as one might a younger sister, even a child.

She smiled. *You don't think I'll last two weeks, do you?*

He was taken aback, though he tried not to show it. *I didn't say that. Anyway, it depends on where you go.*

She laid the *Handbook* on the table next to their drinks. *So where did you go?* she asked.

He brushed the question aside. *You'll notice how slim it is, the* Handbook. *That's because you really can't tell people what they need to know. But read it anyway. Definitely read it.*

He smiled. He explained he was leaving for New York the following day and all he could offer by way of good advice was for her to go home now. Or at least soon. *It's hard enough for a man,* he said. *Though being a woman will have one advantage. You'll be the first on at the airstrip, that's for sure.*

She nodded. She didn't know exactly what he meant and yet she felt to admit this would embarrass them both, so she filed the words away in her head: *first on at the airstrip.*

The drink came to an end. The man smiled and then looked right at her for a single, long minute as though trying to memorize her face.

I'll be fine, she said. It was odd that he should be so concerned. It made her nervous—not of him, but of where she was, what she was doing. These were the earliest hours of the earliest days, long before bullets or chopper rides, before anything at all. She said she'd be fine but she had no way of knowing if this would be the case. She hadn't really thought there could be any other outcome, until now.

He took a long breath. *You're awfully young,* he said, *or maybe it's me. I've gotten old here.* He finished his drink in one long swallow. Then he stood, shook his head as though to push away a thought, and flicked his ash into his empty glass. She extended her hand to shake his, and he took her fingers, drawing her forward and planting a soft kiss on her forehead. He nodded slowly, then turned away, holding a hand up at his shoulder as he went. He left the *Handbook* on the bar table for her as one might an old magazine, disregarding entirely the warning in the pamphlet's introduction that the contents were confidential.

She read that she must bring a canteen, a poncho, zinc oxide, a hat, malaria pills. Never to go out with any unit smaller than a company. Bring pencils as well as pens because pens dried up in the heat and pencils broke or needed sharpening. Halazone, iodine, chlorine. She was told by those around her to be careful; some even recommended she not leave the ever-tightening boundary of the city. In the hotel's narrow bed, she passed her first sleepless jet-lagged nights with the *Handbook* across her knees, scanning a flashlight across the words on each mimeographed page. In the middle of the night, just upon falling asleep, she would suddenly jerk awake, asking herself frankly how on earth anyone thought she could do the job of a foreign correspondent, a war correspondent, because she was quite sure she could not. She told herself it was normal to feel this way, that everybody must have their doubts. Then she doubted that, too.

She discovered it was hard to function in Saigon. The electricity didn't always work. The water came out rusty from the taps. She drew herself maps, wrestled with the foreign money, drenched her clothes in sweat trying to get used to a climate that seemed from another planet entirely. One day she saw school children file past a dog that had died outside the school gates. The children walked over the stiffened legs or hopped above the bloated body. One of the boys got a stick and hit the dog's ribs as though it was a *piñata* that had failed to burst open its sweets. A few others stood around, watching. Then another kicked the dead body. She went back the next day and the dog was still there, most of it.

She had plenty of time to read the *Handbook* because she found it impossible to sleep. The traffic was like some background record that kept repeating itself: screeching tires, honking horns, exhausts backfiring, and engines that moaned and spluttered under the slow poison of inappropriate fuel. That ended shortly after curfew at eleven, but then there was all the noise from the assortment of odd guests at the hotel where she stayed. Some nights they arrived drunk from clubs, speaking at the tops of their voices, playing music, or kicking a soccer ball down the halls. Fights broke out between the drunken ones and those who had regular jobs that required early rising. It was not unusual to hear an argument conducted in three different languages, and once in a while it got physical.

The hotel's owner was a middle-aged balding man named Thanh. He had a mustache like two sets of toothbrush bristles stuck above his lip, and an open, sad face. He seemed particularly burdened by the noisy guests and was concerned, too, about their impact on the quieter ones. Even so, it did no good at all when he knocked door to door along the corridors at midnight with the question, *They boddering you?*, while further down the hall came shouts of laughter.

I was asleep, she always lied.

Even when all was peaceful at the hotel, it was still only a couple steps up from camping. Insects trailed her wherever she went, crossing whatever barrier or combination of sprays she used, bringing up itchy swellings on her skin. When she did sleep, she managed it only by putting a pillow over her head to block out the noise. Reading was good. It helped her to believe she was learning something useful and she knew there was much to learn.

10

In those early days she could not have understood what she had gotten into. For example, she paid no attention to the *Handbook*'s suggestion to pack belts and field straps—materials that could be made into a tourniquet—as she didn't think she was going anywhere she might be shot. She glanced over instructions on first aid because she thought there were specific people who did that—others, not her. Okay, so she had seen some kids beating the corpse of a dog. And she'd noticed, too, how many people with crudely amputated limbs begged along the streets. But she hadn't made the connection yet. She didn't realize that people could play football down a hallway, walk outside and be blown up by a little anti-personnel mine strategically fixed beneath a car. She was still under the impression the war could be contained, a thing over there, something that had to be arrived at quite deliberately. She didn't realize.

A lot of Vietnam correspondents have a story of how they came to the country: chosen by accident, paid for their own ticket by winning a game show, confused with another guy, filled in for someone else on R&R and the person never came back. Susan was no different—the choice to send her seemed random, the end result of a chain of assumptions. She was working for a women's magazine and had a private interest in horse training—it was really the combination of those two facts that had brought her into the war. One long summer in '66 she moonlighted for the police department, desensitizing their horses to gunfire, preparing them to cover student protests, city riots, rallies. The job required learning to shoot a pistol, launch smoke grenades from the saddle, and move the horses away from rings of fire, then toward them again—hours of this until they would happily jump through them. *What we need here,* said one of the officers, a transplant from the Southwest, a guy fond of flicking his hair back, of swaggering cowboy style into the barn in the early hours and staring right down at her

11

ass as she worked, *what we need here is a cow-y pony that can separate one man from another in a crowd, you know what I mean? A bolshie sonovabitch, gelded late.*

She looked up from where she was working, bending down to trim a loose flap of frog off a front hoof. *You mean a mare, then,* she said.

Like hell! Mares can't hack it when the chips are down. I don't want to be right up against it and have my horse go all girly on me.

She took in a breath. She'd worked late on a story the night before and she was tired; she didn't want an argument, especially one as inane as whether a mare was capable of going "all girly". She moved to the next hoof and began clearing one cleft, then another, ignoring the guy. It was the only defense.

He came closer, gave the tag end of her chaps belt a little tug, and said, *I like the way you ride.*

She stood straight, dropping the horse's leg, staring at the guy, the hoof pick held like a pirate's hook. Quietly, as though sharing a secret, she said, *You can fuck right off.* To which he laughed hard, backing up as he did so.

That's good, he said. *That's real good.*

He told her he was biding his time for her. *It won't be long,* he promised.

The horses had to walk through smoke, explosions, throngs of people. It was exactly the opposite of what is natural for them. She taught the small herd of four the same skills as for cutting cattle and slowly the horses began to disregard everything but the job at hand. Before work, on the weekends, late into the Midwestern evenings when the heat gave way to the velvet of a summer's night, the training took up all her free time all that summer long, until she could have ridden beside a firing canon and the horses wouldn't spook, until not even a dog was safe in an open pen because the horses would chase him out. Finally, at the end of the summer they sent a bunch

12

of the officers into the ring with her and she focused her gaze on the one with the swagger, and felt her horse connect with her meaning, hooking on to the guy.

He made a run for it, whooping as though he enjoyed being chased, showing off to the others. He lifted his hat like a clown running in a rodeo; he made a show of pretending he was scared. But it took only four strides to catch up with him and less than ten seconds until she was circling him at a canter as he held up his hands in surrender, laughing. He expected her to let him go now, but she didn't let him go. She kept up the revolutions, the horse rolling on its hocks, the sound of hooves like a drumbeat, so close to the guy he looked as though he'd been corked in a bottle. Now the officer stopped smiling; he stared at her helplessly, unable to move an inch, 900 pounds of horse around him like a cyclone. She watched a window of fear open on his face. He suddenly looked young and stupid; he suddenly looked like someone she felt sorry for. She sat back, bringing the horse to a halt.

Meet Millie, she said, patting a swatch of mane.

At the magazine, they thought horse training meant she was a particular type of person, a kind of rugged, intrepid girl willing to take physical risks—not what she thought of herself, not at all. Spring the next year she was called into the editor's office and given the assignment to collect women's interest stories for a feature they wanted on Vietnam. She was to be there only a few weeks.

War reporting? She was confused.

Her editor kept looking at the copy she was marking, barely registering the question. *As you seem to like adventures,* she said. The editor's desk was littered with typescripts, paperweights, trays stuffed with clippings, envelopes, a grammar, a stamp pad, a half-empty bottle of aspirin, caffeine pills, two dirty coffee cups which sat next to the one from which she was now drinking. She smoked Larks, her lipstick ringing the filters of

13

a collection of spent butts in the ashtray. She wore browline eyeglasses in the style of Malcolm X and had an affecting glare such that one tended not to argue.

Vietnam, Susan said. *Women's interest.* It was more a question than anything.

The editor had a rash around her hairline, some kind of eczema that worsened with stress, and a large vein in her neck that bulged when she shouted, which was not infrequently. She looked up from what she was doing, scribbling over some copy with what might have been a glass marker, and reeled off a list: *Orphans, hospitals, brave young GIs, gallant doctors, heroic captains, courageous American-loving civilians . . . go there, find it.*

Susan nodded. *So, no dying—* She was going to say *So, no dying sons,* but her editor fixed her with a look that brought the entire discussion back to where it had begun, as a set of instructions. Then the older woman scratched her head and told Susan there were newsmen all over Chicago desperate to go to Saigon—didn't she know that? Her fingers unstuck a file drawer and suddenly she slapped a manila envelope on to the desk, her eyes never leaving Susan's.

Open it, she said.

There were photographs of women in combat gear, cameras around their necks, ponytails beneath helmets. She recognized one right away, the late Dickey Chapelle in her horn-rims and pearl studs, squinting through the lens. Another showed a girl with reddish blonde hair, a long, freckled nose. She was smiling at a soldier wearing a helmet that listed the months of the year, four crossed out, a pack of cigarettes tucked into the band.

Her editor said, *That's Cathy Leroy, age twenty-two. Little French girl arrived in Saigon with no job and no experience as a photographer. The way she makes a living is by taking more risks than the guys.*

Cathy Leroy was built like a gymnast, not even five feet tall. In one of the photos she was following a group of four marines as they carried their dead buddy over a field of elephant grass flattened by the force of wind off a chopper's rotor blades. Susan thought it was impressive what the girl was doing; it made something flicker inside her, a rush of possibility as though she had just stumbled upon a vision of herself in that same place, beneath the same hot sun and the same deafening sound of a medevac arriving. She had never, not once, considered a foreign assignment, let alone in a war zone. Now, as she flipped through the photographs her editor gave her, it occurred to her this was exactly what she wanted, or could want, if she dared.

She came across a black-and-white glossy of a brunette with cropped hair and large dark eyes, a pad out, a pen, a casual look on an intelligent face.

Kate Webb, her editor explained. *She's a stringer.*

There was a pause between them, a lot of silent air that seemed solid. Susan cleared her throat. *I've not really had any experience*—she began.

The editor interrupted. *Kate went out with no job at all. Like Cathy. But you have a big advantage in that your room is paid for. You'll be on salary.* She took out a fresh cigarette, waving it as she spoke. *This assignment might lead to more. So think carefully before you say yes.* She gave Susan a long look, brought a match to the cigarette, and inhaled sharply. Then she went back to marking up the pages she was working on while Susan sat in the chair across from her, not sure whether to leave or stay, to say yes or no. Not even sure whether to hand back the photographs.

After a minute the editor sat back in her chair, folding her arms across her chest and frowning at Susan, who had not shifted from her seat. *When I said think carefully before saying yes, I did mean you should say yes.* She dug into her handbag for a new pack of Larks, stripped the plastic seal, and offered one to Susan.

15

I don't smoke, Susan said.

Start. It's good for keeping the bugs off you in tropical climes. It's not that I don't want to go—

I wouldn't have asked you if I didn't think you wanted to go. Of course you want to go. What I'm telling you is this: you won't likely get another chance.

Susan tried to look confident, relaxed. She tried to imagine herself in Vietnam. *I'm just letting the idea sink in,* she said.

The editor attempted a smile, but it came out wrong, the smile was more like a grimace between streams of smoke. *The idea is to have a chance to distinguish yourself,* she said. *The* idea is to be somebody.

And so she had arrived early in 1967. By then there was already plenty of every kind of reporter in Vietnam, almost all men, and she doubted more than one or two of those who gathered at bars and restaurants, who stood in line at the cable office or wrapped up their film for shipment, expected her actually to go out into the field. The magazine, too, had imagined she would remain, more or less, within the protection of Saigon, staging occasional day trips to nearby (secure) bases.

But she soon discovered this was not possible, not if she wanted an actual story. She attended the afternoon press conferences, winding her way through the maze of corridors and windowless, low-ceilinged offices at JUSPAO, chatting to the reporters doing the same, but found nothing in the press releases that would translate easily into magazine articles. The military gave battle statistics: body counts, numbers killed in action, wounded in action, killed by air. They talked about the enemy, but rarely about people. They talked about territories, but not homes. They had a particular way of describing the Vietcong's movements, how they "infested" villages, so that Susan imagined them like the enormous, prodigious cockroaches that roamed freely through cracks in the skirting boards of Saigon buildings, emerging from tiny spaces in plaster where wires flowed, even up through sinkholes. It was part of the jargon— WHAMO, LZ, DMZ, ARVN, PVA, NVA, SOP—that she was learning, that she was trying to learn, and which at first felt as mysterious and incomprehensible as Vietnamese itself. One day during her first week in the country, she made the mistake of drawing attention to herself by asking the lieutenant colonel making the announcement, a man who seemed to dread the afternoon press conference as much as the press who attended (who were said to be divided into two camps: those who did not believe the information, and those who did not care), a question about this terminology. Raising her voice so that it could be heard in the front of the room, she asked the lieutenant colonel to please tell her what "WBLC" meant.

The officer stood on a raised platform in front of a large map on which there were highlighted areas, circled areas, circles within circles, and a great deal of cryptic numbers. He was older than he ought to have been for his rank, somehow stalled at the lieutenant colonel status now for so many years it was certain he would remain there through to his retirement, which was imminent, though he was saddled for the moment with this band of undisciplined correspondents as though with unruly children. His uniform was newly starched, immaculate, with knife-point creases, reminding Susan all at once of something she had forgotten: how her father told the story of how he would examine his own dress uniform with a magnifying glass for wrinkles—this, before state dinners. She wondered if the lieutenant colonel in front did the same, whether he glided the glass across the crisp collar and sleeves, along the pressed seams on which she could not help but bestow a certain feminine admiration. Her own summer dress stuck to her skin, having lost its shape in the humid air. If she'd had to stand next to the lieutenant colonel she would have felt like a servant girl in an inadequate frock, and she was grateful that she was

17

sandwiched, almost obscured, between the men sitting on either side of her.

You want me to explain what a WBLC is? the lieutenant colonel said. He leaned over the edge of the platform in a hawkish manner, his attention directed at her. She immediately regretted the question. She seemed to have ignited something inside the man. The lieutenant colonel had been using a pointing stick made of pale wood to indicate places on the charts and maps that flashed across the screen behind him. Now he slapped the pointer across his palm brusquely so that it reminded her of a policeman's nightstick. His face seemed devoid of expression but she could tell by the way he set his mouth, as though holding back all manner of unsaid words, that nothing good would come of this conversation, which—she was reminded now—was being held publicly in front of all her colleagues, most of whom she had not yet had the opportunity to meet.

She nodded. The way the lieutenant colonel glared at her had an effect she would not have imagined of herself: her heart pounding, the heat lifting from her like a series of veils, her throat becoming uncomfortable as though she'd swallowed a bug. *I'm afraid that is correct, sir,* she said, grateful she was sitting down. *I've never heard of a WBLC.*

Miss, if you want to cover a war it is important you have some familiarity with military terms.

In one of her notebooks, one that she hoped would never be seen by the likes of the lieutenant colonel, or anyone gathered in the press room at JUSPAO, was a glossary of military terms which she had committed to memory. *That is why I am asking the question,* she said. *Sir.*

He grunted his disapproval, twirling his pointing stick in his hand. For a moment she thought he was going to strike the screen.

WBLC would be waterborne logistics craft, miss. I hope that will help with your education.

18

There was a smattering of conversation in response to this remark, a twitchy sort of laughter, exchanges whispered between the correspondents, who, Susan imagined, would either be agreeing with the lieutenant colonel that she was severely unprepared for her assignment here in Vietnam, or who were simply relieved it was the female reporter from Illinois being singled out for attack rather than themselves. She felt her face flush. She felt a beading of sweat along the rim of her skull. If her father hadn't been a full colonel, she would never have dared to ask the next question. If she hadn't grown up watching such men overindulge in every available vice, seen them drunk, heard their stupid off-color remarks, and the ridiculous manner in which they made every conversation a contest, she would never have said another word. But she'd seen it over and again and she was, after all, the daughter of a full bird. She cleared her throat. *I'm sorry, sir, I don't think I know what a waterborne logistics craft is.*

The lieutenant colonel wheeled around, glaring at her, then glanced to the side, shaking his head. It was too much to look at her, so ill-informed, unwise enough to let her ignorance show. It was like seeing a man admit he had no clue, not an inkling, how to do his job, like having some failing fucking New Guy stand in front of him, parroting back the words he himself had instilled in the recruit: *No, sir, I do not have any idea how to perform, sir! How to be a useful part of the US Military, sir!* It angered him, enraged him. He looked across the audience of assembled press, with their unkempt hair, their fat bellies, their ridiculous safari shirts, sneering, he thought. Totally unaware. He was tired of them, tired of seeing them at the airports and officers' clubs, ready to pounce on the smallest mistake made by the lowest-ranking of officers, ready to spread yet more tales of woe when the war, as he saw it, was going very well—magnificently, in fact. It was an impressive war if you looked at it properly, which these reporters never seemed to do.

You don't know— he began, his voice rising with each word.

Someone passed a note to her. It arrived from across the room, hand to hand, over the laps of journalists. She held it in her palm, feeling the moisture of her skin soften its corners. She wished she wasn't so nervous. It seemed completely unprofessional of her not to assume the same lazy confidence of the others in the room. *Sampan*, the note read. *Sampan* = *WBLC.*

She imagined the sampans she saw along canals. Long, primitive boats whose name literally means "three planks". She'd seen them stocked with fish, fruit, paddled by families, by children even, in their black pajama trousers, their broad conical hats. She read the note, then carefully, silently, pressed it back into quarters, then eighths. Meanwhile, the lieutenant colonel was still talking. *I don't have time,* he emphasized, *the US military does not have time, to educate unprepared girl reporters—*

It was that expression "girl reporters" that did it. It lit something inside her she didn't quite understand. She found herself interrupting the lieutenant colonel, then rising up despite how nervous she was, despite the crowded hot room, her face dotted with perspiration, the spectacle of it all. She stood, craning her neck to look taller and focusing her gaze directly at the man who glared down at her from his theater of maps. Her dress was ridiculous; she decided on the spot never to wear such a dress again. Even so, she stood, balancing herself on the back of the chair in front, holding the note, which she hoped the lieutenant colonel could not see, in the clenched fingers of her right hand. *Are you talking about a sampan?* she said, as forcefully as she could. It came out loud enough to hear, not a scornful question, not a challenge, but a genuine enquiry delivered with the assurance of one who will be able to evaluate the answer. *When you say WBLC, do you really mean sampan?*

It was as though a bubble of air between herself and the lieutenant colonel had been punctured, as though she were standing right up next to him, balancing on her toes, stretching her entire, compact frame up to meet the gaze of this large man. She was no longer afraid; she was no longer an observer. She felt herself finally to be among the press. There was a beat of silence between them, then the lieutenant colonel dropped his chin, blinking as though suddenly awakened from a dream.

A few chuckles, a reporter from AP laughing loudly, then a voice from the crowd, Son's voice, the first time she would hear it, his heavy Vietnamese accent in which she could detect distinctly Anglican vowels, his light, slightly nasal tone. *Can we have confirmation that a WBLC is a sampan, sir?*

The colonel stayed his position, breathing purposely in, then out, wetting his lips with the tip of his tongue. After a moment he let out a sigh, turning his face so that the projector etched out the line of the Demilitarized Zone across his left cheek. His pointer, which he had dropped during the exchange with the female reporter, with Susan, he now retrieved from the floor. When he spoke, it was to the map screen. *Yes, that is correct,* he said, finishing the matter.

Thank you, sir! came Son's voice from somewhere across the room. She did not know who was speaking. But Son had noticed her from the start, even that first week. He never admitted this, but later she pieced it together. Marc, of course, had not been at the briefing. She met him the following week, after deciding she'd better get out of Saigon and see the war for herself.

It was on a battlefield. Marc came on a convoy out of Cam Lo, riding in the open bed of a truck with his cameraman, Locke, and a dozen marines. They smoked and talked to the soldiers and looked out over the landscape shimmering with the day's heat. Never in all the time they pitched over the bumpy roads did he think there would be a women ahead; but she had travelled out the day before and was about to beat him to a story.

They arrived at the base of a hill where a row of bodies, faces blackened as though burnt, waited to be taken back in those same trucks, a captain yelling for more bodybags and ponchos, men in gas masks working the duty. He didn't see her yet, not her or any other journalists. He got out his notebook, his recording equipment. Locke trained his camera on the bodies stacked to their right, only briefly of course so as not to be seen doing so. The smell of the bodies was revolting. Marc kept himself from looking and held his breath as much as he could until they went up the hill on foot, out to the camp. They were brought to the observation post. No bodies here, just miles of dusty, red dirt, low-lying shrubs, rubble and artillery and sandbags and men in foxholes.

There was sporadic fire, plenty of incoming but none of it that close. Then an onslaught of artillery. He didn't know when the serious shelling began, but it did, like a storm gathering and settling upon them, ceaseless and consuming. They dived into an open bunker, marines beside them curled up around the edges of the pit, their faces pressed against the shallow walls, their legs and arms seized up beneath them. They could not have gotten any smaller. Locke tried to work the camera, getting as much footage as he could. Occasionally, they became brave; moving cautiously over the dusty grounds standing at the rims of foxholes, desperate to get some good pictures, but equally ready to dive underground as the storm of firing continued. There had been explosions all morning, coming every thirty seconds, every fifteen, landing at first some distance off and now much closer. They thought they were up here doing a story about the morale of marines, asking them how they felt about being there, Con Thien, the meat grinder, the graveyard, three featureless hills right up against the Demilitarized Zone. But the incoming was so heavy there was hardly enough time between explosions to get even a quick on-camera.

The marines were extraordinary. After so many days and weeks of fighting they seemed to know how close a shell was by the sound of it, and would remain on their feet longer than he would dare to. He tried to be that brave but the rockets came cracking out of the sky—no sooner was he standing up than he was flat on his front again. He felt suspended in time, as in a dream when you cannot quite get your limbs to move. They needed the footage and surely this battle was something they ought to record, but they couldn't get much. He would see Locke rolling film across the hills where the explosions followed a line of men in defensive positions, then both Locke and the camera would disappear. He clutched the microphone, trying to record some natural sound, but no sooner had he made the effort than he found himself once more on his face.

Something happened. The earth itself seemed to tip and now he was on his hands and knees, the tape recorder covered in dust, the microphone, the wires, sprawled out on the dirt. He didn't know where Locke was; calling out would be useless. There was constant firing in both directions, the ground lifting up beneath him. Someone grabbed his shoulder and threw him into a bunker. It was Locke. He could tell because the camera knocked him in the face. They'd been up there less than an hour, maybe much less, but he did not know, and would not be able to recall.

No light, the earth shaking, artillery shrieking above. He was aware of other people in the bunker, of the walls of sandbags, the dry earth pressing around them with every blast, red dust showering down from the sandbags over their heads, raining on his shoulders. On the floor, hugging his knees, neck bent, arms over his head, hands over his ears, he told himself that unless they got a direct hit, they'd survive. His cheek swelled, the place where the camera had hit him. He was missing his eyeglasses and then he realized he had them in his hand.

The bunker was only a few feet high, not much wider, hot. He felt the sweat on his back, his chest, running down his face. Another explosion, this one so close he called out, the sound rushing from his lungs as though forced out by the blast, his heart screaming inside his chest. He recalled reading an account by a survivor of the Ia Drang massacre, a soldier whose company had nearly been wiped out. The soldier had told how when his buddies were hit in the belly or chest, they let out a terrible scream and they kept on screaming, until they were hoarse, until the blood filled their mouths, until they died. He wished he hadn't read that account, which had been in the *Saturday Evening Post*. He thought of it now; he didn't know why. The noise was so loud, so penetrating, it seemed to alter the way his body worked. During the blasts he saw bright orange and red behind his eyelids, felt his skeleton acutely within the soft tissue of his muscles. Strange bits of information hung around the edges of his thoughts. Body counts from other battles, a line from a childhood prayer, a drive toward silence, the need for which was reaching desperation point. He was alternately blinded by darkness, then by light. Nothing happening now, not one thing, was natural.

He heard the metallic click of a cigarette lighter; a flame illuminated the bunker. He opened his eyes. Across from him, not ten inches from his face, was a woman. Her helmet was lopsided, the hair hanging beneath its rim coated in dirt, scratches across her cheek. Her eyes were open and glassy. He didn't know her. Didn't know why she was in the bunker or the base, or in the country itself. The world had receded to this one, small place, and here she was before him. The sergeant with the lighter lit a kerosene lamp. Nobody looked at each other, except him and the girl. They locked eyes and kept them locked, as though through doing so they might somehow stay more focused and right thinking. Already, he felt himself begin to settle. Despite the shelling, which continued. Despite the sound of air attacks charging north. He tried to get out his notebook and pen, but his hands were shaking too much. He couldn't write. He dropped the notebook and let it rest by his boot, by her boot. His pen, too, lay between them.

Outside the air was one large fist of sound. It was a constant pummeling, endless, almost rhythmic. The noise seemed to go inside him; he could feel it in his bones and teeth, straight down his spine. He had, of course, been through such things before. This was not his first war. But that didn't matter now. The only thing that had any weight, any significance at all, was this isolated moment, then the one that followed. He felt his legs begin to shake, the adrenaline coursing through him. He felt a low weight in his stomach. The girl across from him began to cry silently, her face frozen in an internal agony he understood, understood completely. His throat was dry, his mouth gritty with sand. His arms didn't seem to have any strength in them. He felt weighted and immobile, a statue of himself, buried in the ground. It seemed to take all his strength to raise his hand, fingers trembling, and touch the girl's face. He looked at her, breathing purposely in and out, trying to calm herself. He put the back of his hand on her cheek, on the soft skin beneath her jaw. He wanted to offer her something. It seemed the least he could do, sitting so close to her, and through all these minutes.

She reached forward and hooked his knee with her arm, leaning toward him. It helped. He couldn't say why. The explosions continued, stretching out so that they seemed to follow on, each from each, in one long, continual crashing song. Occasionally, he moved his hand across the girl's face, and over the top of her forehead, as though soothing a fever. She gripped his knee and he felt her fingers gratefully, needing her touch. The lamp went out, the darkness so sudden it made him almost sick with fear, and then the sergeant wearily, hesitantly, relit the wick. He saw now that the sergeant was frightened, even him, and he felt sorry for him, sorry for them all.

It felt as though they had been tricked. That there had been some terrible swindle and as a result they would now die. He had always thought he would recognize the moment of his death—through some sixth sense or a moment of dread that informs. Now he decided the opposite was true. It would come like fire when it came. It would revolve everything, crush his guesswork, all of his imaginings.

The girl sobbed silently, her shoulders shaking, and he held her until she stopped. The siege lasted twenty minutes or more, and when he and the girl finally, tentatively, pulled themselves apart and climbed, one by one, out of that hole he felt connected to her, as though he'd known her for ever, known her through the very end of the world and now, its new beginning. He held her arm as she climbed up, stood close to her as they crawled up on to the flat, featureless scrub, this place of unending battle, destined always to be so, now and until the end of the war. At some point they moved forward in a column, each man a few meters apart. He watched her walk ahead of him, then run. A jeep was backing up at the foot of the hill, getting ready to go back up the road to Cam Lo and she moved like a bullet towards it. He steadied his eyes on her as she ran, arms flailing, cameras whipping against her back, a notebook clutched in one hand, the other holding her helmet, heading for the jeep. The jeep was full already, no room at all, but she ran and kept running until it slowed to turn and the men inside lifted her aboard among the bodies. They did so effortlessly, as though plucking a flower from the ground. She balanced herself on the rim of the thick bed and he thought he could see her moment of revulsion at having to travel with the dead. Don't look at their faces, he wanted to tell her, and when you get to the other side go straight for the bar. You had to be careful what you focused on in the war, he thought, and he watched until he could see nothing of the girl or the jeep, just the dust rising in columns.

He didn't know who she was, hadn't seen her before. She turned up just like that and he fixed on her in a manner he could not shake.

She learned about taking cover, the things you needed to look for, how quickly you needed to drop. From the pages of the *Handbook* she read, *Look for a tree stump, a wall, a rock. Holes are good, buildings are good. Bunkers are good if you don't get killed trying to reach them.* She learned, too, that diving to the ground under fire is almost an instinctive act, although there are many new to the field who will stand, listening to bullets whiz by them, behaving as though they are nothing more than annoying insects swarming overhead. The *Handbook* had something to say about that. It said, *What you hear are not bees. What you hear are bullets at the end of their range and they are probably too slow now to kill you, but it would make sense to avoid them anyway.*

She had intended to avoid them; she had intended never to come under fire at all, but as the weeks dropped away she became less certain that any kind of safety could be ensured even within Saigon, let alone if she went to crazy places like Con Thien. That had been a mistake; that had been chancing it.

But even on supposedly safer ground there were no guarantees. She'd been a block away when a small bomb blew up a diplomat's car. The next day a bar frequented by Americans took a grenade, injuring dozens and killing two soldiers and three of the bar girls who drank overpriced "tea." Even so, Saigon itself did not frighten her. The assaults she suffered were not by artillery but by the prostitutes on Tu Do Street who called her names as she passed. Or when she walked, trying to stay beneath the thin shade of the plane trees, and soldiers sidled up to her asking where she was from, what was her name, where was she going. The hotel was one street down from the flower market and sometimes the air around it was so fragrant that if she shut her eyes she could make herself believe she was in the lushest garden in all of Southeast Asia. At night, the smell of flowers disappeared and the rats arrived, traveling up from the rivers, feasting on garbage. Beneath streetlamps the air clouded with insects. There were candy shops that sold Belgian chocolates and marzipan flown in from Spain, restaurants that brought in fresh lobster so that you could choose your own dinner from a tank. In the cosy heat of early evening, sitting on the terraces of the better restaurants, she would look up at the colorful sky, its reds and oranges set like a painting above her, unable to imagine anything more beautiful.

But there was contrast at every corner. People slept outdoors in the shaded entrances to shops, or flat out on benches, or sometimes curled on the steps of the cathedral until moved on. Market stalls sold goods quite obviously wrangled from the military post exchange or off the bodies of dead soldiers: combat fatigues, helmets, boots, even guns if you followed the vendor to the back room where they were kept. Old women sold tea, Marlboros and marijuana. Some sold only marijuana. Children sold pictures of naked girls, and the older ones sold the girls themselves. They stole the pens from your pockets, wrangled spare change from your hand. She lost a camera the first week and had to buy a new one. That is, purchase someone else's camera, also stolen, but now displayed on a cardboard box propped up in a makeshift stall.

She was settling in, getting to know the places to meet, who to speak to, where to go, but also she registered an unease that (she would learn later) never truly lifted from a visitor to Saigon. The city surprised her in a million ways. There were mysterious chirpings and whistles that arrived with dawn, along with the onslaught of traffic, a ceaseless commotion that exhausted her as much as the temperature that she measured not in degrees but by how many times each day she had to immerse herself in water.

There were other sounds, too, that required attention. One night, shortly after her arrival, she heard something like thunder that confused her senses, making her imagine a storm when the night was clear. But the storm was not the reason for the noise; it was bombing to the west of the city, which from the street she could not see, but thought she could feel, detecting a kind of vibration in the air. The sound of the bombers was heard not only as thunder, but in a sudden heightened awareness of people around her, who appeared to step up their pace, or crowd themselves at doorways, or create even more knots of traffic in the swarming streets. The war registered itself in the way the window glass rattled, how the strings of lights upon railings flickered and were still. Closet hangers danced, making their tinny sound; dogs that roamed freely began to shout into the night.

In Susan's own small room the pendant lamp above her bed was set in motion, barely noticeable, as rhythmic as a metronome. Plaster broke away and splattered on the floor, the war approaching and receding like a tide. Even if she wasn't in the room at the time, she would notice upon her return the broken tile, the settling of dust, feeling almost as though someone had been through her things and moved them all a millimeter or two in a ridiculous but unsettling act. Sometimes, with a group of other journalists, she stood on the rooftop terrace of the Caravelle Hotel, watching the bombing, tracking tracers and bullets many miles off that poured from the guns of a US airship as though from a firehose. She watched the sudden red of bombs meeting their targets, trying to determine exactly where they were falling. There really was no more to it than that. She hadn't thought about what it would be like to be on the receiving end of artillery, or to be under those bombs. In her cocktail dress recently purchased from Marshall Field's, during those first few weeks in Saigon, while clasping the delicate stem of a drink from someone she'd just met, whose name she couldn't recall as she clinked his glass, she could not imagine such things.

It turned out not to be a matter of time, but of distance. It was a decision you made, where you put yourself in the country, who you traveled with. It began slowly enough, going out with soldiers until something—an angle, a profile, an interview, a sudden, newsworthy event—happened her way. It had almost become a game she played—how close could she get to the war without getting *too* close. She wore chinos and a short-sleeved blouse, interviewing those who set up refugee camps and orphanages, her hair limp in its ponytail, her cheeks newly sprinkled with freckles. A gradual change was taking place; she settled into her role. She realized two weeks into what was now being called her "tour," while trudging through a dusty, crater-filled village, barraged by gangs of children demanding their piastres, swearing in mixed-up English at her if she didn't pay, that it was precisely because she hadn't hungered after battle-fields, and in fact had no definite opinion one way or another on whether the war was ethical or winnable, that she'd been sent in the first place. The magazine would never have chosen a "political" reporter. They'd chosen her because she was quirky enough to train horses in her spare time and because they thought—they really did think—that she would never leave Saigon. That is, all except her editor. She'd received a telegram a few days earlier:

GET STORIES OUTSIDE THE CAPITAL STOP YOU ARE AS GOOD
AS ANY OF THEM STOP

She carried that telegram with her for days. It made her think she could do it, made her know. It was still too early for her to have bad dreams; too early for her to be woken in the night by them. She wished only to understand truly what was happening in this one small country and everything she did was a process of this unfolding. It was not unpleasant. Quite the contrary: it was exhilarating. The trip up to Con Thien had both terrified and intrigued her. She then went to Pleiku and wrote a good story about a small hospital there. That was when she came across Son, whether by fate or by deliberate intent on his part, she never knew. The country was full of random occurrences and anyway it was not surprising that she should meet him—everyone knew him. While Western correspondents

30

came and went, staying a few weeks or a few years, their numbers growing exponentially with each season, Son remained, a kind of ambassador to the war. He'd watched the number of newsmen in Vietnam increase tenfold and more. He'd watched Saigon fill up like a dam.

His full name was Hoàng Van Son. He had a couple of identical Nikon F cameras, a heavy zoom lens which was a recent acquisition, and he filled his pockets with Ektachrome color and a few rolls of Kodak Tri-X black and white just to walk down the street. He had a long mouth that curled up at the ends, blocky white teeth that aligned as though he'd had years of orthodontistry, which he most certainly had not. He was quite handsome—Susan thought so—but in a way she was not used to and which kept her from fully acknowledging it. He spoke English very well—that was the main thing. He knew how to cover the war. They decided to form a partnership, him as a still photographer, her as a print reporter. He was her friend—she believed they were friends—and also her translator and her entrance into combat reporting. One afternoon, still during those early weeks in Saigon, he showed her how to fall to the ground when mortared. That is, he tried to convey how fast she needed to move. But she didn't understand.

Is there a certain technique? she asked innocently. They were at the hotel. He'd been checking out the bathroom to see whether he could use it for a darkroom. The bathroom had a broken doorknob that occasionally locked solid, and for this reason there was a screwdriver behind the tap. The room looked as though a poltergeist lived there: rotting tiles that came off the wall and broke in pieces on the floor, plaster dust, handles that dislodged themselves overnight, doors that swelled with the humidity and wouldn't shut or wouldn't open. The bath was moldy; the grout grew a tenacious fur. Insects everywhere, occasional rats, which she discovered had gnawed spaces in the

31

plaster where the pipes were laid so that they could navigate the whole of the building through the maze of its plumbing. Despite these flaws, Son said it was perfect. The bathroom would be ideal for developing his film. But could they put a board across the bidet (rust-colored water; jammed, immobile taps) and use it as a small table? Could they get rid of the flouncy shower curtain Susan bought because there had been none when she arrived? Could he move the towels? In short, could she do without a bathroom?

You want me to tell you how *to fall down?* he said. His cigarette bobbed in his mouth as he spoke; his large white teeth reminded her of piano keys, and though he was smiling he seemed completely baffled when she nodded and said yes. It was one of those moments between them—one of many—in which he seemed as confused by her as she was by him, by the whole of his country, and especially the war. He could have admitted he was equally mystified by Western women, and particularly by Susan, but he might have thought that this fact was already quite plain. *Fall down?* he said now. *Just* . . . his hands beside his head showed his confusion. *Have you never done that?*

Not deliberately, she told him.

If a vehicle is hit, it can easily blow up, and vehicles of any description are one of the favorite targets of the Vietcong, who attempt to take out as many supplies as possible on their way to the field.

She read this in the *Handbook,* but she had no idea what it meant, what it really meant, until Son threw her off a flatbed in the same manner in which you might throw off a bale of hay. She learned also in those long minutes that once you've heard the shooting and jump over the side of the truck, you should follow immediately wherever the soldiers are running. And they will be running *toward* the bullets. Again, this was not initially for her a voluntary act; she was hauled along by a marine who held her like a bag of groceries in his non-smoking hand.

She was getting closer all the time. She didn't realize how close.

She got a telegram from her editor:

EXCELLENT WORK ON HOSPITAL STORY STOP PHOTOGRAPHS
BY HOÀNG VAN SON FIVE DOLLARS NO MORE STOP

She had to tell Son five dollars was all that the magazine would give him. She was embarrassed by how cheap her editor could be, or whoever it was who decided such things. *Sorry, Son, we can't really argue with them, but you could sell the photographs elsewhere,* she said. *It's so little money, I'm embarrassed.*

No arguing, said Son. *Celebrating, yes, but no arguing.*

But I hear Associated Press is paying fifteen a pop—

Susan, that is blood *money.*

Blood money?

I don't think you understand what is danger yet. The first few months you won't. What were you doing up in Con Thien? You'll begin to judge these things better. Well, I hope so.

He looked at her as though she were a live circus act. As though trying to decide if she'd fall off the wire.

First there had been the bunker in Con Thien, then Marc saw her at a party in Saigon. It wasn't like him to go to such a party. He'd been in Vietnam a long time, been to more than his share of events in hotel rooms and embassies and restaurants, private rooms and villas, hotels and offices and bars. He'd grown weary of them. But tonight's casual, crowded gathering took place in his own hotel, one floor down. He'd have had to make an effort to escape it and there had already been enough talk about him. About how solitary he'd become, how remote. The rumors—

that he kept his own M16 under his bed, that he was never without the dried hind foot of a rabbit, either in his pocket or around his neck; that he, in fact, had a mojo bag full of talismans and holy cards, wore a St. Christopher's, counted backwards from seven before jumping from choppers—used to make him laugh. But lately, he'd come to wonder if he appeared strange to his colleagues, enough so that they thought some explanation was in order. So he went to the party, arriving at the door to the welcome of Brian Murray, about whom no rumors were ever put forward. The man never seemed to travel five minutes for a story these days.

Oh, good, the press has arrived, Murray said. Murray was a print reporter and his comment might have been yet another little dig at television reporters who—it was understood—were not nearly as informed as those who wrote for newspapers. Marc never really understood the rivalry, and he didn't see why Murray always felt compelled to remind him of it. It felt like a reprimand, coming from the older man.

You look well, Marc said. Murray wore crisp cream-colored trousers, a new belt. His shirt had been diligently pressed, undoubtedly by one of the Vietnamese girls who worked in the hotel. His shoes, too, were unscuffed, even glowing, beneath the layers of polish that had been applied.

I'm in one piece, he said.

You've had a lot of print lately.

The wire has. It's Sanchez. He's always out there, him. But not me. Not as much as I'd like. Murray said something else, too, but Marc found it difficult to hear him. The music blared from four speakers, rigged up in the corners of the room. Murray was a quiet guy. He didn't look like he belonged in such a gathering. He looked like he should be at home with his wife and children, with a dog at his feet and a warm drink and a pipe. His hair curled in graying locks and his pale skin showed exactly how little he got out. He probably never left the city any more.

34

He probably was at the door now because it was the quietest place to stand.

You going to let me in? Marc said.

Oh yeah. Sorry, Davis. Come in.

Marc looked for the bathroom, where undoubtedly there would be a tub of beer swimming in melted ice. He looked for Locke, but couldn't find him. He was probably asleep. They'd been up most of the night before, flying the milk-run from Danang, hoping to get back before the weather turned. Marc got a drink and talked with a few guys from a French paper. The French pouted into their drinks and passed each other Gauloises cigarettes. They always looked so miserable at American gatherings; he wondered why they never appeared to miss a single one.

He picked up a *Life* magazine, thumbing through its pages for the stories about Vietnam, but it was all about protestors this week, photograph after photograph of marches and rallies. He glanced through the articles, looking at the images of streets and squares so crowded with people he could not pick out a single feature of cities he knew well. He tried to imagine himself there again, back home in the States. The country—his country—felt far away, almost impossible to reach. Sometimes, when they packed the film to be sent to San Francisco and then on to New York, it seemed to him like magic that the parcel could reach those same streets he knew, that the city blocks and buildings with all their shining windows existed at all, and even more astonishing, that they existed exactly as he remembered them, untouched, unbothered by the chaos he reported daily.

He put the magazine to one side. He looked up and he saw her; he saw Susan. She was by the door, standing in the exact spot he'd been next to Murray. For a moment, it seemed almost as though she had stepped out of his own imagination, or wasn't really there at all, for in his mind she was somehow consigned to the north. He'd expected to see her in Danang or

Chu Lai, or even once more in Con Thien. But of course it made more sense to find her here in Saigon among the press, the crowded bars and restaurants, the hotels. She would have been at the daily press conferences, the five o'clock follies, that he could barely bring himself now to attend. He'd heard from Locke that there was a new English girl in town, *some girl journalist*, Locke had said. The minute he mentioned her, Marc knew it was the same. *I think I know the one*, he replied. But even so, he always thought of Susan up north, not here. It shocked him, seeing her among so many people he knew.

She was framed in the doorway, her hands on either side of the opening. It seemed to him she was hesitating, taking in the geography of the room, the people inside. Murray was trying to talk to her—what was he, a sentry at the gates?—and from this distance she appeared to be answering him politely, her head tilted to one side. She looked shy, sweet, young. He wanted to go over to her but he hesitated, watching, and then she was swept up with a group and he didn't want to intervene. Somebody asked him for the *Life* magazine and he handed it over wordlessly.

Davis— he heard, *Hey, Marc!* Someone was calling his name, a man, not her. He kept walking.

He tracked her, a few steps behind. It was a game at first. To see if she noticed him. He watched her pass through the party in a thin dress, its sleeves shaped like flute glasses from which her wrists seemed surprisingly delicate. He could still recall how she'd clung to him in the bunker, her arm looped over his knee, and the strength of that grip. The dress made her seem more fragile than she was, and in this manner he found her appearance deceptive, as though he was being shown a pretend version of Susan, when he knew full well how strong she was, how fast she could run. He could still see her racing down that hill, her feet swinging up to her hips as she pushed forward through the dust and stones to the jeep. Tonight she looked altogether different, and it was like looking at a beautiful portrait that showed some other new and lovely aspect of her person. He could hardly stand to look away.

He felt a hand clap around his calf and he stopped, frozen, staring down. It was Curtis, a soundman he occasionally worked with when he was lucky enough to *get* a soundman. He was arranged on the floor with some friends, sitting absurdly close to the speakers, which blasted the Stones so loudly you could feel the vibration in the air. The guys asked if they could mooch just a little weed as were down to seeds and stems. Marc patted his empty pockets, shrugging.

I'm all out, he said. The music was so loud he had to lean down, shouting into Curtis's ear. From a distance it would have appeared as though he were telling Curtis a secret.

Curtis said, *Bullshit, you're never out.*

I am. I swear.

We don't have anything even halfway smokeable. Come on, man!

You're out of luck, I don't—

Curtis pushed two fingers into Marc's shirt pocket and uncovered a dime bag he'd forgotten about.

You're not awake, Davis, Curtis said.

It's this new dreamy image he's projecting, another of them said. *Like he's here but not here.*

Very cool.

The coolest.

Probably thinking about a girl.

Don't tell his wife!

Curtis laughed. *I think he was just holding out on us.*

Marc shook his head. He watched Curtis pinch a spray of the weed and stuff it into the blackened bowl of a small bong with dirty water, some marks on the plastic where it had burned.

Keep it, Marc said, nodding at the bag.

They told him to sit down, share a bowl with them, but he shook his head. His eyes floated across the room once more, searching for Susan, hoping she hadn't left already. She was dressed carefully, her hair newly washed. She was probably going off for dinner later. He shouldn't even have talked to these guys. He knew what they were after anyway. He should have just dropped the pot into their open palms and kept on tracking her. But he had honestly forgotten he had any. He wondered if the bag had gone through the laundry.

Over the course of the hour the hallway filled. People filed in from their offices, or on their way back from other parties, from restaurants or clubs or straight out of the field. They came and everyone packed in, some never getting as far as the stairs. He stepped over the legs of those with their backs up against walls, using Coke bottles for ashtrays, sharing rolling papers and pizza brought up, dried and cold now, curled in boxes. He saw some guys from the bureau and fell into conversation about an assignment. Curtis's girlfriend arrived in a miniskirt and unshaven legs, looking like a scruffy cheerleader, and kissed him full on the mouth. Locke showed up, holding court with one group, then another. People called him 'The Information', a name he didn't seem to mind. A couple of guys would go off to find some more beer, or better beer, or more pot, or better pot. A group would bring in a few more records and then, for no reason, a song would be interrupted halfway through as the LP was changed, the great scrape of the needle across vinyl singing in the speakers and someone calling out, *Shiiiiit, what are you doing, man?* A bicycle was hauled up the stairs—it belonged to a student who didn't dare leave it on the street. A guy whose two silver bars said he was a captain borrowed it off him and was now trying to wheel it through the crowd. The captain was here only because his girlfriend lived in the hotel. She was nothing to do with the war, but exported goods to the US.

War talk, all of it. Locke described a particular hill battle near Kontum and how he'd traded cigarettes for grass, ounce for ounce, and all the better ways they could have used the Montagnards as fighting soldiers with American advisers, but didn't, and now they're giving information both sides, what a fucking waste. The guy he was talking to said he'd lost three cameras: one stolen, one ruined by water, and another hit by shrapnel.

While you were using it?

No, man, it was in my bag.

There were correspondents, and soldiers—officers—and two GIs on R&R planning to bunk in the room, guys who worked construction or something anyway and didn't talk about the war or anything but just sat stolidly and drank one bottle of 33 beer after another, lining up the empties in neat rows like game pieces.

It was odd to see anyone sober, or anyone over thirty. He watched Susan and noticed that she didn't drink much, that she didn't know many people. She seemed to flit about, talking only briefly here and there, not entirely at ease. She had some friends among the exhausted nurses, who slumped on the floor with their oversized drinks, and pulled her down to talk to them. There were women: wives or girlfriends, some who worked for the USO or other relief organizations, the nurses who'd been brought in by jeep by some bunch of seriously in-breach soldiers. The women had their moments of peculiar talk and outrageous flirtations, except for the nurses who looked so tired they might lie down and sleep right there across a doorway if that's where they fell. They sat on the floor or lay on the floor, their hair falling all around them like lank seaweed, looking up at the ceiling fan going round and round, or staring at the smouldering end of their lit cigarette, or leaning into the arms of one guy or other, crowding around the air conditioner, laughing, drinking, once in a while bursting out crying.

At last he found her alone at the window, one of three large sash windows with great swags that had grown dusty and old now, the ornate gold piping frayed along the seams. He went to the window next to where she was standing, amazed that she had not noticed him yet, much less recognized him. It occurred to him that she might be avoiding him. The way she studied the sidewalk outside seemed almost a deliberate turning away, and in one respect this gave him hope. That he'd had an impact on her, that she hadn't forgotten the bunker in Con Thien, what passed between them in those minutes, what he thought had passed. If she wanted to avoid him, then it must be that she remembered, that she knew the power of their first, extraordinary meeting when she fled like Cinderella from the ball, holding her helmet with one hand, her notebooks in the other. In his day dreams he had often entertained himself with that last image of her, running toward the jeep, leaping up on to the open bed. It seemed wholly at odds with the woman he saw now, in a dress that hugged her hips, her hair falling in a fan across her shoulders, and the contrast he found dazzling, exhilarating. He didn't know if he dared talk to her.

He glanced through the window and saw army trucks and clusters of careening bicycles, people rushing from the first throes of evening rain. The pedicab drivers leaned into the motion as they worked. The kids traded money and sold things they'd found or scrounged, pens and card packs, pictures of naked girls, all of them getting soaked now, getting drenched. A boy in a T-shirt three sizes too small and a pair of underpants, nothing more, darted across the crazy street like a dog, trying to avoid being killed outright, selling cigarettes that nobody wanted to buy. It began to rain harder and his hair shined with it, his underpants dragged down his hips, his bald little legs splashed in puddles. At some point the boy looked up and saw Marc at the window and called out *Wanna buy?* Marc reached into his pocket and found a clump of notes, dropping a colorful bill down to the boy who stood with his hand stretched out, his chin to the sky, rushing one way, then another as the note floated, swooped and dived to the street below. It felt mean to have made him work so hard for the note, so he threw some change and the boy ran for it, too;

other children, hearing the coins scattering on the pavement, started doing the same. A crowd gathered, rushing in from adjoining lanes, not just children but old men, teenage girls, all of them rushing now. A child with only one arm danced below the window trying to lift the coins from the road with her single outstretched hand. A round woman with long gray hair pushed a child to one side. They were all running for the coins, calling up, screaming for more. But the rain was fierce, banging down on to the steaming tarmac and bouncing up again, streaming down the edges of the road, soaking the clothes and hair of the people below and drowning out their voices.

Suddenly, a spear of lightning cracked across a piece of sky to the west and all the lights went out. The street went black as though it had disappeared altogether, like a stage across which the curtain has been drawn. Inside, too, the room, the party, was suddenly immersed in darkness. He glanced away from the street and into the sudden gray shadows of the hotel—he didn't even know whose room it was—and looked across at the adjacent window, blinking, searching for Susan, but she was gone.

The lights stayed off but no one was alarmed. It was a city of precarious amenities. Water, light, access down a particular street or building, at a particular hour or a different one, were granted or not granted. One night, as the guest of an embassy official (someone he assumed to be a spook), he'd been in one of Saigon's best French restaurants when a blackout had taken hold of several city blocks. The waiters hurried with hurricane lamps and table candles, reassuring the diners that all was well. They had a generator for the kitchen, the food would not be a minute delayed. The waiters carried small flashlights, like theater ushers, and set out a line of lanterns at the station where they brought orders. He and the official carried on with their meal, though the man seemed suddenly quite awkward, straining through the darkness to see the other restaurant guests, who paid no attention at all to the blackout. If anything, they seemed to enjoy it. Outside, the streets were lit by headlamps and starlight; while the restaurant, now cloaked in the candles' amber glow, felt like a festive cavern. Everyone spoke more softly than before, as though the candles enforced a kind of secrecy, and Marc found himself having to drop his own voice, leaning across the table and into the cloud of light made by the flickering flame between him and the official, in order to hear the man speak. They carried on for a few minutes and then he saw the official's face suddenly glaze over. He was staring into a small spray of flowers that had been on the table all the time but, until now, had gone unnoticed. They were tiny lavender buds, each one the size of a thimble, and they let off an unusually strong scent in relation to their small size. In an abrupt move, the official dropped his napkin on to the table. *Let's get out of here before someone takes us for a couple of faggots,* he said, standing. He summoned the waiter for the bill, threw some money on the table. One of the waiters followed them out apologetically, suggesting that they at least finish their main course, but the official said, *Wrap it up, give it to someone.* He looked down at the plate of change the waiter had brought, rumpled bills on a saucer of white porcelain. To Marc, he said, *They give you these dirty notes so you'll leave them as a tip. Why should I give him all that? The place doesn't even have working lights.* Then he said, *Come on, let's get something to drink.*

Marc remembered this now, standing in the darkened party, and it made him smile and cringe at the same time. He listened as someone bemoaned the dead stereo, the unexpected discontinuation of music. Laughter erupted from down the hall where the darkness was almost complete. The party guests, unable to contain themselves in the excitement of the abrupt night, moved in waves in one direction, then another, guided only by the momentary hiss of a lit match, the glow of cigarettes, the few penlights that passed from hand to hand like batons.

And then, just as he least expected it, she was by his side. He recognized her profile in the darkness, her nose, her chin, the shape of her hips in the dress. Her voice was new to him. He'd never before heard her speak. *I know you,* she said, standing at his shoulder. He took her in, straining his eyes to see her more clearly. He remembered how in the bunker a few weeks earlier the darkness had obscured her, and how she'd arrived with the unexpected tide of light from the sergeant's lamp. He could picture her face then, streaked with mud, a few scratch marks, her eyes frozen in fear, pupils wide, her mouth open, unsure whether even to take in a breath. He reminded himself that he had once held her, crying, in his arms. It gave him confidence to remember that, to tell himself that she had found solace this way.

She said, *I wasn't sure, at first, and then I thought maybe— I don't know—that you wouldn't want me to bother you.*

The rain was heavy now, the drops splattering the floor near the window, open for the necessary breeze it allowed into the crowded room. He saw a fat raindrop land on her bare arm, another on her shoulder, and it was all he could do not to reach out and wipe them away. *You're getting wet,* he said, leading her from the window. Lightning came and went; with every bolt she became temporarily visible, the opaque whiteness making her skin seem pale, almost translucent. Then she seemed to disappear altogether as his eyes adjusted to the dark wake of the vanished electricity. He was fascinated by her presence, he couldn't say why. He had anticipated this meeting for weeks, guessing at where he might see her, and under what circumstances. He'd been careful how he asked after her, allowing himself to display no greater interest than he would in any new journalist he might see in the field, or at least not much more. He knew her name, who she worked for, a few places she had been recently. He looked at her now, wondering whether to tell her how he had sought her out, how her memory had dogged him. They had met in such honest isolation, both of them terrified, neither hiding nor able to hide anything about themselves.

43

He had never admitted, nor would admit, to that kind of fear, certainly not to another journalist. But she'd been there, witnessed it, given him the gift of her trust as she clung to him in the bunker. Now she said *I know you,* and it seemed so right and appropriate a greeting. She did know him, had seen a part of him he did not allow himself to dwell upon; he had considered at that time the possibility that they would suffer a direct hit, that the bunker would disintegrate and take them with it, that he would die with her there. He'd thought of that very thing and he knew, too, that she had.

The lightning came and went once more, a kind of shutter through which they saw each other and then did not. When he was able to focus again he saw her blinking up at him, smiling. He had not seen her smile before and he drank it in, greedy for it. She was so alive, so vibrant before him. He had found her once more. That, in itself, seemed a miracle. He wanted to scoop her up in his arms and twirl her.

I wasn't sure whether to come over or not, she said.

I'm glad you did.

I used to see you on the news all the time. Before I arrived here, I mean.

He nodded, at first confused. She carried on talking now, listing some of the news reports she'd particularly admired, one of which he hadn't done at all—it had been a colleague of his at the network—and at some point he realized that when she'd said *I know you* this is what she'd meant. That she'd seen him on television.

His stomach soured; the euphoria of a few seconds earlier drifted away. He felt himself receding, as though he had somehow been suddenly transported to the ceiling and was now looking down upon himself talking to this woman, a young and attractive woman who had no idea who he was except as he appeared on television when he did his best to sound as much as possible like Walter Cronkite. He wanted to

44

rewind to that moment by the window, or even before when he followed her around the crowded rooms. He found himself shaking his head slowly, unintentionally back and forth. She had no idea who he was. Whatever he thought of their meeting in Con Thien, it held nothing for her. She seemed to him suddenly just like any girl, like anyone else at the party. He watched her grow silent in front of him, aware perhaps that something inside him had shut down, that he was no longer listening.

I'm sorry, he said, his voice filled with disappointment, sounding overly contained, even robotic. *I thought you were someone else.*

The lights went on again and a great round of applause erupted from the party's guests. He could see her plainly now, and though the storm continued to rage outside it no longer felt as if it were here in the room, even between them. The record went back on, so loud that the guests raised their voices to shout over the heavy beat. Some began dancing, colliding into those who stood with drinks and some who sat. She leaned toward him so that her mouth was just under his chin, her brow knit, and said in a clipped manner, *Then I beg your pardon.*

She turned and walked in one deliberate, fluid movement, leaving him unsure whether to follow or let her go. He was angry and he had no right to be angry. He wanted to call to her, even to argue with her, this stranger, a woman whom (he reminded himself now) he did not even know. Unable to get her attention in the din of the party noise, the blaring music, the waves of laughter that seemed to come from the corners of the room, he went after her once more. When he was close enough, he reached forward and touched her shoulder and she turned, her eyes fierce upon his. Now he saw her as he remembered her, the strength of her emotions connecting them. It comforted him somehow, to see her once more as strong and clear as she'd been those weeks ago, not hiding a thing about herself. She could hate him if she wanted; that was understandable. He'd humiliated her—he realized that—but it hadn't been deliberate and he wanted to tell her so. Instead, what came out was altogether different, a plea from inside him that he hadn't reckoned on. He said, *You were in that bunker by the observation post. We sat across from one another. You don't* remember *that?*

She looked confused at first and he thought for one brief, dreadful moment that somehow he'd gotten the wrong girl altogether, that it was his mistake. It didn't seem possible that the girl in the bunker was some other English girl. He knew her face, her eyes. But there was no point in carrying on. It had happened, finally, even inevitably: they had met again. Never in all his imaginings did the event have so little importance.

I'm sorry, he said. *Never mind.*

He looked down, trying to decide how best to navigate himself away, out of the room, the hall, the hotel. He thought he could go to the bureau, or somewhere.

Then she said, *Con Thien?*

He felt something between them relax. He looked up and saw her face, the awareness arriving like a slow-growing wave. She began to fidget, holding her elbow with one hand, pressing her fingers over her mouth. She looked at him newly, her eyes scanning his face, his chest, his hands. Finally she said, *I remember that.*

He hadn't moved, was standing close, still holding her arm.

She said, *I didn't know it was you. I mean, how would I know? You were covered in dirt. You didn't have a helmet on and it was all in your hair—* Her hands moved to her own hair as she said the words. He felt the corners of his mouth rise, felt a wash of relief. She remembered. He let go her arm now, sure she would remain with him, that whatever would happen now had already begun, had taken hold. She looked down at the floor, a frown of concentration across her brow. *I thought you were a marine,* she explained.

No— he began.

Your hair is short like a marine and you had a first-aid pouch—

It was a tape recorder. The first-aid pouch is waterproof, so I use it—

You weren't wearing glasses.

They were in my hand.

I was sure—

Susan, he said, the first time he used her name. *Think back. I had no weapon.*

She looked down at the floor as though searching there for something she had dropped. He saw her shoulders move; she looked up and he realized that she was laughing. He tried to smile but could not. When had his life become so weighted he could not laugh with a beautiful woman?

Oh my God, she said. She sounded happy, relieved, a little overwhelmed, even. *I thought I'd never see you again.*

The truest advice she ever heard about combat reporting was that if you were really scared, you shouldn't go. But the amazing thing about being around war so long—one of the amazing things—was how it began to feel normal; healthy fear melted away and was replaced by curiosity. The stories came daily, told at the bar or while waiting at the airport for a lift. They were printed in newspapers, cabled from the offices on Tu Do Street, and with every story of a firefight, a skirmish, a reconnaissance, a bombing mission, a search-and-destroy, came a sense of the increasing normality. It was exactly the way the horses she had trained became used to fire and smoke and crowds and sudden loud sounds: a simple system of approach and retreat. Not that she became immune to fear—in some respects she felt scared all the time—but she reached a place where it arrived too late to keep her from doing the dangerous thing.

She did not feel braver. It was more that over the weeks the battles themselves had moved toward her, moved toward them all, into every city, every ville, so that it no longer seemed such an odd thing to witness and report, then eventually to wait around when a rumor was in the air, and at last to request to be woken at 4 a.m. to go out on an operation. It happened naturally, a slow attrition of common sense.

Now, she packed ace bandages, iodine, cotton. She regarded bits of rope or twine with interest, carried duct tape even though it weighed so much, wore a thin leather belt with a strong buckle. These things became most ordinary, like packing socks or underwear. She didn't think about why she packed them any more, though if asked she could tell you. Almost all battle deaths are caused by loss of blood.

Midnight, miles and miles from Saigon, out with soldiers in the jungle, absolutely riveted with concentration, unable to do anything but walk forward, she strained her eyes to keep track of Son, who was in front of her, and of the man in front of him. The line of soldiers stalked the land under the absolute darkness of a jungle night, putting the flats of their hands against the backs of the guys in front of them, training their eyes on to the tiny pieces of fluorescent tape tacked on to helmets, following the flashes of light that danced in the opaque screen of black as they marched. She held the hand of the man in front, and the man behind. There were no instructions required; they were all so scared that holding hands made sense. She had forgotten that she had not been drafted and had no need to be there, that she was not a useful part of the military machine. She had forgotten, had been in the process of forgetting for some time now, and had arrived at a place in which it hadn't seemed at all extraordinary to go on this search-and-destroy mission. Following the column, part of it now, she thought how easy it would be to become lost, to somehow spiral out of this line of safety. If she were to get herself into trouble, this would be the place. It would be so easy to become momentarily separated and it would feel, she imagined, like losing your way in outer space. And then it happened. Not contact with the enemy, not the sudden rush of incoming artillery in her ears, but the same abrupt, unexpected tide of awareness that she had experienced before. In the middle of that night, in a manner that arrived like its own assault, while walking silently in a string of men barely out of their teens, it was as though she suddenly discovered where she was and how stupid she had been. It was, she realized, like being in the helicopter the first time she was on the receiving end of gunfire—she could not get away. She felt the sweat dripping down the sides of her body, flooding her forehead, her eyes. She would follow the men with assiduous care, with the same steady, silent footsteps, even though now she was out of her mind with fear, even though she would do anything not to have come on the operation. It happened to her the same way every time: the discovery always came too late, or in the wrong place, or the wrong circumstances. Each time that she came, however momentarily, to her senses, it was like being back in that helicopter months before, hearing the bullets like tiny hammers beneath her and wishing she could run.

Then don't go.

Marc would tell her this late at night as they lay in bed. It was his answer to any hint of worry or doubt, any concern at all about things that happened—the chopper being hit, the awful night on the search-and-destroy mission. She wasn't supposed to feel anything. Or she wasn't supposed to admit it.

But I want to go, she said. She didn't say that it was he who had woken her with his restless audible dreams, that she would not be up late at night worrying if he hadn't startled her in the night with his voice. When he talked in his sleep he did not sound like himself. The first time she heard him she was frightened, waking momentarily to the thought that she was

49

elsewhere, with a stranger, listening to a voice that seemed wholly detached from the man beside her.

He kept whiskey by the bed, always a glass of it, or a mug or paper cup. He took a long swallow now, then searched the ashtray, using a penlight so he could see. *I've got a jay in here somewhere. Hand me those matches. Look, you go back to sleep. You'll feel better later. It's always worse at night.*

What is worse?

She looked at him slyly. She wanted him to admit he had the same fears as she, though it would do no good even if he did. He shook his head, pushing himself up, so that his back leaned against the wall. He had a pillow on his lap, the ashtray on the pillow. *Everything*, he said. He might have said more, about how the dreams rise with you in the morning, that you eventually find there is no rest, but he did not. He sat in bed and smoked diligently until she fell asleep. In the morning he told her it was nice that she slept so well. He told her he was jealous.

Like everything in Vietnam, their relationship seemed to be on fast forward. They'd met for the second time at the party, and after that night he'd disappeared up north again and she was forced to put him from her mind. His face, which she had known from television when she used to watch from her apartment in Chicago as he broadcast from Vietnam, was now part of her daily thoughts. She associated him not with a network but with that bunker in Con Thien, that hotel room where they stood by the window, an electric storm, a particular song that kept being played on the record player. Back when she watched him as part of a news report, it had seemed as if he was broadcasting from a world far away and unreachable. Now it felt as if the television image of him was from another world, a ghost of him that visited the living rooms of people across America. She thought of him altogether too often, and then one day he arrived unannounced at her door, telling her he knew a very good restaurant, and asking if she had time for a bite.

She wasn't all that shocked to see him. He'd somehow managed to get a cable to her, letting her know when he'd be back in town and asking if it would be all right to get in touch. Apparently, get in touch meant come and fetch her from her room.

It's three in the afternoon, she said.

Should I come back later?

No.

Am I allowed in? Or are we going to stand here in the hall?

We're going to— She didn't know what they were going to do. She had a page of copy in her hand. Her fingers were stained from fixing typewriter ribbon that had gotten twisted. She wondered if there was black ink on her face. She wanted to appear bold, decisive, to be someone he would take seriously, who could surprise him. *We're going to your hotel,* she said. *I prefer it.*

He tried not to show his delight. He looked around him— at the peeling walls, the scuffed floorboards with tiny holes throughout from some kind of insect damage, at the bare bulbs and places on the ceilings where water from long ago leaks, had stained the paint. *I think I agree with you,* he said casually.

She would have changed her clothes but there was nowhere in the room to undress except in the bathroom and Son had crowded photographs in various stages of development there. She ended up brushing her hair and checking her face with a hand mirror.

I didn't know you were a photographer, he said.

I'm not.

He indicated all the black-and-whites clipped along the walls.

She told him they belonged to Son. *I think you know him,* she said. Now his expression changed and so she added quickly. *It isn't what you think.*

51

Where is he now?

Son? She thought for a moment. *I have no idea.*

He just pops in when he feels like it?

She smiled. She didn't like the way the conversation was going. *He doesn't have anywhere to live. No money. He sleeps on the floor, on a mat. I know it must seem very odd.*

Very. He took her hand. *You'll need an umbrella*, he said.

He wasn't especially tall but in her recently purchased flat canvas sandals he seemed so to Susan. He guided her as they walked along the sidewalk, which smelled like a mixture of overripe fruit and urine. He told her about his most recent story. He offered her a cigarette. Whenever the conversation strayed from the subject of the war—what was being said, where he'd been, descriptions of the men in the company he'd gone out with, or who he'd recently spoken to from an embassy— he seemed all of a sudden nervous. She let him talk, learning from him but feeling, too, that this is what she could expect, a wildly attractive tutor, an alluring purveyor of knowledge about the war.

Where are you from? she asked.

New York, he said quickly. Then told her how he'd grown to prefer Danang to Saigon, how he really didn't like it down here any more.

You're married, aren't you? Her question, injected into the conversation as it was, made him lose his train of thought.

Currently, he answered.

She didn't mind. Not at first. In the circumstances in which they found themselves, it didn't make all that much difference.

Marc was what Son politely called "not so cautious," by which he meant the guy had a death wish. Susan's and his was a misguided amorphous, sprawling kind of relationship with no obvious direction or end in sight. In other words, perfect for the time being. They met between stories, holing up in his hotel or anywhere else they could find, disappearing for a day and then emerging again, rushing out to get another story. It was exhausting and addictive. And among many other things, it had the effect on Susan of knocking away whatever remnants of common sense and perspective she had. She went out on more missions. She took more risks.

I'm thinking you might get killed soon, Son said one night. They were sharing a meal at the Eskimo, sitting shoulder to shoulder, eating off each other's plates and talking about something else entirely—how the Americans had brought over enormous pigs from the States in an effort to increase the size of Vietnamese pigs, a silly operation that had resulted in no demonstrable gain as the smaller pigs ran away from the atrocious, slow monsters from the West. In the middle of laughing, Son had suddenly gone quiet and then issued his concern. *If something happens to you—* he began.

Nothing will, she interrupted. That was on the eve of an assault mission they covered. And she'd been right that time. Nothing happened—or rather, nothing happened to them.

Another telegram:

```
EXCELLENT STORY BUT FEEL YOU ARE TAKING TOO MANY RISKS
STOP MAGAZINE CANNOT BE RESPONSIBLE FOR RECKLESS
REPORTING STOP BE MORE CAREFUL STOP
```

She could imagine her editor sitting in her houndstooth skirt with its matching jacket, the vein at her temple throbbing, her skin itching as though she had fleas, sleeves pushed up away from the clutter on her desk. Cursing Susan for making her sweat like this, she would dictate the wire to some trembling young secretary. The cost per word of such a wire was too high to include the expletives, which the secretary would understand must be deleted from the final dictation. *That's it!* she'd say when she had completed the message. *Now bring me a fresh pack of matches.* Then she'd ball up some paper as the girl fled tfrom he office, the dictated cable in hand.

Susan was fond of the woman; she did not want to cause her an early stroke, so she returned as follows:

BEING MORE CAUTIOUS STOP FOLLOWING SUPPLY CONVOY TO
REFUGEE CAMP STOP HOPE THIS COMPLIES WITH REQUEST
STOP STOP WORRYING STOP

She and Son were traveling with the 9th Infantry to what she thought would be a safe enough place in the Delta, an area where huge camps were being set up for what were being called "refugees," that is, people emptied out of villages thought to be enemy strongholds. Her reason for choosing the story was simple: she wanted a story that did not require her to walk miles or sleep on the ground or sit in a hole in the rain. Besides, there was her editor to consider. This was meant to be easy, the refugee story, with photographs of children and mothers and smiling soldiers. She wore a pair of utility trousers, a T-shirt and field jacket. The rain was easing off so that she could flip back the hood on her poncho, enjoying the cool air, talking to the guy next to her on the armored personnel carrier about his collection of fighting fish that—so she learned—were a species that originated in Vietnam. They'd been traveling over an hour now, a slow, uneventful journey; it might have been a tractor ride on a wet summer's day.

She'd run out of water and was drinking from Son's plastic bottle, the canvas flaps jigging with the movement of the track, her sunglasses making her nose sweat. She was handing him back the bottle when she heard gunshot. The bottle dropped. She wheeled toward the sound, the air cracking around her as though blocks of wood were being exploded close by, then a huge booming explosion that made everything shake.

It was as though the world was erupting beneath them. Great spouts of earth rained down as the ground, blasted with mortars, sent mud flying as though an enormous force was kicking it straight into her face, over her head. The M60 mounted on the hull of the track burst into life; she was deafened by the gun's noise, which soared through her, lifting her up, making her weightless as though she were floating. She had always thought she was protected if only by the firepower of the men with whom she traveled. By the guns, the boxes of ammunition, the ever-squawking radios, the sheer volume of artillery. Joining the convoy, so heavily armored, hadn't given her any concern, not a moment of worry; they were heading for a refugee camp, not trying to take a city. And now, this.

The first few blasts destroyed the vehicles in front and the ensuing attack came straight at those who stalled. She was traveling on the open back of the APC; there was no place to take shelter, and she realized suddenly that the feeling of floating was due, in part, to how hard she had to work just to hang on to the vehicle. They were reversing now off the road, bouncing over uneven ground, churning up mud, scraping against the brush, which itself sparkled with gunfire. The track was tipping one way, then another, lunging into the jungle, then reversing up again, the men above her yelling to each other, firing madly, the spent casings dancing on the track's deck. She saw tracers to the rear, flashes from the enemy guns. She looked at Son, indicating wildly the attack which was coming from behind, hoping he could somehow alert the gunman. Instead he grabbed her arm, pulled her down and together they jumped off the track, running, wheeling and diving, tripping, getting up again. It was a crazy thing to do, to run blindly toward the bush, away from the approaching gunfire, but there were soldiers on the ground now, too, and they didn't know what else to do.

They survived the initial, lethal minute. That was the first thing. They missed the ammo log that exploded, the fragments of burning metal, the small-arms fire that rang out around them. It was the right thing to run. They might have made it, too, but there was a kind of disorientation; the jungle seemed to swallow them whole. The fighting continued, went on and on. They didn't know which way to move. They heard screaming; they heard the long cracking sound of machine guns. But they were out of voice range and never heard the call to mount up. The convoy moved on without them while they were still trying to figure out where the road was, where the shots were coming from. All around them was jungle, elephant grass and vines, the air full of carbine, the heat like someone holding a blanket over her head.

She didn't feel frightened. When she saw the ammo log blow she imagined that the blast would roll toward her. The burning metal tumbled through the air so cleanly, she thought it would fly straight to where she was sitting on the track. One of the crew on the track had already been injured. She saw him crumple in a single, smooth motion, as though someone had suddenly removed all his bones. He fell on top of the track, amid the burning copper shell casings which would blister your skin if they touched you, then he slid toward the edge. She might have hoped the soldier wasn't dead, but she couldn't hold on to such a simple, humane thought. She'd seen him fall, his body halfway off the edge of the vehicle. She'd seen the people running and crouching, throwing themselves this way and that, falling, dying, all of this happening beneath the heat of a rising sun. It seemed impossible that they had been so effectively ambushed and, then, that she had survived by running toward the jungle. In the thick of the jungle, she felt amazed to be standing, to be whole, stunned so that for a minute she ran her hands over her arms, her legs, then turned to Son and did the same to him. To think that she was still alive! Even her friend, too, even him. She was not afraid, but grateful. Grateful to every animal and bird in this harsh land, to the sun and wind and to everything she observed, suddenly free, standing, breathing, sweating, living.

Now it was only a matter of getting back to the convoy. She did not realize it was already moving. She pulled Son's arm, told him they had better get out of there. But he stood silent and immobile, as though he'd been planted in the ground like wood. She began to grow concerned. She took his shoulders and shook him, frowning into his still, frozen face, wondering if he had some injury she could not see, a hole in his body like the holes she'd seen in bodies before, a dial of blood rimmed by charred black flesh, sometimes small enough you had to look for it, hiding an enormous, tattered exit wound. But there was no bullet and anyway, he was standing. Though his breath came in shallow gasps and his eyes stayed fixed on the air in front of him, he had no injury she could detect, and there was no explanation she could imagine.

At last she saw him move. He swallowed, sucked his lips in, and spoke in a hoarse whisper so that she had to lean toward him to hear. She realized all at once what was happening, what held him there, unmoving.

Behind us, he said.

II

The targets were known to everyone. For example, the men who carried radios were targets. Her second month as a correspondent, a Spec-4 was killed in front of her and his radio, still squawking, was hit two more times before she had the sense to crawl back out of the way. Son was screaming at her, *Get down! Move!* The lieutenant whose radio the Spec-4 was carrying was nose down in the dirt, yelling like mad for a medic. There were more bullets; they sent up spirals of dust only a few yards from where she was, splintered the branches of nearby trees, made hard cracks in the air around her. She could hear all this, the lieutenant going crazy, his cheek to the ground, his mouth open, calling and calling for help for the dying soldier, Son shouting her name until his voice was hoarse. But she was stunned; she could not bring herself to move. She dropped on to the dirt, her eyes level with the radio operator's shoulder. She kept staring at his chest where smoke spiraled up from two neat holes, looking at his arms stretched out casually on the ground, the plastic handset still resting in his open palm. He wore a wedding ring. She thought about it, but she did not touch her camera. Had he been a dead Vietcong she would have gotten out the camera, but this was an American. He had a letter from home folded carefully in the band of his helmet, his face toward the high, white sun, his eyes large, empty, no longer focusing, and still the smoke rising from him, his chest on fire, his heart.

There was more shouting and bullets and the *whoosh* of rockets overhead. She heard the radio calling to the dead soldier, asking his position, calling over and over, a desperate voice demanding his coordinates, until finally the next bullets came and then even the radio stopped. Suddenly, she woke up as though from a stupor, felt a rush of fear gathering inside her, the sensation so strong it was like having the wind knocked out of her. All at once she cried out, then crawled as fast as possible to a nearby anthill, a huge mound, baked hard, bigger than a rosebush. She hid there, her hands over her head, her chin in her chest, wondering what she'd been doing—what on earth—sitting in the open like that, so easy to pick off.

The lieutenants leading platoons were targets. They allowed her to tag along with her steno pad. They allowed her to ask questions, to share C-rations and cigarettes, to dig a hole at night and sleep among the men, but not to walk point with them up front. They did not want her killed. It wasn't that a lieutenant had any reason to favor her. She was of no use to them—if she died, if she didn't—but she would not know to be wary of dried leaves, which can sometimes be old camouflage hiding an explosive. Or that an unusual object on the ground—a VC scarf or helmet—would blow her arm off if she touched it. They protected her by keeping her among them, and she cherished that protection. The commanding officers would not say this to her face, but a dead woman was not good for morale.

Son they did not worry about. Put him up front. Put him behind, in the middle, anywhere at all. He was male, Vietnamese, a journalist—who cared?

Radar equipment was a target. Artillery pieces were targets. Anything was a target, but there were values attached. A helicopter was worth a great deal. A reporter was not worth much, possibly nothing at all. Most of the ones who died were shot by accident or tripped a mine, at least before the war moved into Cambodia. Then it all changed. September 1970: twenty-five reporters killed that month alone. By then she was out of the war. She got a letter from a friend who was still there telling her Kupferberg was dead. Sanchez was dead. Jenkins was missing. Ngoc Kia, dead. She hung up her coat. She sat down on the steps. She thought, *Everything in my life is poisoned.* She thought, *Don't let me go back.* But of course she wanted to go back. She would always want to.

But in 1967 she did not know any correspondents who had been killed, did not know any personally. You *could* die. Anyone could die; you didn't even need to go out on combat assaults for that. Poisoned in a crowded street in Saigon from a hypodermic needle, or blown up while standing exposed at a bus stop waiting to board one of the military buses with steel mesh bolted over the windows to stop grenades. If you went out, or if you didn't. Hotels were bombed. Church buildings. A secretary for the CIA heard a noise in the street, went to the window, and was killed when a car bomb exploded. Nobody meant to kill her, her specifically. There would be a lot of blood shed, then nothing for a week, a month, so that you began to relax. Then it started again. Marc's cameraman, Locke, called it "the life cycle," an ironic name, she thought. Marc was even more philosophic, saying "If it happens, it happens." But one thing she thought she knew was that she herself was not a target, was never a target.

Yet here she is, with three guns trained on her.

The three Vietcong stand in a formation, one more forward than the others, rifles out, balanced in their hands so that the muzzles are aimed straight at her. She has not seen guns pointed in her direction before. She is used to seeing the sides of the barrels, the curves of the magazines, the focus of the soldiers who carry the weapons directed at some far-off target, not her. She remains completely still, as though for an X-ray, frozen in place, not sure whether to raise her hands. The soldiers must be assessing how dangerous she and Son are, studying their belts for weapons, searching the brush behind them for soldiers, for the green army uniform, the canvas-sided boots. Suddenly, one of them lowers his weapon and comes forward under the protection of his comrades, who stand ready to fire.

The soldier who approaches them is tall for a Vietnamese, with a narrow head like a rocket. There is a ferocity to his movements so that it feels to Susan as though a wild animal is charging them. He directs his attention at Son, whom he regards as though he has been hunting him for months, for years even, as though he knows him and hates him, as though there is some dreadful business that needs settling and which gives the soldier every right at this time to knock Son hard in the chest with the butt of his rifle and send him sprawling to the ground.

She sees Son's head rock back, his knees collapse. She watches as he goes down with a grunt, his head rolling back as he falls. Her hands fly to her mouth, her eyes stare; she wishes she could turn away. He is on the ground, on his knees. The soldier turns now to her, glaring as she reels back, her body tense, expecting a blow. But he does not hit her. He shouts at her in Vietnamese, kicks Son, and issues an instruction she doesn't understand. Son manages a response which includes the words *bao chi*: journalists. There is a pause as the soldier takes this in. He mutters a short sentence also containing the word *bao chi*, and Son responds once more, his focus still on the ground, unmoving. The others remain ready to fire.

She feels so tense she thinks she may faint, and she wonders if they will shoot her as she falls. The first soldier nudges Son with his foot. A second approaches, this one smaller with bushy hair sticking out every direction, and Susan sees that he has a sword in one hand, his rifle in the other. He starts speaking in a rapid, insistent manner, pointing to the sky with the sword, a crude weapon that looks as though it has been made from burnt metal. All around them are flying insects, the sun so bright she squints and still cannot see. It is like being inside an overexposed photograph. Her vision fades at the edges. For a moment she thinks they are going to kill Son with the sword, bringing it down upon his head as he crouches on the ground. She cannot take this in, how they are going to kill them now as easily as if the act were a culling of stock. But the soldier seems more interested in what he sees above him, in the pale, hot sun scorching from its height above the scrub and trees. The sword does not come down on Son's neck. Nobody is to be killed, at least for now.

Son is told to get up. He rises, his hands arranged behind his head, his neck bowed. The third of the young soldiers is with them now. He has an air of certainty about him, and circles as though assuming ownership, his weapon more loosely held than the others. They are talking, a rapid exchange that means nothing to Susan until Son speaks to her in French. His French is as good as his English, much better than hers. He does not meet her eyes.

"They want us to move fast now," he says. "Before the air strike."

Being captured, she discovers, is a feeling of being trapped, but worse even. Being trapped and buried alive. Son carries himself stiffly, his shoulder swollen from the earlier blow, one leg of his trousers torn at the knee with a gaping hole that seems to get larger by the hour. Her field jacket is tied around her waist, slightly damp from the morning rain and her own sweat, smelling like warm grass and mold. She has lost her hat and has only a scarf to keep her hair out of her face, the sun off her head. For now, the sun is not a problem. They walk through a dense stretch of jungle that allows in only the darkest green-hued light. The jungle has a fairytale aspect to it, with huge leaves, vines that hang like snakes, tongues of fungus that poke up from the ground. It has a smell, too. Rotting vegetation,

65

stagnant water, hot wet earth. Her breath feels scorched in her lungs. She takes in the air and it feels empty to her, unable to deliver the oxygen she needs. She wonders how she stays standing, walking. She thinks she can feel the gaze of the soldier behind her, his eyes on her back, his rifle close enough so that she could reach back and touch it. She listens to the sounds of the jungle, the whistles and rustles, the birds through the trees, their own footfalls on the jungle's floor. Everything spooks her. If she thinks too much about the soldier behind her she will scream.

These first hours are like no others she has experienced, not even when she pressed herself into the earth under fire. They are almost unbearable. She knows she is lucky to be alive. During the ambush, when she reeled back from the first explosion and saw the truck in front buck and collapse on its side, then heard the small-arms fire open up, she squeezed her eyes shut and listened, had no choice but to hear the cries of the wounded around her. That, too, was terrible. The battle had lasted only a short while. A matter of minutes, not even a quarter of an hour. They had run so that they would not be hit in the crossfire, and because they feared the vehicle might explode. They'd run because running was instinctive. Now, of course, she wishes they had not. She always knew it was possible to be wounded, to be shot, but it never occurred to her that she'd stumble upon the Vietcong in the same sudden, slightly incredible way that you might come across moose in a forest, and end up captured.

The plain, dark uniforms, the bushy, unkempt hair, the faces which appear younger than they are make the Vietcong seem more like a small band of lost boy scouts than enemy soldiers. They were separated from their unit when it scattered during the firefight. They had been as lost as Susan and Son were at the moment of their meeting. It was all a dreadful coincidence. Two have AK-47s. One has what looks like a Soviet semi-automatic.

They have grenades and Chicoms, the appalling sword. The sword is what disturbs her most. The soldier who has it seems to enjoy swiping the air with the blade as he walks. It bothers her more than the guns and grenades, more than their acetate map that they carry, discussing where to go. The map is blackened with mildew, with little pockmarks like the actual craters that gouge the land. And it belongs, she realizes with a start, to the US Army.

"What are they going to do with us, Son? Please talk to me—tell me what they are saying—"

He won't reply. For some reason, whatever she asks Son, he will not answer. He scowls and moves one leg in front of the other, sometimes rubbing his palms along the sides of his shirt. The sweat trickles from his forehead, his sideburns, making a damp patch beneath each arm and across his chest. She wants to know if he has any idea where they are being taken, what his guess would be, whether he is injured from where the gun struck him—anything. But he will not reply or turn her way. Perhaps this is what happens to people in such extreme circumstances. They go inward, forgetting the allegiances they once had, thinking only of survival. The minutes, then hours, pass in a dull, tense silence.

By noon, the jungle is a dark oven through which they travel. In only a few hours she has endured capture, marching, abandonment, with no prelude to these lessons. They walk, all of them tense. The Vietcong have the guns, which is why they are in charge, but there is a feeling they are as miserable as their captives, obliged to fasten themselves to these stray, anonymous people, to take charge, to point the weapons at them. Though they began the march with purposeful, angry strides, now in the early part of the afternoon they have sunk into a steady, weary step. They chat infrequently. There is a concentration of movement, on placing one foot in front of the other, every action slowed by the heat. This is no different with them than all the times she has been with the Americans, though now she is expected to move more quickly. Even so, the rhythm of their steps, the steady, almost mechanical pace is the same.

The only animation the Vietcong have shown came shortly after they set out, once the air strike had come and gone and they could hear it in the distance. The trees hid the billows of black on the horizon, but she could imagine the spiraling smoke, the planes disappearing one by one. Susan had a bag of watermelon seeds in the pocket of her fatigues, the sort of thing you buy before the Tet holiday and eat with friends. The Vietnamese soldiers took it, along with everything else she owned: her papers; a "women's interest" story—about a triple amputee, six years old, who with remarkable prosthetics was now able to walk and use a spoon; extra socks; money; MPC notes; a signaling mirror; T-shirt; compass. They sat with their canteens and passed her comb from man to man, giggling. They tested her pens for ink. It was as though these unremarkable personal things were valuable bounty; they examined each item carefully. Then they took her boots—a means of controlling her movements, kinder than tying—her gold cross, hairbands, a letter from Marc.

"Anything more you need?" she said as they tried to figure out what the Kotex was, holding it against make-believe wounds as though it were a dressing.

They have taken Son's map, binoculars, matches, insect repellent, gum, and his cameras, which he handed over only reluctantly. They have taken everything she owns except the clothes she wears and her hammock. Without the weight of her possessions she is looser, lighter, able to move more freely, and yet Susan feels more exposed. If she could cloak herself in the things that are hers, she might stave off the disorientation which is arriving, she knows, not because she feels it yet but because it has been described to her by others, by women she once interviewed in an Illinois State Prison, for example, who were locked up for such crimes as "lascivious carriage," which meant they had lived with a man out of wedlock. Once the women's clothes and possessions were confiscated, once they had been dressed identically and doused with lice powder, their personalities themselves began a process of unraveling. The draftees she had interviewed some months previously reported the same feeling after their civilian clothes were discarded, their heads shaved so that they could not recognize themselves in a mirror, and every ounce of privacy annihilated to the extent that even the toilets were set out starkly in rows on a long wall with not so much as a screen between them. It did something to you, set in motion a kind of uncertainty that was easily manipulated by whoever was in charge.

She reminds herself that the men in control now are only three youths who somehow became separated from the rest of their unit during the ambush. It was almost by obligation that they took her and Son prisoner. And though their rifles are menacing enough, they have immature, bland faces. They only want her things for the novelty value. When she reminds herself of all this she feels more herself, and she can believe, however fleetingly, that the whole thing is a game. As if any moment they will release her and Son, and then all scatter behind trees, count to twenty and start again.

That is how she will tell it, she decides, if she gets the opportunity.

Hours later she is not sure she will get the chance; the mood of the soldiers has changed. They'd been excited at first by what their prisoners had in their pockets, but now they appear bored with the whole thing. Miles into the march she is surprised they don't just shoot her and Son and have done with it. They are weary. When they pass under low branches they are attacked by red ants which seem to wait for their prey, dropping down on them as they pass and biting at their collars. Like Susan, the Vietcong have to dig the ants out or squash them beneath their clothes. They swear in Vietnamese just as she would swear in English, if she dared to speak at all. The soldiers look at Son and Susan as if the ants are their fault. At rest stops they glare at them with hatred, Susan thinks, as though it is they, the VC, who have been taken prisoner by these inconvenient others.

She supposes it is the responsibility of guarding that weighs on them, especially in the heat of the day. For her part, she is too frightened to hate them. There are times she is so certain they will kill her that she almost wishes it would be said aloud. She thinks the admission might help prepare her for the act, like anesthesia. By mid-afternoon her head is swimming. There is a pain in her left temple that tracks her pulse. All at once, almost without meaning to, she says, "They will take us some-place and shoot us. Near a swamp or a rice paddy. In a field." After many hours of saying nothing she is suddenly talking to herself, talking to Son. He doesn't answer, but he is giving her a curious look as though she's inexplicably sprouted a tail. She's feeling giddy; perhaps that is why he is staring at her. They sit beneath a cluster of trees. Her feet are numb all the way up to her knees. She is being allowed some water and she wishes there were enough so that she could drink for as long as she wanted, pour it over her head, over her feet which are dead to her now, so that it feels like she is walking on stumps.

One of the soldiers has collected some bamboo that he is carving carefully for reasons she does not understand. She is aware of the heat, the air swollen with moisture, but she no longer seems to be sweating. She hears herself speak and it sounds like someone else talking, not her. "They'll stand us on the side of a bomb crater, shoot us, and then we'll fall in," she says. Her mind flashes images, sometimes disjointed, as though she is dreaming. She sees craters and bones, tall dry grasses, the white sun. She shivers and wonders why; thinks it must be her own fatigue making her imagine this. The craters look like convenient graves. She's seen them full of water, newly alive with marine life, and wondered then how the fish managed to find their way into bomb craters. She has seen soldiers bathing in them, peasants fishing in them. She's also seen a body or two. She thinks this is remarkable, that she could die now in a hollow of the earth, in the footprint of an explosive whose origins are from some Midwestern town half a planet away.

Her skin has gone strangely cool. Her lips taste of salt. Son is staring at her. The soldiers seem not to notice, perhaps not to care. For a moment she thinks she might fall asleep, right here, right now. Her head begins to dip, her eyes closing. She realizes she is becoming a heat casualty. She has seen troops medevac'd on stretchers in the same condition. Her awareness of this startles her. She recovers long enough to ask for more water.

"Can you walk?" Son asks. These are his first words to her in many hours and they feel good, like the water itself. But though he has spoken only once, the sound echoes in her mind so that it feels he is asking again and again: *Can you walk, can you walk?* Part of her, the part that is thinking straight, still rational, knows that it is heat exhaustion that is the problem. She drinks as much as she is able, then nods and stands up. Her feet are bleeding, she realizes, but she can walk.

They reach a clearing made some time ago by US troops who, judging from the look of the place, had apparently wanted to land a helicopter right here in the jungle. She studies the tree stumps that have been blown up, charred wood, charred ground, a lot of sudden sunshine that comes through like a knife. She feels almost drunk, her legs jelly, her arms shaking, the cool sweat like the glistening oil of a snake. She is glad there are no craters near by, even though she knows she is only imagining what might happen, that nobody has told her, told her anything really.

The soldiers are busy scouring the land, looking for left-over C-rations, matches, cigarettes, gum—anything the soldiers may have left behind. There is a fair chance they'll find something valuable. Marc once told her it was not uncommon for the Americans to bury a whole carton of C-rations rather than carry it. He told her this as they stood in a wooded area, a fire behind them from where the troops had burned a Vietcong hideout. She watched a GI walk to the river's edge to dump a load of rations, then get another box and do the same again. *What's he doing?* she asked. Marc looked up from his notepad, blinked into the sun, and explained. She'd had no idea. It was like a thousand details of this war that were a mystery to her. She looks now as the three Vietcong soldiers pick up bits of garbage, an empty Salem pack, a cracked Bic lighter. If found, rations are treasure to the Vietcong, better than money, which they seldom have a use for except to surrender to their superiors.

She imagines the Americans back again, the soldiers who made the clearing. With their M16s, their bandoliers, grenades and knives and helmets. She wishes them back and for a moment she smiles, picturing the face of a captain she met while out with Marc on a story in Gio Linh. She didn't think she'd paid that much attention, but there is his face in front of her now, the slightly wild glaze of his expression, the thin upper lip, the whites of his eyes bright against his face, which is dark with earth and sun, with insect repellent and dust.

He'd stood in a clearing waving an ice-cream cone as he spoke. There'd been a story about how the troops were under-supplied, with TV footage of them describing how they might run out of C-rations at this rate. Command had reacted, first by getting after the reporter about "misreporting," and second by sending barrels of ice cream and ammunition out to the soldiers immediately. She watched the captain talk between slurps of ice cream, which melted faster than he could eat it, running down his sleeve, attracting insects which he picked out with his fingers. They'd blasted out a temporary landing zone to get in a chopper for a wounded soldier and it looked like the clearing where she sat now. She half expected to see the white wrappers, the Popsicle sticks, packaging from dressings, cigarette butts. She half expected to see that captain's grubby face, the dusty, sagging uniform, the reassuring gun.

You shouldn't have said what you did, Davis, the captain had told Marc. *Ruins morale, a story like that.*

Wasn't me, Marc said. *I didn't even know about it.*

It might not be you who did it, but it was your network, that's for goddamn sure. I mean, why can't you people get on the team?

Marc sighed. *I didn't know the guy who did that story. We're not all that friendly, the press. To each other, I mean.*

I don't know. You look awful friendly to me, the captain said, moving his gaze from Marc to Susan and back again. *Getting altogether too friendly, I'd say.*

She'd only known Marc a few weeks then, the charge of electricity so strong between them it was as recognizable as an army flag. They could deny it—to the captain, to a dozen others—but it was obvious, palpable, a disaster in the making.

Under normal circumstances, if she were to think about the captain at all, she would have recalled with a small stitch of resentment the way he looked at her as if she was a nice little can of rations tucked into Marc's own pack. But that is not what seems important now. What she thinks of now, what she wants most of all, is the ice cream. She is almost exhilarated by the thought of something cold and sweet and wet.

Son is studying the Vietcong, the ground, the treeline. She imagines he is assessing the chances of running into American soldiers. He frowns into the distance, then looks away, and she concludes that nobody is coming. The only sounds are jungle sounds: the rustling of unseen animals, of scurrying birds and monkeys and rats. Occasionally, she hears a series of long,

piercing cries and she imagines that one of the hidden crea-
tures is murdering another of them, and she is reminded of
the cries of the men she heard during the ambush. She blames
herself for being here now. She swats at the insects that flutter
next to her head, confusing her in the heat and dust with the
vibration of their wings and the constant stimulation of movement near her eyes.

As they begin again, moving out of the clearing, she asks
Son once more if he thinks they will be shot. They are walking
over splintered, dead branches strewn with new vines that grow
easily over the broken land, around torn stumps already
sprouting new buds, the land so fertile and determined it is a
force of its own, as powerful as the war. For a moment she
thinks she sees Son nod. This sends her into a desperate,
pleading burst.

"Is that right, then?" she says. "Is that what is going to
happen? *We'll be shot?*"

He has no chance to respond. One of the soldiers indicates
with his gun that she needs to keep moving. Walking is increasingly difficult. Her feet hurt; she is drying out. In a minute
she'll begin hallucinating, or perhaps she will fall. She feels
invisible to the soldiers, who move them on like cattle. She
feels invisible to Son; perhaps in his mind she is already dead.

Salt pills, the juice of a dragonfruit, water and shade. She is
nursed with these simple things and when she wakes she has
no idea how long she has been asleep. She thinks it has been
a long time, but judging from the light still left in the day, it
has been less than an hour. They begin again to walk. She feels
better than before, but not great. She wishes Son would talk to
her, just a few words every once in a while and she would be
satisfied. He still does not turn around or slow his pace. Perhaps
he has no choice. She is handicapped by her inability to understand what is said when the soldiers speak to him. Before they

took her wristwatch, she had checked the time every ten minutes, comforted by the thought that it was the same time everywhere else as here in this wilderness. Now she feels adrift, out of synch with the world. The soldier with longish hair is ahead, the other two behind. The guards keep their rifles on their shoulders, or use them to point, like extensions of their arms and hands.

You get ground down to powder, then you get greased, that's what a GI told her once, his summation of the life of an infantryman. He was missing two teeth, knocked out when he dove during an attack on a firebase that was nearly overrun. He struggled with the gap in his mouth, his tongue escaping so that he developed an unwelcome lisp. *Then you get greathed,* he said. *You thtart getting religion. You thtart wanting God.*

She understands now what he meant. It was this right here. Her feet ache. Her hands are scratched so that the blood beads against the skin, attracting flies. She watches the soldier with the long hair, the one in front, and wishes he'd trip a wire and leave nothing left of himself bigger than a stone. Then, just as she has this thought, the soldier gestures behind him, putting Son up front to act as his personal bomb squad to clear the path ahead. It bothers her to see Son there, a rifle trained on his back. She notices with relief when the guard lets the rifle drop once more. It is not difficult to imagine the soldiers getting bored with prisoners, shooting them for convenience's sake, bringing their bodies to the river. It is unfortunate, she thinks, that she has such an imagination that she can envision the execution, or, as she walks the narrow, difficult path, almost see a booby-trap exploding. To be brave, she thinks, you need to be right here, right now, with no sense of what might happen in a few hours or days. To be very brave you need never to imagine consequences or sudden turns of events. You need, really, to have no imagination whatsoever, which is why (she concludes) good writers are not usually good combat reporters.

Wrong temperament. Like bringing a race horse to a rock concert.

They rest, squatting on the jungle floor, sitting on their ankles in the fashion of the Vietnamese. The one with the narrow head, who was carving bamboo earlier, lays the shavings in a pile and then rubs two pieces back and forth, strikes a spark with a flint and makes a fire. The flames shoot up unexpectedly and he jumps back as though something live has sprung at him. This sends the others into giggles, their grubby faces smiling in a manner that seems genuinely warm. They are friends, Susan can see that. She observes them the way she might a herd of exotic animals with their own unknowable social order. A part of her understands they may be like her and Son, who have traveled together so long that they have become a kind of family, but she doesn't dwell on this. Instead, she tells herself they are killers—all soldiers are killers—but she hopes they are not yet completely dead inside.

The flame is for bits of fish and rice produced from a bag. The fish are old, dried, and yet her hunger makes it smell delicious. She longs to eat. She longs to talk to Son. They have bound her wrists with green wire. She does not understand at first why they find it necessary to tie her now, after so many hours without, until she sees that once they have tied her and Son's wrists they can put away their weapons, lie down, relax. One of them stretches out on a rock; another makes a seat out of a log, then rushes back when he is attacked by ants. The soldier who lit the fire makes up the meal and brings it to the others. The soldiers eat, chatting as they do. They drink from their canteens and make jokes, particularly the smallest of the three, the one with the sword. He lies on his back, his sword above him, splicing the air with the dark blade, commenting in a manner that occasionally brings chuckles from the other two. They might have been friends together on a camping trip.

When finally they have finished eating they offer some fish to her and Son, getting out cigarettes and smoking while she and Son eat awkwardly with their hands bound.

A few minutes later they turn, all at once, and stare at her. She would be startled, but she is too tired to be startled. All movement has been made slow by her exhaustion and the heat. It takes more than a tough look to raise her heartbeat, but it feels as though a pack of wolves has just woken up to her presence.

"What?" she says in English.

The thin one, the one who clubbed Son with his rifle, is the first to speak. He has a soft, high-pitched voice that is difficult to take seriously. "How long you work for American imperialists?" he asks in French.

To her it sounds like a line out of a propaganda leaflet. She ignores it at first, but the soldier repeats the question.

She looks to Son for guidance. He meets her gaze, then looks away.

"I'm not sure what you mean," she begins, and the question is repeated, same as before.

"I don't work for them so much as explain to American women what is happening over here."

He looks confused, probably because she said "women," so she answers once more. "I describe the war for Americans in their own country. So that they know what is going on," she says.

She thinks she should put up some sort of resistance, that at least she should refuse to answer certain questions. There would be dignity in opposing their efforts. Instead she answers casually, as though she is answering questions for a stranger on a bus, or when introduced to somebody at a party, rather than being interrogated. She would like to be the unyielding, self-possessed prisoner that Son is. He looks away from them, or straight through them. He answers nothing or shrugs. It

77

makes no difference if they tie his hands or not; he behaves as though he is their superior in every way, speaking only when he wishes and refusing to be bullied. Even the food, which he picked at as though it were something he might discard at any moment, did not appear to interest him.

But there are no questions that require her silence. They interrogate her in a half-hearted way, mostly asking again and again whether she works for the American army—*No.* Whether she helps the American officers—*No.* Whether she knows of the atrocities committed by the Americans. *What atrocities?* The napalm, the killing of civilians. *Yes, of course, I know about that.* What do you think? *I think it is bad.* You are American? *No. My mother is English. From England. I was born in Buckinghamshire.* She does not tell them that it was on an RAF base, that she grew up eating Raisin Bran and peanut butter as often as Weetabix and marmalade, that she has lived in the US for almost the whole of her adult life. She does not say that the clearest memory she has of Buckinghamshire is an awful boarding school in which girls were not allowed blue jeans or tampons, the use of which was tantamount to declaring oneself a slut. The Vietcong soldiers confer for a moment. Then they say, But you look like an American! *All white people look alike,* she replies. The small one laughs. He is missing a front tooth; she can see a centimeter of curled pink tongue in the gap of the cage of his teeth, a snail in a shell. The missing tooth makes him look even younger. They've been captured by evil children, she thinks.

Because they have no idea what to do with her, or what to ask her, it seems, they move to questions about how people get engaged in America, and other odd questions about sex and marriage. American brides are not virgins, they say. Doesn't the husband feel cheated? *No.* They don't believe it. And perhaps because they don't believe it, they go back to their original questions: Are you working for Americans? *No.* Do you help the American military? *No.* Do American girls sleep with several men before they get married?

They can't speak English; their French is awful, a tangle of words beneath a heavy accent that itself would make communication difficult. They must think her French is terrible, too, because they wince and shake their heads and ask her to repeat everything. *Moi no compris pas toi parler,* they say, which means *me not understood you to speak* and is unlike any French she has heard. It appears no more refined language is possible between them unless Son acts as a translator, which at the moment he appears reluctant to do.

Finally, the one with the long hair says, "What does your father do for a job?"

"He's dead," she tells them. It is true. He died of an aneurism last year. She thinks, with some regret, that he'd never have approved of her working in a war zone, that he'd have done everything possible to prevent her from going.

"Dead?" He studies her carefully. "In the war?"

"No. He was too old for this war. He was sixty—" This is too much information. She doubts these soldiers know how old they themselves are, what day they were born, let alone how old their fathers are. She repeats, "*Mort. Il est mort long-time.*"

They nod, satisfied. Their fathers are probably dead, too, she concludes.

Apparently, the green wire that held her wrists during their meal is necessary also for this period of interrogation. Afterwards, they free her and ask her to take photographs of them with Son's camera. They want her to take the pictures but only when the barrel is pointed her way, and only as they appear to be taking aim. She asks to stop—again, her imagination is too fertile for this game—for what if they thought it would be amusing to have her take a photograph as they pulled the trigger? She tells herself to stop thinking so much and tries

79

to take comfort in the fact that it is only through the frame of her camera that she sees them training their rifles on her. She comes to this realization—that they've relaxed their guard, that they don't seem the least interested in killing—and it serves as a tonic to calm her. Even so, she asks them to please allow her to put the camera down. She does not want to take any more pictures, she explains. She'd like to give back the camera now.

They appear mildly disappointed. The thin one spits, then turns away abruptly. The one with the long hair gives orders for them to carry on marching. Their new manner is to carry their weapons with the absent constancy with which small children carry their favorite teddies. The guns are there, are always there, but they have all grown accustomed to the guns, herself included, so that they seem almost as though they aren't real, or are never fired, or contain no bullets.

"That's an interesting sword," she tells the soldier with the sword. He holds it up, smiling at it as though it were something he has made himself. It's an ugly sickle with a crude handle, but he presents it now to her as though it is a work of art birthed from his own genius.

"This is from an automobile spring," he tells her, running his finger along the air above the blade. "And see this handle? From a howitzer."

She nods, amazed. So he did make it. Seeing it as a composite of its many parts, she has to admit there is genius involved.

A soldier's relationship to his weapon is complicated. She recalls the time a platoon she was with fired continuously in a "mad minute" because they heard a branch snap among the trees. The noise came from every direction, even from the ground, rising up through her feet, her legs. It passed through her and she felt her body as a thin veil, a kind of skin through which sound pulsed. There was no real reason for the explosion of fire. It was only that they'd been carrying so much ammunition; they were tired of hauling it all. Afterwards, she could not hear properly. She sat on a stack of ration boxes and wrote messages on a steno pad to Marc, who was with her. Smoking, listening to that single sound *eeeeeeeee* spinning in her mind like an insect, her writing pad out, her water bottle almost empty, she felt suddenly exhausted, running only on nervous energy. She might have curled up next to Marc but it was too hot for that and, anyway, she would never have shown him any affection in front of the soldiers.

I keep thinking that somebody is just there, or there, she wrote, then indicated the treeline, *watching us and deciding exactly when to shoot and which one of us to shoot first.*

Marc sat with his legs folded, knees bent, his shirt loose around his neck. His utilities had a tear in the pocket from overstuffing them with TV batteries and cables. Through the hole, she could see the white skin of his thigh, a strong contrast to the brown of his arms, his hands. He shook his head, dismissing her fear.

It's like a movie in my head, she wrote. *How do I make it stop?*

He got her to play a game in which he wrote a line from a song and she had to guess the song. Then another game in which you filled up boxes on a hand-sketched grid. He drew her away from her thoughts. He wrote, *You're beautiful.*

They played hangman and he wrote out *PEACE.*

She thinks how far away he seems now, belonging to another time. She recalls his face, his dark hair with a crown in front so that if he cuts it too short it sticks straight up. The war had produced a few early gray hairs that clustered by his temples, some new lines by his eyes from squinting in the sun. She has known him six months and in six months he has become far too important to her. She blames the tide of her affections on the war, too. It seemed to transform everything to extremes.

"Here, look! Look, you!" It is the soldier with the sword. He is frustrated because her thoughts have drifted. He commands her attention again as a pesky younger brother might. A younger *armed* brother, she reminds herself, and nods quickly at the soldier and his sword, indicating she is paying attention. "This is *very* sharp," he says, and holds the dark sharp edge near her palm. He wants her to admire the blade, which he has honed to a thin, lethal plane; the handle which allows a strong grip. She looks down at it, but will not touch it. It is how Marc would behave, unimpressed, a little bored. Along with the sprinkling of gray hair, Marc has also acquired here in Vietnam a bold, incautious wit that she is able to assume at times, as though having been with him so much she has assimilated this part of him.

"What you think?" says the soldier. He looks proudly at the sword, holding it up in front of him.

"I think you could use it to shave," she says. "That is, if you ever needed to."

The soldier nods, unsure of her meaning.

In Saigon she had become accustomed to sudden violence, expected but nonetheless surprising. People speculated; there wouldn't be anything today, or this week, or until such-and-such a time. She walked the streets with reporters in tiger suits—their canteens and cameras and tape recorders strapped on to them, some holstering pistols—and just in front of them would be civilian women on their way to a tennis game, looking sporty and white, like women in country clubs all over America. The expats ate lavishly, whatever else was going on; the best restaurants were run by Corsicans, the best clubs by Vietnamese women. A restaurant on the Binh Loi Bridge was blown up— partially blown up—not once, but three different times and still they gathered there because of its position along the river and because it was built on stilts and was therefore irresistible for at least a single visit. Once, while between courses at another restaurant near by, she pointed out the window to where she swore she saw a VC soldier. Her companion, Marc's cameraman,

Don Locke, said, *Yeah, wouldn't surprise me,* and asked the waiter for more fish sauce for his chiko rolls. She tried not to worry. The magazine liked her stories; they wanted more. Her editor cabled her to tell her she could sell her combat pieces elsewhere if they couldn't use them. Locke ate his chiko rolls. She thought, *Maybe I'm just seeing things.*

And (mostly) she did not worry. Few reporters were wounded, fewer killed. What were the chances? The tennis players rode in their air-conditioned elevators; French women sunbathed at the sports club, lying on their backs and squinting up at the F-100s soaring overhead. The helicopters dove low so that they could see the bathers, who rolled on to their backs and waved with their fingers. These women weren't afraid. They pointed their breasts to the unseen pilots above, smiling as though to a friend. Vietnamese officers' wives had grand social schedules. For them, Saigon was one big party. She became friendly with a girl named Nicola, who was having a long-standing affair with a lieutenant colonel who'd re-upped twice just to stay near her, and who frequently flew her to his base for parties. Hippies traveled from around the world just to check the place out. No one thought they were taking risks. And when they went home they told their stories, exaggerating all the dangers that they never themselves truly believed.

"Son, I'm so scared," she whispers now. She is in a hammock, he is on the ground. Even at night the jungle smells like a stagnant pond. Tonight, the world around her is so black she cannot tell if her eyes are open or shut. It is difficult to assume a relaxed expression or focus her gaze normally. Her vision seeks a destination and she finds herself straining to see in the darkness so that she has to blindfold herself with her hands. She wonders if they will kill them in their sleep, why they haven't killed them already, why they haven't let them go. She doesn't know anything, she despairs, not even if her eyes are closed. It seems unfair, all this confusion.

The guards take turns sleeping. The one on duty sits as though in a trance and may be asleep; he has not moved in at least an hour, though time is distorted now and she cannot honestly tell. He has not moved anyway.

Nothing makes sense. In the morning they will either be killed or get up and march. She doesn't know why she should die, or why they are marching, because she has no idea where they are heading anyway. Perhaps the Vietcong soldiers are lost. They certainly seem unable to find their unit. They are as stranded and alone as she and Son, but it is they who have the weapons.

"I've had enough," she says now, a phrase she might have used about a bad phone line, no seat on the bus.

From Son comes a whining noise, like that of a dog, and when she hears it she realizes he has, indeed, been listening, noticing, that he has not been nearly so removed as he appeared all day. She feels his hand on her back through the thin material of the hammock, and with that touch she becomes calmer, more solid in herself. He rubs his palm in a short circular motion, then leaves it still for a long time. She cannot remember anything being so comforting. She'd like to reach to him, but dares not. It is the first time—the only time—he has touched her.

She met Son in a hospital in Pleiku about a week after her arrival in the country. He'd come in from the bush with a bunch of soldiers from the 4th Division, his lip cut, the blood all down his shirt, making the green cotton black. The lip looked awful, swollen so that he appeared to be pushing it out like a pouting child. It was the end of the day now and he was arguing with a nurse that he didn't need any stitches, just give him a needle and thread; he'd do it himself. He claimed he'd stitched himself before in the field and it hadn't even gotten infected. *Please*, he said as the nurse clasped his chin. *Ah do it!*

The nurse held his jaw in her hand, dabbing iodine on his face. *Don't move, Tarzan!* she said.

Da nun show may! he said. He was a scrapper; he never stopped talking.

Why're you moving so much? You want to split that lip worse? The nurse had her eye on his lip, squinting into it as though down a scope glass. She was angling his face for better light. On her smock was her name, Tracy Flower, sewn neatly in what might have been the same stitch being applied now to Son's lip.

Da nuns! he tried again. *Dey show may!*

Nuns? Are you talking about nuns? I'm not a nun. Stop moving. Tah so!

She let go his face and he cupped his hurt lip behind his palm to shield it. He saw Susan watching and pretended he had not. She could tell this by the way he moved away all at once, as though discovered. She'd seen him earlier while walking the lines of beds, trailing the triage nurse, passing through screens thin as kite silk that separated the living from dying, and again outside the muddy exit where the grim drums of gasoline lined up above their nests of fire. She had seen him and had felt instantly drawn to him, a feeling powerful enough that she had needed to remind herself it was invisible. It was as though he knew her, or wanted to know her, and she felt it that way, as a kind of invitation.

The nuns showed me how to sew, he said quickly before the nurse could grab him again. Susan realized now why he had got her attention. It was not the wound to the lip, not Son himself, but how he spoke during the temporary moment he had his jaw back. It wasn't only that his English was good, though that in itself would cause her to take notice, but that the vowel sounds were British. That is what had seemed so oddly familiar to her. She knew the voice. She'd heard it that day at JUSPAO when she'd infuriated the lieutenant colonel by insisting he tell

85

her what a WBLC was. Sampan, she remembered, and the voice of a young Vietnamese journalist who said, *Can we have confirmation that a WBLC is a sampan, sir?*

Son tried to smile now, but the lip prevented it. Susan smiled at him, but only for a moment. The nurse was giving him instructions again. She had a soft but commanding voice, reminding Susan of one of her father's sisters, who had that same way of telling you what to do in the nicest fashion, but with an authority that meant you better do it.

Nuns? she was saying. *Well, that's just grand. Now keep still!*

The nurse was as tall as he was. Her hair, pinned at her neck, had come loose from its clip and she blew it away from her eyes, still holding on to Son. He finally gave in, sighing into her palm, and stood quietly for the stitches. Susan could see the grit on his neck, the red mud smeared on his trousers, the caking of dirt around his fingernails. He was just in from the field and he'd sweated so much his hair rose straight up from his head as though the light were sending a current through him. He seemed to be trying to move away from the nurse and stand still at the same time, almost jogging in place. Finally, he gave up the struggle and stood without wincing as she put line after line of neat stitching across his mouth. In the middle of the procedure, in a gesture as casual as a wave, he held up a camera, angling it on to the concentrating nurse, and snapped several shots of her stitching his lip.

Who is that? Susan asked another nurse, someone she'd tagged herself on to, a woman named Donna who did not object to being followed around. Donna held two bottles of urine pinned under one arm and a third in her right hand. They didn't have anything as useful as Foley bags but had to improvise even in this regard, using empty water or saline bottles to collect urine. The hospital operated out of little Quonset huts, corrugated-iron buildings, like pig arcs, maybe half a mile from the landing strip. Sometimes rockets intended for the airstrip hit the wards by mistake. They used to operate out of tents, held in place by sandbags, and the sandbags still lined the walls.

You're still here? Donna said. She dried her palm against her thigh, pushed a swatch of heavy bangs from her forehead, and gave Susan an amused, slightly disapproving look. She wore a long smock with sleeves that she rolled as high as they would go on her arm. The smock was stained a rust color with damp patches beneath the arms. She nodded down at her bottles. *You want a job?*

Susan said, *I really wanted to interview a surgeon, but I haven't talked to one yet—*

No, and you won't, Donna said.

Then you'll be stuck with me a little longer.

That's okay. You on a deadline?

Susan told her yes, though this was not strictly true.

You can bunk with us. But really, I should make you do something! Donna moved with purpose, with the stamina of a plow horse. Everywhere she went in the ward she picked up one thing, deposited another; she carried rolls of bandages, ringers, drugs, sheets, plaster, splints, these items balanced across her chest or on her hip. *You're a nice girl, Susan, and we don't mind you being here. But a reporter in a hospital! I mean, no offense, sweetheart, but really. Titties on a tomcat, you are.*

They ran into Son in front of a supply room. *What are you doing here?* Donna said, and he slouched off, was herded off, in truth. Susan nodded at him, then looked at Donna, making a question with her hands.

Who knows? the nurse answered. *Some gook with a hurt lip. Who gives a— Hang on—you carry this for me. We got to get these dressings changed!*

Earlier, on a cigarette break, Donna told Susan they stored water in empty napalm tanks with holes cut into them and that their penicillin was out of date. That in the operating room they had lap tapes, which were like cotton bandages, to mop up all the blood, but they'd soon run out of the tapes and found themselves having to re-use them. The nurses cleaned the tapes in drums of boiling water before sending them to the laundry. When Susan asked to take a photograph of these drums Donna pulled back her chin, recoiling slightly at the question of why on earth anyone would want such a photograph. But she told her the system was set up in the back of the hospital if she really wanted to see it.

This is not, you know, standard operating procedure, Donna said. *It's just what we do.*

I'd like to have a look anyway.

Suit yourself.

The drums were raised up on steel grates, surrounded by large patches of mud. The water was boiled, the bandages skimmed off with a wooden trowel, then placed into the next drum. Sometimes the nurses boiled the tapes three separate times before they were clean enough to send to the laundry. Donna also explained that amputated limbs had their own place, a drum filled with gasoline, which they burned.

Over there, she said. She didn't look, just gestured with her hand in a reluctant manner. The barrel was like the others but further away. At first Susan couldn't bring herself to step toward it, imagining the nurses—imagining Donna—hauling a severed arm, a foot, a leg, burying them in the fuel, setting them alight. She got closer, looking back at Donna, who arched her hand up, the one with the cigarette, indicating she could not go near the fuel.

She saw Son again then, his wild hair, blood on his mouth, a swollen lip. He was skirting by the door, patting his pocket for a cigarette. He seemed to know her; she could feel it, the way he regarded her, the contents of her reflection through his eyes. He made a show of getting out his cigarette, putting all his attention into that one small task. But something in the way he looked at her caught her attention completely. She knew exactly what she saw, a recognition. He wanted something from her, she thought, but she didn't know what.

On the second day, early in the morning, the soldiers catch a monkey. It screeches at them, reaching with its claws like a cat, trying to fight off the hand that holds its neck. She turns away, unable to look, but the image of the monkey's face remains with her, as does the sound of its screams and the way the soldiers laugh. They kill it quickly, dragging the body, now slack like a child's doll, over to the flame to cook it for breakfast. She thinks sadly that if they are willing to risk all the smoke the monkey's carcass makes, they must be quite convinced there are no American troops near by.

They eat what they want, then give her some of the meat. She is hungry, so she takes it. She has to push away thoughts of what it is she is chewing; she struggles to imagine the meat only as necessary protein and fat. Later, they also give her a gift. It is a ring of dull metal, fashioned out of the remains of a downed American gunship. The ring in her hand feels like some part of the dead pilot, his teeth, his eye. She drops it on the ground and it is returned to her at once. She tells them she does not want the gift. She does not tell them it makes her sick to look at it. The monkey they ate was strung up with a vine and cooked over a fire. She cannot look at what is left of it now, knowing she has eaten the flesh. She hadn't wanted to eat it; she was driven by hunger. But there is no need for the ring. She gives it back; they press it into her hand once more. She throws it at them and it is returned as though this is her wish. It is a game. They laugh at her distress, just as they had laughed at the monkey as it fought for its life. The ring ends up in her pocket. The monkey is left charred on the grass, its skeleton not unlike that of a human baby. She feels suddenly like giving up, but she cannot think of what exactly there is to give up on. Son watches and says nothing. She thinks he looks ashamed.

She asks them for the hundredth time for her boots, explaining she can no longer walk like this—barefoot, with cuts newly infected across her soles and the tops of her toes, along her heels. She begs them for the boots.

"Tien!" they call. There will be no discussion about boots.

"No tien!" she says back. "I can't walk!"

Finally, even Son tells her to stop arguing. The boots have been booby-trapped with explosives and planted along the trail, he explains. He whispers this information. Stop talking, he tells her, or you'll be more thirsty. All she can think about is water and her boots. She has become a true prisoner, with her bare feet, her parched throat. The sores on her feet fill with clear fluid. They pain her, become numb, then ache. She looks down on them as though they belong to someone else. She feels sorry for her body as though it is a thing separate from herself to which she longs to be kind but cannot be. She makes herself walk, imagining her body as a dumb animal, carrying her head, her brain, all her thoughts.

The heat is a hazy, invisible force through which they travel, made worse by the nauseating stench of the jungle floor. When they stop, she tries to pick off the body crabs, rub the hurt out of her heels. She figures out later that they did not understand that her feet were soft, unused to being exposed, incapable of stepping across a jungle floor. All over the country the children walk barefoot. It was inconceivable to them that she would not be able to do even that. At one point Son tried to give her his own shoes, but the tall one with the long hair signaled no, then called out a warning in Vietnamese. Son turned toward the soldier as though to attack, spitting out something she couldn't understand. He began firing off words so fiercely that for a moment she thought the soldier would have no choice but to shoot him. The two stared at each other for a good half-minute, the energy between them like two bulls, and then Son leaned over slowly, dropping on to his knee as he did so. He ripped the bottom of his trousers, held up the torn portion and slit it into strips and then began to bandage her feet, the insects hovering around his head as he worked, one landing on his lip, the same place that the nurse in Pleiku had stitched. He spat it out rather than take his hand away from the job of doctoring her feet. The soldier didn't like what Son was doing; he stood with his gun ready, but he didn't really intend to shoot them. It was half-hearted, a show of strength, nothing more. By then the boots were miles back, and had she tried to retrieve them they would have blown up in any case.

It is this soldier, the one with the long hair, who is in charge—she guesses he is in charge. He seems to be the one who decides about such things as food and cigarettes, which direction they go and for how long. During a moment of rest in the afternoon, she shows him her feet. He looks surprised at how they have split and bled. He is sorry about that, he tells her, then gives her the remaining water in his bottle, helps her up. He tells the tall, thin one to give her some medicine and he does so from his pack, unloading the iodine that was originally hers. The bottle has a leaky cap, she notices, so that when she moves it her hands are stained by the brown fluid. She does not want to lose a drop of the liquid, which is all she has by way of defense against infection. When she hands the bottle back to the soldier, she says to him, "Be careful with this; don't let it roll around in your pack." But the soldier, the thin one, pays no attention. She thinks of this man as the thin one because he is so much taller than the others and he looks as though he has been stretched. His feet are long, his ankles and calves. But she notices, too, how little muscle he carries and that his fingernails are overgrown and shelly, lending an oddly effeminate character to him. He seems to disregard her even more than the other two. He gives no indication he understands about the iodine and deposits it into his sack with no special care, turning away impatiently as though the idea of giving her any medicine—including that which belonged to her in the first place—is unnecessary.

She follows the soldiers, trying to keep up with them. The swelling in her feet means she moves with a short-strided rolling gait, pulling herself with whatever foliage she can hang on to and sometimes regretting it when a vine splits into sharp fibers that cut her skin. The one with the long hair shows her which leaves to avoid, those with saw-like edges. He looks angry when she hurts herself, tells her not to drink water during the day. It will only make you stink, he says. And your feet will swell more. The feet have become an embarrassment to them, a source of argument. The thin one seems especially resentful, as though it had been her choice to become their prisoner, to chuck out her boots, to hurt herself walking.

At one point the soldier who she now calls Long Hair lends her his own sandals with rubber tracks tied to the bottoms and she is amazed to see how he himself glides easily barefoot. After several hours he still shows no signs of discomfort. No wonder the soldiers find her complaints mysterious. She believes they practice walking barefoot in order to force themselves to be careful through the paths, avoiding mines. She notices, too, how quietly they move, even in the difficult areas. American soldiers might hack through the jungle with machetes. They might try to plow an armored vehicle right through dense brush. Bulldozers, tanks. What they really wanted was to clear the whole damned thing.

Not that they weren't capable of more subtlety. The patrol teams that went out at night were stealthy, cat-like, silent. But the Vietnamese soldiers, who she watches and cannot help but admire, are more so. They march without any sound at all, barely disturbing the vegetation. Sometimes, they are more quiet than usual, scowling at her when she makes a noise, as though she does so on purpose. She gets the sense that if she doesn't follow instructions, stepping softly, warily, they will find her a liability, even shoot her, though they never say so. Perhaps she imagines this, the way she imagined the captain's face. She hopes the need for silence is because of the proximity of American troops, and that somehow, miraculously, they will stumble upon a group on reconnaissance. That would be lovely, if by accident she was to walk into freedom. For an hour or more this hope swims in her thoughts, then her mind goes blank, concentrating only on the next step and the next. She is exhausted by the heat, the air that feels as though it contains no oxygen, the physics of movement. All she can tune into are the mechanics of her body that signal the need to drink, to eat, to shit. When she sits down, she sleeps. Her body tells her to do this, too, even through rain.

In Pleiku, where she met Son, she'd found it difficult to talk to the doctors. When finally she got to them they seemed so buggy, troubled, and exhausted that sometimes they couldn't even answer a question. One of them, Howe, had been on shift for twenty hours. By the time she interviewed him, he seemed almost incapable of thought, let alone language. He was shaky, pumped up on Dexedrine, which a nurse dropped into his mouth like a gumball while he was working on a patient. She watched the way that happened, how he lifted his chin toward the ceiling, parted his lips for the nurse's fingers, made an effort to swallow. His breath was sour, his pupils wide. She couldn't understand how he could operate on one more person, let alone the dozens or so who were waiting.

There had been a push, the medevacs arriving like a swarm of bees; they kept bringing in the wounded and bringing them again. Howe stood in the operating theater like a mechanic. Susan heard a young man—he might have been a teenager—

bargaining for his legs. She'd had to leave then. It was just too much, listening to the young soldier asking so politely for the doctor to try to keep at least one leg for him. *You already took the other,* he said. *Let me have that one.* She walked around outside, shaking, the boy's voice echoing in her head as she stood in the cooling evening air. She stood on the wet ground, staring out at the landing strip and the open red sky. A few minutes later she was surprised by Howe, who appeared outside for a break. He cupped his hand around a burning match to light his cigarette, then looked out over the muddy landscape, untroubled by her presence. She clutched her elbows, hugging herself, trying to forget how the boy had begged for the one remaining leg. Howe smoked assiduously, preoccupied, his attention turned inward. Susan paced, then stood still, thought about going back inside, then couldn't. Howe dropped the cigarette in the mud and went back and she could have sworn he hadn't noticed she'd been there at all.

Later, as she held her notebook over her wrist, angling her pen, she asked him what sort of changes he'd seen at the 18th Surgical. He said, *Yeah, a lot of changes. An awful lot,* but he wasn't able to name a single one. He blinked often, rubbing his eyes. He didn't look right. She tried another question and that one, too, seemed to bounce off him. She relaxed the notepad, repositioned her pen in her pocket. Howe seemed at times to be looking up, over her shoulder or listening to the air. She noticed he had a revolver belted on, a small Smith & Wesson, known as a "hush puppy." She couldn't think why he'd need such a thing during surgery and wondered if he even knew he was wearing it. *Yeah, so it's been a day,* he kept saying.

She asked about the boy's leg and he said, *The first was a . . . uh . . . traumatic amputation. The other, well. We couldn't save the foot.*

She had to pause just then. She thought of the boy, now a double amputee. The barrels outside, the smoking fuel. *I see,* she whispered. She had to work to remember her next question.

She asked him about the triage system, a method of sorting casualties as they came into the hospital. A great number of hospitals across the US were now adopting the same method based on the experiences of field hospitals, and she wanted to know how they felt about the system here.

Yeah, well, you get the Immediates right away, he said.

The Immediates were those needing attention the fastest. The Walking Wounded would wait.

How do you feel about the Expectants? she asked. These were the guys they put behind a screen, the ones they did not make any effort to save. They were Expectants because they were expected to die. She'd sat with a few already that day. She'd meant to take a photograph. She really *ought* to have taken a photograph. But she did not. She'd recently been told a story by a photographer. He'd been standing in front of a line of bodies that were bagged and awaiting transport and they'd run out of bodybags—they ran out of everything in the Highlands—and some of the bodies had to be wrapped in ponchos. The troops saw the photographer and told the guy to put the camera away. They held their rifles pointing upwards, a sign the safeties were off. *Don't you want people at home to see what you're going through?* the photographer reasoned. The response, *Get rid of the fucking camera NOW,* sent the photographer's hands into the air. He backed away. She imagined those troops, the ones ready to shoot the photographer, the look in their eyes, the hurt, the anger, every time she wanted to take a photograph of a dead body. They'd said, *How about we kill you and take a picture?* Even when the guy had walked away. They said, *You know what, you'd stink just as bad and never believe any different,* and in her mind's eye she saw the photographer nodding as he left. The story stayed so strongly it felt at times she'd actually been there. She had not. But she thought about those men and she found she couldn't photograph bodies in the hospital. And she couldn't photograph those waiting to die.

There was another reason she didn't take pictures that day in Pleiku. It wasn't just that she felt wrong about doing so. The fact was that the Expectants were not always unconscious. As often as not, they were awake but dopey. One of them started a conversation with her. He thought she was his girlfriend. Then he thought she was his mother. He said, *I need a doctor.* A few seconds later, he died.

The triage system? she reminded Howe. He seemed to have forgotten she'd asked a question, or even that she was in the room. A desk fan had come loose from its cage and the blades clacked against the casing. From somewhere behind them came a long, low howl, then a man's voice saying, *Shit, shit shit.*

Howe nodded, blew out his lips. There was a slow twilight outside the high windows of the Quonset and he seemed to concentrate his vision there, outside, where the incoming arrived and arrived. *That's okay,* she said. *I'm sure I have enough.*

They march at night, for hours at a time without pause. They march through showers and she discovers that her clothes stay cleaner because of the rain. Except in the mountains in the north of the country, the rainwater is hard, and the volume of rain during a downpour is such that it will wash your hair almost as well as a weak shampoo. She is astonished by this. She is astonished when one of the soldiers shouts a warning to her and pulls her toward him with surprising strength just before a tree falls across the path. The high humidity of the jungle means that trees rot from the inside out, falling with no warning. She asks him how he knew the tree was about to fall and he looks at her with an expression as though she is mildly retarded, or pretending to be so. Finally, unusually, he answers. "I know." It was the one with the gap in his teeth, the pink tongue. Long Hair. Gap Tooth. The third she hasn't a name for, then she realizes of course that he is the Thin One, which is ridiculous because they are all so thin.

She runs into a cactus. The thorns pierce her thigh and she cannot get them all out. They give her a funny feeling in the muscle, as if menthol has been poured into her veins. The part that is disturbing is that it doesn't hurt. If anything, she feels an increasing numbness. By the end of the day there is a red mark like an asterisk forming at the center of the wound. Son hauls Long Hair over and shows him the infection. He seems to have no reaction as Son shouts and points. She feels the numbing around the circle of red skin on her torn fatigues, checks to see where the normal sensation begins again. It hurts and itches and then goes numb again. They give her more of the iodine, which she notices has been dripping into the sack the Thin One carries. She dabs it on to her feet, on to her thigh. She wishes they'd let her be the one to carry it, but they will not. The next morning there is a swelling on her thigh, rising like a tiny volcano beneath her skin. She uses a thorn as a needle, puncturing the inflamed skin, then watches as a stream of brown pus flows.

She asks for the iodine again and, reluctantly, they hand it over. She does her best not to spill a drop, and she thinks about the tree, how it rotted from the inside.

The soldiers find it embarrassing to wait for her as she takes a measure of privacy in order to relieve herself. The three argue between themselves as well as with Son. The arguing has increased, but always in Vietnamese, so she has no idea of the content. Finally, it is agreed she can go on her own to a discreet bush, though they keep three rifles trained in the general direction in which she squats.

This is ridiculous, she thinks, to be shot while peeing.

*   *   *

They take turns lending her their sandals. She thinks they probably regret giving up the boots for bomb-making.

"You have more seeds?" asks the Thin One.

"Of course not. If I had, I'd have eaten them."

"Look for more."

She shakes her head. She has nothing on her and they know that. The soldier is impatient so he grabs her hand and pushes it into her front pocket.

In English she says, "Oh yes, do help me, please, as I have no idea how to search for items in my own clothing."

They are nearly out of food, she finds out. And now they are stingy with the iodine, not letting her use it often enough, though Son keeps arguing for it.

Son has grown thinner, his clothes torn, embedded with filth, his hair dirty and disheveled. Hour by hour he seems to look more and more like their captors and less like himself. It scares her, this transformation. It is almost as bad as the guns and the bullets, the rotten feet, the fact that she has no choice. No choice at all.

Normally, when they didn't want to be understood by Americans, she and Son spoke in French. Now he has clearly decided he doesn't want her to understand and he is suddenly, resolutely Vietnamese, talking to their guards, walking with them as though he is part of their team. At times she hates him almost as much as the three others, who are silly and young and don't even inhale when they smoke their cigarettes. Son is older than they are; he knows the agony she is in, the fear, the desperate desire to connect, to connect with anyone. He knows how to help her, to reassure her, and she is stunned by his refusal to do so. She thinks of all the things she would like to say. Dramatic damning conversations between herself and Son. She plays each scene out in her head, then suddenly dismisses them all in favor of some kind of resolution. She misses him. He is never more than five feet away and she misses him.

She listens to the soldiers arguing, having no idea what they are discussing. She always imagines it is over whether or not to kill them. They have been attacked by fire ants and sweat bees. They stink and swear. Their unit is nowhere to be found but they plow on with a ferocity that sweeps her forward, too, carrying her along. Although Son is holding up well, she is exhausted and ill. Her feet bleed and swell further, with creases developing around the ankles, even though now she has sandals. Son tries to give her his shoes again but the Vietnamese shout and gesture and threaten until he is forced to take them back, so she continues with the pairs of sandals they lend her, which are all right, really, perhaps better than shoes in some ways. But why is Son allowed boots and she is not? Why do they let her borrow their own sandals but not boots? They are capricious and stupid, she concludes.

On the third night, she listens as they sit in a circle, facing each other, smoking, sharing their dried fish, the last of her sunflower seeds, cigarettes. She cannot understand them, but they seem to be discussing something serious. The way they bow their heads together, the tone of their voices even though she cannot understand the words.

What she needs is some sense of what is in store. Ever since their capture it is as though she has been free-falling through space and it is this, as much as anything, that makes her crazy. She hears the sounds of monkeys, of flapping birds and all the hundreds of unseen insects. She itches and aches. Her clothes hang on her, oiled over and over by sweat.

"They are deciding whether or not to shoot me, right?" she asks Son now. "If they are going to keep us they have to feed us, and they've run out of food. Is that it?"

He shakes his head, doesn't want to talk. His hair is greasy, pushing over his eyes in thick dark locks. His skin has a muddy cast, as she imagines does hers. "Son, talk to me," she says, but he shakes his head.

"Okay, look, fuck you, okay?"

Still, he says nothing. He is listening to them, she knows, and he cannot both listen and talk at the same time. But it doesn't matter any more. She wants some information. Now.

"If you don't answer me, I'm going to go over there, make a grab for one of their goddamn guns, and get myself shot," she says. She crouches in the leaves, holds her wrists up to remind Son that they haven't tied her this time. "Are you getting this?"

And now, remarkably, she finds herself rising, obedient to her statement, one that had come out of her mouth without any thought at all but seems nonetheless to have momentum. She will get herself shot. If nothing else, it will serve as a kind of destination. A stopping point.

Son puts out his hand, closes his palm over her kneecap. "They aren't going to shoot you. They just don't understand who you are."

"What about you? Why haven't they—" She can't bring herself to finish the question. What she'd been told about the VC is that they kill any man of fighting age. And anyone aligned with Westerners. Certainly, Son was both these things. By rights he ought to have been shot in the first few minutes of his capture. She's seen the bodies of men just like him, caught out at the wrong time, made an example of, left with notes stuffed into open cavities in their bodies, sometimes a dreadful mutilation adding to the details written later on to the form under Reason For Death. "Why haven't they shot you?" she asks him.

"Same reason," he says, but she doesn't understand.

She remembers the hospital in Pleiku and how, on her way back to the nurses' quarters where she was bunking for the night, she heard some commotion from the POW ward.

The POWs did not always get the first or best treatment. She'd already figured out that it was hit and miss for them. In a situation in which the nurses and doctors were already over-stressed, they got what they got. Today there was a young North Vietnamese officer guarded by two soldiers. He'd come in the day before covered in red dust, his clothes moldy, his skin like leather, with a serious belly wound. You would think he would be left on a litter and placed to one side. He wouldn't be allowed in the Expectant area as he was North Vietnamese and they would always be kept separately from Americans, even when dying. But in his case, he was not left to wait, much less to die. Every effort was being made to save him. He was a high-ranking North Vietnamese officer. He had a "city accent," was educated; they needed him for questioning.

He knows something, maybe a lot of things, one of the soldiers told her. He was chewing gum, leaning against the wall. His ears were crusted with bug bites and sunburn and he had a tattoo, she noticed, a necklace of barbed wire. *It took some doing, getting him here alive,* he said.

Five American soldiers had choppered in with him, two of those were already dead, and the three live ones were ready to take him out with their own hands. The company had lost thir-teen men in a day. Thirteen dead, more wounded, and here was an enemy officer with lines coming out of him, everyone fretting as to whether he was going to make it. The grunts didn't like that. It had been touch and go all the way to the hospital, whether someone behind an M16 was going to find it impossible *not* to kill him.

He doesn't look like he's going anywhere, Susan said. She found it difficult to believe he was an officer. He didn't look like the US officers. He was as thin as a child; had a pinched face. His mouth sagged open, revealing a white film that encased his gums. He smelled like earth and urine and sweat. Where the tubes entered his veins there were flecks of dried blood, dark bruises, swellings where fluid collected stagnant beneath his flesh. Donna arrived every so often to suction him as he lay mute, handcuffed to the bed, conscious, but barely. Susan was willing to bet he couldn't turn over, let alone run. She didn't like to see him in handcuffs when he couldn't breathe on his own and she asked the soldiers why they kept him like that. She'd never heard of such practice.

Yeah, well, one of these gook bastards got a hold of a pair of scissors and tried to stab a nurse last week, so we're staying put, was the answer.

She asked what happened to that guy, the one with the scissors. The soldiers looked at each other, then smiled. The one with the barbed wire tattoo flicked his hand at her dismissingly. The other said, *Think real hard, and you'll get there.*

A few minutes later, one of the soldiers had gone off for a smoke and the other was checking on a buddy of his who had come out of post-op and was now on the ward. The hospital was so small that everyone was squashed in together. You could hear conversations from behind the screens that divided the wards, shouting from outside when instructions were given, the moaning of wounded soldiers. Footsteps, clanking trays, the rattling wheels of instrument trolleys, a rush of water from the tap, doors opening and closing, and occasionally the *thwack-thwack-thwack* of more medevacs pouring in, bringing their own windstorms, bringing new men to fill up the small space where the medical staff worked—constantly, it would seem. The soldiers who were guarding the North Vietnamese officer hadn't gone far. The officer was alone, but not very alone.

But when one of the soldiers returned from his smoke to where the officer lay, he thought the guy didn't look right. A mustardy hue had gathered round his eyes, a blush of lavender ringed his lips. His fingernails were blue. His eyes were pinpoints. He didn't respond when the soldier yelled at him, when he pointed his gun, when he shook him.

He's dead! he called. *Fuck, Evans, get in here. He's dead!*

Evans was the one with the tattoo. He collided into Susan

as she came rushing in to see what had happened, and it felt like running into a door. Suddenly there was a team of nurses, Donna screaming for a doctor, yelling that the prisoner had coded. Howe arrived, absolutely crazy, shouting at Donna that she shouldn't have left him so long.

Donna looked down at the POW, her lips pressed tightly together. She didn't join up to take care of POWs, you could see it in her face. You might have judged her for that, but her feet, her ankles, were swollen. She was wearing boots two sizes too large, looked ten years older than she was. The war was putting on her and putting on her. *He's not dead!* she said. *Until I say he's dead, he's not dead!* She might have been speaking to the soldier who was not Evans, the one who had been yelling, or possibly to Howe or to herself. The soldiers crowded around the POW now, rifles behind them, staring intently. *Sit down!* Donna ordered and they dropped back like trained dogs.

They worked on him. Susan stood to the side and watched as they shot him with adrenaline, as they tried to stabilize his heart. He stopped breathing and they vented him. He arrested and they resuscitated him. He was dead, then he was not. He floated between two worlds for a good five minutes or more, during which they lost him several times. Susan had never seen anything like it. Like two sides of revolving door, either side easy enough to step through. The officer was alive one moment and dead the next, his body struggling in some small way, then collapsing again.

What the hell happened? moaned Howe. Nobody knew. Belly wounds were a bad affair. They studied the lines, looked for where he might be bleeding, checked his airways. Another five minutes and he was dead. Even Donna had to admit it. When finally they gave up, standing away from the bed, catching their breath, looking down at the body which was more of a mess than before, Susan could see him clearly, his vacant staring eyes, his blue fingers, his clothes which were pockmarked with mold, torn, blood-soaked, muddy, hanging off him in long strips where they'd been cut away.

Ah, man, said one of the soldiers, holding his forehead. *I can't fucking believe it.*

Nobody said anything for a moment, and then Donna shot into action. *I'm taking bloods,* she said. Howe looked at her. He looked at her and in that glance Susan realized that these two, working so closely and for so many hours, had somehow fused together. They understood each other. Her eyes met his and communicated her determination to get to the bottom of this. He said nothing and in that silence acquiesced to the fact she was going to take bloods and he was not going to stop her. Not even if he had another emergency surgery right now, this second. He understood and stepped out of the way, then marched outside for another smoke.

Susan said, *If he is dead— I don't get it. Why do you want a blood sample?*

I don't give a rat's ass if he's six feet under, I'm taking bloods. He's had some kind of suicide pill or some such, I just know it.

Donna, honey, said the other nurse. She shook her head as though she was sad for Donna. As though the young nurse were losing her mind. *He couldn't even move his hand.*

Meanwhile, Howe was walking out of the hospital, his head low, holding his arms away from his sides, as though he'd touched so many people that day he couldn't bear to come into contact even with his own flesh. The soldiers seemed to recede into space. Donna got a syringe and a set of phials. She didn't *let* him die, she said. Something happened. The needle she used was a fair-sized gage but even so the blood wouldn't flow. So she told Susan—she ordered her—saying, *Massage the arm.*

It took her a moment to understand Donna's meaning, and then to contend with the fact she needed to touch the dead body. She approached the North Vietnamese officer's arm, squeezed it, and released. Donna said, *I don't know what he did, but he did something!*

Susan squeezed the arm again, watched the slow intake of blood into the syringe. At her knee, on the floor, was her pen and pad, all her assembled notes. She wondered what the hell she was doing.

Like this, Donna said, demonstrating. She worked the arm vigorously, patting it, kneading it like bread. *Work it down.*

She did as she was told. It felt like milking a cow. She couldn't bear to look at the man's face. Instead, she looked past the curtain and there she saw Son, whose name she did not yet know, watching as though from the other side of a plate of glass. He was standing in a doorway looking at the officer. His lip was purple with black spiky pieces of gut sticking out, the stitches he'd protested about. His eyes were gloomy and full. It was unlike Son to look anything other than happy, enthusiastic, even playful. Only late at night, only when he thought he was alone, did you see the expression he wore then, watching as she and Donna drew the blood from the dead man's arm. If she'd known as much, she'd have paid more attention to what might have been the reasons he was sad. As it was, she looked at him and then returned her attention to the North Vietnamese officer, trying to imagine the arm was, in fact, a loaf of bread and not a man's limb. She wondered what they did with the bodies of enemy troops, whether they fed the bodies straight back into the earth, dumped in rivers or rice paddies or bomb craters. In the Delta the US troops defended bridges, regularly shooting into the water so that enemy frogmen could not swim under the current and plant explosives. Bodies floated down rivers as regularly as driftwood and splintered sampans. She didn't know what they would do with the officer now. It was one of those questions, like how to dispose of severed limbs, that she couldn't help but ask herself.

*   *   *

105

Surrounded by the screeching, whistling, croaking, cawing sounds of the jungle, hunkered down, her knees to her chin as though pressed into a small space by the darkness of the tropical night, and all around her a pungent, rotting vegetable smell so strong it leaves a taste in her mouth, she misses Marc. He has always been that person who somehow linked Vietnam with home, who made it seem perfectly normal for her to be here. The small routines of meeting up at restaurants after many days of being apart, how they compared notes, talked about people they both knew, holding hands, touching their legs together under the table. Being with him made her feel part of something larger, something important. Not just the press corps, more than that, part of a history that was unfolding. She missed the milky coffee he brought to her in bed, how he set a battery-operated radio on the edge of the bath and read the papers there until they became soggy under his wet fingertips. If he were here, she would not feel so foreign, so completely disoriented. He would ground her, she thinks.

Sometimes the feeling of wanting him with her is so powerful it seems to gather color and texture, occupying a place just beneath her eyelids so that when she tries to sleep she sees his face, feels his body beside her, imagining the breath of the soldiers is his breath, that he is here with her instead of them. She misses him so much the aching becomes a part of her no longer attached, a phantom limb, every nerve on fire. If he were here, he'd know what to do. He'd have a solution, or at least an idea. If she could have had any one thing just now, even more than her boots she'd want paper and pen to write him a letter. And among the ways in which she drives the Vietcong soldiers to distraction is repeatedly asking for paper to do this. They do not answer her when she speaks English, when she speaks French. Finally, she says, *"Giấy! Giấy viu lòng!"* and even then they behave as though she has said nothing, not even turning in her direction, so that she begins to doubt her own ability to be understood. Dear Marc, she thinks.

She wants to touch him, to write to him, to dig out the letters in the layers of rotting leaves on the jungle floor if that is what is required. Instead, she forms each word on the roof of her mouth with her tongue. She scowls at the guards. She thinks as hard as she can, spelling out a message for Marc in her brain, hoping that some invisible power she does not believe in will transport her thoughts to his. She considers that death begins with just such a desperate, impossible cry. She has seen young men die and often they were still trying to speak as they did so. For the first time she deliberates whether it is inevitable that they will die here, die in the next few days or weeks, or that she will, anyway. Not necessarily by gunfire, but because that is what the jungle does to you. You leave it or it kills you. She can think about this rationally for the moment. They've given her a bit of rice and it has cleared her head for now, so she can think about such matters.

Maybe they were just arguing about which direction to take, but she always imagines that there is one of them who thinks they should be shot, while another wants to spare them. The Vietnamese soldiers stand in a huddle like a three-man football team. Their voices have a high, light tone for young men and contain a musical quality that might seem beautiful if she didn't imagine they were speaking of death. She wishes she could tell which one was arguing for their lives, as she'd like to thank him. She wishes she could know who has been persuaded to their side, for she would like to thank him, too.

At the end of the third day, after a long heated discussion, she hears Son say, "It's okay now." He's been listening, his head alert on his long neck, bent like an antenna in the direction of their captors.

"Son, *please*, tell me what they are saying. Tell me exactly."

He sighs, looking away and then toward her again. "They have to present you to their officer in charge, which means they have to take you with them—for now. But they think they are likely to run out of rations, so the question was whether they should release you, which would get them in trouble—if it was ever discovered, that is."

"Let me go now? Where? *Here?*" In the middle of the jungle, she thinks, without any idea where she is and with no food, she is willing to bet.

"They don't themselves have the authority to release you. They don't have any rank. But they are also worried that you are becoming a burden, that you are slowing them down."

She is silent. So she had been right about what they were discussing. Though she had guessed as much, she is surprised. Though she *knew*, it comes as a shock.

"Because they are running out of food," she concludes.

Son nods. "They need to find their unit."

"Are they going to shoot me?"

"Susan, they don't *need* to shoot you. They could just walk away from you and you'd perish. Unless they let me go with you, but they will not—" The look on her face silences him. He pauses, saying nothing for a minute or so, then changes the direction of his conversation. "Anyway, they aren't going to do that. They are keeping you with them."

He states this flatly, without any joy in his face. She knows there must be more. She thinks—she knows—what it is he will not say.

"They are considering whether to stop *feeding* me?" she whispers.

Son swallows; his eyes are heavy, burdened. She can see he feels he is failing her. He is not failing her, but she has nobody but him, and she is hungry. She is tired.

"There are plenty of fruits," he says cautiously. "We have coconuts, dragonfruit, breadfruit—"

"They're going to stop feeding me!"

"Susan," he pleads, "at least they aren't going to leave you here alone. You would die. As surely as if they dropped you in the sea, you would die."

"But why not *you*? It's like you're one of their own! And *you*, according to every understanding I have of this war, are an *enemy*!"

He wags his chin, dismisses the question. He will not look at her. She thinks this means that he knows already that they will kill him. She will be spared, perhaps because she is *co anh*, an English girl, but he will be taken somewhere and shot, left there. She suddenly sees his body slumped at the base of a tree, the black red blood seeping into the earth, his skull in pieces. She shields her eyes with her hands in an effort to erase the vision from her mind. Meanwhile, Son rises and goes over to where the guards are standing, ignoring their guns, treating the AKs as though they are nothing more than disused sports equipment. He speaks to them so boldly that her attention is drawn away from the thought of hunger, of possible starvation, and is suddenly, acutely, located upon Son, whom she admires and thinks remarkable. He's not afraid; he never has been afraid.

He returns a few minutes later, twiddling one of the guard's cigarettes in his fingers. "We're going to keep marching north," he says. How has he managed to get them to give him a cigarette? They only reluctantly share their food with her, Susan thinks, but *he* gets a cigarette? And why is it that he said *keep* marching north? He must have known they had been marching northwards and had not told her. He knows exactly where they are going, she concludes, and has known all along.

"Tell me where," she demands.

He lights the cigarette, drags deeply then offers it to her on the end of two dirty fingers. "Hanoi," he says casually.

Hanoi is hundreds and hundreds of miles away.

"They are out of their minds," she says.

"But I don't think we'll have to go that far. Their unit will be in one of these hamlets along the way."

All she can think is *Hanoi?*

"In these stupid sandals! With no real food?! Look at me, Son! *Look at me!*" She slaps her hands against her collarbone, her thighs. Her clothes are grimy with little holes puckering through. She is covered in scratch marks, swollen, infected insect bites, the oozing thigh, the pus-filled feet. Welts from the red ants, black grime all around her fingernails, her toes. The only clean part of her is her eyes, shining through a film of dirt and sweat that makes her appear almost to be wearing a mask. She turns to the three soldiers now, all her anger directed at them. They look up with alarm as she yells, "Hanoi! Are you out of your *fucking* minds?! You stupid little *shits*! How *thick* can you be? You might as well kill me now as—!"

She stops when she hears a rifle bolt pull back, then another, a third.

In Pleiku she slept in the nurses' hootch. Donna found her in her bunk, waking her from what wasn't exactly sleep. It was the middle of the night or early in the morning— she had no idea. Donna was whispering in her ear. *Morphine overdose*, she said. *And nobody remembers giving it to him.*

She felt the weight of her head against the thin mattress. Her limbs were heavy, immovable. All she had done was *follow* the nurses and she was this tired. What was more remarkable was that Donna was still awake. She looked at Susan with an alert, nervous energy, passing on this information about the Vietnamese officer.

How would he have gotten any morphine? Susan managed.

I don't know, but he did. Must have stolen it from somewhere. They all have suicide contingencies, these gooks.

But he couldn't even move! He was so bad—

110

He was a train wreck, but damn if he didn't get hold of a syringe. He probably had it hidden under the mattress. They are not like you and me, these people; they have unbelievable physical resources. You should write about that. They are not the same kind of human. Must be some kind of genetic thing, super strong, believe you me. I don't get it.

Donna sat on the end of the cot, nearly lifting it from the ground. Susan got the impression she'd been a rather stout woman when she first started in the army. She still had substantial hips but the flesh hung on her arms and throat as though she'd suddenly lost whatever it had been attached to. She thought she never wanted to have to work this hard, the way Donna worked. The way all of them worked out here.

They're just people, Susan said.

I know they're people! I've seen them inside and outside, and you are right they look the same, but I am telling you now—

They were interrupted by a sound outside, an explosion, not too near.

Don't worry about that, Donna said.

In the dim light Susan could make out the shadows under Donna's eyes, the hollow between her brows. Her face looked ragged. Her hair hung in sections, unwashed. She'd changed from the smock she'd had on earlier, but the way she sat, the way she held her arms in her lap, showed her fatigue. Susan wondered if this was what happened to a person if they spent enough time at a hospital in Pleiku. Maybe their biology changed so that they no longer slept normal hours. Maybe they felt wired all the time and there was no way down, no place to land after flying an all-day adrenaline high. She imagined Donna falling asleep, her body finally collapsing, limb for limb, like a camel dropping slowly to the ground. It would almost be a forced thing, she thought, an insistence from the body, like a sudden blow.

What's in your canteen? Donna asked.

111

Water, Susan said. *I've got water in my canteen.* She gave her the canteen, sitting up now.

That's good, 'cause I've got some whiskey! Donna patted her hips for matches, looked on the table, and found a lighter there, swigged out of the canteen, wiping her mouth with the back of her hand. *He wasn't going to talk, that VC.*

I thought he was a North Vietnamese regular.

Yeah, well, they're all VC.

Outside the bombs continued, not too close, the sound like a thunderstorm. That was okay. That was safe. When it felt as if you were on the inside of a drum, being pounded from all sides, was when it was close. Donna didn't look worried, but Susan felt each distant explosion inside her like a little hammer on the casing of her ribs. What she worried about mostly was if one of their own fell short.

That is outgoing, right? she asked meekly.

Oh, yeah. You'll know when it's incoming. Now that the Russians are giving them rockets, what you really want to listen for is the whining sound before the explosion. You hear that, take cover and say hello to Jesus. I'll tell you when.

Take cover, Susan repeated. She wondered where. She wondered how you get to a place where you can calmly smoke a cigarette as Donna was now doing and listen to artillery as though to a song on the radio. She wanted to get back to Saigon where the illusion of safety was much greater.

Aren't you scared ever? she asked. She knew Donna would have had no idea what was in store when she signed up. The enlistment people told nurses they couldn't be posted to Vietnam unless they volunteered. That was the first lie. Others followed.

Donna shook her head as though to say no, but out of her mouth came, *All the time.* Then she said, *That little fucker, I still don't know how he got it. Must have grabbed it out of one of our pockets. Or maybe it fell.*

Susan tried not to remember how she'd massaged the arm muscles to work the blood down, what the arm felt like in her hands. She wondered if he'd been afraid of being tortured, and that's why he'd killed himself. Or maybe it was a case of not wanting to give information. Whatever the reason, he was dead, and the war continued very well despite this fact.

There were high windows in the hootch. From her angle, Susan could see red tracers in the night sky; the white flares that suddenly illuminated, then were gone. She could hear the shelling, like a constant Fourth of July. *They're making more work for you out there,* she said.

They're always doing that. Did you get the story you wanted? I'm fine.

That photographer asked about you. The gook with the lip. He wants to show you his pictures.

Oh yeah?

They're always trying to sell you something, these guys. Just be careful.

They smoked their cigarettes, listening to the bombs. Donna dumped the rest of her scotch into Susan's canteen and took a long swallow, offering it back with a nod. She told Susan that when they dropped white phosphorus it just made her crazy.

You have to keep neutralizing the burn or else it continues right to the bone, like it's aiming for it. I wish they'd stop that shit. We don't have the time, you see, to do what you have to do to treat those casualties. Napalm is bad but the Willie Pete takes full up every minute you've got. Hey, how about you put that in your article?

The scotch had a lovely, warming effect. Susan began to feel a little more relaxed. She smiled at Donna, who slouched on the other end of the cot.

Man, I'm beat. I'm going to hit the hay, Donna said. *Write that thing and let me see a copy. We don't get anything interesting to read up here. Stars and Stripes is all. Closest thing we*

113

get to a women's magazine is a Sears Roebuck catalog. Tell them
not to strafe with the Willie Pete, please. We're already flat out.
And send me a copy.

I'll tell them, she said, though of course nothing like that
would make it into the article. If she wrote in the problems of
treating burn victims it would be edited right out.

This night in the jungle she is thinking about Donna, about
the white phosphorus, the fireballs of napalm, the VC captain
suiciding in a hospital bed. It didn't seem such a bad idea now,
she thought, a suicide pill. Some kind of poison. Reporters who
carried guns often did so for this one reason. A kind of Plan
Z when all the other plans fail, if you had any plans to begin
with. She can't think of any right now, except to try to eat
enough, to drink enough, to rest enough. Maybe to hide, she
thinks. Wouldn't that be nice? Just hide and wait and let it pass
over.

All the bits that your god had left over after making the world,
Son once told her, *he heaped into the jungle and they grew there*
in a big tangled mass. You see, all the trees, vines, fronds, every-
thing piled on the smoking, moldy floor of the jungle is nothing
but spare parts. A celestial junkyard. Buddha's rubbish heap.

She laughed when he told her that.

That's religious lesson number one, he said. *I will teach you*
more about your god tomorrow in religious lesson number two.

Your god? she asked him. *Do we each have separate gods?*

What do you think I am? A pagan?

What could you possibly know about an English god anyway?
she teased.

That he built the world in seven days. That he brought the
animals in seven by seven—

Two by two, she corrected.

No, seven by seven. Only the unclean ones went two by two.

Son, you are remarkable.

Good with numbers, he replied, touching his temple with the tip of his forefinger. *We Vietnamese very good with all things numbered.*

Numerical.

Indeed, it is! A miracle!

You pretender! she said. *You know* exactly *what I said!*

You said miracle—

Numerical.

New miracle? I'm sorry, perhaps I misunderstand—

He was teasing her, of course. His English was perfect. She knew he was teasing and he knew she knew. But it was all part of the joke, somehow funnier because he play-acted.

Oh, Son, youuuuu!

He would do that, pretend to be the awkward, fumbling native, struggling to please colonial powers. At cocktail parties she would watch him as he lit another man's cigarette like a waiter, or insisted he had no idea how to dance until she dragged him on to the floor for a waltz and he glided with her so easily it was clear he'd been taught. He would behave as though he was nothing more than a translator, a Saigon orphan grown now into a useful coolie, and then she'd turn around and see him talking to an admiral with all the confidence of his equal. He was quiet one minute, and the next a small crowd would gather round him as he explained what he thought about a particular political leader or the strategy of the communists. Everyone knew him. She had no idea how he became so educated in Western ways, but of course the French taught them, were still teaching them. And he was Son, therefore unique.

Religious lesson number two went like this. *There was all this water not good enough for the ocean, but too good to throw away. Plus, really, there were no drains. So your god combined water and grass and mixed it in a big rice bowl and that became a large*

115

portion of our country. Every day he tries to cook the water and
grass to make stew, which is why it is so hot.

I've read nothing of this in my King James—

This is Hoàng Van Son's version. Official, original edition.

So your point is that we are actually in God's kitchen?

Exactly. But Buddha disapproves of this practice and so nothing
ever gets done and your god goes hungry. Poor chap.

He'd always been like that and whatever warnings people
like Donna might give her, she found him irresistible. After the
night she sat up with Donna, she had gotten on a chopper out
of Pleiku to An Khe, and there was Son, one among others.
She recognized him right away, of course; tall for a Vietnamese,
stitches on his lip, alone, as was she.

She was still so new that helicopters scared her. She decided
early on that they had the aerodynamics of a chest freezer and
was never sure whether she should move her leg or shift her
weight when riding one, lest it topple to the ground. Unlike
airplanes, helicopters seem to struggle to stay airborne. They
cannot glide. It is difficult to fly one in the rain, and it rained
all the time in Vietnam. Every noise was a piece of the rugged
effort to keep the thing flying and there was no room between
her and all the parts that made it fly. She couldn't stand helicopters. Riding in them felt like being inside the heart of a
giant machine, but there was no choice. She got used to them.
She even got used to how the doors were left open for the
gunners, so that the wind came through in a wild and constant
rush. And to the fact you could not hear unless you wore head-
phones, and then you could only hear the pilot's transmissions.

A helicopter is not a great place to hold a conversation, but
Son was determined to do so.

He was sitting on a couple of mail sacks. His buff-colored
trousers were so loose he had to strap his belt up high to keep
them on his waist. Holding on to his ball cap, hugging himself
with his free arm, he smiled at her, shivering a little. She pointed

116

at her lip and mouthed the word "ouch." He pointed at a star on one of the bags, the stripe of his open neck shirt, and mouthed "American?" They conversed like that, in an odd mix of mime and charades. He managed to tell her his name, where he was heading, and that he loved birds. She wasn't as good as he was, not nearly so precise and communicative. When she tried to mime typing, he got it into his head that she was an entertainer. Later, they had their first real conversation.

How long have you played the piano? he asked.

I don't play the piano. That was supposed to be a typewriter. I'm a reporter.

So does that mean you are not twelve years old either?

Not recently.

You are American?

Yes. My father's side. My mother is English.

Well, I really do love birds, he said. *It's a shame you can't play piano.*

He convinced her to meet him in Saigon the next day. He said, *Good! Excellent! I will show you my photographs and perhaps we can work together. I would love to work with you!*

He said it so easily, as though there was nothing more to explain or decide upon. When she didn't respond, he said, *I'm a good photographer.*

She told him she was sure he was good, but it wasn't up to her what photographs were bought or used. *Someone else pays me,* she explained, *and they don't have much money either. Or at least they aren't very . . .* She thought of her editor, how she never once took her to lunch or asked her how she was feeling when she came back after a sick day or offered anything that could possibly be construed as a raise. One time she came by Susan's desk with a package she presented as though it were a gift, handing her the crisp brown paper bag and saying, *I've got something for you.* Inside was a can of Crisco oil and a couple of lemons. She wanted Susan to cover a riot. *For you,* she said.

Useful for getting the tear gas off. Susan looked at Son. How could she explain someone like this editor to such a man? *They aren't very generous,* she began, hoping he'd understand her meaning. She remembered, too, how her editor had left the package on her desk and swept out of the newsroom. *Oh,* she added, looking over her shoulder, *oil for the skin, lemons for the eyes.*

Son said, *Never mind about that, whether they are generous or not they will see the photographs and decide!* He had a youthful, almost innocent aspect to him that was fetching.

You learned English from a Brit, didn't you? she said.

Who told you so?

Nobody told me, she said. *It's the way you pronounce your vowels.*

Ah, yes, of course. The BBC. I've been copying it for years.

You learned English from the BBC?

Indirectly. Directly, I learned English from a Vietnamese actress who always hoped to go to London and star on the stage. The West End. Can you imagine?

No, she could not. *Did she ever make it?* she asked cautiously.

No, but she had a little dog and one day a famous English actress came through Saigon for some reason and saw the little dog and bought it from her. So the little dog went back to England and the story goes that the little dog became a stage celebrity! So, the actress teacher did not become famous, but she had a famous dog. We were all so happy!

Son, are you unusual or are all Vietnamese like you?

We are all of us unusual, he said. *But, Susan, surely you want to know the dog's name?*

How would she know to stay away from such a man? There were no clues, except if you took that single, facile, ignorant one that she would never adopt: that he was Vietnamese.

Leave a box of vegetables in the sun and that is the smell. Lie on asphalt at noon on an August day and that is the temperature. The heat rises from the ground, bombards you from above. The dense brush, the banyan trees, their branches intertwined, connect at the top to form a canopy above, allowing no breeze. Her hair, her clothes, stay wet and wetter still with no chance of drying in the humid air. Even in the cool mornings, the foggy mist is wet. During the sticky heat of noon, the air is wet. She has been on such marches before, always with a company of Americans, always with Son, who carried the bulk of the equipment. It is different now. A kind of timelessness has set in. She keeps thinking she is dying, that she is walking with a ghost.

She feels best when they are passed by scout planes, droning above them like giant insects. Sometimes they are so low she cannot believe the pilots do not spot them. She looks up longingly, wishing she could signal.

"Stay perfectly still or else we will shoot you," they tell her. Or, "Don't run or we will fire."

"Where exactly would I run?" she says. She wants to put her arms up and embrace the plane. She wants to jump so high she can catch it.

Long into the night, she is scheming how she will make it through the jungle. She wishes she had a gun, but the gun would do no good at all—she doesn't know how to shoot straight and she isn't sure she could kill a person anyway. She might try, but she'd be too late. To kill a man in Vietnam requires complete conviction that this is what you must do now. Otherwise, he will shoot you. She has no such conviction. She has never considered the possibility. She feels that in many ways she is no different from the Saigon women in their tennis dresses, or all those overfed French women along the beach who smiled up at the pilots. She hadn't really thought she'd need to know so much, or do so much.

She wishes she had her compass. Wherever you are in the jungle you are in the center of it. There is no way of getting any perspective except if you climb a tree, and the trees are hundreds of feet high. She remembers interviewing some of the soldiers in Mike Force, a mixed bag of mercenaries and Montagnards, a few Aussies thrown in, who apparently crawled along the brush, unwilling to stand, often stopping to evaluate the next twelve inches in front, looking for trip wires before continuing, burying their waste. She thinks now about all the questions she wishes she'd asked them.

Once, with Son, she'd visited a captured Vietcong village which had been made into a training ground for new recruits. The traps were set up so that you stepped over a trip wire with your right foot, but missed a different one with your left. The doors were rigged, the grass alive with explosives. It is hard enough to see a full-grown man in a jungle, much less the wires of American mines, or the vines of the Vietcong's. In the ersatz village she had set off ten explosives in almost as many minutes. She thinks about this as she lies awake now, concentrating her thoughts, already separating herself mentally from the four men around her, sleeping.

If she could find a road, she could set up a kind of ambush, wait for ARVN or the Americans to come along, and try to get their attention and identify herself before they opened fire. With this in mind, she could make a white flag out of some bamboo and her underpants. But then she thinks how they have not crossed a road in four days of marching; she thinks she would tire of dragging the pole. The previous night, she washed her underpants in the water of a tree stump. They dried in a stiff shape as though starched, smelling of earth. She picked ants off them, then put them back on and discovered that the elastic had stretched. That, or her thighs were much thinner; the pants sagged on her as though they belonged to another woman. What was she going to do when they wore out completely?

Commonplace things—roads, plates, bedclothes, running

water—feel unreachable, the thought of them absurd. Where would she find new underpants? She falls asleep for a few minutes, dreaming of fresh water and roads.

Son always said he hated the jungle, even though he would agree that the view from a helicopter is beautiful. *There are two times when it is best to avoid the jungle,* he joked. *Night and day.*

A few weeks ago, what feels like years now, she told Marc that joke, pretending it was her own. He didn't laugh. Instead, he said, *You don't have to go.* He wasn't trying to discourage her. He was issuing information. He routinely accompanied soldiers into the field, carrying his recording equipment strapped to his back or chest, his pocket stuffed with batteries, cables, film. He was thin, no extra meat. He sometimes smoked while he walked. He sunburned badly. He went because if you didn't stay with the troops you would listen to all the crap being said in Saigon and begin to believe it. He went because the only way to properly cover the war, he said, was to film it. Otherwise nobody would believe what you reported. You'd contradict the stories from the military, stories that were repeated by the hundreds of reporters who did not leave the city. If you contradicted those stories without proof, without footage or at least some photographs, you appeared mis-informed, that was all, or as though you simply hadn't observed correctly. The camera was key. But he didn't want her to go. *Why don't you stick a little closer to home for a while?,* he said to Susan. *You don't need to be out there all the time.*

This was a night when he was a little drunk. He sat close to her, breaking their recent agreement to avoid each other, to put their relationship on hold, to check it back. They were supposed to be only "friends" now. His wife had written him that she was pregnant. However abstract that felt—an unborn baby thousands of miles away—the affair had to end. But they were finding it difficult to end it. Sitting together, she could feel the proximity of their bodies by the small change in heat between them. If they touched, the places their skin met would grow moist as though they were melting together. She knew this, just as she knew that if he ran his hand through her hair, his fingers would stick, and that, undressing, their clothes would peel away from their bodies like a rind. Once, after making love, they'd bathed together and she remembers tasting the water and being surprised by the salt in it, as though they'd produced their own kind of brine. Perhaps he, too, was remembering this. He looked at her for a long while, then he said, *Come see me. Who knows? Things may have changed.*

If he had made some small gesture, laced his fingers through hers, pushed her hair back, placed his palm against her cheek— something, anything—she might have been more kind. If he had said, *I want to do whatever it takes to keep you.* Or, *Please, I want to see you so much and we could talk about a solution—* she would have given in. It really would not have been difficult to hang on to her, if that was what he intended. And no, she didn't expect a solution, not really.

But all he did was issue an invitation for her to take a chance, come and see, poke around once more in his life and decide for herself whether it was safe to come in. That's the way he makes nothing his fault, she thought then. He made suggestions. He made proposals. He believed entirely in an individual's responsibility to himself, to his own life and aspirations, and took no responsibility for another's choices. It seemed to her there was a certain deceitfulness in this.

She preferred Son's way of being, how he tried so hard to please her. He would arrive in her room, having raced up the steps, carrying something he'd found for her in the market. *Here is a new teacup and saucer for your collection. Do you like it?* He took responsibility for everything, would ensure she had the right bug spray, apologize when they got caught in a rainstorm. There was a woman in Hué whom he loved secretly and sneaked off to see. He claimed it to be his fault, his fault that he was so devoted, that he could not leave her alone. She, too, was married. They were both of them in love with married people. *Why do we always love the wrong ones?* she asked Son one night. They were sharing her last cigarette. She'd already gone from three a day, to five a day, to ten a day. As she turned the butt of the cigarette in his direction, he brushed her hand. *That is our nature,* he said. *And not the worst of our nature, I am afraid.*

From Susan, he asked nothing. Sometimes she thought he must find her ugly or ungainly, for he almost seemed not to have noticed she was a woman. For her part, she was completely at ease in his presence, taking his arm sometimes as they walked, trimming his hair, a flowery towel draped over him like a cape, her scissors a delicate bird hovering at his ear. Much of what they did was more intimate than anything that happened with Marc. And yet, she was in love with Marc.

In the bar, the last time she saw Marc, sitting so close to him so that there was no mistaking they were lovers, hearing his fractured invitation, she said, *I'm sorry, Marc, but please explain: what would have changed? You have a wife, and now a baby on the way.* She spoke in a rational, logical voice that did not match how she felt. She could picture herself as he must see her, sitting stiffly in her chair, the chill of the air conditioning reflected in goosebumps along her bare arms, a tight smile, a slightly dark, wise look in her eyes. *I mean, I can't see how anything would have changed,* she said. *Or even, let's face it, that you want it to change.* She did not allow him to see how he hurt her, but she regretted the words, or rather the way they had come out, stinging, bitter, with no purpose other than to wound. It made her feel shrew-like and therefore less attractive. She kept thinking that if she were just a little more beautiful, he wouldn't be so casual about her. A man who her father introduced her to years ago, a colonel like himself, once looked at her from across the dinner table, and proclaimed, *Young women are wasted on young men*. She'd taken it as a line of simple flattery, but now she saw there was a certain truth in what he had said. We are all in such abundance, she thought, like shiny fruit in a market stall.

I'm sorry, she said, a little softer, though she was not sorry. He was silent.

If there was someplace we could go with this— she began. Wasn't he a man who liked order and logic? Who made decisions easily by weighing up alternatives? But there was no place to go that brought them to the end they wished for. She didn't want to hurt him. She wanted some kind of purpose and that was the one thing he could not offer. There had been talk early on of his getting a divorce, but that was gone now. *It's probably better to leave it this way,* she said. She didn't mean it, but she didn't want a man she had to bargain for. And she didn't want to think of what a divorce would mean for his wife, for the baby. She wasn't sure how she felt. Without a vote, is how she felt.

Marc nodded. He gave her the beer he'd just ordered and got up to get another for himself. The bar was full of journalists, most of whom he did not like. It was an odd truth that while the camaraderie among soldiers increased, that between correspondents sometimes splintered and died. Susan watched him negotiate a small circle, trying not to get snagged into conversation. She remembered how he once told her never to trust anybody. That had been an evening on a firebase when they lay together and watched tracers blazing overhead. You could pretend they were fireworks on a hot July night. You could pretend the man next to you was your husband. *Don't trust anybody*, he said. She shook her head. The pot made him paranoid, she thought. He'd been smoking earlier with two guys on his crew. He had his face in her hair, his arm across her stomach. *Don't trust the kids or the laundry maid or the plantation owner,* he said.

Shall I trust you?

Me? Of course you should trust me. On second thought, don't.

She laughed.

For practice.

She sat in the bar, remembering that previous conversation, how they watched the sky and he told her not to trust anyone, and then explained what was being fired and where. *That's just H&I. Our guys having a little party. Nothing to worry about, Stay near me. I can't remember when I've been happier to be on a firebase. It's fun with you. It will be even more fun if we don't get hit tonight.*

She'd turned to him. *Will we get hit tonight?*

He made a puzzled face. She'd honestly thought he would answer the question, that he could know such a thing. She understood this wasn't possible, but it didn't stop her from asking, asking earnestly as though he could tell her.

In the bar, having made his bid and lost, he went to get his beer and she thought: I love him. It was an admission that angered her; it was an uncomfortable feeling, like wearing clothes that were too tight.

He returned with a full glass, a change of subject. He could do that, discard his own emotions like a coat that he removed. He said, *I don't like Son.*

I think I knew that.

I don't trust him.

Why would you trust him? You don't trust anyone.

I'm serious.

I can see that.

If I were you, I'd quit with him. Walk away. You don't need to tell him why, you don't have to have a reason—

She interrupted him, setting her glass abruptly on to the lacquered table in front of them so that it landed with a crack. *No,* she whispered.

Susan, listen to me—

She shook her head. *Stop it or I'm leaving.*

He's not who we all think he is. I don't know who he is, but I am certain—

Stop!

Maybe it's just you he wants, but he wants something!

All this taking place in shouted whispers, their heads bent together. From a distance it would be possible to believe they were exchanging messages of love.

Oh, for God's sake—

He's so damned slippery, Susan. I know everyone thinks he's great, but I don't—

—if you want to finish with me, finish with me, but don't try and pat me on the head and send me home to Chicago. Don't poison every contact I've made, or friend—

She thought he was just talking, that his bilirubin counts had jumped again. Or maybe—ha ha—he was jealous. She had never asked him to divorce his wife. She'd never asked him for anything. With everything else that was going on, why would she expect him to make plans with her? Before they could make any plans for the future, there had to be a future. And being in a war zone didn't make you think like that. It made you think only about right now and maybe the next day.

But now he'd received word from his wife. The news came in a short note, written in his wife's florid hand. She had flown out to meet him in Singapore the way the wives of reporters so often did and that was when it had happened. The pregnancy was well into the second trimester now. He claimed he hadn't known about it until this recent letter. It changed everything. She felt she shouldn't—no, indeed, that she could not—carry on with him. They'd agreed to stop seeing each other, but here they were again, going over the same old ground.

As he continued, talking about how Susan should stop working with Son, she believed that what he meant was that he couldn't bear the thought of her with another man. Perhaps now that she no longer visited him in his room at night, he imagined her with someone else, even with Son. Maybe that was why he tried so hard to extract her from Son. It was a way of getting her to be closer to him. He seemed to have let her go easily enough, but no, it hadn't been easy. It hadn't worked. She could not understand why they did this to each other, why they'd gotten involved in the first place when both of them knew it could not end well, or why they did not separate now. Because he couldn't stop himself, that was the reason; and she did not want to stop either.

But sitting in the jungle with the soldiers and with Son, and remembering back, she recalls the conversation differently. It hadn't been only about their relationship; he'd been telling her something else altogether. When they'd gotten through the most awful part of their conversation, he had said, *Who do you work for?*

She didn't answer the question. It seemed like a non sequitur. She was thinking how far they'd come from the way the evening had begun, a glass slipped into her hand, his head near hers, the words: *Come and see me.* In only a few minutes, it had devolved to this. She would not be able to stop thinking of him now, not for a long while.

Have you lost your memory? she said, wearily. She wished she could curl up with him on the bed in his big, airy hotel room, lay her head on his shoulder, sleep. She didn't see why, if they were going to spend time together, it had to be arguing.

He smiled. He had large brown eyes, an offset nose, his teeth small and neat and white. For a few seconds, he appeared to have forgotten his question and they looked at each other, sitting close together in the leatherette sofa at the bar. She touched his face. She couldn't help herself. I love you, she wanted to say. She thought these words so strongly that for a moment she was afraid she'd spoken them. She was startled by the possibility that the words might erupt no matter how she tried to contain them. A musician she admired, a pianist, once told her that at the height of a concert, when the bassist and the drummer and he were in a lock, and the music was being discovered, plucked out of the air as though it had always existed somewhere in the ether, occasionally, without meaning to, he'd make a noise, calling out. He couldn't help it, he explained; the body insisted on its own emissions. For a moment she thought that for sure she had told Marc she loved him. Or that the information had slipped into him invisibly, a parcel of thought from one heart to another. She removed her fingers from his cheek as though from a hot pan. He noticed this. He noticed even more than when she had touched him.

Why are you asking me this? she said. He knew who she worked for.

Susan, he began, sadly. His voice was low, so she had to lean forward. Now she was way too close to him. She could smell his clothes, the sweet, sooty scent of marijuana. It was the same smell of his bedsheets, the same as his hair. She did not particularly like the smell, but it made her long for him. She wanted to pull away, but she couldn't. She wanted to put her head on his chest, but she couldn't do that either. He said, *I can tell you every article you've sold, and to where. Half the time I can tell you when you filed. There's almost no place you can be where I haven't imagined you. I know who you work for, yes, but that's not my point.*

What are you saying, then?

That you better ask yourself who Son is working for.

Every day is as hot as the last, and every hour seems exactly the same until nightfall, which comes suddenly. Then the temperature drops but the sounds remain, spookier now in the darkness. The jungle is alive with birds and monkeys, with sudden snapping branches and snagging vines and leaves, with invisible insects that buzz and swoop and form clouds in the air. The noise is constant, the heat rises and falls. She has never been alone, not once, since arriving in this loathsome, magical, indomitable country, and now she feels utterly alone. It gives her a feeling of panic. Like a trapped animal pacing behind bars, her mind weaves back and forth. She is caged in trees and heat. The way the soldiers press on suggests there must be an end to the monotonous green, but she does not believe it.

There is also the matter of the way Son is behaving—the early pretense of disregard, almost as though he had contempt for her. Even now, he speaks to her only when the soldiers cannot hear. Otherwise, he ignores her, sometimes for half a day or more. She believes it is an act. This man who taught her to ride a Vespa, taking his life in his hands as he did, who woke her up once in the middle of the night because he'd had a dream in which they were riding in a commercial jet somewhere, possibly to America, and wanted to tell her, who bought her a whistle in case she got into trouble in a crowd and needed to signal him. He adored her, and yet he'd changed completely since their capture. She sees now what she hadn't seen before. It is like suddenly noticing the magician's bluff, that trick of the eye, a form of misdirection in which a larger action hides a smaller one. It is a ruse, the way he ignores her. He pretends not to know her, and that it was a coincidence they were found together in the jungle. In front of the soldiers he behaves as though he has no real feelings for her, only official ones. She sees through it now. It's a con. Not to fool her, she has come to realize, but to fool them.

She is about to tell him this when her thoughts are interrupted by Long Hair. He sees something. He is pointing and shouting. Gap Tooth runs ahead, pushing her aside in the process, and she sees, all at once, what the soldiers are excited about. They are arriving at what looks like a small hamlet, its tidy order contrasting with the chaos of the jungle. She sees huts on stilts, shaded walkways, areas for animals. The path becomes wider; the brush and trees dissolve to a clearing.

"Oh, my God," she says. She does not know whether to hope this might be the place where things will turn around, that the soldiers will be given word from the villagers here about where to find their unit. There is the possibility that the unit is nowhere near, or that they will find it and still not release her. She is suddenly frightened that something awful will happen now. As the soldiers quicken their pace, then run, she is filled with anticipation and dread. She does not know what to expect. Once the soldiers' unit is found, there will be others to contend with, and it is these faceless others who worry her now.

The hamlet feels like a small, shaded oasis, though in truth it is no more than some houses set upon stilts. She is so stunned by the hamlet itself that she does not at first notice how quiet it is. No barking dogs, no grunts from pigs or other sounds you'd expect, no smoke from cooking fires or slapping of children's bare feet against the swept earth.

She and Son wait as the soldiers go in and out of the huts, their guns ready, checking who is around to greet them, to feed them, to give them information about their unit. But it is cemetery quiet. Not even a rooster crowing.

"Don't be scared," Son tells her. He smiles. He makes a funny face to lighten the mood. Out of sight of the soldiers he is as he has always been toward her, and she feels herself soften toward him, feels a prickle in her throat as though she might cry. Maybe this is why he doesn't talk to her much, because it makes her more easily upset. Why else should she begin to cry now as opposed to hours or days before?

She is distracted by the soldiers, who are moving faster and faster through doors and walkways. There is something wrong. They call, bewildered, turning to each other with expressions that show their confusion. At some point the people who live here will appear, she thinks, and they will know where the unit has gone, and everything will change. But the soldiers look increasingly disturbed. Son, too, becomes absorbed in what is happening in the hamlet.

"Oh," he says, as though he has just been issued a piece of information.

"What's wrong?" she asks. To her, it seems like an ordinary hamlet. She looks to her left at what is almost surely a pig corral, like many she has seen before. She recognizes the churned-up earth, the bays of mud, a broken bucket, a pile of empty straw. Everything, she realizes with a start, except pigs.

And then she understands: the hamlet is deserted. Even the animals have been taken. They find chicken feathers, clay bottles, clothes for a baby, empty houses and empty baskets, everything in disarray. The soldiers are upset. Long Hair drops down in the middle of the open space, leaning his forehead into his hand. The thin one slouches near by, his mouth stretching toward his chin in a frown. Gap Tooth swings his sword loosely at his side, swears a few times, kicks the ground, and shouts something to Son, who answers back in French, so that she can understand, too.

"It's nothing to do with me," is what Son says. "Anyway, they might have left some food behind. By accident, of course."

Gap Tooth considers this, then moves off like a scolded child. Long Hair shouts something in Vietnamese and Gap Tooth answers yes, and keeps walking. The Thin One stands quietly to one side, staring at the ground, until he is told to go search the hamlet, too.

"There may be clean water," Son says to nobody in particular.

A few minutes later, she hears a whooping sound and now Gap Tooth runs out, holding a small sack of rice above his head as though it is treasure from the ocean. Not only rice, but the pearly white rice that is preferred, not the bran that is fed to the animals. The soldiers crowd around the sack, delighting in it, weighing the rice in their hands, sniffing it, holding it up for inspection. The anguish of finding the hamlet deserted is replaced now with this new, festive mood. The soldiers sift through the rice for dud grains, talking excitedly, then they disperse once more, racing through the hamlet searching for more food. It might have been a treasure hunt. Long Hair calls out excitedly that he has found a few C-rations and they all run to where he stands, holding up the cans like trophies. So peasants hoard US military rations. Perhaps the whole of the country was surviving on them, she thinks.

"This could all be much worse," Son tells her.

"I won't get any."

"You'll have hot rice, warm broth. I'll make sure of it."

"You told me they would stop feeding me."

"Ah, but now it is different! There is food! One day you can tell the story of how your life was saved by a bag of rice."

They boil the rice and add some flavor from what is left of their dried fish. She stares at the pot, her stomach making audible groans as she watches. Finally, they give her some, and then more. They have found some rice wine, too. It's in a cloudy bottle with a medicinal smell, but it is strong alcohol and it makes them optimistic. She hears Gap Tooth say he's going to hunt for rats as surely they will be among the huts, easy to kill. He stumbles out, swaying from the rice wine, a rifle in hand, and the others laugh. Rat meat, found rice, who would have imagined she would call it a feast?

She eats until her stomach is full, the feeling like a new sensation, something to celebrate. Nobody knows what time it is. It might be midnight. It might be eight o'clock. The soldiers finish the last of the food and get out a pack of cards, inviting Son to join in. For a few hours, it seems, he will not be a prisoner. She hears them chatting together, the shuffle of cards, the ebb and flow of conversation. It sounds as though they are old friends.

She should feel relieved, but she does not. They sleep in greater comfort, a roof over their heads, the dry earth beneath them, her hammock set up in a corner. She is warmer than she has been since they were captured. Son was right, everything has changed, and yet she is even more uneasy.

"Where have all the people gone, Son?" she asks. He is near her, asleep. The soldiers have given him some rice wine, too, and he is completely out. He begins to snore. It is the same with the Thin One, who is meant to be guarding. She watches his head drop back, his shoulders relax, the gun lowering slowly to the ground. For a moment she considers taking the gun, or perhaps just walking slowly, quietly away, but then he wakes up once more, and she thinks anyway how foolish she'd be to try to escape. They would wake and shoot into the brush, and maybe they'd get her. Worse still, they might injure her just enough so that she died slowly of septic poisoning. And even if by some miracle she managed to escape into the jungle, where would she go? The jungle was emptying out, she thought. Deserted hamlets, lost troops. Even if she could get away, where would she get *to*?

A belly of rice, the promise of a dry night beneath shelter, a fire indoors so that the heat is kept. She ought to be able to fall asleep, but she has enough comfort now to lie awake instead and think. She is regretting the decisions that have added up to this occasion, all those small choices, the tiny determinations in her life that have brought her here, right now. She is thinking of how it might have been different if she'd gone to Marc's room, knocked on the door, stood beside him in the grim neon lights that shined through his windows, and told him she was finished with Son, that she'd quit him, as he had suggested.

Good, because a guy like him is a chameleon. You can't know him, Marc would have said. He may have said something like this before. She hadn't believed him then, of course, but she believes him now.

*   *   *

By the time the guards are up, by the time Son is awake near her, she has figured it out. A lever in her brain turns; the thoughts line up. The realization arrives effortlessly and she accepts it: an unwanted gift of her own imagining.

"What happens to spies when they are caught?" she asks Son. She wants him to know that she knows. Or thinks she knows. She sees no other reason why the soldiers have not already shot him. After all, he is Vietnamese; he is of military age; he is traveling with a woman who was almost certainly aligned in some way with enemy forces. Under most circumstances they'd have shot him outright—there would be no question. There was no reason *not* to shoot him, no weight in the decision. Old men, women, pregnant young wives, sometimes even children, the everyday kill of such soldiers. And here they are, drinking with a man who by all rights ought to be considered their enemy, playing cards with him.

She says, "You must know something they want to find out. Or maybe you have a high rank and they don't dare kill you."

He says nothing. The soldiers are making some kind of tea from curled leaves that give off a smell like freshly mown grass. She tries again. She says, "What will they do to you when they find out you spy for the Americans?"

There is a long silence, then, "I don't spy for the Americans."

Her stomach lurches and it feels for all the world as though the earth has suddenly swayed. A lever in her mind, and now she understands and wishes she did not. He's a spy, all right, but she hadn't understood correctly. Now she does. "You don't spy for the Americans," she says.

He shakes his head slowly.

"Not for the Americans," she says again. She hates what she is learning. It enters her painfully, this information.

"You do a good imitation of a photographer," she sighs. "Though I guess a spy has to have a convincing counterfeit profession to hide behind."

"I *am* a photographer. You know that."

"I don't know anything," she says, "except you hold powerful sway with these soldiers."

There is a pause. It would seem that Son is quite willing to forfeit the conversation entirely, to let it stop right here.

"So explain this: why me?" says Susan. "Why did you choose me, of all people?"

He says nothing.

"I remember how you found me at Pleiku. That look on your face. You pegged me. I know you did."

All this she says easily. No emotion to her voice. She does not want the soldiers—if they are listening—to guess at their conversation, or to imagine that they are arguing. She keeps her voice light, her inflections playful. Judging from the tone of the conversation you'd think she was reminiscing about a nice summer's day.

She continues, "What will the Americans do to you when they find out? Or are you planning to go underground now? Or join these guys? Or live in Hanoi, if we ever make it that far? And you know we won't. *I* won't."

She hears him sigh. Or perhaps it is a yawn. "I've told them you are English," he says, finishing the sentence with her name; not her given name, Susan, but a nickname that she allows only him to use: "Susey." "And that you've been a help to me."

"Well, that's certainly the truth," she says. "Did you mention I had no idea what kind of help I was providing?"

"I have told them to take me with them and verify my identity and position. If you make yourself into my enemy, you may be in danger. Not from me, you understand."

"They have my papers. And those say I am American. From Chicago. It's all there."

"They have no papers."

"Of course they do."

"No. They do not yet realize, but they do not have them."

"Why not?"

"I ate them. Last night. With the rice. They weren't paying so much attention."

In other circumstances, it might have been funny. "What about my MACV card?" she says. "Did you eat that, too?"

It was hard plastic-coated card, like a driver's license, that identified her as press.

"You have your MACV card," he says.

She feels in her pockets and there it is, a rectangle of stern plastic. It is there, like an egg conjured up by a magician, appearing at once from behind her ear. "You stole it back," she whispers. He says nothing. "What will happen after they figure out who you are?"

"They may be glad they didn't kill me."

"Will you be released?"

"I would hope."

"And then what happens?"

"Then? It is up to you what happens."

Up to her? "Son, who are you? Who are you exactly?"

With the new supply of rice the soldiers are more relaxed. The next day they give her back her canteen, which she tops up whenever possible from the small pools that collect in the jungle's wide, oversized leaves. Gap Tooth shows her how to get clean water from a bank, and even how water comes out of bamboo. She has already learned to tie the thin branches of low trees into a canopy that creates shade, to squat on her heels when eating. Long Hair removes his necklace on which hangs a P-38, a US Army tool that opens combat-ration cans, and shares one of the precious cans of rations with her. It holds peaches, and when she realizes this she feels overwhelmed with gratitude, her dry mouth suddenly moist with the thought of eating them, the juice so good it might be from another world. If this is how she feels about canned peaches, she wonders what her response would be to other foods. She imagines grilled trout, lemons. She imagines black cherries and bacon. She forces herself to stop thinking about food, because it is almost unbearable to do so, but she finds once more her mind drifting: lemonade, a cold sweet orange.

Her actual diet, apart from rice, is now crickets and other insects, brought to a smoky crisp in a small bowl of charcoal carried on a pole like a kind of mobile barbecue. The bowl is another of the treasures discovered at the hamlet. It serves as a kitchen and a focus for their attention, too, as they collect worms and termites from the jungle floor, charring them in the charcoal one after the other. The rice makes all the difference. It smells a little like mildew (not that she cares), and the peaches are a godsend. *Thank you*, she says in French, and again in Vietnamese, for it is one of the few phrases she knows. *Thank you, thank you.*

There are places so thick with bush that the soldiers could shrug their rifles over their shoulders, give a command, and all disappear into the bush. Other areas are like a dark, dense forest, the sunlight filtering through in small spiky bursts of light, so that it feels like living inside the green glass of a bottle. They march at night, and though it is cooler she is spooked by the phosphorescence of the jungle floor, a ghostly swimming light caused by fungus on the ground.

She is given a mixture of water and lime juice to pour on her feet. She does this, shuddering with pain. They bring out the iodine next. She looks hard at the medicine, trying to judge how much has evaporated since last time and pressing the cap with her fingers, trying to repair the damaged threading that makes it leak. Lime juice, then iodine. She can almost feel the goodness of this combination in her flesh. Afterwards, Son tears strips of his trousers, tying them just below her knee to keep the leeches from climbing up her legs. As he bends over her, carefully arranging the leech straps, whatever vestiges of anger from the day before vanish. He is a spy but right now it does not matter. He's negotiated with the soldiers for her food, her medicine. He is helping protect her from the leeches she dreads. This is all that she can consider at the moment, and that she is alive because of him.

She puts her hand on his cheek.

"Don't," he says, jerking his cheek from her palm. "I don't deserve it."

He is the Son she has always known, the boy who taught her how to play Tien Len, who slept on her floor, who sometimes grabbed her thumb with his hand and lurched along the street like a chimpanzee, who could make a sound like a cricket, who taught her to blow smoke rings, and once showed her the magnificent scar from his burst appendix. She does not want to leave him—whatever he has done or is doing. If they let her go but keep him, she thinks how hard it would be never to see him again. Not to go with him to milk bars in Saigon, watch him working on his photographs in the small hotel room that has become a kind of office and home, not to travel with him beside her, or to see his face which is more familiar to her now than her own. It feels to her the universal theme in this country: departure and loss. Everyone is always in the process of leaving. Everyone is dying or disappearing or going away or being sent home. You never got used to it. Even the soldiers who had served two or three tours, even they didn't, and certainly not her.

"Son—" she begins. She thinks the worst thing about his being a spy is that they will have to be separated. Or that one of them will die.

He does not let her finish. He pats her knee, stands up all at once, and turns his back, walking away. They are now moving again through the brush, making slow headway, the whole process tedious and uncomfortable.

*   *   *

The next day it is she who holds the smoking charcoal pot and Gap Tooth who goes barefoot. Gap Tooth's sandals fit her the best, the outline of his feet being covered easily by her own. She is more comfortable now; walking with less trouble than the day before. Even so, it is a wonder to her that these soldiers can march barefoot without pain or injury. At a rest stop Gap Tooth sits beside her and she finds herself staring at his feet, at the tough soles that are caked with calluses. He notices her doing this and takes the opportunity to show off his feet the way he once showed off his sword. He points to the leathery skin, brown and smooth. He explains that the soles of his feet are shoes.

"Yours, maybe. Mine are casualties," she says.

"You need work," he says. "You need practice."

She is supposed to use a long wooden pole with a fan at the end to catch insects for the charcoal pot. The pot smokes and crackles as she moves down the path, giving off a heat that causes her to sweat even more. Try as she might, she cannot target an insect correctly and little makes its way into the pot. Long Hair takes the pole from her and shows her how to sweep the fan. He scoops up several insects and drops them quickly on to the hot charcoal, then pushes one into his mouth as though it were popcorn. She tries again, but she is no good at it. Finally, she is allowed to pass the project on to the Thin One, who stares at her as though she is utterly useless, so that she cringes under his gaze. But at least he takes on the pot and fan.

She is settling into the walk again when suddenly the soldiers freeze, speaking rapidly to one another. There is the sound of airplanes, like a rumble of thunder that grows louder by the second.

"Don't move," she is told.

This has happened before, planes going overhead, never spotting them, never even swinging back to take a second look in

139

case what they saw down there was a person. You would think spotter planes would see the five of them walking, but it seems never to be the case. However, this time feels different. She knows it is different even before anything happens, though she cannot say why. The planes are screaming; she can feel the earth vibrate. She yells to Son that it is an air strike and, just as she does so, there is an enormous explosion. The soldiers have their guns out but they do not move an inch. She wants to run. She begins to argue but Long Hair grabs her arm and demands that she not move. "Stay!" he growls, pinching her elbow. But then another explosion; this from napalm, and the soldiers' reactions change abruptly. Long Hair lets her go, pushing her aside now as they run, crashing through the thick brush.

She tries to follow. It is the natural thing to do. She is shouting but the noise is so loud around them that she cannot be heard, the jungle exploding, ribbons of fire sailing above them. She can feel the heat from the flames, the air changing around her; she runs as fast as she can but Son and the soldiers have disappeared. She cannot find them and she is racing forward now through brush that scratches her face, tears her clothes. The sandals cannot protect the tops of her feet from thorns and vines. The air seems to hold no weight to it—it is as though she is breathing in a vacuum. Then within minutes, within seconds even, the sound of the planes lifts, leaving in their wake clouds of black smoke rising from all around her, so thick it might be solid matter, a small planet erupting. She doesn't know where to go now. She drops to the ground, her feet bleeding, her toes balled together, the whole foot arching inward in pain. She can hear the planes on their way out. She looks up, her eyes stinging, a sharp throb across her forehead. She can see fires all around her. She wonders if she's been hit.

She is suddenly terrified of being alone. She thinks about the field hospitals, how the dying are put behind that awful curtain, some of them begging not for a doctor but for the comfort of a friend, a nurse, a buddy, the face of someone to reassure them as they die. She feels the same way now, the frantic need for connection, the unwillingness to be left behind. The planes could come back and drop more napalm. The napalm terrifies her like nothing else. She's seen cans of it, ribbed, innocent, silver cans that might hold apple sauce or peanuts, rather than jellied gasoline. She has heard the stories of how soldiers are cooked inside the flames, their skin falling from the bone as they dance in the fire that pours over them like water. Now, as she is surrounded by fires igniting the jungle as kindling, she begins to panic. She searches frantically from side to side and she sees, as though waiting specifically for her, a cluster of steel straws protruding from the ground, a set of ignites camouflaged so well into the earth that it is as though they are naturally part of the jungle, as much as the giant fronds, the elephant grass, the canopies of leaves. Her eyes fix on the mine and hold the rest of her completely still. She has to force herself to exhale, to look for a firing wire. Her vision begins to fracture and she uses every ounce of her concentration to bring herself back to the task at hand, to figure out how the mine has been set up, so that she can avoid it.

She has seen such a mine before, just once, close up, when a young sergeant held one up in front of a group of new guys and said, "Gentlemen, meet Betty." Then, it had been isolated, contained. Seeing the Bouncing Betty here, ready in the jungle, is like seeing a rare, lethal animal that you have seen before only in a zoo. She feels herself swimming in heat, in desperation. She begins to tremble, to push herself back, to spin her head wildly around looking for where the wire leads. She must stay clear-headed or she will die. She knows this, but she feels herself unraveling.

The next explosion she thinks must be the Bouncing Betty. She covers her head with her hands, rolls into a ball; she feels time like a slow and expanding moment, like a dreadful weight.

141

She is waiting. But a mine can explode only one time and these explosions continue, over and over, waves of sound coming from everywhere. She digs her chin into the earth, pushes her face as far down as she can, unable think at all. Even with her eyes closed she sees a wall of red, a dazzling constellation of colors against the backs of her eyelids, the drum of the explosions coursing through her. She has not been hit. She knows this and it mystifies her. She feels as though she has been propelled up into the air, away from the earth, preserved through some miracle of physics. Only later will she realize she hasn't left this patch of earth, that the Bouncing Betty remains where it is, that the explosions are not here but a quarter-mile away. For now, she is sailing along the rolling explosions, feeling the vibrations against her teeth, the bones of her nose, the tender hollows of her temples. The noise is through her and around her. She clutches her knees, presses her chin into her collarbone, waits for it all to end, as she knows it must. But the planes recede; they always do. And as much as they try, they cannot obliterate the whole of the jungle or the people within.

III

There is a rotting smell in the taxi, like overripe fruit, its scent lodging itself high inside his nose. He cranks the window down. The smell takes him back to a taxi ride with Susan, looking at her beside him on the balding cloth seat, her hair wild across her face, her pale eyes blinking against it. He remembers how she tried to comb back the locks with her fingers, but the hair escaped, streaming like kite tails. They'd rolled the windows down then, too, because the smell was so strong and sick-making.

That was not long ago, a couple of months, though of course in the curious manner in which time stretches and condenses with its own, peculiar logic in Vietnam, it seems a long time. This same smell—what is it? Cabbage, rotten food, dirty clothes?—draws him right back. Susan had buried her head in his chest. She'd shorn her hair from its previous length so that it was harder to collect all at once, and he remembers, too, how he'd walked into the room late one night and seen her there in front of the mirror, her reflection in the glass, the scissors in her hands. She turned to him, the length of her lopped hair in pieces across her shoulders, the corners of her mouth turned up, the hair like confetti all around her. *I've always wanted to do this,* she said, as though talking about a place she'd always wished to go to. She stepped to greet him, her neck newly exposed like some part of her he had not seen before. He

145

took the scissors from her hand, sifted his fingers through her hair, lifted her chin up to him, and kissed her.

He feels her absence now like a sudden space once comfortably filled, a solid piece of himself now missing. He is no longer anchored by her, is drifting dangerously. To say he misses her is an insulting, ridiculous statement. He is frightened for her and there is no relief.

The taxi in which they'd traveled, like the one he is in now, had been filthy. It looked as if it had been buried, then excavated. That's what he'd told her. *Thing looks like it's been exhumed,* he said, and felt the satisfaction of her small laugh.

Sometimes the cars in Vietnam were constructed out of several other wrecks. Susan had told him this, not then, but another time. Another of the many taxi rides they'd taken together. She'd likened the ingenious recycling of auto parts to the Vietcong practice of making mines out of dud howitzer shells, houses from flattened cans of Cola, and told him the only waste there was left in the country was what happened to the people. That was true, he'd agreed. That was true.

There had been the smell of a soldering iron among the other, less pleasant scents. She pointed this out. Rust on the inside, the outside. If it had been raining, the roof would have leaked. He could see that from the watermarks darkening the upholstery above him. But there was no rain that night, only dust and noise. His foot rested on a sandbag that almost certainly covered a hole in the floor.

I don't think the doors match, Susan said, laughing.

Beside him, she looked crisp and pale, out of place, a cool glass of water on a summer's day. She wore a white blouse he particularly liked, jeans with embroidery, a slim military watch, a gift from a colonel who had also given her a ticket to Hawaii which she'd had to decline, although she was quite willing to have dinner with him in Saigon. The colonel had shown her how by pulling the watch's crown one could stop the sweep

146

hand, allowing soldiers to synchronize the time. *The guy is so old*, Marc had said, *probably that watch is from World War II.* Susan laughed at him. *You're just jealous*, she said, to which he grunted, *Don't be ridiculous. I have no right to be jealous in any case.* It was true he didn't like it when another man showed her attention. One time, it had been so hot when they'd been together on a patrol that the soldiers quickly ran out of water. A private, some nineteen-year-old kid from Michigan, let Susan have the last slug from his canteen. Watching her head tipped back, the workings of her throat as she drank gratefully, the soldier standing close to her, admiring her, Marc had to look away, pretend it didn't matter, that he hadn't noticed. He'd run out of water a mile ago and it had never even occurred to him to share it.

You're all right? he said as they crossed into Cholon in the taxi.

I'm thinking about Thanh. Thanh owned the hotel where she stayed. He was a fat, balding little guy who gave Marc disapproving looks whenever he entered the hotel with her. *He brought me another lizard.*

They're not lizards. They're geckos. Or anoles.

He says they will eat the insects.

Bug spray. And a new lock on your door. Basic stuff. Tell him you would like running water, for example. He didn't like that hotel. He was always trying to get her to leave it, find a room elsewhere.

You don't have to hate him.

I don't hate him.

The taxi glided down the road; he kissed her. *Stay in my room. If I'm there, if I'm not,* he said, though he knew she wouldn't. She did not keep a change of clothes in the room, not so much as a pair of socks. She didn't belong to him—that was the truth—and he often felt that the way in which she left no trace of herself was more revealing than if she were to keep

147

an extra pair of underwear in his drawers, or a comb, or a toothbrush in the echoing bathroom with its high ceilings and black and white tiles.

He found the nape of her neck with his thumb, whispered into her ear: *It's paid for and half the time it's empty. You can get room service. The windows don't leak when it rains.*

And leave my lizards? Sorry, my anoles.

Bring them. I'll stick them to the walls myself.

If you're not going to be there, then why would I want to be there without you?

Well, there's a lot more room, he said. He was thinking of Son, how the guy slept on her floor like a tramp.

Ah, the truth reveals itself, she laughed.

This was weeks ago—six, eight? The taxi seat had a tear mark, he remembers, the foam beneath it rising up like proud flesh. She pushed the foam back into position, smoothed the upholstery, put her hand on his knee. The window, when he'd rolled it down, became stuck in position. He could not move it unless he got out and lifted the glass. He apologized for this, but Susan shrugged it off.

I like the breeze, she said.

He spoke again but the sounds from the road drowned out his words. Pedicabs, motorbikes, the heaving drone of an ancient bus. The noise awakened inside him a feeling he associated only with this city. Whenever he was in Saigon he began to feel a kind of controlled desperation, something he picked up from the place itself. The size, the dense clusters of people and buildings, overwhelmed him with its mad logic, its combustion of heat and energy that cloaked him like the fine dust that he washed off in the evenings. He felt all of it, all at once: the discreet corner swindlings, the meetings of money-changers, the pickpockets, the girls dressed up to attract business, the courteous hotel staff who tolerated, more than tolerated, who *absorbed* the indiscretions of their Western guests. All the hundreds of vendors, floating markets, corrupt police and restaurants in which this group gathered, or this other group, he seemed to take the whole of it inside himself, swallowed in one big gulp. He tapped his chin, his fingers fluttered, his leg vibrated in a steady rhythm. He couldn't remember when he'd acquired these habits. It was part of the electricity that coursed through him and to which he'd become accustomed.

What's the matter? she asked.

Nothing. Put your hand back. Keep it there. If I move, press down.

Yes, sir.

I'm sorry. I'm a little strange tonight.

Tonight?

Ah, ha, ha. I've had an awful day.

I know, sweetheart, she told him.

And it was true. That afternoon, he'd been threatened by the police because he had brought a camera to a student protest. The police were everywhere, an army in white, and among the pale uniforms of the Saigon police were Westerners, too, men in crisp shirts, cropped hair, pale uncallused hands. The CIA advisors looked like thoroughbreds before a race. Charged up, even sleek, in their pressed trousers, their almost identical blue blazers and ties. He watched them among the crowd, noticing the air of authority they projected, something they seemed to acquire in training. Even the youngest of such advisors had it. One of the men broke away from his companion and approached Marc, his eyes leveled at him, fists clenched, head hunkered down upon his collar. Marc knew the man's name, had even had a drink with him once at an embassy party. *We wouldn't want you to get shot, Mr. Davis,* the man said. *Stray bullet.*

Marc had nodded at the statement, showing no sentiment one way or another. Part of the treachery he was able to bring upon such people was his ability to hide his emotions.

He issued his own question coolly, as though grateful for the advisor's admission of violence. *Are you planning to shoot people this morning?* he asked in his reporter's voice, the recorder on, his cameraman, Don Locke, to his left, just behind him, the camera resting on his shoulder, the film ticking through.

There are always stray bullets, Mr. Davis.

Marc was not on camera. The steady focus of Locke's camera was on the CIA man, whose face was as solemn and angry as though he'd had altogether enough of newsmen, of cameras and notepads, of the press demanding special rights and access—who had agreed to all that in the first place?

Marc pretended he did not notice. He smiled as though the man was making a joke, and said, *How many stray bullets are you expecting today?*

The advisor turned away now, out of the frame of the shot, pushing past the Vietnamese policemen. *One may be enough*, he whispered as Marc stumbled along beside him, trying to get his tape recorder in range.

It was not the first time, but he'd never grown used to such intimidations. They filmed the American as he spoke and then watched the Vietnamese policemen with their billy clubs, their white gloves, their Honda steeds. The students were beaten, shot at, dispersing after not much fuss. It was over so quickly it was hardly a story. Then they came upon a girl, maybe seventeen, eighteen, her hair wet with blood, lying on the hot asphalt. Locke put the camera on her, following her as she was lifted by another student who himself was struck, hauled off by four officers who met his protests with their clubs. Another student arrived at the girl's side and he, too, was pushed back. They kept the film rolling. The arrival of ambulances, shouting, circling police. Twenty seconds, maybe half a minute.

Suddenly, there was gunfire; he and Locke ran backwards, the camera still pointed toward the girl. The commotion continued. Locke tried to keep the camera up to film as a group of students, newly determined by the sight of the injured girl, fought off a line of police. The students could only hold their ground for a few seconds before being set upon by another group of police and forced back; in this way they surged and withdrew, forward and back like a receding tide, dropping their banners and signs. The girl was there, then gone, then there again. Marc held the recording equipment up and away from him, exposing his chest. It forced him into a vulnerable pos ition but he had no choice. Locke lifted the camera high above the reaching arms of the police in the same manner. They had minutes of good footage, enough for a story.

Then the police hit Locke's arm so that he dropped the camera on to the street. Marc jumped for it, grabbed it, then was kicked, his arm stepped upon so that for a moment he let go the camera. Somebody booted him across the shoulder, trying to turn him over now that he'd tucked the camera beneath him. But he rose up through the blows, bent over, the camera at his belly, shielding it with his body. The girl was gone and in her place, he saw now, was a fan of smeared blood. He would have loved footage of that, too, but the camera was huge, unwieldy, and he kept getting pushed back, down on to the street again. He got up, turning as he did so. The police were pulling at the camera, prying it away from him. He held on; running, trying to run. His feet didn't seem to make any progress; it all happened in a compressed moment of time in which he felt trapped, overpowered. He looked over his shoulder and saw another journalist being hit in the face. The man fell down and was kicked. He saw it and stopped, held the camera up, trying to film. The journalist was dragged back, smacked in the ear with a boot. Then someone dropped a gun—he saw this—dropped a gun right next to the journalist's hand. By then he was being pushed back hard in a rush of people. The recording equipment wagged on his hip, the camera was harder and harder to protect. He could film nothing. He looked wildly around for Locke, but could not see him. He saw the gun inches from the journalist's elbow. He wished he could yell to the journalist, *Don't pick up the gun.* He ran forward, colliding into people; he heard the journalist crying out. There were sirens everywhere, shouting, gunshots, CS cans rolling down the street spewing their pummels of smoke. *There are always stray bullets, Mr. Davis.* He thought what might happen if the journalist picked up the gun that had been planted there, how easy it would be then to shoot him, to justify it, even to insist on the necessity of yet another assassination. The police hovered over him until tear gas drove them back. He couldn't see the gun any more. Either it was obscured by the gas or the policeman who dropped it there had picked it up once more. Someone had gotten the journalist to his feet and he saw now who it was: Brian Murray. His eye was swollen; he had blood over one side of his head. He was ducking his head one way then another as though fending off blows that were no longer coming. Though Marc did not manage to get that on film, he watched it, and the sight of Murray protecting his face from assailants who were gone, had scattered, fled, became so embedded in his mind that for many years he believed he'd seen the footage, that he'd filmed it and that it had been shown on the news.

Locke grabbed his elbow and spun him around. Already their eyes were streaming and stinging from the tear gas. *Let's go!* Locke said. Marc handed Locke the camera. *Get Murray*, he said. He meant get him out of here, but Locke thought he meant film him.

We've already got enough!

No, I mean, go get him!

Murray had lost his eyeglasses. He was trying to find them, patting the ground, his hands filtering through papers, coins, cards, keys, shards of broken glass, other bits of debris, but he couldn't see with his swollen brow, the tear gas overwhelming him, the glasses undoubtedly smashed to pieces anyway. Locke and Marc reached him, yelling already for him to stand up.

Move! Locke yelled. *Stand up, for fucksake!* They took him by the elbows, hoisted him up. He rose with enormous resistance, shoulders first, making a squealing sound, then stopped suddenly and vomited on their shoes. Locke yelled, *Run! Run, you sonofabitch!* At that point Murray finally registered that it was them, Locke and Davis, and opened his mouth in surprise. They ran down the road, escaping the tear gas, the riot, Murray clinging to them, Marc hoping the guy wasn't seriously wounded, that they weren't leaving a trail of blood. He hadn't checked; there had been no time. He had the sudden, awful thought that Murray had been shot, or had been hit so hard in the head that his brain was swelling.

They got a taxi to the radio station ten blocks away, Murray holding the front of his head, patting the wound there. It did not look so bad once you could see where the injury began and ended, a broad scraping that had taken off the skin across his forehead. Locke pushed a bloody handkerchief against the back of his own head where he had been kicked. That wound was of a different kind. It had a caved-in look that made Marc nervous. He was inclined to tell the taxi driver to keep driving, to pass the radio station altogether and head out to the dispensary by the airport to have the gash seen to. But Murray was half mad with fear and it took both him and Locke to keep him calm. No change of instructions was given, about a dispensary or anything else, and so the taxi stopped duly outside the radio station.

They all piled out. Murray recovered himself enough to curse the whole of the Saigon police department, particularly the Commissioner and a few other high-ranking officers. The blood on his head wasn't too bad, but his hands were a mess. Standing on the sidewalk, Murray stretched his fingers out and back again, or tried to, checking if they were broken. One of his wrists had a purple bruise that seemed to grow by the minute.

Let's go, said Marc, and they charged into the radio station, climbing the stairs to the cloakroom, where they washed under the disapproving glare of Madam Ngô, who ran the place, and who began to yell when they took turns ducking their heads under the faucet, trying to get off the traces of gas and blood. Murray couldn't work the taps; his hands were too swollen. *They must have stood on you*, Locke said. Marc turned the taps for the guy, brought him some paper towels. At the adjacent sink the blood from Locke's head wound mixed with water and filled the bowl. Marc told him he really should go get some treatment. Murray finished at the sink and set off downstairs once more, saying he was getting a taxi to the dispensary. He was worried about his fingers, one of which was blackening at the tip. *Go with him*, Marc said.

Locke frowned down into the sink, then spit. *We'll do the spot first.*

Madame Ngô clucked and stomped around them. *What you do my floor!* she said. *My towel! Why you take all my towel?* They dripped water over the tiled floor along with flecks of blood. Locke made a compress of paper towels, pressing them against his swelling skull. Madame Ngô pointed to these infractions, shouting at them as they piled back down the stairs to the studio. By apologizing profusely and promising to send someone to clean it all up, they convinced her to connect them to San Francisco, then get a patch through to New York. She made it clear she found them boorish and demanding, impossible even, worse than disrespectful children. If she could have spanked them, she would have. Marc did a one-minute spot on a New York station while Madame Ngô pouted and stamped on the other side of the studio's soundproof glass, berating Locke, who had the bad manners to continue to bleed despite all her ravings, marking the green linoleum of the radio station's floor. Marc stepped out into the area where Locke was leaning against the metal shelving that held cables and production equipment, all the mysterious black boxes and wiring and reels of tape, ignoring the woman who bent at his feet, scraping spots of blood with wads of tissue paper from a roll she held tightly near her person, lest the enormous American man above her try to use that, too, for the problem with his scalp.

They got a taxi to the bureau. Locke went through the sequence of pictures, first this, then that, guessing at how much time he'd got on each set of images, as Marc typed out the words for the voice-over. He read it through once more, then wrote out the changes in longhand, editing where he could. What he wrote did not entirely capture the drama of the event. It did not include the warning from the CIA man, the attack of the journalist, Murray, the last fan of blood left by the dying girl. But it was a sound, accurate report that he was glad to conclude. It had been a misery, the afternoon; in the end, they had to ride out to the dispensary because the blood was still seeping from Locke's skull.

What a pain in the ass, Locke said.

It's no big deal, said Marc. *Might as well have it checked out.*

Marc felt all right. He thought he was all right. He'd been in Khe San only a month before when North Vietnamese gunners were firing three hundred rounds a day. This little student protest didn't even figure by comparison. Even so, in the taxi on the way back from the dispensary, Locke's wound neatly joined now by a line of new butterfly bandages, he didn't feel entirely all right. He'd had a coffee with cognac. He'd had half a joint in the stall at the dispensary while they tended to Locke. *Fuck if I'm doing any more work tonight,* said Locke afterwards. *I'm getting sufficiently stoned and that's it. Goodnight.*

The traffic coming out of the dispensary slowed, then stopped. They stood in the baking heat, Locke slumped against a door, asleep or close enough, the sun like a knife, the only slight shade at one edge of the seat, which was burning hot, as though the vinyl might melt altogether. Marc ran out of cigarettes. Normally,

155

he would have asked the driver to stop and get him some, never having to move from where he was sitting. You could do that in Saigon, sit and wait and have things brought to you. But the taxi hadn't gone more than a mile in twenty minutes. They were flanked by every kind of vehicle, stalled by the sheer weight of traffic because (he learned later) a military convoy making its way slowly over a cross-section had experienced some type of mechanical problem. Meanwhile, he wanted a smoke. This fact and the way in which the sun was angling into the cab, searing them like meat, made him so crazy he banged the roof of the cab and howled at the driver, who quivered and was silent. Locke didn't move from his stupor. He leaned his head on the half-open window, a neat pink line from the window's edge dissecting his cheek. He was completely out of it. He didn't care who yelled at who. The traffic was one long unmoving chain; Marc was thirsty as hell. No cigarettes. He flung himself upwards from his seat. The driver shrunk down as he roared.

What the fuck? said Locke, then closed his eyes again.

Marc felt himself become suddenly aware of his own crazy anger; he felt the sweat beading on his lip, wished he'd shaved that morning. His face was hot. He rubbed his collar, wiped his palms on his shirt.

Sorry, Marc told the driver, but it came out all wrong, as if he was issuing an order, as if he was expecting the driver to be sorry. He tried again. *Je suis desolé.* But it was too late. The driver had cloaked himself in the same invisible shield he'd seen in many of the Vietnamese. A shouting American, a Vietnamese taxi man. It was the same story all over the place. Who could blame the guy that he didn't respond to the apology, that he appeared not even to have heard it?

Marc wanted to tell the driver that only hours before he'd had the back of his knee kicked out so that he went flying on to the street, that his arms had been stepped on when he

156

grabbed for his equipment, that he'd seen a colleague beaten and could do nothing. *Your goddamned police,* he wanted to say. And why? Why did he want to berate this man driving the cab?

He could not be alone. He needed a drink. That's when he decided to find Susan. By the time he arrived at her door he'd reached a new place altogether, a leveled anxiety that pointed inward. His heart was pumping, the heat rose from him so that he felt his shirt sticking to him like a second skin. He was unable to relax, standing in the hall with a newly purchased pack of Camels, smoking one after another like he was going through a box of chocolates. When a maid came in with her bucket and rags, he fixed a glare on her that shooed her away. He felt like a bully. He hated himself. He pulled on the cigarette, blew the smoke up to the ceiling, used the floor as an ashtray, then marched downstairs and got a scotch. Susan still wasn't back so he went outside to a newsagent. It began to rain, the sky opening just as he left with his newspaper, stabbing warm raindrops, then thicker ones that felt like someone were cracking eggs over his head. He ran back to the hotel, flew up the stairs. He stood impatiently outside her room door making the carpet wet. When Susan finally appeared, back from the five o'clock briefing, he greeted her as if she were expecting him. She was not. She wore a trenchcoat, loafers, some sort of ridiculous rain hat that floated around her head.

What's this? He touched the hat. It was transparent plastic with a brightly colored cord that tied beneath the chin. Something a child would wear. He seemed to recall that back home they sold such things in gumball machines for a quarter. He wondered how much she'd paid for it here in one of the Saigon market stalls. Some crazy price just for Americans, three dollars for a piece of plastic glued to nylon. *Looks like something you'd wrap a sandwich in.*

Well, it's an improvement on the plastic bag I wore last time

I got caught in a storm, she said. *What you need in this place is a shower cap, really. It's like standing under a waterfall—what happens during monsoon season?*

He thought of the all-day deluges, the washed-out roads, the sucking mud that went up to his knees. Not here in Saigon, of course. Here it was only a matter of constant rain and steam and floating garbage and people with worsening health. *You might need more than . . . uh . . . that,* he said, meaning the plastic rain hat. He held a log of soggy newspapers under his arm. The floor below them was darkening with water.

I keep losing my umbrellas.

You're not losing them. They're being stolen.

She had her keys in her hand. Her fingers were wet, the cuffs of her blouse, her shoes. *Why weren't you at the briefing if you were in town anyway?*

I couldn't face it, he said. *Give me your keys.*

I can do it.

Well, come on, then.

He told her he'd been at the student protest. She'd been at the protest, too, but had arrived too late to see anything. He told her briefly about the girl and about the wall of students who challenged the police. He didn't mention the fight for the camera, that Murray was beaten, that a gun was dropped on purpose. She wanted to hear more of what he'd seen, but he didn't feel like talking. He shouldn't have arrived like this, in this condition. He felt everything inside him was coming unglued; he could only be a burden to her in this state. It occurred to him, not for the first time, that he'd been in Vietnam too long.

She finally pushed the door open.

You want dinner? he said.

She shook her head, dropped her keys on the arm of a chair, kicked her shoes off.

You're probably hungry, he said.

I'm not. I'm fine.

The room had a stagnant feel and smelled vaguely of dust and insect repellent, like all hotel rooms in Saigon. She set the fan in motion; he felt the movement of air across his cheek, caught the scent from her hair. He looked at her portable type-writer with its set of skeletal keys, the ribbon beside it which she'd apparently been trying to wet down or re-ink. In a better mood he'd have offered to send her a carton of new ribbons. Instead, he looked at the bed, the rumpled sheets, the inviting pillow, and wanted to lay his face on that pillow, stay there for ever.

Shut the door, he said.

She smiled uneasily, shook off her coat, rubbed her watch against her blouse, drying it. There was a drumming of rain along the rooftop, the mild mechanical sound of the revolving fan.

Is he *here?* He took in the walls of Son's prints, the elabo-rate iron tea set, an empty bird-cage which was most certainly his, as were the lens filters, the small pouch of tobacco. In the corner, next to the window, was a box set upon one end in which someone—undoubtedly Son—had made a pair of thin shelves.

No. Son's away. What's the matter with you? You're acting funny. Is something wrong?

Nothing's wrong. Same old stuff. You know.

He dropped into a chair with a sigh. She regarded him as one might a bad-tempered dog. He handed her his jacket and she hung it up over the bath with her trenchcoat, stuffed some dry newsprint into his shoes. His socks were stained from the dye in the leather. She knelt on the floor and removed them, then put her head against his knees.

Keep going, he said. He let her coax off his shirt, unbuckle his pants. He wanted her to get her clothes off. It was really all he wanted right now. The rain stopped as abruptly as it had

159

begun earlier and the room rapidly filled with too much light. *Hang on a second,* he said. He went to the window, pulled down a blind. He rifled through her small record collection. She waited for him by the bed. *Don't move,* he told her.

He couldn't think of this now, traveling in the taxi through Cholon, remembering that horrible day—the riot and the dying girl, the camera being wrenched from them, the planted gun, Murray on the ground and the awful, shrill screech he made, thinking that he and Locke were more police when they lifted him. He couldn't bear to remember how he'd stormed into Susan's hotel, how he'd yanked shut the curtain in that small room, swung the needle carefully on to a record, then much more recklessly attended to her skirt.

He has no idea where she is now. No idea.

He hadn't been able to calm down that night. And that was why later they'd left in the taxi, the one with the window stuck into position, the tear in the seat, the smell of cabbages and stale sweat and ash. The one he was reminded of now. He couldn't sleep and so they headed through Saigon's doomed, impoverished neighborhoods, the alleyways of shacks with dark, doorless entrances that Locke always called mouseholes, the gangs of children who no longer acted like children but prowled and scrounged, and yelled at you if you didn't give them enough money. They wound through streets and then crossed out among the canals, where the people lived in sampans, their clothes strung up with fishing line, motionless in the still skies of the heated night. Arriving finally at a fragile, undecorated squat little house, closed and bare and flimsily decorated with scarves and bright gauzy draperies that separated the small rooms. *Here!* he told the driver, and tapped the roof of the taxi. He paid the driver and stood in the street. It was a nice night, apart from the smells all around them—sewage, rotting food, fires and burning fuel. Susan said nothing about where they were, this alley they'd come through barely wide enough for the taxi, the derelict little shacks that stood end to end. It was a kind of slum, really: that's where he'd brought her.

The house where they went was better than the others. It had several rooms, a cement floor, solid walls, a door. Inside, waiting for the opium he'd come for, he looked at Susan differently, a well of emotion building inside him. Maybe it was sex that made him feel this way, a kind of chemical afterglow that played upon the emotions. Maybe it was because he'd brought her out here to this awful part of the city when it was entirely possible to avoid such places. He wished they hadn't come. There were so many beautiful parts of Saigon, yet they rarely went anywhere but to a restaurant and then back to his hotel. He always treated Saigon like a bus station, like a place from which he was waiting to leave. But he wished at that moment to find a quiet spot within the core of the city, to take her hand and lead her to a terrace decorated with flowering plants and oil lamps, to kiss her among all those glossy foreign leaves. He wanted to wander with her in the gardens behind the sports club, where lovers touch fingers and learn to walk as one; and they whisper, and they tell each other things. To go there and sit with her on a bench, studying her eyes in the glow of the evening's vigilant moon: that was what he wanted.

She was wearing the white peasant blouse, her jeans with a flower sewn on, and her hair picked up the gold from the glow of the small flame in front of which the hostess worked the opium into a ball, then a series of smaller balls. She turned to Marc, opening her face to his. She pressed her palm to his palm, and he felt a fluttering of nerves as though her fingers were electric. He wished they'd never left the hotel. He wished she were sitting in the armchair at the foot of the bed, that he was kneeling in front of her, removing her shoes, touching her ankles, her knees, that he could bury his face in her lap, wrap himself around her. They shouldn't have come here at all.

Mr. Davis, good man, the hostess said now. The hostess had the fragile frame of an addict. She warmed the opium over the fire of a wax lamp, kneading it between her fingers and on the back of a metal cup. She smiled as she did this. Her teeth were black, her lips pulled away in a tight grimace. She might have been Marc's age, but she looked much older. Her cheeks were so drawn it appeared as though someone had taken a piece from each side. The bones stood up beneath her eyes, her collar lolled around her neck. She had no breasts, this woman, no shape at all except the casing of her bones. She had a wide, proud forehead, a well-defined nose, the outline of her face regular and even. She might once have been beautiful. She spoke to Marc in a mixture of Vietnamese and English, encouraging him to lie back among the dusty cushions on the floor as she molded the opium.

Are you all right? he asked Susan. He wanted to know if she was comfortable, content, if he'd scared her this afternoon, arriving through the rain, pushing her on to the bed. She nodded and he nodded with her, whispering. He watched the hostess select a small, black nugget of opium, spearing it with an iron rod and setting it above the flame once more. Susan glanced toward him, then away again, her attention taken by the bubbling in the charred bowl. He directed his eyes on the hostess as she concentrated on the sizzling ball of opium, noticing the glazed, pleased expression on the hostess's emaciated face. He saw how thin her wrists were, the way in which her body seemed nothing more than a hanging place for her skin. He suddenly wondered if she'd be dead next time he came, if he would arrive at the door and see everything shrouded in funereal white. He had experienced the profound pull of the drug, had at times craved it, sought it out, then broken free of its hold once more. He understood how the hostess had come to look as she did.

He took up the long, arched pipe, pulling the smoke inside him. Drugs were a way of calming down, a way of revving up.

He remembered, or thought he remembered, that William Burroughs once said that the single greatest appeal of heroin was how it simplified life, by which he understood there was no longer fame, aspiration, wealth, relationships, family, country, and certainly not war—only high or not high. Marc hoped Susan wasn't frightened by the sight of the addicted hostess. He understood it had been a mistake to come. But he took in the drug and felt almost instantly better, once more that familiar peace, that easy presence that enveloped him, held him. He allowed no one to give him what the drug delivered, that soothing, elegant calm. He breathed out, lifted the pipe again. He felt a change inside himself, as though finally the clockwork of the war was winding down. He stopped worrying about where he was, why he'd come, even how they would get home. The drug gave him a nice place to occupy, containing him within its aura.

Your turn, he told Susan, passing the pipe, lying back on the addict's pillows. He finished a second bowl that evening, then a third, allowing Susan to take charge, lead him home. He cannot remember the rest of the night. He told her he loved her. He did love her, but he told her so that night.

He woke with a start at four in the morning; they were in his room, with its high ceilings, its green stucco, the windows taped in case of air raids, the shutters drawn against the city lights. He was staring up at the ceiling fan revolving on its short stem and thought for a moment that the revolving blades were lowering down upon him, to kill him. Even after he understood this was just some kind of nightmare, a play on his imagination, he still felt an urgency to run. He often felt the need to go somewhere but with no idea of a destination. A flight response, sprung out of some place in his brain that suddenly came alive, as though an electrode had passed over it. It happened like this more often than he wanted to admit; it had begun happening all the time. *This is the problem,* he said, meaning the need to run, the confusion. *This is what is wrong.*

You're dreaming, Susan whispered. She was wearing one of his T-shirts, the sleeves reaching down to her elbows. Her hair smelled of chamomile and opium resin. Her skin was hot where she'd been sunburned. He wanted to hug her, but he was sweating so much. *You might have overdone it last night.*

I'm not dreaming. He was thinking about the gun that had been dropped purposely next to Murray. He was thinking how he would have found it impossible in those circumstances not to pick up the thing and shoot, and how he would, in turn, have been shot. It felt so sure a thing, as though it were happening right now: his hand on the grip, the stony muzzle of the police's gun pushed against his skull. He wanted to tell her he was afraid, not of any one thing, just afraid, but he said nothing. She thought it was a dream; she thought it was the opium. He wanted to say, *Look, if you keep going out there, this is what is going to happen to you.* He wasn't talking about the drugs. He was talking about the war.

He found a fair-sized roach in the ashtray, just a few tokes. It gave him another hour or two of sleep.

The next day he fought the urge to return to the opium den. Instead, he and Locke headed out to a firebase in the Highlands where he heard there were daily small-unit battles going on. It was this search for news—for the most recent battles and missions and losses, and sometimes, too, the oddly measured, unmaintainable gains—that allowed him to shake off whatever remnants of violence lodged in his mind. One set piece replaced another set piece, one chopper of wounded lodged into his memory against another chopper of wounded, seeming almost to erase it. The sound a bullet made entering flesh, that dull thud, became in his mind just a single bullet, a single body, something he witnessed once, not dozens of times. Everything could be forgotten under the hammering noise of heavy artillery. If he kept moving, he felt better. The flooding of images drowned each other out, so he put himself in the worst places, worse and worse. Perhaps he hoped that by doing so he would one day remember nothing.

It had worked, this strategy, which was not so much a strategy as his job. Until now, it had worked very well. But the war was a kind of horrendous wind, like one of the many tropical storms that blew over the narrow country, making water out of land, scattering the animals in every direction so that you found a snapping turtle in the middle of the jungle, a crocodile in a garden pond. The careening, blind power of the war seemed to suck up, dislodge, or destroy everything, and these days he was struggling to forget.

With Susan gone, there really is no forgetting. He's been tossed so thoroughly into the war he cannot bow out, as he'd believed he would do someday—even a day very soon. It is not the first time he has realized that he cannot leave, but it is different now. He cannot leave the country without her. He cannot leave her behind.

He has not been back to the opium den since Susan's disappearance, though the urge to visit is great now, at its height.

Now, in the taxi, with its peculiar smell, rolling slowly over a narrow bridge strung with white lights, he wishes tonight was a simple case of returning to the opium den, taking up the pipe, lying back on the pillows. He sees the bony arm of the pipe, the sticky black of the bowl. He sees Susan's face in the amber flame of the lamp and the thought of her causes a sinking in his gut which anchors him in the taxi, flattening him, making him feel a tide of regrets, almost unendurable. He rolls down the window and the glass sticks in a familiar manner, sitting unevenly in the frame of the door. He realizes all at once that it is the exact same taxi in which they traveled together those weeks ago, that the seat beside him is exactly where Susan was. He looks for the tear in the seat, the eruption of foam, and finds a line of neat stitching.

He tells himself she is not dead. There has been no body and therefore no death. He tells himself he will see her again. But it is all he can do to stay in the cab. It is that feeling again, the need to escape, to flee, to take cover, the one that until recently only visited him upon waking from a dream. He raps on the window, tells the driver where to stop. He is meeting some people who might help get word to the Vietcong that she is politically neutral, that she is not a spy. He has spent the past twenty-four hours getting out cables, and now he is meeting with men who promise to personally bring word to the North Vietnamese embassies in Paris, in Britain. He has to keep himself together. He needs to get out of the taxi and walk, breathe slowly, drink a glass of water. In a satchel he wears over one shoulder is a photocopy of her passport, her British passport, with a photo in black and white. Also, copies of articles she's written: about orphanages, hospitals, an accurate, short account of an ambush that went particularly well for the North Vietnamese—none of them in the least bit political. If anything, they show compassion for those whom the war has inadvertently affected, compassion for the Vietnamese people as a whole. He has met everyone who will see him, everyone he can think of who has connections in Hanoi. Czechoslovakians, Russians, Poles, Germans. He has written, or caused his friends to write, desperate articles describing who she is and articulating in the clearest terms possible that she is not a spy. Even tonight, he is traveling to meet more people. In the morning, he will go down to the Delta to the place where she was captured. All of this he does without any idea of whether it will do any good, and without any real help from the military.

The official word is that no search can be made for her.

He found out a week ago. He had been in Loc Ninh with the Special Forces. He watched a US artillery piece leveled at the airstrip, burning metal showering the rubber trees to one side, the branches cracking, now on fire. They'd filmed the early, desperate attempts air support made, trying to zero in on an enemy artillery battery without using the airspace over nearby Cambodia. Then it became too dark to film. He watched through the glass of his binoculars as an American gunship platoon worked away at the enemy anti-aircraft guns, the sky bursting with color. He and Locke couldn't get out because the fighting was all over the airstrip. He sat in a foxhole, feeling the water seep into his boots, the words he would write later already forming his thoughts. Beside him, Locke waited out the fight, his helmet on, the camera sleeping in its case. Occasionally he looked out, staring into the evening sky.

Marc said, *I can't believe we aren't getting any of this.*

It wouldn't look like anything.

For a long time the only successful air attacks were from helicopter gunships, flying in a formation that merged their lights, making it difficult for the enemy to see how many were there. He admired the pilots. It seemed remarkable to him that they continued to fight, continued and continued. In the A Shau Valley he'd seen helicopters knocked out of the sky arcade-style by enemy fire. They'd been unable to report the correct number because the information had been embargoed by MACV, which shocked him almost as much as the exploding helicopters. The story had not been completely killed, but they were told to fudge the number of downed choppers. Reduce it. The justification was that to do otherwise would aid the enemy's awareness of the battle, and there was a caveat in all the press's access to military events that they report nothing that might help the enemy. Even so, he would not lie. Instead, they did not give a number at all, but ran as much footage as possible, choppers rocking, spinning, flailing, falling. Let the people count them themselves—it didn't matter. It looked like they'd been badly hit by the enemy, and they had.

Now, artillery rounds exploded somewhere on their side of the airstrip, the ground shaking. The enemy was down to only two guns. Two guns, then one. It was a beautiful attrition and MACV would surely have liked this to be filmed, but they couldn't do it in the dark. More planes arrived and the napalm began, the cluster bombs, explosions tearing through the trees, shattering the rubber plantation, the enemy's guns destroyed.

That was impressive, Marc said. He slipped a cigarette from a plastic case.

Too bad we didn't get five fucking seconds, said Locke.

He went to sleep with a joint on his lips, held by a paper clip twisted around one end. He had several small burn scars on his lower lip from this practice, but it worked to put him under. He woke the next day in the same clothes, and in the same position in which he'd fallen asleep. He shook Locke awake, stuck an unlit cigarette in his mouth, slapped a pack of matches on his chest, and said, *It's morning.*

It was early yet, the air still cool. He went outside. The streets were muddy, rutted by tank tracks and tire wheels, but it was quiet, almost peaceful.

For the first time in three days, they were able to get into Loc Ninh itself. He stood in what had been the police post, daylight where the roof had been, wreckage all over the floor, so many papers it might have been a ticker-tape parade. No blood, no bodies, the place had been abandoned long before it was struck. Outside was a burnt-out truck that looked like the enormous dead husk of an insect. Locke appeared, his camera on his shoulder. He stood outside, focusing the camera through what had been a wall, filming the police post, the broken plaster, the shattered table, the debris on the floor.

You think we can scrounge coffee? he said.

In the distance they could hear a few rifle shots, occasional shouting. They moved to the market, what had been the market. The place was deserted, all the buildings burnt—the government buildings, infirmary, post office—leveled entirely or else smashed so that you could see through them one side to the other. There were piles of rubbish, pieces of thatch and cooking pots, twisted metal, great sheaves of bamboo, piles of filthy clothes, papers, a chair back, a plastic tub. Everything burning or smoldering. Locke got a few establishing shots, then Marc stood between piles of burning rubble and spoke into the lens. *After three days of unrelieved fighting, US Special Forces have successfully taken back Loc Ninh. But the provincial capital has suffered five solid days of violence. Its buildings are shattered, its people gone.*

What was left of the city was defended by the soldiers, who guarded the streets, rifles in hand. Some stood around smoking and drinking beer. No civilians. What few people he saw seemed to be gathering their remaining possessions together, then heading down the road. From the air he'd be able to see a long line of them, families clustering together, their clothes in roped parcels, their food in wheelbarrows and wagons or carried on their backs.

They did some on-camera interviews.

We were surprised, said one sergeant. *It took longer than we thought to clear the city.*

A private said, *They just kept coming and coming. We'd shoot 'em, and they'd still keep coming! Hey, when will this air?*

A couple of days, Marc told him. He checked his volume levels, scraped a dead insect off the microphone stem. *You never know.*

The guys wished it were longer so they'd have time to tell their families. It took eight or more days to get a letter back home.

A couple of GIs claimed the Vietcong were drugged up, high on some kind of suicide drug that made them keep moving no matter how many bullets they put into them.

It's like they didn't notice, one said.

It made for a dramatic piece, the tattered, blackened buildings smoking behind them, the deserted streets, the occasional *rat-a-tat-tat* of machine-gun fire, now this talk about a suicide drug. But he signaled Locke to turn off the camera. Locke looked back at him like he was crazy, but he switched it off.

What drug do you think it might be? Marc asked. No mike, just the question.

I don't know, man—heroin?

No, really, Marc said. *Seriously.*

Heroin, like I said. That'd do it.

Someone found some white powder, said another.

It's not heroin, Marc said.

Then what is it? one asked.

The powder? He smiled. *Washing powder? Soap? Rice flour? Something to brush your teeth with, maybe?*

Heroin, man.

Or some other shit. Is this getting on TV?

They were running straight into our guns. It was like they didn't care.

He took a Camel out of its crushed packet, unbent the end, offered the pack around. *Oh, I think they care,* he said. He scared up a flame on his lighter, pulled on his cigarette. *I think they care a great deal.*

There was a pause. The soldiers looked at each other. They were good soldiers; they'd been fighting solidly for days and they would have continued to fight, if needed.

It's their country, said Marc now. Then he walked away. He turned once and waved, smiling weakly at the soldiers, who he realized now he had not treated as he had meant to. They deserved more respect than he'd shown, but there would have been something deceitful in allowing them to believe a drug was influencing the Vietcong. Enough nonsense was given to them without that, too. The way they were sent out under orders that were often ill conceived, the way they were never told what was really going on. How many times had he sat with soldiers just like these, explaining what was happening elsewhere, correcting their notions of territory gained, of body counts, all sorts of information they were not being told in their truncated briefings? *Thanks for getting us out of here alive,* he told them.

He found Locke filming some ARVN soldiers loading up a bunch of ducks they were pilfering. When the soldiers discovered they were being filmed, they abandoned their cheerful faces to appear grim and serious for the camera. Not an easy thing to do when your hands are full of feathers.

Marc made a face, then, mimicking himself on TV, he said, *Here in the district capital, soldiers from the Army of South Vietnam detain ducks—*

Locke smiled. *I had some battery left.*

This war isn't just about defeating the enemy. It's also about poultry. Specifically about which side gets the ducks.

Damned straight it is.

They got a lift back to Saigon on a Chinook, sitting in the dim light on the two long benches that ran the length of the fuselage, covering their ears as the unwieldy chopper, listing one way then another over the broken tarmac, passing above a C-130 that lay shot-up on the runway. The roaring engines drummed in Marc's ears. He stood up to look out of the portholes above him. He watched the runway disappear, the Special Forces camp, the abandoned city once inhabited by seven thousand people, many of whom were heading south along the highway. The artillery piece the Vietcong blew up was still in fragments at the end of the runway; F-100s were dive-bombing positions just west of the city. He watched all this amid the crushing noise of the Chinook and the volume of sound had the bizarre effect of making it feel as though he were watching it in silence, scanning this piece of Vietnam as though from a great distance, not part of it, not really there at all.

They arrived back in time for the five o'clock briefing in which the American military was claiming a total victory in Loc Dinh, one that pointed to future victories, ultimately, to the end of the war. Nobody mentioned that the city had been held for days by the Vietcong, nor that its inhabitants had all abandoned it now.

Marc had not changed his clothes, not even his boots. Locke, the same. They had a rich, greenhouse smell to them along with all the sweat. Their boots were muddy, their hair unkempt. All around, the press wrote down what was being reported by the officer up front. There had been others there with him at Loc Ninh, of course, and they would have their own stories, but there hadn't been many, and the dozens of reporters here were diligently taking notes on what was being said in this room, right now. He wanted to stand up and scream.

Instead, he asked a question. *How many people were forced to evacuate before the city was captured by the Vietcong?*

The officer, a major, stood stiffly at the center of the platform, his uniform starched, his face scrubbed. A handsome man, standing squarely in front of them all. He was smiling. *The city wasn't captured,* he said politely. *Check your facts.*

It was there in his steno pad, but he didn't need to look. *During the period between October 29 and November 1,* he continued.

Again, the major smiled. *The city was not held by enemy forces.*

Sir, we witnessed many of the city's inhabitants leaving. I am asking if the US military has some idea of the number of refugees. Five thousand? Six thousand? How many homeless are there tonight because the city was destroyed during enemy occupation? Sir? Sir?

But the major had already taken another question and was answering it fully, slowly, and with the concentration of a surgeon.

Later, Marc went to the hotel room, showered and changed, then to the offices, where he made himself a drink and promptly fell asleep at his desk. He got a call an hour later from JUSPAO, waking with a start as though the phone were inside him, rattling against his rib cage, or straight against the throbbing behind his eyes. He had a headache, as usual.

It was a colonel asking why Marc seemed to want to report Loc Ninh as some kind of defeat when quite clearly they'd prevailed against enemy forces despite the aggression of the attack.

A thousand enemy dead, only light casualties on our side and you are reporting it as an indication of our *weakness?* The military line made the colonel's voice sound as though it were being broadcast from the end of the earth. He was shouting the words, in part so he could be heard at the other end, but for other reasons, too.

Marc pressed his right temple with the pads of his fingers. It helped contain his headache. Then he said, *I'm sure we never used the word "weakness."*

I'm using the word weakness because that is the image you've delivered!

The film was already shipped. He told the colonel so. *We got statements from the briefings which we have also included in our story. But the city was held by enemy forces for three days. That is what we saw, and we have to report that, too.*

That would be a mistake.

Marc listened to the line sizzling with static. He wondered if the colonel meant that the reporting was mistaken, or filing the story was a mistake. He said, *Thousands of refugees, the city now almost completely destroyed. I believe that is correct, isn't it?*

There was a pause on the other end of the line, then the colonel's voice once more, this time heartier, more encouraging.

Go back in a few days' time and it will be up and running.

173

Our guys will put it all back together. You'll see. He sounded lighter, almost friendly. They might have been talking about cleaning up after a hurricane, how the people would be happier once the flood water had receded and the village hall was restored.

It's a matter of confidence, Marc said. *Whether the people believe we can keep them safe. If they think their city is going to be an area of contention between forces, they will not stay.*

Of course we can keep them safe.

So they were back to square one. He might have pointed out once again the three-day loss of the city, but instead he promised a follow-up. He tried to get off the phone but the colonel wasn't done yet.

I'd be grateful if you could alter the story as it stands today, he said.

The story is gone. It was gone even before I got to the briefing this afternoon.

I have some news just breaking you might like to hear about. Down in the Delta. You'll get briefed by Lieutenant Colonel Halliday. Take a trip down there. Talk to Halliday.

He had no interest in going to the Delta. He'd been asleep when the colonel rang. He wanted to go back to sleep, this time in an actual bed, preferably for half a day or more. His head felt as if there was a nail boring through it. The thought of another chopper ride anywhere near a battle made him groan. *I've got a lot going on right now,* he told the colonel.

You'll want to know about this, the colonel said. *It isn't confirmed yet, but for you, I would think this was a bigger story even than Loc Ninh. Much bigger.*

If you are asking me to kill that story, I won't. I can't.

You could call your network and explain that when you reviewed the situation, you realized there were a few inconsistencies in the reporting.

There were no inconsistencies.

You may want to change your mind.

He was getting more annoyed. He held the phone against his ear and listened to the confident voice on the other end, thinking he didn't have the energy for this. He fished out two aspirin from his pocket, downed them with some flat cola that had been left on his desk. He was searching for a third aspirin and talking at the same time. *Thank you for your call, Colonel. I will welcome any help on a follow-up on Loc Ninh.*

Davis, you need to change your original story. Special Forces will help you as much as possible if you do.

He'd had enough now. He was about to say as much when the colonel spoke again. *Your friend, Susan Gifford, and her photographer are missing. In the Delta. Are you aware of that?*

The words seemed to hang stinging in the air. Her name coming from the colonel's mouth, sounding so far away on the dreadful line, the word *missing* that hissed from across the miles.

No, he was not aware of that. Not aware. He heard what was being said and was plunged into this new understanding as though pushed underwater. He could not accept it, tried to stop it from entering into him. Suddenly, it was as though some essential part of him had dropped right out; the only thing that seemed to hold him up was the desk, the chair, perhaps even the telephone which he clutched now with two hands.

Davis, are you still there?

He cleared his throat. *I am.* He'd been swallowing the third aspirin when the colonel dropped the announcement into the conversation, and the place where it slid down his throat felt like glass.

We really do want to help you with this one, the colonel continued. *It would be a favor to us and we'd be grateful. Give the Loc Ninh story some time. Meanwhile, we can help you with this new, uh, incident.*

Go on.

She had been missing sixteen hours. The first fact. The rest

175

came in quick statements, just as he'd heard all the news of the war: the snatches of information, the reeled numbers and positions and dates and times. All the loaded shorthand of the military that might mean that bodies were being collected in ponchos and bags, that napalm had splashed down on villages, that half a platoon just got wiped out, that Vietcong suspects have been captured, detained by the US, or tortured by ARVN, who the US military could not influence away from such practices as beatings and water torture, even if they tried to, which they did not. He was used to writing dispassionately about the entire business of the war, and in this same manner he wrote down the information about Susan on his steno pad. The words sat on the soiled blue-lined pages alongside other news of the war: the names of those he had interviewed, the home towns of soldiers, things he wanted to remember later, or which might later become important. He wrote down everything the colonel told him and when he'd finished he suddenly wished the man would not hang up the phone. He had a feeling that when the conversation ended he would find it difficult to know what to do. His job had only ever been to gather information, not to act upon it. He'd only had a few hours' sleep, and even that had been sitting slumped in a chair, fully clothed, so that his head now swam and throbbed.

Do you have any more for me? he asked, his voice different now, plaintive, grasping. *Do we know what condition she, they, were in when captured?*

On the other side of the crackling line, the colonel took a breath. *No, son, we do not,* he said, speaking as he might to one of his own men. *But you get down to where I told you and Halliday will help you with any further developments.*

And so he had learned. In the dead hours just past curfew, while walking back to his hotel in deserted streets, hoping to God he wouldn't come across anyone, that he could get back to his room, the information sank into him the way that a burn settles into the skin. Surely, Son would be killed outright. He was almost certain this would be the case. He hoped they hadn't executed him in front of Susan and told himself they would not have done so, as they would hope to return Susan to the press with a story of their compassion, not their blood-lust, with a nice positive spin on the patriotism and humanity of the communist position. No, they would not execute Son in front of her. In fact, it was possible they would march him miles away to kill him. Or maybe they would not kill him. Or maybe they would kill them both. It was difficult for the Vietcong to understand that a woman could be a reporter, and therefore valuable for their own propaganda. They might think she was a spy. He hoped she had her press tags. Of course, she would. She never went anywhere without them. None of them did.

He tried not to think; he was too tired to think. He was glad to be breaking curfew; it gave him something immediate to worry about, as the police would shoot on sight at this time of night.

Flying to the Delta this November day he decides that after the war he will never again fly in a C-130. There is a whole list of things he will never do again—eat food from cans is another example, or wear anything in olive drab—but flying in C-130s is at the top of the list. The planes are unlined and, of course, have no seats. He sits on the floor watching the levers on the ceiling move the wings, enduring the deafening noise of the engines, waiting for the appalling landing. It is the landing that disturbs him most, how the plane spirals down, tightening its turn as though trying to fix itself into an ever-narrowing tunnel. That's the beginning, the anticipation of which was worse than anything, when the plane dives at speed, gear and flaps down, as though deliberately crashing. It takes on even more force just before the ground opens up below, when the pilot raises the nose, moving to a less angled approach. Then the nose wheel drops and the cargo compartment makes a tremendous jolt, rattling as though the whole plane is coming apart as it goes careening down a runway.

The runway held its own perils. It was often a bit on the short side, coming to an abrupt end in front of a line of rubber trees, or so narrow the wings hang out over brush. At night, if the runway has no lights, the landing area will be lit with battery lights mounted in what look like large bean bags. Sometimes an oil drum or two. Once, because they were riding with badly needed blood, they landed by the headlights of two jeeps. He turned to Locke and said, *This will be interesting,* because inside the cargo area it seemed as though they were landing into absolute darkness, which could only mean they were landing in water. When he got out and saw the headlights, two jeeps angled with their brights on, he thought perhaps it was all becoming a little close. A little too close, all of it. Since then, he has dreamt several times of crashing in such a plane, and in each of the dreams it is nighttime. There is a fire outside. The plane tumbles down in darkness with that same deafening roar. He tries to think of this dream not as cautionary but as only a dream and nothing more. Whenever Susan asks him what he is dreaming about, he always says he can't remember. Fear is a kind of disease, like the tuberculosis that plagues the peasants, and he didn't wish to visit it upon her. She was still new to the war. He thought she had months, maybe even longer, depending on where she went in the country, before anything would bother her like this, staying with her while sleeping. He hadn't wanted her to think the way he has come to think, or dream as he now dreams. There have been times when he has envied those who stayed in Saigon and reported whatever was given them by JUSPAO. It undoubtedly made life easier.

It has been a long spell of changeable weather. They are lucky because a tropical storm has moved away, allowing them to travel. Even so, it is windy. All through the flight there have been great troughs of turbulence. He can hear the force of the wind against the skin of the plane, feel the way it pushes them up from below, or presses down like a sudden wave from above. Puke weather is what Locke would call it. But Locke isn't here, isn't speaking to him, is still fuming over the fact he killed the Loc Ninh story.

What in hell did you do that for? he'd said when Marc told him. *You believe it will make any difference anyway? That our boys are going to launch some all-out effort to find her because you decide not to run* one *story!*

She's not her. *She's Susan. Use her name.*

You've lost sight of exactly who you are, Davis. Nobody here gives a shit about your story! And they don't give a shit about her, either.

Susan.

Okay, that's it, fuck you! Locke said.

Marc turned away. The end of their friendship was set in motion. He heard Locke's words, directed now at his back. *I was out there for five days to get that story and you think I'm just going to roll over and say, "Fine, Davis, it's your call"? I'm saying no such thing. That was my story, my footage—*

I'm going to try to get some information. Be reasonable.

Reasonable? You've lost your mind!

He pushes Locke out of his thoughts, distances himself once more from the whole Loc Ninh affair. It doesn't matter anyway. It was only a story. Perhaps he hadn't gotten a fact or two correct. There was always that possibility. Besides, someone else will run a similar story; that always happens. There would be no consequence for killing the story, except the fallout from Locke.

As the plane turns now into its descent, he feels a shift in himself, a kind of relief that finally all they have to do is pass through this last, dramatic finale. He fixes himself into position, sitting on a metal cargo pallet, holding tightly with one hand while the other pulls his satchel closer against his rib cage. He is surrounded by concertina wire, bags of cement, boxes of ammunition, pitchforks, shovels, hessian bags, drums, so much it might be a warehouse of the stuff. He works out the exact path to the emergency exit, watching the loadmaster to see if he seems at all concerned. The loadmaster, his face gray in the dim light, smokes through the flight. He nods at Marc as they begin to fall straight down, landing as though through a hole in the sky, the hole that has opened up hundreds of times before, and it feels just the same every time.

There is a crosswind and the plane crabs on the approach, then it straightens momentarily before the pilot lowers a wing into the wind to kill the drift. As the nose wheel touches down, Marc feels as though the ground is rushing beneath him. Then a strong pull to the left, all this happening in reverse throttle. Marc presses his own feet down into his boots as though braking, and the feeling is so real to him that it is almost as if he can feel the cycling of the anti-skid system. He's been in the cockpit with these guys and he's seen how their whole body is engaged in landing the plane. Feet working the pedals, hands gripping the steering wheel, pulling on the throttles. Every inch of the craft, rudder to nose wheel, controlled all at once by limbs and toes and fingers. He has watched the pilot's eyes lock on to the end of the runway ahead while he works these subtle physics, studying the line where the runway meets the jungle, the treeline arriving disconcertingly fast, as though being pushed forward.

"Hey, man, we're here." It is the loadmaster. He stands by the door, his arms full, the cigarette bobbing as he speaks.

Minutes have passed and the plane is still. In his pocket, by necessity, Marc keeps a small flask of bourbon. He reaches for it now, ignoring the loadmaster's gaze. When finally he steps from the plane, he feels as though he is pulling himself from a wreck. Suddenly out into the noon-day sun, he can see as far as his eyes will take him. The Delta is flat, a mouth of land ready to take back in the salt water of the South China Sea, with air so wet it seems to have a texture, thick, viscous, a force he has to push himself through as he navigates the airfield under the strong glare of the sun. The bourbon heats him further, a little fire of his own. He crosses the airfield, the heat rising in waves from the ground. The plane ride is forgotten, already behind him. He ducks beneath the overbright sun, so close and hot it feels prehistoric, belonging to a place of tar pits and dinosaurs, of men dwelling in caves. He is here now to find something out, at least one thing, that was not in the report on Susan.

Son he does not care about, isn't even looking for. On the phone, while making the arrangements to come down, he purposely avoided mentioning his name. What he has been thinking about, despite every attempt to push it from his mind, is that the last time he was in this area, about eighteen months ago, he reported on several killings in a small village. Six people had been murdered by the Vietcong, two of them women. It was alleged that the women had hung lanterns in the village as a warning to government troops that the Vietcong were there, scrounging rice and gathering up men to fight for them. He had seen the bodies, decapitated by scimitars which, it would appear, had not been sharp enough to make a clean job of it. All he can think about is how the women had been believed to be spies and how they had been executed with those dull blades, the bodies left to the flies. He has little comfort in the fact that there has been no report such as this, no report at all, in fact, about Susan. That is the reason he is here, to make such a report, if indeed anything has happened. Spies are not toler-ated, their killings are public. The women's heads were placed on stakes, fierce trophies set out as a warning, staying there until villagers had the courage to remove them, to kick the dust over the fallen blood, burn the stakes, hide everything, even their grief. He'd seen all that, and done the story, then flown back and forgotten it until this day.

He is met by a jeep, courtesy of ARVN, thoughts of Susan so full in his mind that he cannot bring himself at first even to talk to the driver, a Vietnamese man a few years older than himself who crouches behind the steering wheel, a serious expression on his face.

"Davis?"

He nods.

"Welcome," says the driver, whose bored expression suggests the opposite. The plane was way off schedule. He's probably been waiting in the jeep for an hour.

As it happens, the driver doesn't want to talk either. Nor does he accept Marc's cigarettes when they are offered. Marc has come to associate this kind of behavior with the older ARVN officers, some of whom remember well the last war with the French and find the Americans patronizing. They may have had family members, a brother, a father, an uncle, "recruited" by the Vietcong—that is, taken away—so now they are suspected always of being Vietcong themselves and treated badly by the US military. It all spills over into a general disdain for Americans. He is used to it. Quite frankly he is so used to it that he does not care.

The heat is made tolerable by the breeze from the moving jeep. Though it is not raining now, there has been rain and the roads are not too dusty. His sunglasses guard against the worst of the afternoon's glare. He has water on his hip. He looks confident. He looks like he knows exactly what he is doing, but he has no clue. No fucking clue, he thinks to himself. He wonders if the driver knows this, if he can tell.

"I'm interested in a journalist who is missing," he tells the driver.

"Yes, I hear about that," the driver says. "Two are missing."

"I'm looking for Susan Gifford, an American."

"A woman. Oh, I see," says the driver. "You should get to the radio that she only *bao chi*."

What he means is to get word to the press in Hanoi, particularly to the communist radio stations, that a non-combatant, a politically neutral journalist, has found her way into the hands of the People's Liberation Front, and that she is not a spy. The choice of words is important, the language itself somehow infused with propaganda. To appeal to the Vietcong, one must use the term People's Liberation Front. To his jeep driver, and to any American he might meet, Vietcong would be the correct term.

"I've done that," he says. He hopes the guy will suggest another idea, that there is something he has overlooked. "I've told everyone I can think of," he continues. "My friends, other correspondents, they have, too. They have gotten word to Hanoi."

He gets out his cigarettes, offers his driver a smoke once again. This time, the man nods, so Marc lights the cigarette for him, placing it in his fingers.

The driver says, "You do right things, you maybe get her back. Who the man?"

"A Vietnamese."

The driver makes a clucking noise. "That not so good," he says.

He thinks about Son. He has never trusted him and never liked him. The way he drifted quietly into Susan's life, the child-like manner he assumed whenever questioned about his past, about where he's been when he disappeared for days at a time— it was all very odd. He was at best an opportunist. At worst, perhaps he was also a spook, keeping tabs on the press. There was always this tension between the government and the press. Even with all manner of embassy parties and invitations to dinners, of private drinks, of information slipped graciously to newsmen, it was there. A strained demarcation of territory. A kind of fixed unseen barrier. He was never sure how Son fitted into it all, but always assumed he spied on them, reporting to the government and to the American military who among the press were the real trouble-makers.

"He's a journalist, too," he says now. "*Bao chi.*"

"Vietnamese will be different," says the driver. He means Son will be killed.

Mark feels tired. If he closes his eyes long enough, he thinks he'll probably fall asleep—that is, until he's bounced out of the jeep. But asleep, he has nightmares. Awake, he pushes away the most unbearable of imagined consequences of Susan's disappearance with a tablet of Valium, five milligrams every four hours, another of which he takes now.

The jeep bounces and swerves, racing beside the rolls of barbed wire overgrown with weeds edging the road, while further back, fields of rice lie tranquil for the moment, churned up in places where bombs have fallen. They pass a mile-long path of evenly spaced craters made by B-52s, now filled with water so that they give the appearance of ponds set out along a flat land.

His driver keeps the accelerator down, swooping past stacks of earthenware crocks being loaded on to a wagon, a flock of chickens, a cyclist trying to make it down the damaged road with two enormous sacks of rice braced on the handle bars. The jeep makes dramatic sweeps through potholes and often straight across whatever debris is in the road—an empty crate, a broken basket. The physical jolts help to refocus his thoughts. Like this, he can convince himself he is on assignment, like any assignment, and feel a momentary peace. A bus pulls out and the driver brings the jeep to an abrupt halt, giving the bus driver a fierce glare. All at once there is stillness; the heat gathering around them like a cloud, insects collecting at his face as

184

though they'd been waiting for him right here at this resting place. His driver, punching the horn so that it sends out its useless bleating sound, calls out to the man driving the bus.

"Let him go ahead," Marc says. The road has been torn apart and put back together dozens of times from bombs and mines. It will be abandoned tonight, as every night, even by the army. "Let him go first and sweep for us."

They pass stagnant marshes, low-lying mangrove swamps, rivers with their fish traps, their small tributaries over which might be a wooden footbridge, shallow banks on which the muddy-bottomed sampans are stacked next to houses on stilts, perched like bird hides along the water's edge. Children swim at the edges of the docks, rising out of the water, their skin sleek and shining. In Saigon he has seen so many amputees, driven from their homes into the crush of the city, that he has gotten in the habit of counting the limbs on children. It no longer surprises him when he sees a baby gurgling up from his mother's arms, a stump where his leg should be. Or when, along the street, he follows the unsteady gait of a ten-year-old with a pros-thetic leg. Now, as he passes through a market taking place under parasols and tarpaulins, conducted out of baskets and clay pots and sacks which might hold rice or dried beans, he sees that here, at least, the people are whole. The children wear school uniforms, ride bicycles, looking much like children everywhere. A pet dog, a pair of sisters sharing a single bicycle, a couple of brothers playing soldier. It all looks very normal.

They pass through a village. It is wash day and the women have strung lines house to house, looping them from telephone poles and drainpipes, scrubby trees with their tangle of small branches, wooden stakes, porch pillars, anything upright around which they can wind their spools of twine. The clothes weigh the lines down so that sometimes a pair of black trouser legs or a white sheet drags in the coarse grass and Marc finds himself looking twice to check if it is a body.

The air smells of wet grass and mud, a kind of earthy reptilian smell. The whole of the Delta feels to Marc like a ragged, wet landscape, like some dubious treasure dredged up from the sea, rich with the eyeballs of lizards and birds and fish. As they pass some women filling a mine hole, he is reminded how the Vietcong put charges on the edges of roads beside potholes, knowing that Americans will drive around the potholes. In their black pajama trousers, their shaded hats, their sandals, the women work slowly, methodically, in the 100-plus-degree heat. The driver doesn't slow—would never slow for anything, just in case it was a set-up—and so the women move back from their work, wiping their brows, making room for the jeep, which passes so close that Marc could have reached out his hand and taken the hats from their heads.

Finally, after what seems like miles and miles, they come to a stop.

"Here," says the driver.

He is not sure what he is being shown, or even why they've paused where they have, out in the wild among ant hills and elephant grass. To his right is a wild thatch of green bamboo, the same verdant bushes he sees everywhere in the Delta, an opaque greenness that closes the country in. He can hear the insects with their swell of sound rising and falling like breath, smell the brackish water hidden by shrubs. It feels good to be on his feet after so long in the jeep. He lights a Camel, offering one to the driver, who gets out his own pack. They stand together, smoking. Then the driver speaks in a casual manner, as though filling in a small point. "It where that girl was taken," he says. "Your friend."

And now he knows why they've stopped.

"Man, Charlie is ingenious down here. The suicide squads strap themselves with dynamite and dress up like trees. They got

186

Chicoms and AKs, sure, but also all this other shit: flying mace, spear launchers, arrows, crossbows—"

"Russian fucking rockets, that's what you got to worry about—"

"—all kinds of knives, not to mention the traps, like punji—"

"Punji, fuck that, this marine—this riverine—he stepped into a bear trap. And that was *it* from the knee down."

"There are no damned bears in the Delta. Chinese flamethrowers, they got. Plenty of *them* around."

"I said trap, man, just the trap."

He listens to the soldiers, sitting inside a small hut in a row of others beneath some palms, the only shade in the camp other than beneath the open-sided marquis-style tents set up for the refugees. He stares out the entrance of the hut, his eyes crossing the humid, swimming air to the command tent, empty for the moment, like most of the tents. No sign of Halliday, and there hasn't been since he arrived. Just scores and scores of Vietnamese peasants, looking aimless and bewildered. There must be hundreds, thousands, in the camp. He has no idea.

The refugees don't think much of the tents, which trap heat. The insides of these newly erected structures have the same smell as a terrarium, with hot, unmoving air like a henhouse in summer. Though the tents provide some shade, there is more shade within the bordering jungle; its trees and creepers and broad shadows of larger leaves block out the imposing sun. Some of the people want to go there, but are prevented from finding the natural shelter of trees by the perimeter which has been set up all around, rolls of concertina wire arranged untidily on the ground, guarded by ARVN soldiers who look tired and bored. Marc feels any minute the atmosphere could shift from this sleepy steamhouse to one of violence, not by the peasants, who appear too disheartened even to raise their voices, but from outside the camp. He keeps waiting for the explosions.

"Bear paws are considered a delicacy. You know, they eat them. Hey, you," a soldier says to Marc, "I'm just saying bear paws are a delicacy, you know that?"

"No," Marc says. "I didn't know that."

"What're you, a reporter?"

"That's right."

"You seen any bears in the Delta?"

He shakes his head.

"How long you been in country?"

"Twenty-three months."

"No shit? Twenty-three months? I don't believe it. And you seen no bears?"

"No. None."

"See, there you go, no bears in the Delta. What did I say?"

There are half a dozen of them there, escaping the sun outside. It is as though the earth has taken a fever and all of them have to wait through these elongated afternoon hours until it recovers. He has seen toads baked in such sun so that they became hardened rocks that the children played with like toys, making the stiff bodies hop as though still alive. He has seen the heat dry up the soldiers so that the thinnest skin between their lips tore away when they opened their mouths. The flatness of the Delta made it all the worse, a shallow dish of land under a hard white sky. The soldiers are lucky they can take refuge in the hut, and he is glad to have found it, too.

They haven't seen the lieutenant colonel and they don't know where Halliday might be. Marc established that within the first minute, so it is only the shade that keeps him here. The hut is cool, dark, the mud walls filtering out the worst of the sun. He looks around and sees a table pushed against one side, a few pegs on the wall. In a corner is a basket of unwinnowed rice, some laundry, a swatch of straw attached to a broken wooden pole making up what must be a kitchen broom. He is sitting in someone's house, he realizes. The soldiers talk, smoke, drink Coke out of cans which they crush on to the floor.

He hears, "So maybe they were just trying to catch a bear?"

"There are no fucking bears here. Crocodiles, maybe."

"It was a fucking bear trap."

"For the river bears?"

"Fuck you."

"Glad I didn't step in it."

Outside the hut, a water truck has arrived, the women gathering around it, getting fresh water and wringing out soiled clothes. One mother brings her baby to the front, undressing him beneath the spray of the tap. The baby cries, frightened by the shower of water, as the mother smoothes her palm over his skin. Marc listens as more trucks roll in, bringing refugees from a village forty kilometers north, mostly women and old men, children by the score. There is the frantic squealing of muddy pigs, baskets of hens held down by cord, bags of rice like the sandbags of bunkers, sometimes a bundle of clothes in twine, sometimes a bicycle. The camp is nothing more than an area of plowed jungle, the bulldozers working through the mud and scrub even now, pushing back more and more trees to make room for the refugees. The tents are spread from one end of the camp to another, end to end, in garish yellows and reds, like a lost circus.

He asks the soldiers how long they are here for. And they shake their heads impatiently.

"We're done already."

"It's not us that runs the camp. It's ARVN that runs it."

"Yeah, we're just waiting to roll out."

He nods, feeling his blood pumping thinly through his veins, his pulse quick with the heat, throbbing like a wound.

The water truck goes lumbering between tents, driven by an ARVN soldier whose hair falls almost to his eyes in a weighty black curtain. Another truck rumbles down the other side, transporting a public address system that plays songs, sung in a popular style, in Vietnamese. The music is designed to be lively, festive, entirely contrasting the expression of the truck's driver, who frowns at the people who pass near him and waves his hands in agitation, shooing the children out of the way. Marc asks one of the ARVN officers what the songs are about and is told they are educational, to teach the people about the benefits of the government. The songs continue, blaring and screeching from a tinny system that distorts even further the high flat tones of the singers. Few seem to be paying any attention to the songs or their message. If they can understand what is being said over the speakers they show no sign of it.

Dogs trot among the people, sniffing the ground. They eat the shit from the pigs and they sniff the bottoms of the younger children until they are slapped away by scowling young mothers. It looks like a gypsy camp, made haphazardly in the mud. Near by they are given vaccinations. Mothers and old ladies stand with their small families in the sun, in long lines that run in three different directions from the medical tent, a knot of confusion at the entrance. The mothers look hot, bored, their children clinging to their legs. There isn't anything for them to do, so they stand silently, fanning their children with their hats and looking vacantly into the distance. When the PA system arrives alongside them, they turn their backs against the blare of the music. When the water truck passes they look at it longingly, but let it go.

It is a blistering afternoon. Every time he comes to the Delta he thinks the same thing, that it could not get any hotter. He can't stand to leave the hut for more than fifteen minutes at a time. When he returns his clothes are plastered to his skin, his hair wet, and he feels slightly light-headed. He looks out at the women waiting for vaccinations, at the children with their mahogany skin, moving slowly up in the line. The hut is fuller each time he returns, soldiers wilting in the heat.

He hears, "I don't know, though, I wouldn't mind some bear meat."

He hears, "They got some chickens around here, you know. We could fry 'em."

They ask him what he is writing and he explains about Susan. He repeats what information he has on the ambush and gathers from those around him other details of the event. Halliday is still no place to be found when he goes out searching, asking anyone who looks as though he might know where the lieutenant colonel in charge would be. When he returns to the hut it is as though he's run a fast mile in the sun. He slumps on the floor, pours water from his canteen over the back of his neck, wipes the collar of his shirt over his face. The heat makes him ache, makes his nose block so that his headache blooms inside him. He looks outside at the refugees, who seem entirely dispassionate, sitting in groups, their faces blank, allowing the ARVN soldiers to carry on constructing the site.

There has begun an effort to spray insecticide throughout the camp, and clouds of it drift between the tents. The peasants regard the canisters as dangerous, leaning away from the spray, their hands held to shield their eyes. They get up to move, some only a few feet, some rushing off altogether. The truck with the PA system still makes its rounds, as do the ARVN soldiers distributing leaflets warning that VC cadres might be in their midst and to report anything suspicious. The refugees seem like all displaced people, hopeless, remote, squatting beneath the colorful tent awnings, chewing betel or casually swatting at mosquitoes, not talking. They are not even refugees, as such, not like those in Loc Ninh who had taken their belongings and run down the road while their city raged with fires and artillery. There had been no true battle in the villages of the people here, but they were made homeless when the army evacuated them, then burned their houses down, burned the school house, the rice stores, the sheds for the animals, everything. There was never any sort of battle, other than the charge of American forces, arriving in a cloud from the air. This he discovers from a sergeant, who he interviews while standing next to a bulldozer. The sergeant explains that certain villages in the Delta were being used by the VC, and that they needed to put a stop to that.

"By evacuating the villagers?" Marc asks.

"We don't leave the enemy an empty village," is the reply. "We level the goddamned thing."

"So all the people of South Vietnam may one day find themselves in camps like this one?"

This makes the sergeant laugh, as though Marc is telling a joke. "It may happen yet!" he says, and wipes his eyes. Then more seriously, he adds, "We leave the friendly villages to themselves. We're looking for VC and hostile civilians."

"How many refugees are there here? Two thousand? Three?"

"Four is expected. It may climb higher, let's hope so."

"And these are *hostile civilians?*" He's never before heard the term.

The sergeant looks annoyed. "No, they are not!" he states emphatically. "Not these, no! These are victims of the Vietcong. They've been coerced to pay taxes and their men have been made to join their forces."

"And you've made them leave their homes to come—" He looks out on to the newly plowed earth, the sun a white light that makes the ground colorless so that he might be staring at the moon. There is so much dug-up ground that if it rains (and rain is inevitable), they will all be knee-deep in mud. As it is, it feels like being on a beach with no ocean and no ocean breeze. "—to come here."

"We're helping them," says the sergeant. "You stick around and I'll find some time to explain to you the *why* of what we're doing here. Right now, I've got men to organize."

He must mean to feed, Marc thinks. He could see the flame

from a barbecue in the distance, smell some charcoal and wood. It would not surprise him if they sat and ate right in front of the refugees, would not surprise him at all.

"How many villages are you set to evacuate?"

"We'll let you know on that one," the sergeant says, then walks off.

In the command tent there are fans hooked to a generator, a cooler of beer and Cokes swimming in water that may have been cold once, but is now tepid. Some tables and chairs. He waits there for a young Spec-4, who finally arrives, coated with dust, smelling like cigarettes and stale sweat, unsure why he has been singled out for an interview.

"Are you the reporter that wants to see me?" the soldier asks. He creases his forehead, straining to see in the tent, which is not dark but is considerably darker than the searing sun outside. His eyes are irritated, bloodshot; he has sunburnt lips that are flaking. He might have been among those unloading the trucks that keep arriving, lifting down the possessions of the villagers, helping carry everything across acres of rutted ground. His uniform sags on him, the collar on his T-shirt is dark with sweat. He walks into the tent hesitantly, as though he thinks he might be in trouble, his lips pushed together, his eyes like lead. Enright is his name.

"This about the ambush?" he says. He's been debriefed on it before, probably many times, Marc thinks, and looks even more fed up when Marc nods, explaining he's doing a story about what happened, about the reporters who went missing.

Enright says, "Yeah, I'm sorry about that. They must be friends of yours?"

The tent is nearly empty. Just him and the kid and a couple of American advisors who stand in front of a fan, going over a list. The advisors seem annoyed, glancing over their shoulders at Enright and Marc. Then, all at once, the two men leave in a single abrupt movement as though following an unseen command.

Enright isn't sure where to put himself. He fidgets until Marc tells him to have a seat. The kid is so nervous Marc doesn't get out a notebook, just his cigarettes. Enright sits uneasily, parking his gun beside him. He looks at Marc as though he isn't sure whether or not to trust him. His eyes scan Marc's face, his pale shirt, the pen tucked into the pocket. They both smell as bad as each other. Marc smiles, then he rises and goes to the cooler, digging through the water which is only barely cooler than his own skin, until he finds two beers. He sets them on the table as though the tent is his home, Enright his guest, and nods at the kid that he should drink.

Enright says, "That looks about right. Now all we need are the Goobers."

"They probably have them around here someplace, too. How was lunch?"

"I didn't get no lunch."

"They're frying something out there."

"Yeah, well, not for me. We worked through."

"Not for the people here either."

"They'll give them something."

Marc looks at him, blows out his cheeks. Then he wets his lips, feeling the rough edges of skin there, and pushes a cigarette into the corner of his mouth.

"Am I supposed to be talking to you?" Enright says. "I mean, I'm not sure I'm *supposed* to be talking to a reporter."

The kid shifts from nervous to angry and back again. He turns his face away, out to the entrance of the tent, as though there is something there he needs to track. But there is nothing but dust and sun and people milling around.

"Why wouldn't you want to talk to me?" Marc says.

"I don't do anything I don't have to."

"How long do you have left?"

"Three months, one week and a day."

"You're getting short."

"Not short enough." He shifts in his chair, picks a few flaking bits of skin from his right earlobe, and lets his teeth show, a big horsey grin. "This going in the newspaper?"

Marc shakes his head. "I just want to know what happened, as best you can remember."

"I've already said all that. You sure you're a reporter?"

"I'm a reporter."

"You don't work for the CIA?"

Marc laughs.

The kid says, "I didn't do nothing wrong out there and, anyway, I've already told what I know."

Marc nods, takes a long drink of beer. "Yeah, well, we got a fan and beer in this tent, so I'd appreciate the long version."

Enright keeps his pale eyes on Marc, scratches his nose, takes a sip of his beer. "Not bad," he says. "I agree."

It takes some time, but eventually he talks.

It had been a convoy of armored personnel carriers and supply trucks—ammo, fuel, C-rations, building materials. They were just bringing the supplies down to the camp, that was all. Susan and Son sat with the soldiers on the open space on an APC between the two guns. Enright was among them.

"They were probably on their way to do a story on the camp," Marc says. "That's why they were with you."

"Doesn't seem like there's much to write about here," Enright says. "Nothing happening."

"Maybe not, but that was the plan." In fact, Marc thought there was plenty to write about. If Locke were here with the camera, they would need only an hour or two to get a good story. And he could easily imagine Susan and Son out interviewing families. It was how they worked best, with Son translating and taking the photographs, Susan persuading the women to open up to her. She was good at that. She had a way

195

of entering into whatever they were doing and he'd often witnessed her engaging in some deeply Vietnamese act—drying joss sticks, wrapping pork rolls—while interviewing the women. But he tried not to think of her too much right now. There had been a moment earlier, glancing across the crowded walkways between tents, when he spotted a reporter he knew, a woman, with the same narrow hips and long back, her hair in a ponytail under a ball cap. He thought, for one brief, exalted second, That's her. But of course, it wasn't. The woman was six inches taller than Susan, with darker hair and darker skin. Older. As he came nearer, his footsteps fast, then slowing until he stood motionless ten yards away, he thought, Get a grip on yourself. He thought, God damn it. Now he said, "They might have been having a look down here, that's all."

"She took a lot of pictures," Enright says. "The other one, too. The Viet. He took a lot of pictures."

Marc recalls how once, on a convoy much the same, Susan and he had passed an old man with a water buffalo standing in a rice paddy. She had leaned over Marc, lifting his camera from the lace of leather that looped his neck, and taken a photograph. They had passed a temple and she took a picture of that, too, using his camera as her own was out of film. He imagines the same scenario now, her head just in front of Son's chest, the camera at her eye, her fingers turning the lens to focus.

Enright smiles. "It was kind of cool having a woman on board. You don't get many of those." He chews gum, poking it with his tongue, setting it in his jaw as if it is tobacco when he speaks or takes a swig from the beer. His face could go completely from one mood to another, Marc notices, like light passing through a tunnel. Now he smiles, his teeth stubby pieces of chalk. "We were all trying to get her to ride with us. I had my eye on her."

I bet, Marc thinks.

"We were talking about my fish."

"*Fish?*"

"Some fish I used to keep back in the world."

"*Pet* fish?"

"Fighting fish."

Marc finishes his beer. He thinks he'd better get another one and that if he plans to spend any more time in the camp, he'd better find a whole case and install it right here. Enright is explaining about the fish now, how they had to be kept separately in small bowls or they'd kill each other. Some kind of specialty bullshit fish. Marc really has no interest. "Okay, and then what happened?" he says.

"Well, nothing. Not if you keep 'em apart. They can't fight through glass!"

"I meant the day of the ambush."

"I've told all that."

"Well, tell it again." He wants to smile; he tries to smile, but nothing. He reaches for a cigarette, his hand touching the foil pack of valium. He takes out a Camel, trying to remember when he last had a pill. Enright goes quiet, turning away so Marc can see he's got chewing gum lodged in his cheek. "She was a nice girl."

"She's missing!" The words come out differently from how he wants. He needs to keep his annoyance in check. He blames the heat, the stifling heat that makes him feel bound and gagged, makes him feel as though somebody he didn't know is sitting behind his eyes.

Enright shrugs. "We lost men on that ambush, too," he says. "Lots of wounded, three KIAs. It's bad, losing a girl. They shouldn't be out here anyway."

There is a silence between them. Enright slowly drinks his beer, seeming almost to have tuned out entirely, revealing nothing. He breathes through his mouth, a rasp of breath that is the only noise other than the fan that sweeps across the empty space of the tent. A minute goes by and still Enright isn't talking.

"Tell me about the fish," Marc says.

Enright nods. "The fish," he repeats. "I kept them in my bedroom, one next to another, so that if you bent over you could see a kaleidoscope of fins, just like a kaleidoscope, too."

"Really?"

"Yup, just like that."

Another silence. Marc waits, timing it. Three minutes go by. He begins to think talking to the kid was a mistake, one of many. His first was believing the colonel who promised him help in finding Susan. It looks as though Locke was right. This is a dead end, a decoy, a way of ensnarling him and using up all his time so that the Loc Ninh story would die a death and be forgotten. They should have come to his hotel room and sealed the door with him inside. It would have been kinder. At least he'd have had air conditioning.

Enright begins to speak again, his voice sounding as if he's dredged it up out of the mud. He says, "She was nice to me, that girl. She asked me if the fish watched each other. 'Maybe they spent their lives wishing they could escape the glass walls and have a battle,' she said."

He stops talking again, puts his finger in the air as though to speak, then doesn't. His hands shake. Marc notices a behavioral tic: every so often he touches the end of his ear. He'd thought at first it was sunburn there, but he sees now the kid has dug a little sore, picking at it the way he does. He's so inside himself that Marc wonders what on earth he's still doing in the field, why nobody has noticed. He wonders if the kid's odd movements are just because of the heat. He's seen that before, how men start acting crazy just before they dry up. But though the kid looks sunburnt, he does not look dehydrated.

"I said, 'Yeah, that is exactly what the fish are thinking. Fish

198

think so much.' And she said, 'You're just prejudiced, because they have no lungs.' And then all the shooting began."

Enright stops there and Marc waits again. A minute passes; the kid makes a pattern in the air with his finger, touches his earlobe once more. He seems to be sifting through his mind as though through shards of broken glass, connecting the pieces. Marc gives him a cigarette and he brings it unsteadily to his lips, takes a long time to connect a match to the end, a long time to suck in the flame.

Marc wishes the kid would go now, go back to whatever he was doing, evaporate. He can't bear to watch him any longer. He can't remember if he has had three or four doses of the diazepam today. He hopes it is three because he's about to take another.

"What're you looking at?" the kid says.

"I'm thinking you better go eat something," Marc says. He waits a minute, again in silence, and then says. "Do you remember anything else?"

The attack came out of nowhere. One of the artillery loads was hit. Some stayed with the machine guns; everyone else jumped off the vehicles to fight. That is what he can discern anyway, from the confusion of words that come from Enright.

"And these two reporters, where were they?"

"How the fuck should I know?"

A fair enough answer.

Enright stops talking again. A few minutes go by. "I keep seeing the men, my buddies, tumbling through the air when that ammo log went up in front of us. Like acrobats, like they were flying."

Marc nods. He knows what the kid means. Knows exactly.

"A friend of mine, Tim Ayers, he's dead now."

"I'm sorry."

"He was hanging off the back of the track and got knocked under it. But he was dead by then. I'm pretty sure he was dead."

"Was the woman off the vehicle when Ayers was hit? "

"I don't know. Someone said they saw her running. Not me. I was trying to get Tim up, but I couldn't. And he fell. But he was dead by then, I think. I sure hope he was dead, because we ran over him. Right the fuck over, too."

"Who saw her running?"

"I don't know. I don't remember."

"Running where?"

"I didn't see it. I was looking at Ayers."

Marc reaches into his pocket, chews off a tablet of Valium from its foil pack. He nods. Someone really ought to talk to the kid's commanding officer. But it wouldn't be him. Not today.

"We had a lot of wounded, a lot of wreckage. It was a bad deal. There was a fire. The woods started going up, too, all this black smoke. I can still see them, flying through the air—"

Enright angles his body toward the tent entrance, hands between his knees, his back stiff, talking now, faster and faster, so that his big teeth seem to flash in the shadow of the tent. He didn't see what happened to Susan. He didn't even know she was a reporter until afterwards. They had that conversation about fish. Are there any more questions? No? No, okay. He better get back to what he was doing. The ambush came. He saw Tim Ayers hit. Maybe she ran for the jungle. They were all over the place. It hadn't been a bad guess to run like that. He might have done the same. But the jungle was on fire. Maybe she got burned to death. Maybe she's still alive. He doesn't know. He was holding on to Ayers, holding on to his arm— but Ayers, he didn't move at all, not to wrench himself up or look in Enright's direction.

"And the track started to move," the kid says, "turning to clear the kill zone. And Ayers was still hanging there; I needed to get to the gun, you know? There was nobody on the M60. I really needed to get to that goddamned gun. I'm sure he was dead."

200

"I'm sure he was."

"He wouldn't hold on."

"No."

"So I let go."

"Same as I'd do," Marc tells him. "Same as anyone."

"Really? Is that true? You'd have let go?"

Marc breathes out, leaning forward toward the kid. He shakes his head. "I'm sure I would have," he sighs. "In fact," he might as well admit this, "I don't think I would have held on in the first place."

Seven hours later he watches the bulldozers roll through the ground, sliding into the undergrowth, their scoops angled to uproot trees. The noise from all this work has become a loud, droning constant, mingling with the babbling public address system, the blaring tinny music, the hundreds of people in every direction. He watches concertina wire being thrown out of a truck bed, bouncing on to the ground in thick, lethal coils, from which it gets pushed out and arranged to form an uneven boundary. A blue bus arrives, pouring out clouds of smoke and unleashing a group of teenage girls, beautifully dressed in white *ao dzai*s which flow like water around their legs and make them appear as though from another world. At first, Marc thinks they must be performers of some sort, but in fact they are part of a "nation-building" group. They clasp their clipboards and smile at the refugees, who regard them long enough to determine whether they have any food or clothing or any power to get some. The pretty young girls might as well be performers as they have no other obvious use to the refugees. They bring nothing to eat or wear and so the refugees ignore them. The girls move through the camp in their flowing robes, the white *ao dzai*s that remind Marc of the sails of ships, attracting the children, who they also seem to have no idea how to care for. He cannot imagine why they are here.

201

There is not enough rice, not enough food generally. Rumors of some families hoarding, taking more than their share, abound through the camp. There are not enough blankets, or fuel for fires, or water to bathe in. The refugees, like all Vietnamese, wash frequently during the day. One old man, thinking Marc is an official of some kind, does his best to explain that he needs water for a bath. He holds a rusted bucket with holes on either side through which a ragged length of brown twine is threaded to make a handle. The man moves his hand into and out of the empty bucket as though scooping water, bringing his palms over his head, his cheeks, under the folds of his arms.

"I'm sorry," Marc says, the old man following him as he walks away. It is the fifth or sixth time he has been asked for something by the Vietnamese, who assume he must be an aid worker. They have no idea what a reporter is, so they tag after him and will not leave him unless he behaves rudely.

He watches an irate woman lambasting a young ARVN lieutenant and discovers that she is angry that she is not allowed to return to her house to get more of her belongings. Someone else is explaining she has left one of her grandchildren behind. How is it possible to leave a child? he wonders. One of the officials of the province scuttles round in a station wagon with the back open, serving as a kind of taxi. Occasionally, he jumps out and uses a bullhorn to give ad hoc speeches to those around him. An obnoxious little shit, Marc thinks.

They have run out of tents, but nobody tells the soldiers with the bulldozers, so more bare ground is created and left uncovered, the rutted soil collecting water in the afternoon rains which blow through the camp and then fade away once more as the searing sun takes over. The heat regains its hold on the camp so that the whole place, now swimming in mud, is also steaming like the mouth of a volcano, sending forth the smell of plowed earth and dung. There is no more vaccine— they ran out—but after the rains the line outside the medical

202

tent forms once more, perhaps in hope that more will be brought. He watches the children playing in the puddles, none with an entire set of clothes, their mothers, soaked, miserable, staring down at the wet ground or up, beyond the perimeter and treeline, looking at the sky as though there may be an answer there. Some leave the line and then re-join it. Finally, as the sun discards its most searing whiteness and late after-noon settles over the camp, he checks once more and they are all gone, the medical tents empty. On the ground are plastic wrappers, gauze, some cotton balls with tape across them, little specks of blood at their centers.

"I'm looking for Lieutenant Colonel Halliday," he tells an American aide. How many times has he said this today?

"Yeah, see, I don't know anybody here," the aide says.

Around evening he runs out of water and drinks a sweet-tasting powdered drink called Keen. He finds his driver there, the one who brought him by jeep to the camp, standing next to the large vat of Keen that is protected from insects by mosquito netting. The drink is available only for the soldiers, it would seem. His driver turns out to like Keen, and fills his cup, then downs it all in one go. Marc asks him why the refugees don't have any.

"VC say it poisoned," he says. "The people don't drink."

"But surely they can see you and me drinking it."

They stand in silence for a moment. The hours earlier, when the driver brought him bouncing through the dirt roads to the camp, seem as though they took place days ago. The driver says, "You expect someone take you to that girl?"

Marc laughs out loud, a miserable little laugh. "No, of course not."

The driver seems satisfied with the answer and turns to go. Suddenly, Marc wants the man to stay with him, at least for another minute or two. "I don't know when I'll get Halliday to even talk to me," he says, rushing the words. "I'm beginning to wonder if Halliday *exists*—" The driver looks confused so he says, "If he's real, or not."

"What you expect?" says the driver.

Marc shakes his head. In the center of a large, round tent, someone has tied a bunch of pigs, now all tangled in their ropes and squealing loudly. To his left, just fifty yards away, two old women are trying to get through the wire to a clump of bushes they prefer to the newly erected latrines. Children stand, pantless, crying, waiting for their mothers, who cannot find them in the crowd. The PA system is now broadcasting some kind of report on the new way in which the government will help these peasants, help them in every way.

The driver continues. "What you think going happen?" he says. "You see here. Chaos. Even more chaos in the villages. What you want happen?"

He thinks about how he killed the Loc Ninh story, about how he'd been brought down here for some sort of "help." Where is Halliday? Not anywhere in the camp, as far as he can tell. Locke and he have worked together now for nine months solid, but he knows without having to ask that there will be no more teaming up with Locke. You don't kill a story like that, not one that took days to develop.

"Nothing," he says. "I don't expect anything to happen."

"Good," says the driver, as though they've agreed on something. He walks away, balancing two paper cups in his hands.

IV

In her hotel, that place she has begun to think of as home, are her books, her typewriter, an aluminum coffee mug she uses as a pencil holder, her stacks of notepaper and clippings, her stained coffee cups and the little area they've made into a kitchen. There is Son's tidy collection of chemicals and processing trays, his photographs clipped to a web of gray wire that runs against the wall. The bed is still as she left it the morning of her departure, unmade, the sheets crumpled, gathering dust so that if someone were to sit on it now there would be a cloudy puff noticeable in the broad sunlight of morning.

The pillow, sunken with the weight of her head, yellows in that same sun that pours through the glass, unprotected by the blind which she left up. The leaves of the plants that Son bought to purify the air and to bring into the room a scent other than traffic fumes and insecticide are covered in a film of dust so that the leaves no longer shine. Gathering like ash, the dust also creates a mask of downy white on the desktop, the typewriter, the chair seat, on Son's things, too, which were left folded in a small corner of the room as he always left them. When he spent the night, he always arranged his clothes perfectly, making a neat small square. He was a man accustomed to small and crowded rooms; he could make anything fit into the tiniest of spaces. He never complained about the water turning rusty, the electricity being cut off. He would work by moonlight and candlelight. His dark profile, the outline of his shaggy hair, his untucked shirt, its sleeves wagging unbuttoned at the wrist, his lean legs shifting silently across the darkened room are as familiar to Susan as her own reflection. If there was no water, which was the case now and again at the hotel, he washed with what was left in his canvas-covered bottle, using a handkerchief or a thin washcloth, a sliver of soap you could see through. He was able to sleep amid any noise—even gunfire— and she has never seen him with a bed fancier than an army cot.

The plants are dying, their soil cracking in chunks in their pots. The fern's rumpled leaves fold in at the tips; the bushy ivy yellows, the lilies that had blossomed, have dropped now, the whole plant sagging. Son hung a map of Vietnam on the wall above the bed, not a map like Susan's own, with the war zones and bases in thin ink, but an illustrated map showing the soft green hills, the wide expansive valleys, the mists that flow up and down the landscape. Tigers were portrayed in the jungle, porpoises along the eastern shore, parrots flying off the edges, the whole thing opening out, inviting, magical. The map was like something you might see in a child's room, completely useless, except it was not: it has given Susan comfort to look at this map, to see Vietnam not as a place of war, with bases and field hospitals, the Demilitarized Zone, the 17th parallel, but as a magical place with parrots and monkeys, tigers hiding in thickets of bamboo, dolphins rising in arcs along the shore. The map is not old, but the sun is making it seem so, carving fissures in the corners, giving it the texture of drying leaves. She had always closed the blind, opened the window, protected the room from all that bright light, but she is not there now.

Instead, 100 miles away, she pushes her face into the ground as the landscape explodes around her. It is not the Bouncing Betty that has detonated. That mine remains like a sleeping python in her line of vision, miraculously quiet, while the onslaught of air strikes further away blast through every thought she tries to gather, so that she is left with nothing but the most basic of instincts: to make herself small, to draw in her arms and legs, curl her back, tuck her head into her chest, round her shoulders, ball her fists. Really, however, she needs to move. There is a thing called sympathetic detonation, an explosion resulting from a shock wave, from a sudden change in pressure, which is exactly what is going to happen to the Bouncing Betty if the air strike gets any closer. She begins to crawl back, enduring the combustion of bombs, a confusion of noise that comes from every direction. She feels a weight passing through her so that her bones themselves seem to catalog the blasts, so that she feels—she could swear this— her brain slosh against the inside of her skull, one direction, then another, with every blast and shock wave. She tells herself to keep moving, is engaged totally in this inch-by-inch retreat. She keeps hoping for something, but she doesn't know what. There is just this single, raw desperate hope, like a cry from deep within her, inaudible but fully intact. It is what keeps her going.

And then, out of nowhere, Son appears. She sees him in the thick brush, a sudden, unexpected arrival. He has come back for her, shouting as he approaches, though with all the noise around them it appears as though he is silent, that she is watching him from behind a thick wall of glass. He is in front of her, yet unreachable; he is yelling at her but to no effect; his mouth moves, his hands; he strains to communicate but the sound is only articulated in the corded muscles of his neck, the open cave of his mouth. When the bombing began he must have run back to retrieve her. She cannot imagine risking such a thing. She cannot understand how it was possible for him to find her in the thick green of the jungle. From the moment she spots him, his legs stepping high over the brush, his head shaking with the movement, his arms out balancing against the thin, odd-shaped trees, she wants to yell to him about the

Bouncing Betty. But it is hopeless. He is so close and even though she is screaming he cannot hear her. If he runs into the mine, they will both be killed. As futile as it is, she yells loudly into the deafening air, pointing and gesturing and begging him to move away. But she can only watch and gesture and trust that somehow he will notice. He is already reaching for her, pulling her toward him as though she has no legs. She rises, pushing him away from the mine as she does so. Either he's seen it or by luck he is avoiding it anyway. They run, fumbling through the brush, bent double, hands over their heads. They are together again while only minutes ago she thought surely she was both alone and dead.

He leads her to a shelter, nothing more than a hole in the earth. The entrance requires her to push herself down a vertical shaft no bigger than a chimney, arms above her head, wiggling to force herself down, holding her breath, hearing even through the layers of earth the great swells of noise that shake through her as she plunges steeply into what might be anything at all, a man-trap, an underground jail cell, a volcano, for all she knows. She doesn't care. Suddenly, she drops a foot or more, banging her shoulder and hip, dislodging bits of earth as she moves, scraping her cheek, and getting an eyeful of grit. She reaches a landing and scrambles for footing, sliding along a trench no wider than her shoulders until the passage suddenly opens out. She balances on the floor of the shelter, her legs askew, feeling as though she has landed in a wet grave, for there is mud and water and slime all around her, oozing into her clothes, squelching between her fingers, coating her knees and elbows, her feet, her hands.

She cannot speak. It is hard enough to breath. She holds her knees to her chest, leans her cheek against the mud wall, and feels the wetness there, too. Son lands through the same narrow chute that she has clambered down, putting himself near her and wrapping his arms around his head, trying to

210

shield himself from the noise. She cannot see, but she can feel the presence of others. She is spooked as much by this as by the darkness and wetness, the heat and booming explosions. She begins to tremble. She can feel the discrete measure of elevated heat between herself and someone else, one of the soldiers. Her head pounds, her shoulders shake, her arms tremble around her knees. The smell of the wet earth is like urine and like rot. It feels as though a giant is marching above them; with every blast come sprinklings of earth from close above their heads. The shelter is a boggy, unstable hole. She wonders if it will cave in.

The blasts continue. She is sure they will throw down more napalm. She remembers what the nurse in Pleiku said about white phosphorus, how it keeps burning to the bone. She looks at the spine of cotton wood which props up the walls of the shelter, the crumbling ceiling, the dark, damp corners. If it caves in, they will all die, as there will be nobody there to dig them out. If they rush from the shelter, they will have the Willie Pete, the bombs, the jellied gasoline to contend with.

She would not have guessed it would be so hot here this far under the earth. There is no ventilation except through the narrow shoot that runs six feet up to the surface. The darkness itself seems to produce a heat. The noise outside suddenly fills the area around them, then there is silence, then another great sound. When the bombs hit, the small bit of space they occupy seems to contract like a muscle. At those times it feels to Susan almost as though they are sitting on top of each other, as though they are inside a live animal, consumed by this beast of earth.

As her eyes adjust she can see the outline of the soldiers. A flashlight is switched on, the same one she has carried for months now, and through its dim glow comes the face of Long Hair. He has his weapon beside him, at his ankles like a loyal dog, and is tightening one end of the flashlight, shaking it, then tightening it again. The bulb is dying but in the darkness of their shelter it casts a fair-sized glow. She can see Gap Tooth and the Thin One on either side of the cave-like walls, but she doesn't look at them; it is the light that holds her. The light from the small flashlight given to her by Marc, who tossed it her direction one day as she was setting off. At various times she has worn it around her neck or kept it deep in the front pocket of her fatigues. If the soldiers were to unscrew the stem of it, they would find a letter written to her by Marc. She keeps the letter hidden there the way that some women keep their own love letters in jewelry cases. *Nothing happens as we imagine it,* it begins. The letter describes where he is, the soldiers he accompanies, how they march, probing like bait into what they believe to be enemy territory, waiting for an ambush. *During the lull times, they sleep and smoke and listen to their small transistor radios. If I hear "Windy" one more time, I may have to shoot the DJ . . .* He describes a little of what they've filmed, and a great deal of all the different ways in which she enters his thoughts, how she had cost him a chess game because he kept daydreaming of her. Of course it does not mention the future. No love letter does, and anyway they were always careful never to speak of the future. Of the end of the war, of the world back in America, of his wife. Now, of course, it doesn't matter. She does not think about Marc the way she used to. He occupies a different world, one that feels far away. Nothing matters now, except what happens in this minute, then the next.

Nobody speaks. They endure the air raid each in their own way. Son with his hands over his head, Long Hair with his head on his knees, his rifle tucked between his legs, Gap Tooth staring at the walls, his eyes glassy, the Thin One holding on to Gap Tooth's shoulder, as though for balance.

She watches the flashlight bulb like it is a thing alive, comforted by its meager glow. She rubs some sweat from her brow, and then there is a huge explosion so near to them she screams. She feels a spasm in her gut and begins to vomit. She is scared. She imagines what would have happened if she was still out in the brush, close to the Bouncing Betty at the moment of the last explosion. So close. She thinks to herself, *I am scared to death*, and then empties her stomach once again. She wipes her face with her sleeve, dabs her eyes, tries to swallow. Long Hair gives her water, for which she is grateful, but as she lifts the canteen to her lips she smells the ooze of the shelter's floor on her fingers and vomits again. She tries to dig a hole in the earth floor to bury her vomit, but as she digs she reveals only more wetness, the ground nothing more than a thin layer above boggy, sodden terrain. She feels she must cover the vomit, but this is impossible. She becomes immediately and acutely aware of the air supply, feeling herself breathe in and out more rapidly now, her skin clammy from being sick, worried now about suffocating in this gap in the earth. Her fingers glide over the dark floor. The smell will stay with them a long time, she thinks, mingling with the scent of stale sweat and new sweat. The soldiers say nothing but look at her slightly disgusted, she thinks, as though they cannot believe they are stuck with her once more.

As time passes, the bombing grows less frequent, then stops altogether.

She tries to speak, but all that comes from her is a long, slow whine that she does not recognize as her own voice. It is a sound like a siren, like the stammering beginnings of a cry. The sound rings out in the well of earth in which she sits and she thinks surely she has gone mad if she cannot even make a noise with volition. Long Hair, too, must be wondering what she is doing. He gives her a puzzled look as though he, too, is confused by the strange whining. Their hearing is so distorted now, their heads ringing with the aftermath of the air strike, it is not surprising they hear phantom noises, and that sounds ring unusually in their battered eardrums. The air itself is dense and close, vibrating as the skin of a drum. She feels like at any moment the place will combust.

She folds her arms over her knees. Son takes her hand, her arm, pulling her toward him, holding her there now that the mortars have eased, the vibrations ebbing back, the world once again left in stillness. He appears no longer to care if the soldiers see the depth of their friendship. He is covered with the same stinking mud, the same dirt and slime and sweat that is plastered over her. She is glad to have him near. She does not want to think of what it might cost him later—a man who evaded execution by claiming to be Vietcong but is now sitting with his arms around an American girl. She has no sense of "later," of time itself. The thought of a timepiece—a watch, a clock— seems a folly to her anyway when death is so at hand. She has no idea why the Americans called in artillery on this particular patch, and wonders if it was an accidental strike, the sort that happened all the time and which usually resulted in scores of unnecessary deaths and might, this time, have caused her own.

Through the ringing in her ears she hears again the high whine and realizes now that it is not her voice but that of one of the soldiers. Their senses have all been so distorted that it is difficult to tell what is happening, who is making what noise, whether there is a noise at all. She looks up and sees that the Thin One is crying. He is shaped so differently from most Vietnamese, taller, with long, flat bones, a tubular rib cage, a narrow head as though someone once put it in a vise. He is crying as a child might cry, from fear and confusion. She has never seen a Vietnamese soldier cry, let alone a VC soldier. He seems entirely surprised by the event himself, his face registering astonishment at the tears which spill, so that he touches his face feeling for them as one might feel for blood. He speaks to the other two, who observe him as though he has just grown gills. At last, he turns to her, his fists clenched by his chin, shaking like a crying child's fists will shake, the muscles at his brow swelling with the effort of his emotion. He looks, in fact, like a child. Like any number of the large-headed underweight pubescent boys she sees half-naked in the villages. It suddenly occurs to her that he may be no older than fifteen.

He lunges at her, grabbing her neck with his hands. She is so startled that, at first, she does not resist. She feels the pressure against her throat, a stabbing pain, her eyes beginning to lose focus, a sudden darkness, the whole thing happening so fast she does not have time to scream. She feels the weight of the soldier's body, his knee against her chest. She feels herself braced against him, her hands grabbing uselessly at his, trying to pull his fingers from her throat. There is a jarring sensation as he bears down on her, her ears ringing, her eyes seeming to pop out of her skull. It happens so fast and yet each second expands into the next as though they exist now in a balloon of time in which a minute is an hour. All at once, she realizes she is passing out. The edges of her vision cloud. She cannot move her head or arms. The soldier recedes from sight, far away, then close again. Her focus wanes. Just as she thinks surely she is dying, he suddenly, unexpectedly, drops his hold on her throat.

He topples off her and she struggles to breathe again, terrified because it appears she cannot. Her eyes feel as though someone has taken each eyeball and squeezed it like a lemon. Her throat throbs and expands. She can see again, but cannot move her head. She can hear a fight beside her and realizes that it was Son who pulled the soldier off and now the soldier is hitting Son, who kicks him in the face, the whole thing ending with Long Hair threatening to shoot them both, then grabbing the Thin One and throwing him off Son, so that he knocks into her again.

The soldiers continue arguing loudly in Vietnamese. Son tries to talk to her, but she is still too preoccupied with trying

215

to breathe. There is a sound like an engine in her throat and though she tries to gain some breath, it feels at first as though the damage to her windpipe is too great, the swelling too large. After several minutes she is able to get enough breath and the awful roaring noise inside her subsides a little. Some time later she is able to breathe normally, without gasping and sputtering and feeling she will be sick. She pulls herself up out of the slime on the ground and says, "It's not *my* fucking air strike!" to the soldiers.

"He is upset because we cannot find our unit," Long Hair answers.

"And that's *my* fault?"

"The hamlet was deserted and now we have to find the next."

The Thin One tries to say something and Long Hair raps him with his knuckles. He pulls back, making a great effort to control himself now. He wipes his eyes and then blinks as the mud irritates them. He is sniffling; they are all so covered in filth that there is no way he can wipe his nose or clean himself. Susan looks away. She does not care if he is upset, if he is worried or hungry or half mad with fear. If he is angry about Americans or air strikes or the whole of the damn war. She'd just as happily kill him herself right now.

She puts the soldier out of her mind, concentrating on the dim glow of the flashlight in the corner of her vision. Son wraps his arms around her like a cape. He does not speak, nor does he need to. He has saved her life. She is certain that if he had not been there, the other two soldiers would have let the Thin One kill her. Not because they hated her or because they thought she deserved to die, but only because they were distracted and because if they cannot find their own unit, she cannot be handed over. And if she cannot be handed over to their commanding officers, she is of no value. She will eat their food and slow them down, bringing them no reward at all. But Son had been watching out for her, as he always did. She concentrates on the feeling of his embrace, on the miracle of the bulb that has not given out, on the letter hidden within the stem of the flashlight, a letter she cherishes. She is grateful that they have survived the bombings, that her throat is clear now. She reaches behind her, feeling for the still erect walls. She breathes deeply and thanks God for the presence of oxygen in the air.

In Saigon, Son sat with her at night as she brushed her hair, getting ready for bed. She dressed and undressed in the bathroom, balancing against the walls. They had so often found sharp splinters from broken tiles embedded in their feet that they wore flip-flops in the room, the rubber thwack of their heels a background noise, like the passing cars outside. She did not hide herself from him, but nor did she go braless or wear shorts. He appeared to have no desire at all except for her company—at least, she thought this was the case. He read aloud to her from newspapers, or chatted as he fixed his developing trays, dousing negatives, watching with anticipation as images arrived on the treated paper, occasionally holding one up for her to see. Once, when she had a head cold, he brought her soup in bed, but usually after she lay down to sleep he did not look in her direction. Out of respect or embarrassment, she did not know. It was just one of the many ways they managed to live as they did in that one small room.

Occasionally, on a particularly beautiful night during which they might be walking through the last haze of evening together, talking quietly, glad to be away from the fighting, or pleased with the outcome of a story they had covered, she felt like taking his hand. She had never done so, but it was there: the wish for an increased connection. Was there nothing more to it than that? To take his hand: what did that mean? It was innocent, she thought. Nothing more than an occasional desire to demonstrate the closeness of their friendship.

There were times when she wondered, too, if he would ever

do anything to test the waters of a possible romance with her. She did not broach the subject with him—it would have been unsettling and, after all, they spent so much time in harmony, in that familiar closeness that was precious to them both. She did not want to disturb that. In truth, weeks if not months went by without her considering whether he felt any attraction for her or, indeed, whether she was attracted to him. However, it did not go entirely unasked. Once, early on in their friendship, she edged toward the subject and he told her he knew she was in love with Marc.

The way you look at him, he said, as though that finished it. When she seemed perplexed he added, *The way he looks at you.*

We don't always get along. It was easy to say this, but not entirely accurate. What she meant was that they had lives that were separate, that must always be so, it seemed. She did not mean they argued, because they did not.

He loves you.

Like that would matter, she said. *I mean—*

She didn't know what she meant. The statement seemed coarse and she immediately regretted it. She was not suggesting that love was meaningless, only that the question of such allegiances went unasked in Vietnam. It was its own small world, a theater of extremes, and it was temporary. She had borrowed Marc. That much was perfectly obvious to her. She had loaned him from the world in the same manner in which the GIs were on loan, the missiles and the aircraft, the supplies that arrived daily in the harbors, the tanks and helicopters. Not that these temporary arrangements did not matter. They were crucial, critical, without which none of them could be here. But one day everything would go back or be destroyed, or sold on, or thrown into the ocean. Nothing could remain as it was. But she could not explain this, not at the time, how she knew and had always known that Marc would leave her. Anyway this was not how Son would see it; Vietnam was his home. For him there was no place to retreat, no getaway, no other life or world.

So she said, *You must have a girlfriend.* She might have added that she was not used to men who slept on floors, who spoke gently to her when she had a bad dream, who did not appear ever to look at her, except as a brother might. *Perhaps you even have a wife?* she said. Had he been American, had he been white, she would have asked this question of him a long time ago. Did she think he was any different for being Asian? She must have thought so, because one of the first questions to the soldiers in the field was always whether they had someone back home. She'd asked dozens of different GIs that question, so why hadn't she asked Son? Now, whispering, with a certain dismay at her own odd behavior, she continued, *Don't you have someone, Son?*

They were at a market. He had spent the morning trailing behind her with a string bag and a plastic sack. The bag held condensed milk, coffee, dragonfruit, batteries, limes, the pork rolls that Son always bought, a few oranges. Beside them was a newsagent, stocked with newspapers, almost all of which were censored. Great gaps in the print, whole headlines blackened as though with a giant's mighty pen. The papers with their blocks of blank newsprint, their darkened boxes, their tales of government victories, were crammed on to a rusted metal rack or stacked, like most of the goods in the market, on sagging cardboard cartons, piled in rows.

Son stood near; anyone looking at them would have assumed they were lovers, deep in conversation over the things lovers whisper about, those forgotten questions and declarations, so important at the time. His gaze, angled at her, showed tenderness. Because of the bags in his hands, he could gesture only with his shoulders. A moment later, she took his elbow and walked closely beside him as he steered them through the crowd. She was talking quietly, head bent, her mouth near his collarbone. She would not dare to have such a conversation in the room. To speak of these things required the presence of market stalls, the busy movement of people, women cooking in blackened pots over small fires, the pickpockets and money changers, the flasks of dark tea, the bold children pushing Cola they sold to Americans for ninety cents a can. Otherwise, it was too intimate, too close.

You must have somebody, she said. *I can't believe—*

I won't say, he told her. *But you are my best friend.*

But, Son. Don't you ever, you know . . .? They stopped again. He faced her, standing with her bags as a good husband would. She took a long breath. It confused her, all this. Everywhere she went she was propositioned by soldiers, not always in a bad way. Some were polite, asking her to dance at a club or complimenting her in some small way, offering their cigarettes or pop, or just smiling and saying it was nice to see a woman who was a "round eye," that they hadn't seen one in months. Others were more direct, occasionally obscene. She let those comments bounce off. In truth, she really didn't care what the soldiers said. She was too aware of how they spoke to one another, and how the officers degraded them with abuse that would be shocking if it weren't so commonplace. It was all very impersonal, really. Even when men in the press corps teased her, or spoke in their brusque manner, so false, so full of bravado, she really didn't care that much.

But she *did* care what Son said. She looked at him as he smiled awkwardly, glancing up, then away, anything not to look directly at her. He was blushing. His hair had grown a little so it fell on either side of his head like a newly thatched roof. His cheekbones, his chin, his teeth were all so large, and yet he had a delicate face.

No, never, he said, then his mouth formed a small smile which grew, erupting into laughter.

She smiled and slapped him gently on the arm and said, *All right then, enough of this.*

Eventually, she broke him down. She thought he broke down. This was weeks later. They had spent a difficult few days on a story about a hospital in Dak Nhon and had arrived back to Saigon once more, feeling that same relief and, for Susan anyway, a mild guilt that she could take refuge in the cramped comfort of the hotel, far away from the bombing, while those about whom she'd written her story could not. The moonlight streamed through the window, sliced by the slow rotation of the ceiling fan. The crickets chimed from the corners of the room and from the balcony outside. It was neither hot nor cold. The afternoon rain had cleared the dust and given the air outside the pleasant smell of a flower shop. They'd had pork rolls, the ones that Son always got from an acquaintance at the market who he said used the best meat, and they'd had a little to drink in order to celebrate the beautiful night. She was tired from traveling. She was half asleep when he began his confession. At first, when she heard him speak, she thought she might be dreaming. *There is somebody,* he said, and it was as though his voice passed through her dreams, alighting there.

He was on the floor only a few feet from her bed, his clothes folded into their small package, his map dark against the wall. It was midnight, perhaps later. The papers from the pork rolls were torn and pressed into the bin. Their empty glasses were set along the window sill. The rice wine they'd drunk that night had come in a glass flask, like something you might find in a chemistry lab, and had a deceptively light taste she distrusted. She'd been unwilling to let it remain on her tongue and swallowed it all at once the way she had once been taught to eat oysters, feeling the effects almost immediately. She'd been drunk, but she was not drunk now.

Son said, *In Hué. But she is married.*

Her eyes opened. She realized he was telling her something important.

Her husband is in the army—

221

So that explained it.

She turned toward him, folding her pillow in half to lift her head, nodding into the darkness. She wanted to hear everything, wanted to encourage him, but was afraid that saying so might have the opposite effect.

They met at a relative's house, he explained, so that nobody knew. She was four years younger than him, a mother.

She is not so fond of her husband, he said. The way he said this caused Susan to smile for a moment, but she wiped the smile away when he spoke again, his voice serious. *It was not her choice to marry, but that did not bother her. It was that he left, forced into the army.*

The woman's husband had been chosen for her by her family; they met at the engagement, the wedding day having been decided by a fortune teller. When they knelt beside the ancestral altar, the bride who would one day betray her soldier husband had felt the heat of the incense against her cheeks, her eyelashes, and believed the warmth was a promise from her ancestors for a secure future. Now she had a house with a courtyard and a child, but her husband was never there. He'd been drafted into the army. She never saw him. Not even his family looked in on her and so she was on her own. Son discovered she was married long after he fell in love with her. He returned to Hué again and again, pursuing her. It wasn't her fault, he explained, it was his. Too late, he discovered how impossible the situation was. But now he was in love, trapped by it, betrothed in a manner that felt more final than if he really were married.

The way he described it, she could see that there was as much pain in the mix as there was joy, sex, passion. She could also see now why it was possible for him to sleep night after night on her floor, the moonlight shining through the window and, even tonight with the slight drunkenness from the rice wine, never think of making love. He was in love up to his eyeballs and it pained him.

222

It sounds to me that you've brought something wonderful into her life, Susan said. *How could that be such a mistake?*

I have made it so very much harder, he said. He sounded sad. He sounded resigned. *You can love a person and by doing so make everything harder.*

It was true. The moment she heard it from his mouth, she knew exactly what he meant. Not just in this case, but in all cases. She and Marc, for example. Though she didn't intend to make it hard for him. She wasn't going to hang on to him unduly.

He sighed. *And there should be no secrets.* And with that he closed the conversation as one might close a door. In silence, she looked at his face, his eyes far away, burdened. He would say nothing more. She knew this. She drew in a breath, felt herself sigh inwardly. After a few minutes she turned over and watched the ceiling fan with its slow revolution, her mouth dry, her head throbbing lightly with her pulse.

I'll get you water, he said, reading her mind.

From then on, whenever Son was gone, disappearing as he did every now and again, she imagined him in Hué, the turns of desire and guilt so powerful that they could be endured only for a few days. Sometimes, upon his return to Saigon, he stared out the window of the hotel room, his thoughts, Susan imagined, condensed into a single moment of intense vision. She believed that he was dreaming of the woman in Hué, a beautiful young Vietnamese wife who betrayed her soldier husband with a photographer who roamed the country taking pictures of the dead, of the dying. He took photographs of grieving soldiers, of mothers clutching their children, of elderly farmers watching their crops exploding, of orphanages so packed with children the floor was obscured so that the children appeared almost to be floating on air. Everywhere, he recorded the disastrous state of things. One disturbing love affair—she didn't know what the consequences would be. Everything in the country was so political. Being caught by the Vietcong speaking to some marines, a chieftain is executed, his head adorning the gates as a warning to all. Being seen running from an American unit on a search mission a farmer is shot down in a rice paddy, his body left to float upon the glasslike reflection. What was the consequence of a betrayal of mere love? Probably nothing. Son would not tell her the woman's name so Susan gave her one. She called her Han, which means faithful and moral. She couldn't see a lover of Son being anything less, and she did not know what she may have suffered, this young woman. They were all suffering so much. She saw her as just so she called her Han.

When he was not with Han, he was with Susan, working, or beside her on the floor near her bed, or occupying her room when she was with Marc. It was a marvelous game of musical beds. Outside, the Saigon streets were flush with sleeping children with only newsprint for blankets, with ordinary citizens whose every available room became someone's bedroom at night. The streets filled as a vessel might, spilling over so that homes were made on the canals. In a city that had been designed for half a million people there now slept three million or more, pouring in from the countryside as the war ate up village after village like a hungry dog.

In such circumstances, it was easy to become casual about where one lay down. She was used to stepping over Son's slumbering body on her way to the bathroom. She was used to moving half a dozen things just to sit on the toilet. She didn't mind. She liked falling asleep with him working on his still photographs, washing them, hanging them, correcting the errors that only his eye caught. Sometimes he would sit on the floor smoking Kools, streaming the smoke out the window, and tell her stories of an older Vietnam, the Vietnam that existed before the Americans came, before the French. That is how she learned how old he was, thirty one. He did not look more than twenty; he shaved at either end of his lip and one small patch of stubble on his chin. Only his hands, as rough and callused as those of a laborer, gave him any age at all.

Last night, she wanted to tell him she had never believed there was a Han, that she had known from the start he was lying to her. She wanted to tell him she had only pretended to believe him, not because it would make any difference, but because she could not bear the thought that he had betrayed her for so long, that he'd convinced her with such an easy lie. He had guided her judgment of him. The way he'd locked on to the fictitious Han seemed to set him apart from all the men she met, the journalists with their singular vision, their consuming passion to beat others to the big stories, their ambition almost grotesque, consumptive, as bad as if they'd shaved their heads and joined a cult, however talented they were, however bold. She had thought Son was different and he was not. She'd been fooled. And not just her. He had fooled the entire press corps, the embassy officials, the American and Vietnamese military. This soft-hearted boyish man who carried her groceries and made her tea in his decorative pot, who spoke quietly and laughed at other people's jokes, who blended in and caused little stir, had walked among them and tricked everyone he met. It occurred to her, too, that he may still be deceiving her.

But buried in the earth, covered in mud and slime, none of that mattered. He'd run back to get her while the bombs exploded around them. He'd pulled her to safety, led her to the shelter, wrapped his arms around her, and shielded her as best he could. He'd even wrenched the stupid soldier off her when he tried to strangle her, stood up for her even when it was the others who had weapons. He had, quite clearly, risked his life for her. That was a fact. For surely the VC soldiers were as capable as any in this war of shooting someone who was attacking one of their ranks. *You can love a person and by doing*

225

so make everything harder. He was certainly making it harder for himself now, on her behalf. And she had to set the fact that she was still alive against the fact he'd been in command posts and seen maps that would have been important to the communists, that he'd used her in that way, in order to find out information, plans of operation, to infiltrate and get knowledge about American forces. He'd lied to her and would even right now be continuing to lie to her, had they not been in the ambush together, had they not been taken prisoner.

But he is remarkable; she feels herself drawn to him newly. He is not falling apart the way that she feels she is falling apart. And look at their captors: Long Hair is so covered in mud he gives the appearance he's been unearthed from a tomb; Gap Tooth drags his sword with him up through the narrow chute that serves as an entrance to the shelter, looking as though he no longer cares if he lives or dies; the Thin One is still sniffling. Son is behind her as she pulls herself up from the muddy surface of the underground hide, her elbows and knees making the climb. He helps her through and then, in the open air once more, smiles at her encouragingly.

"We were lucky," he says.

Lucky? She cannot imagine how he can say this.

He says, "It's so hard to hide in the Delta. Everywhere you dig is water, you see, so you cannot rely on a foxhole or an underground shelter. What a lot of luck we had."

"I don't call what's going on here luck," she says.

"Susan." He touches her elbow. "You are *alive.*"

And it is true. Despite everything that has happened, she is still alive, unharmed. Emerging into the evening, she is amazed by this. She finds the evening itself remarkable, as though she had forgotten, or never truly known, the wonder of a breeze. The air is fresh, cool; it seems to have weight, like a tangible presence she might hold. Though there is the smell of carbine and sap, burning foliage, and another scent, a woody, dark taste

226

to the air that she cannot identify, it all feels brand new, to be savored. When she breathes she does so with her whole face— mouth and nose, her tongue slightly aloft between parted lips. In a clearing, she looks out into the darkening sky, grateful there are no more bombs, no great surges of fire raining down, and she has the thought—almost comical—that she will never again enjoy walking in the woods. She will never want to be one of those ramblers she has seen in her mother's home in Buckinghamshire, who in waxed jackets, gaiters, and boots, disappear off to trek from one end of the Pennines to the other. She has had enough of heat and sweat, of clinging mud and painful feet. The insects bombard her, crashing against her body as though unable to sense her presence at all, and she thinks that if she ever gets out of here she will come no closer to nature than a window pane's distance.

"You are brave," Son says. She does not feel brave. She feels grateful to this man next to her, who in some ways, she realizes now, she does not know at all.

Every day in Saigon the sun burned a white hole in the sky so that by mid-morning the temperature was already climbing skywards from 98 degrees, the air claustrophobic and unbreathable. Her skin was forever damp; her hair took on a new texture, no longer silky, no longer smooth. It kinked up around her face and ears, tangling at her neck. It felt like heavy drapery. If not for vanity, she'd have cut it off. Occasionally, in the afternoon there was a sudden rain shower, which offered some relief. The rain was so abrupt and powerful it swept garbage along the street, making the flimsy stall coverings sag or fall, creating large puddles through which the ceaseless traffic splashed. But after the warm, startling rain, the atmosphere only became more humid so that it was like a hot kitchen, the steaming air so wet you felt you could reach out and lick it. Cutting through the sky once more, the over-bright sun lit the earth, stinging her eyes, so she wore sunglasses almost all the time, looking down upon an ever more ragged Saigon, whose contents tumbled and flowed. This was when it was all so new to her. A distant, exotic city in which she had recently become resident.

The Vietnamese did not seem to notice any discomfort. Not the heat, not the extraordinary banging of constant construction, not the noisy traffic that ran lawlessly, its fumes laying low upon the road in a blue haze. They were not bothered by the raucous antique engines, the mopeds with their beeping horns, the cars backfiring because of the cheap, badly mixed fuel that they ran on. Along Tu Do Street teenage girls stood in the doorways of drinking establishments, their job being to encourage the GIs into the bars. When Susan passed, they hissed or swore so that she walked faster, her head bowed.

Everywhere there was someone trying to sell you something: stale cigarettes, warm sodas, stolen radios and other small electronic devices, black market currency which was set at a better rate than the official exchange. People crowded through markets, which extended from shop fronts into narrow, covered walkways, selling everything from dried shrimp to army-issue canteens. Old women cooked in wide, dark vessels that turned out delicious smells, lost among the influx of traffic fumes. There were garlands of flowers, black market stalls stocked with Prell shampoo, Crest toothpaste, melting chocolate bars and brands of tampons and hand cream that she knew from back home—clearly the ravages of illegal dealings. Every few feet she was approached by beggars, often children, holding out their hands in search of piastres. They knew enough English to insist on the money. That first month she made the mistake of giving someone a dollar bill, which caused a virtual stampede.

She met Son in a coffee house, entering cautiously, her eyes taking time to adjust to the sudden darkness after all the dazzling sun. She saw him there, his lip still swollen, the stitches in their stiff little x's just as they'd been sewn in Pleiku a few days earlier, and she smiled automatically. He waved and gestured with his hand. He saw that she was temporarily blinded by the cool dimness of the coffee house, that she had to move slowly, her hands held slightly outward as though to protect her from unseen walls, and so he came toward her, leading her back to the table with him.

He was wearing the same pants as he had in the hospital, but clean now, except for a few stains at the cuffs. He wore a fresh dress shirt, a silver watch with a wide band. His face lit up as though her arrival was everything he'd ever wished for. His broad smile strained the stitches on his lip. It looked a little painful and she asked him about it. He told her it was nothing. He was more concerned about her. Was she all right? She told him she had only been in the hospital to report, not because of an injury. He nodded enthusiastically. He seemed so eager to agree with anything she might say that she wondered if he was paying any real attention at all. Finally, he asked if she'd like a coffee. She nodded and he pulled a chair out for her to sit, then swept toward the bar, firing off orders to the waiters, who he clearly knew.

He'd evidently been studying a map. It was there, unfolded, lying across the table. There was an ashtray set on a long, silver stem that rose up from the floor, now full of spent butts, and a couple of dirty coffee mugs and a beer glass. There was another man at the table, and she was left to introduce herself to him. He was a cameraman, she discovered, named Don Locke.

Is that your map? she asked.

It's for you. You look lost, Locke said. The map showed an area in War Zone 1, hundreds of miles away.

She laughed. *I hope not. I only came from the hotel, though I admit it was a bit of an adventure.*

You'll get used to it here. Everything about this place is weird,

*but you kind of get to understand its weirdness after a while. And
then, of course, you yourself grow—*

Weird?

We like to call it acclimated, but yeah. It's inevitable.

There it was: the place. Whatever was bothering you could
be blamed on the country and its resident war. Who she was,
what she would become, the distant years, the uncertain,
alluring future, was all enveloped by a country in which she'd
arrived with her ambitions and apprehension, her need to
escape or to discover. Locke blamed the place; they all blamed
the place. It started immediately, even upon arrival, and lasted
a lifetime. He invited her to think so, and without speaking
she accepted.

She said, *I've only been here a couple of weeks.*

Son arrived with the coffees, making what seemed like a lot
of noise with the spoons and milk jug, the saucers and cups,
drawing Susan and Locke's attention to him. She grabbed at a
wad of paper napkins before they fluttered to the ground. Locke
took the tray from Son.

Are you trying to tip it on us?

I'm not such a good waiter.

I think you'd make a fine waiter, said Locke. *But meanwhile,
you might let the pros do it, you know?*

They are too slow. I wanted Susan to have a drink—

Well, don't pour it on her!

Son looked at Susan. *Davis isn't here,* he said. *That's why* he's
*here. Locke usually won't talk to me—only to Davis—but this
morning is different because Davis is away.*

Marc Davis. He's gone to see his wife, said Locke. *Singapore.*

*So we get to talk to Locke. I always talk. I can even talk with
one lip in a paralysis state.*

In a state of paralysis, Locke corrected. *To Susan,* he said.
I don't have a wife, just in case you were wondering. He was a
giant of a man; you could see it even when he was sitting.

His shirt billowed over his waistband. He looked like he outweighed Son by eighty pounds or more. Nice looking. On his hand was a gold wedding band which she did not bother to point out.

We work together, Son said.

You work with Mr. Locke? said Susan.

Don, said Locke. *And hell no is the answer to that one.*

I work with you, Son said, directing his words to Susan. *I hope to work with you.*

Just as a matter of interest, Locke said, *this is why I don't ordinarily talk to the guy. He makes no sense.*

Susan looked at Son. *I'm not sure I understand,* she said.

Son, you can't spend your life bullshitting, Locke said. *You really are a consummate bullshitter. Everyone thinks you're so wonderful, but Davis and I are on to you. We don't believe anything you say.*

Son giggled. He clearly found it all very funny. *I should explain. I am trying to work with you, Susan. I would like to work with you.*

Locke interrupted. *Your English is perfect. You only make mistakes when it's convenient. You are full of it. And that,* Locke said, pointing now to Son's lip, *was a fistfight.*

I banged it in Pleiku.

On somebody's knuckles, Locke challenged, *at UPI.*

Don't be silly. I don't fight. I cut my lip in the company of your competition at NBC. I was hit in the face with a TV camera. They are too big, your cameras.

I heard you hit someone.

No. I don't hit people. You are the one who hit people—

Hits, corrected Locke.

You work for UPI? Susan asked.

I did, said Son. *I used to.*

They dropped him because he kept disappearing for days at a time and nobody knew where he was, said Locke.

Son said, *I never understood what they mean. Sorry—* he looked at Locke apologetically. *What they meant.*

They fell silent. Locke seemed to be studying Son, who quickly scanned the room as though looking for a friend hidden in the crowd. Susan found him irresistible, however much he annoyed Locke. It was with some reluctance that she said, *You can't work for me. I don't pay people. I work* for *people.*

Son said, *We've been through all this. The other day, on the helicopter.*

She gave up. Locke shrugged. Son continued to look over the room at the people at other tables.

Locke said, *Son, one day we're going to find out the truth about you. The whole secret life of Hoàng Van Son.*

You are talking rubbish.

Rubbish, Locke corrected. *Or gibberish. And I'll tell you what else, buddy, you won't be able to cutey-pie your way out of it when—*

Son dropped ash from his cigarette on to the map on the table, the one they'd been studying before Susan came in. A little hole began to burn, quickly consuming one of the northeast quadrants. Locke grabbed at the map, stubbing out the flame with his fingers. *Give me that!* he said.

She's very modest, said Son about Susan. *The people will like her.*

You mean they won't spit on her when she walks down the road? Locke said. He folded his map again, shaking his head at it, brushing away some ash. Then he looked up at Susan. *They spit, just in case you haven't noticed. Another thing you get used to.*

That's you, Son said, *because you look like a soldier. Your hair. And muscles.*

My muscles, said Locke, rolling his eyes.

Nobody spits on me, said Susan. *But the girls yell a lot. On Tu Do Street.*

232

Locke smirked. *They yell at me, too, but I can't believe they are saying the same thing as they do to you.*

Please, let's not discuss this, said Son. *Why must we reduce our conversation to what is being shouted on the streets?*

I was a little shocked, she said. *They don't look fifteen.*

They're not, Locke said.

Susan, they are afraid of you, offered Son. *That's why they shout. You are beautiful and, to them, exotic.*

You're the competition, said Locke. She gave him a sharp look. *Sorry.*

I have to say, they don't look *afraid,* said Susan. *And they are awfully loud.*

Locke said, *Their only verb is fuck.*

Did you know Tu Do used to be lovely? Son said. *But not any more. It is best now to avoid—*

Or more precisely, "fuck-fuck," continued Locke.

Susan, you must absolutely not pay attention to that place. Or this man. His partner is much more refined. Locke, you get worse when Davis is away.

Locke wagged his head slowly back and forth. *He's with his wife,* he moaned. *God, I wish I had a wife.*

It looks as though you do, said Susan, nodding at his ring.

Locke caught her gaze. *That,* he said with some disgust. *That's old. She ditched me and I can't get the damned thing off. I'll have to have it cut or something. But look around you. Would you go asking here for someone to cut the ring off your finger? They'd chop off your whole hand, stuff it in their pockets, and run to the next market stall to sell it!*

Oh, said Susan. She wished she'd said nothing. But Locke began to laugh.

Someone said put my finger in ice long enough, it'll shrink.

Ice, she repeated. She was still reeling from the idea of the chopped hand.

Now, Son said, *let's have a look at something else, shall we?*

233

He kept his photographs in a bag with his cameras and film. The bag was waterproof and light, the thick strap fitted over his shoulders, lying cross-ways against his chest. He unbuckled the bag and took out a short stack of black-and-white photographs, laying them out on the table. Susan instantly recognized the staff at the 18th Surgical in Pleiku. She saw the nurses in their stained smocks, the soldiers laid out in bed after bed so close together there was only room enough to walk between them. Right now, as she was sitting down with her coffee under the restaurant's cooling fan, Howe would be scrubbing his hands, debriding a wound, teasing out a jagged bit of metal from the pink flesh around it, trying to think about this one patient in front of him, instead of all the others who waited. She thought of Donna, who moved with enormous speed on her swollen legs. Donna had explained that if the swelling climbed higher than her ankle, they made her take R&R. *But they don't send me to no Hong Kong or nothing,* she said. *R&R here, in Pleiku, I mean, what good is that? The least they could do is let me have a few days in Saigon!*

Donna was in a number of Son's photographs. She had a wide open face, big dark eyes with a series of concentric circles around them, as though she hadn't slept in years. She was going prematurely gray and had colored her hair; the effect was that it frizzed a little, looking like an ill-fitting cap on her large head. But she looked cheerful in the photographs. She had a lopsided smile, an off-center front tooth. Susan remembered watching Donna turn a patient and how the muscles in her forearms stood up. She'd trust Donna with anything, she thought. Even in the photographs she came across as competent and in charge.

There were photographs, too, of each of the men, the casualties who lay in beds by the dozen. Some of the pictures showed more bandage than soldier. Some showed the cheerful smiles of those who, she supposed, were just grateful to be alive. They held up peace signs to the camera, looking like big kids.

What about the POW who died? Did you get any of him?

Son seemed not to remember who she meant, which she found odd. She was sure he would have noticed him. But he said he had not. He hadn't understood the importance of the prisoner, he explained. He'd just been taking pictures with American papers in mind. And besides, if he got in the way that nurse kept at him like a chained watchdog.

That's because she knew you were trouble, said Locke. *She saw through all your disguises.*

My disguises! That is a good funny joke, Locke.

Susan shuffled through some more photographs. Howe looked just as strung out and exhausted in the pictures as he did in real life. There was one of him changing his shirt and you could see his hipbones sticking out, the sunken belly, the wasting muscles. It was the Dexedrine. It did that to you.

And there was one of Susan, kneeling in front of a wounded marine, her Leica aimed right at him, his eyes locked on to her own. He was bound into a metal transport stretcher, freshly lifted off a helicopter. He was high on morphine but even so the muscles around his jaw were clenched in pain. Two minutes later he would be lifted straight into surgery with no time for X-rays, but in the photograph there is just him and her, and the effect was chilling, as though she didn't have any other goal but getting him framed in that lens. As though she didn't care.

I thought you might use one or two for your piece, Son said now. *Free.*

Don't you believe it, said Locke.

Susan said, *We can't use your pictures and not pay you.*

Oh, you'll end up paying, all right, Locke laughed. *The guy is Vietnamese. You hear me? Vi-et-nam-ese. He'll find a way of getting the money out of you.*

Please, Son said. He looked at her urgently. *I would like so much to be in an American newspaper.*

235

Your work's been in plenty American papers, said Locke. To Susan, he said, *Don't let him charm you.*

Son said, *No money. Just a credit.*

Again, he's bullshitting, said Locke.

She told Son she wrote for an American women's magazine. That she was here to cover stories of particular interest to women.

Yes, he said, nodding his head. She was almost sure he had no idea what she was talking about. There was no such magazine for women here in Saigon, not one that would offer the same kind of features. The women in Vietnam were a diverse bunch. You'd see them filling sandbags, or breaking up concrete with pickaxes, doing laundry, cooking in the street, calling out to GIs, riding their bicycles in their flowing *ao dzais* which made them even more beautiful than they already were, but she had seen nothing to suggest that they read anything.

It is a national magazine? was his only question.

She nodded. *Of course.*

She told him she had two rolls of film of her own that the magazine could use for free, though she admitted his pictures were better. If he really wanted her to try for him, she'd send the prints with the film, but it didn't mean anything would happen.

Son smiled. He stacked the photographs for her and placed them carefully into a manila folder. On the back of each was faint pencil, indicating his name, the place the photograph was taken, and a description of the contents. For the one of Susan photographing the marine, the caption read, "American journalist, Susan Gifford, working in Pleiku, 1967."

May I keep this? she asked.

Of course! I am delightful! he said, giggling.

You mean, delighted, said Locke.

Well, wouldn't you be? said Son. *If you were me, that is?*

I'd be trying to get my job back at UPI, Locke said, then quickly glanced at Susan. *No offense,* he said.

236

No offense taken. I am not an employer.

Son packed up the rest of his bag and left her with the photographs, going to the bar once more for coffee.

I'm warning you, said Locke, *he's a sneaky bastard. He has something planned. Maybe he's hoping for an American girlfriend.*

She didn't know how to answer that. She wasn't sure she liked Locke and so, if anything, his disapproval of Son worked in the other man's favor. She was thinking anyway of how, if she worked with Son, she would have no problems with language. Her ability to write about people in the countryside would open up. Her inexperience, the fact she was a woman, that she did not have an association with one of the wires, would be less of a hindrance. Son looked over from the bar, smiling. Nothing about his manner made her feel he was looking for a girlfriend. The man genuinely appeared to want a job. She looked down at the photograph he'd taken of her, imagining his seeing her just so, her face through his eyes.

How does he know my last name? she asked Locke.

Locke frowned. *Goddamn Son, he knows everything.*

She prefers Long Hair to the other two. He is older, for one thing, and seems to possess an intelligence she can connect with. The Thin One is a wild card—she will avoid him as much as possible. Gap Tooth, with his sword and the giggling triumph with which he captures the insects to barbecue in his bowl of smoking charcoal, fascinates her. She hears him talking to himself, entertaining his teenager's mind with stories, she imagines involve great heroism on his part and not a small amount of bloodshed.

Long Hair is a leader. She has seen him squatting on the ground explaining to the other two where they will go now, what they will do—at least she assumes that is what he is saying. He uses his hands in a manner not unlike one of her professors at university, who brought out the gravity of words through gesticulations so concise and well timed they seemed to contain a language of their own. The other two nod, occasionally asking a question. They do not challenge Long Hair, but neither are they afraid of him.

Susan once heard her father explaining how they were able to pick out the soldiers with leadership potential, those who would one day guide and direct the very men with whom they stood shoulder-to-shoulder in lines, with whom they ate and bunked and endured long drills. It was a matter of looking not so much at the individual as the way in which others responded to him. Did he offer practical solutions that made sense to the other men? Did they listen to him? Had her father been present, had Long Hair been one of the thousands of young soldiers that her father must have seen through his years in the military, he'd no doubt have selected the boy for officer training. Of course, for the Vietcong, there would be a much different system. Or so she imagines anyway. Before now, she has only ever seen VC as prisoners or casualties. How the three before her fit into the larger picture is anyone's guess. Long Hair is not an officer. And there's nothing about his clothes—plain, washed out, threadbare—to indicate he had any rank at all. Even so, he is a leader.

Long Hair's true name, she discovers, is Anh. He has not told her this, but in the hours listening to the soldiers' conversations as they course through the jungle, she has picked out the name Anh associated with him. She has noticed that Son addresses him this way, and that Anh speaks to him more often than to the others. It would be like Son to ingratiate himself to the man who mattered, though not in his usual manner of appearing innocent, harmless, unthreatening, not the same charm with which he had moved so easily among the Americans. He seems to understand that, in this case, such a ruse would be useless, even dangerous, and so instead presents to the leader the opportunity of a right-hand man. She has noticed how Son often walks point with Anh, how he positions himself next to him when they sit down. He is entirely different from how he was when in Saigon, suddenly himself a soldier, an equal, a fighting man. Perhaps in the end, Son will convince his captors in the same way he has been able to persuade everyone else to do what he wants, by assuming whatever traits of personality are required. She thinks that this quality is not one that was ever described by her father when listing the attributes of a leader, and she wishes now she'd asked her father how the American military undertook recruitment of its spies.

She calls to Anh, using his name, and he turns as naturally as if she has always addressed him so. He is holding a water coconut that they will eat later, a thing the size of a pumpkin. His hair, parted down the middle, is less caked with mud than hers, but even so it clings to his scalp, dry now. He looks at her casually. The days of narrowing his eyes at her, baring his teeth that small amount, steadying his hands on his rifle when looking her way, those days are over. She has become so unthreatening she might as well be a mascot, like one of the dogs seen with American units, inevitably named after a fighter plane or perhaps the place where they picked up the dog or where it began to follow them. Anh steps toward her, his shoulders relaxed, flicking a mosquito from his arm. He uncases a cigarette from a box he keeps in his pocket, bending over the flame as he lights it. The cigarettes are not one brand but a mix of different brands and roll-ups, which cast a smell that does not resemble the tobacco of Americans. In the same box as the cigarettes he keeps half-spent butts, and broken wooden matches that she supposes he might use again, though she has no idea why. She has seen him lining up the broken match-sticks on top of the map he studies, which darkens with an encroaching fungus, so that it appears at times the landscape is narrowing into a shadowy fuzz. She has no idea where they are located now in this jumble of wilderness. She must remember to ask Son. He would know, or at least have a fairly accurate guess.

"Anh," she says. "Could we find some water to bathe in?" She imagines he is just as uncomfortable as she is. She has seen him scraping the mud off the backs of his hands with his fingernails. She has noticed, too, how he twiddles locks of his hair between his fingers so that the mud flakes off. The discomfort of the dried mud is such that Susan holds her fingers apart, rubbing the skin between them. She brushes her hands over her clumped hair, wipes her forearm across the cracking mud in the folds of her neck. She knows she has leeches, too, and it occurs to her now, all at once, why Anh has kept his spent matches: to relight as torches in order to burn off the leeches once his cigarettes run out. The matchsticks are a good tool for the job, though not as good as cigarettes, which do not require being relit. She wonders if the careful manner with which he holds on to the matchsticks means that Anh does not believe they will come across the rest of their unit any time soon. She hopes as much as the soldiers do that they find the remainder of their unit. The alternative is being hungry, tired, with no real rest or shelter or end to all the marching. That is what she really wants: to end this now. She indicates the mud on herself, shrugs her shoulders, and says, "Il pourrait nous faire malade." Anh nods in one swift movement, then carries on walking. He's gotten used to her schoolgirl French. His response, however, is usually the same. A nod, the command, "Tien." Sometimes he points with his arm, sometimes his gun.

"The mud is awful," she says. "And unhealthy."

But he only tells her to keep walking, nodding in the direction they are going, concentrating on the path ahead.

"Yes, all right," she says, rolling her eyes. In English she adds, "I have not forgotten I'm your prisoner, Decision Boy."

Son hears this and gives her an amused glance. Then he looks at Anh and mumbles something, possibly a translation

240

of her comment into Vietnamese, because suddenly Anh looks back at her and, for the first time, she sees him smile.

There is no longer any distinction between inside and outside; she feels part of the jungle and moves through it as though through a roomy mansion, discovering always some new feature. Some details are not important: the way the branches contrive to find space to grow, the way logs disintegrate under the savagery of termites. But just as she has discerned Anh's name, she has also begun to make out the signs the Vietcong use to signal to each other which trails are safe and which are not, and it is as though she has discovered a new language. The gathering of grass together, knotting it in a particular fashion, the breaking of branches at certain turns of the trail so that it could be followed safely without fear of booby-traps, these are the things that Anh watches for. She wondered—she used to wonder—how it was that the Vietcong didn't die in the same mines that killed and maimed Americans by the thousands. It was because they set messages for each other in the grasses and trees, reading easily this code of the bush. The language has evolved through decades of war. It seems so remarkable, this discovery, that she wishes to share it. In her mind she taps out the keys of a typewriter. She can picture the keyboard exactly, and so imagines the letters G and H on either side of the central bone of her palate. The P is next to her second molar, the T and Y form her eye teeth. The way she keeps her sanity, one of the ways, is to tap out words in this fashion. With her tongue, she now writes, *We think we have been at war a long time. Three years now, depending on where you begin to count, but the Vietnamese have made war against intruders for many decades. There are signs of this everywhere, in the knotted grass, the snapped-off branches, the twisting trails that wind in a manner that seems pointless to an outsider. There is a point to everything. Communication lines coil through every mile of the jungle. The landscape itself is set up for war.*

241

Son looks at her, no doubt noticing the way she is moving her mouth. She shakes her head, indicating there is nothing the matter, and they walk on.

Once the evening has lapsed into darkness, they have to bunch up to stay together. It is then that she realizes how much they all smell; not that this small matter bothers her. The night is alive with the sounds of insects. They walk in a blur of darkness surrounded by the unseen vibrations of wing tips, of whistles, crackling branches, the wormy glow of fungus on the jungle's floor, all of them filthy, all of them tired enough they might just lie down at any moment and sleep like enchanted, doomed children. Before now she thought of the Mekong as a place of endless water, and this description is true for the most part. But the jungle is a troublesome tangle, difficult to get through, and not all of it is water, not in the least. It is mud and rot and mist, but not water, not clean water, in any case.

She thinks of Marc, who said that when he first came to Vietnam he memorized all the different names of the trees there, banyan, ironwood, umbrella, rubber, teak, aquilaria, aloeswood, and then forgot them all, deliberately, aggressively. *Why,* she'd asked him? *Because I didn't want to know any more,* he said.

She understands now what he meant, that you reach a kind of saturation point. Whenever possible, she tunes out of the jungle, pushes the Delta from her mind, absents herself from her present company and concentrates instead on things in the past. She does not want the giant dark leaves, the gnarled peeling bark, the vines and roots and mysterious, poisonous berries, everything for the moment shrouded in darkness so complete it is as though a cape has been thrown over the whole of the rainforest, to become so familiar that it replaces what she still thinks of as her real life. She struggles to recall as much detail as possible about Saigon, the bend of the roads, the canopy of shade allowed by the plane trees, the clamor of traffic, the silky warm evenings in which she wore dresses with bare shoulders.

She thinks of Marc, of how he waited for her outside the hotel, or rested his hand on her back as they walked, or how he kissed, or talked, his head bobbing slightly as he recalled something important about a story he'd covered. She remembers the sound of the air conditioning in his hotel room, the ornate molding on the ceilings, the olive carpet, the great swags of silk that made up the curtains in his favorite restaurant, how they waited at airports, never sitting together lest she endure the gossip, how they arranged to see each other by cabling:

STAY IN DANANG STOP AM ON THE WAY STOP.

She prefers to think of these things rather than the fact that the bandages on her feet (the torn fabric of Son's trouser legs) are now caked in mud, the sandals embedded with the same. Her fatigues are loose and she sometimes twists the waistband around her finger to make them tighter because, of course, the soldiers have taken her belt. How much harm could she do them with a belt? She supposes she could try to strangle one of them, but how far would she get before being shot by one of the other two? She considers asking for the belt again, or making one out of dry reeds. Her hipbones stick out, her shape more boyish by the day.

"What's that one called?" she asks Son, nodding toward Gap Tooth.

"Minh," he whispers.

The name sounds familiar to her. As soon as she hears it she thinks how she ought to have known this was the case. She imagines (perhaps incorrectly) that it was not Anh who decided to take her boots and make them into explosives but Gap Tooth, Minh, who seems always to be searching the jungle, looking for something to sabotage or kill or scar with his sword, which he no longer plays with quite so much, but which he carries nonetheless, as a boy might carry a toy pirate sword. The Thin

243

One trails behind, somehow deflated by his earlier outburst. She notices that Son walks between the Thin One and herself. She is grateful. She does not trust that soldier; he could attack her again at any time; he could shoot her through the back as she walks and she would never know. In the dim light, she cannot easily see him and anyway she is drained of energy. From the bombing, from what happened in the shelter, from the mud and insects, from being scared and sick, from being attacked and getting up again, from walking through the absurdly dark night, from the whole concentrated, awful effort.

She pulls up her fatigues once more and her hand catches on the plastic edge of her MACV card that Son stole back for her. She thinks of how he held her through all the artillery down in that terrible hole. She could feel anything toward him right now—love, betrayal, gratitude, need. She has felt all these things at different times, but there is no room for emotions now, for the five of them must walk, must keep walking. She cannot imagine getting back to Saigon, being again among the busy lanes, seeing the women gathered in the area outside her hotel, gossiping on the steps. An aging colonial building, the hotel had a grand sweep of stairs, showing signs of decay now, with troughs of rough earth in which silvery stems of weeds and grasses poked through. She cannot imagine climbing those crumbling steps, passing through the heavy, unguarded doors, requesting her key, finding her room, her bed, her clothes. To think she has so many clothes: cotton dresses and collared shirts and blue jeans and summer slacks, clean towels and underwear, a nightgown, coat, belts, scarves. All of them stacked in drawers, set out in a basket by the window, hung up over doors or on the small rail in the cupboard. It seems to her extraordinary, all those clothes. She feels a swell of homesickness; she feels herself wandering like a lonely ghost.

The blackness of the night is solid like a wall. They are hidden from each other and from the world, and the darkness, like darkness everywhere, makes her honest and foolish, makes her bold. Nobody can see as she reaches back, taking Son's hand. His fingers encase her own so effortlessly. They walk easily together, though they smell of rotting earth and have so much mud on them it is like they have taken a second skin. Even with this, they are comfortable with each other. It is an intimacy she will never know again, and she would do well to notice it, even more than the croaking of frogs, the abrupt, jarring sound of branches overhead, the unbearable darkness, or the fading memories of the city she has left.

"The third is named Hien," whispers Son. It is a miracle how he can time his words to the exact moment of another sound— this time of Minh coughing—so that their conversation is between them only, contained in the small space between them. She thinks, not for the first time, that it is as though Son possesses a sixth sense, or that he is aware at all times of everything around him. She forgets, or perhaps has never understood, that the jungle is not so foreign to him, that hunger is a condition he has passed through many times and that he treats it as one might an inconvenient virus, like a cold. That he is not truly captive, as any day now they will find the rest of the unit and eventually the officers who will know who he is, or take him to those who do. He is one of their own, not among the enemy, as she reminds herself they must properly be called. If Son is fearful it is only for her sake. He holds her hand with its coating of mud, touching the delicate fingers. She feels for the reassuring pulse in the crook of his thumb. Her fingers are longer than his, though his palm is blocky and wider. They fit together; they have always fitted, always belonged as one. She realizes this now and the thought, arriving in such circumstances, is as unexpected as the call of a nightjar in this dark forest, a sound she knows so well from home.

Weeks earlier she and Son made a trip to a civilian hospital in the Highlands. They flew to Kontum, skirting the blue-green hills, heading for a wide, dusty track that served as a runway between them. She looked down at the houses with their lush gardens, staked with bamboo, ringed now by the same concertina wire that surrounded American bunkers. She thought how once long ago this would have been a pleasant place. They were flying with equipment that was being delivered to the hospital in Dak Nhon, just south of Kontum, some kind of barter with the military. There were always these excursions with equipment or food or blood or mechanical parts. At different times they had traveled with ammunition and crates of grenades, which made her nervous, but it did not seem to bother Son. He'd sit on top of the boxes, resting, relaxed, his eyes closed.

Closer now she could see the goats with their dainty legs and low-slung bellies, ambling among rusting Food-for-Peace cans embedded in the dried mud near the runway. An ambulance sat near by, a jeep trailer attached to it, empty. She thought how ominous the ambulance looked, parked by the runway, as though anticipating somebody's disastrous landing, but it turned out the ambulance was their taxi, the trailer a bed for the generator the hospital staff thought they were receiving. There was no generator, of course. Only batteries and a few other parts.

The driver was a thin German wearing a T-shirt and jeans. He had watery blue eyes irritated by the sun, a lot of dark blond hair and the beginnings of a beard. He waved, then pulled his hand back to shield his eyes from the small pebbles and clumps of dried earth sent up from the ground by the windstorm created by the chopper rotors. When the rotors slowed he jogged in their direction, then walked the rest of the way as if the effort to run had defeated him.

Not a smile or a handshake. *Welcome*, he said, but he didn't appear at all interested in Susan and Son. He put his head inside the chopper door, looking for the goods he hoped had

246

arrived. The staff believed they had bartered for a new generator, not just parts to fix the old one, which hadn't worked in months. It was a disappointment to discover this was not the case, and when he saw that there was no generator, only parts, he became agitated. He marched to the pilot, explaining that they were meant to have an entire generator, that they didn't have a mechanic and though the car batteries might come in useful, could someone at least come out to help them fix the generator, assuming it was not beyond repair?

He sounded impatient; it was not the way Susan was used to hearing civilians speak to military. She and Son hung back, trying to distract themselves from the conversation, which ended with the German shaking his head and turning in a huff toward the ambulance, its dented fenders and fading paint giving it a dry, reptilian appearance, like a crocodile in the sun. *This is typical!* said the German, as the chopper pilot smoked a cigarette and surveyed the surrounding countryside, the desolate houses, the bushy, low trees, his face registering a lazy indifference which seemed to further annoy the other man.

Are you coming, then? The German said, glancing over his shoulder at Susan and Son. He pointed his chin to the ambulance and they followed a few feet behind as he walked, his steps purposeful, his hands balled into fists. There was a splatter of ink across the hip pocket of his jeans, a water bottle on his belt. He muttered, *We cannot get any supplies and when we do, they spoil. Primitive refrigerators, no reliable electricity!* He dropped into the driver's seat, his boots resting on a worn patch of carpet rugged up so that it showed the metal underneath. *We have no blood, you know,* he said. *No blood bank.*

The door creaked loudly as he slammed it shut, the window rattling. Then he reached across the seat and pushed open the other door for Susan, while Son found a place in the back.

She got out her pad. She thought perhaps the man was telling her this because he wanted her to write down the information.

Has this always been the case, or only recently, when your gener-
ator went down? she asked. Perhaps that was the trouble, that
they could not keep the blood cold. She assumed it was a new
problem. She couldn't imagine how they could have coped very
long without any blood at all.

How would I know? he said. He couldn't look at her because
the sun swept through her window straight at his shoulder,
blinding him if he turned in her direction. He drove with one
hand on the steering wheel, another spread like a visor over
his eyes, ducking and peering through the bright sunshine.
There was a fly on his hair and on his thumb, Susan saw, flies
on the dashboard, buzzing against the windshield. *I've only
been here six months,* he said. *It seems a lifetime, but that is what
the calendar says. Only six.*

The ambulance seats were split, the torn vinyl stiff and sharp.
The dashboard looked slightly melted. The doors were wired
on and they rattled with every turn and pothole as the ambulance moved along a dusty, gray road pitted with craters. The
trailer bounced behind them, empty. In the back, amongst an
assortment of other boxes, including a set of tools which might
have been kept there in case of breakdown, were the batteries
and parts.

The German told them his name: Jonas.

How do you get blood? Susan asked. *When you need it, how
do you . . .* For a moment she had the awful thought his answer
would be that they did *not* get blood. That they did without,
and that the patients died. Hadn't she seen similar, unbearable
circumstances already in the country? Burn victims whose
bodies resembled unfinished wax mannequins, a starving baby,
lying in a cardboard box, an old man smoking a pipe through
the bones of his amputated forearm?

We have a card catalog of names, Jonas sighed. They were
heading south across the Dak Bla, Kontum's river, past the
sprawling Command Control Central, out into the jungle. *We*

go directly from one person to the other, checking the dates they last gave.

I see.

It is very—he hesitated, searching for a word—*strenuous.*

They drove in silence now, the landscape increasingly rural and wild, until at last they reached a cluster of low buildings arranged around a dusty courtyard. The hospital was run by a woman doctor from America. She was waiting at the door when the ambulance arrived.

What's going on? she said. *The trailer is empty. Didn't they meet you?*

No generator, Jonas said. He walked past her, shaking his head.

The doctor followed. *Where are you going? What did they say? I should have got out my damned self!* she called.

Jonas wheeled around. *There was nothing I could do! If I'd let him take the parts back, then we'd have nothing.*

No, I mean I ought to have gone and watched and made sure they loaded the thing!

Susan and Son followed the woman doctor inside, where the air was stale but at least somewhat cooler. The doctor was well known for helping the Montagnards, an indigenous group who came under pressure from both the North and the South Vietnamese. Among the Montagnards, infant mortality was so high they didn't celebrate a child's birth before the age of two. If a person died outside the village, their body was not allowed back for burial. Sometimes grief-stricken parents kidnapped their own sick children from wards, stealing them back in the night so that they could die within the village, where their spirits were believed to stay for eternity. The nurses were always on guard for such thefts, but many of the nurses were themselves Montagnards, and they understood. Even so, they lost children to this practice who would otherwise not have died.

She learned this upon entering the hospital, within the first few minutes, listening and nodding and writing as quickly as she could while following the doctor, who walked briskly ahead. The doctor had shock of light hair that stood up, a narrow waist, long legs. A man's watch hung from her belt loop and she frequently pushed back a stethoscope that kept working its way out of her front pocket. The doctor explained who these mountain people were, why she'd come to the Highlands, what the hospital tried to provide. She showed Susan and Son where to put the car batteries, which they were carrying. Between the commentary and instructions she interrupted herself to address her patients, using a mixture of English and Vietnamese, sometimes a bit of French, and wrote notes to herself on the inside of her arm. When she greeted Susan, a cigarette hanging in her lip, the first thing she said was, *You look fresh out of high school.* To Son, she only nodded. She seemed to take an immediate dislike to him. Susan noticed this; she was used to Americans reacting this way to Son. The soldiers were worse.

We get mostly orphans and young mothers, said the doctor. *Nobody over the age of forty.*

Why is that? Susan asked.

The doctor wore an expression as though it was tiresome to explain. *Well, it isn't because we refuse people over forty. I am over forty.* She looked up at the ceiling and sighed. *The life expectancy of a Montagnard is, let's see, about half of an American's, though not an American over here, I must say.*

Was the doctor making a joke? Susan thought so at first, but this was not the case. The doctor's gaze trailed a Montagnard nurse in a nun's white habit, its hem dusty, the nurse's hands dry and small. The nurse brought water to a patient, cradling the man's head as he drank from a polished gourd. It made a nice photograph and Son framed the image in his lens, the doctor watching with a mildly disapproving look.

Do you not want him to take pictures? Susan asked.

It isn't that.

Then . . . She wanted to say: Then what is the trouble?

You know what the Vietnamese call them, don't you? the doctor said. She slapped at a mosquito, gave Son another dark look.

Call who?

The Montagnards. The people here. The ones in the damned beds. You know what they call them?

Susan shook her head.

Moi, said the doctor. *Savages.*

I see.

Do you think that's right? She was glaring at Susan as though examining her thoughts, which Susan reminded herself were unknowable to the doctor, however much she stared.

The doctor said, *What about your friend? Does he think that's right?*

Susan put her pen in her pocket and said, *You'd have to ask him.*

The doctor leaned back against a wall now, looking down at Susan from what seemed a great height. Susan cleared her throat, about to speak.

She was interrupted by Son, who said in French, *Tell the lady doctor that it was the French who first spoke of them as Montagnards. They call themselves the Degar people, but mostly they refer only to their individual tribes.*

What is he saying? the doctor asked. She stepped toward Son. *Que vous dîtes?*

I said thank you for allowing me to photograph your patients, Son replied in English.

You might ask them! the doctor shot back, then moved on so swiftly that Susan had to hurry after her through the crowded ward. The hospital smelled of disinfectant and urine warmed in the heat. There were other smells, too: camphor, stale sweat, the musty wetness of wounds, discarded dressings, iodine, salt. The doctor was regularly interrupted by the relatives of the sick as she walked her rounds, which made everything take twice

251

as long. Surrounded by relatives of the wounded—who wanted baby food, penicillin, injections, food, tablets of various kinds— she looked like Gulliver among the Lilliputians.

Pardon me, Susan said, as she stepped over a child who might have belonged to a woman who sat at the bed of another girl (her daughter?) who had taken shrapnel to her face and neck, a few other children playing idly on the floor.

Dysentery, tuberculosis, malaria, injuries from mines (very common), injuries from burns, the doctor was saying, calling out these ailments as Susan followed, trying not to step on the baskets and water bottles, piles of clothes and native blankets, the occasional dog.

We got some mysterious *parasites that seem to kill within a few days,* the doctor said. *A fair bit of plague—*

Plague? Bubonic plague?

Yeah, bubonic. There's a number of different strains. Not too hard to treat, if you get it in time.

A naked toddler wandered into Susan's path and she stepped over him, nearly colliding with someone else. The child belonged to a family who sat on the floor beside one of the beds. The mother—Susan assumed it was the mother—was arranged over a fold-up metal chair, from which she leaned down over a mattress, asleep. An older child, perhaps seven years old, was in the bed. She did not look awake, or asleep; most of her face was obscured in an arrangement of bandages. Above her, an IV bottle perched precariously on the thin arm of a metal stand.

Burn victim. The doctor shook her head. *I don't like that one.*

At midday there was soup in wooden bowls, fed to the patients with hand-carved spoons. The soup was either brought in by the families, or prepared on the hospital grounds over wood fires. Perhaps it was just as well that relatives helped provide meals, because there did not seem to be enough, not for the patients, not for the staff. Susan and Son were offered some weak coffee but nothing to eat. She grew hungry. Son had the habit of stuffing boiled eggs into his pack, and she thought about how she might make an excuse and go find one now. Her stomach rumbled and she coughed, trying to hide it.

What's the matter? said the doctor. *Lunch reservations cancelled?*

She might have disliked the woman more, but the doctor attended to the sick with inexhaustible patience and concern. She did not berate them, as Susan had seen army doctors do when setting up field operations for peasants, telling them with frank disgust that they needed to keep their children *clean*, that they needed to feed their babies *more*. This doctor, by contrast, seemed to understand there was never enough of anything. Food or water, soap, medicine, medics, milk—the list was endless. There didn't even seem to be sufficient bandages to change the dressings as often as she would like, and she was cross when the filthy bandages could not be replaced. The nurses could be seen scraping the residue off old dressings and reusing what was left of the cotton, a practice that the doctor seemed to object to even as she helped. *That one is finished,* she said of one of the dressings. *Throw it away. But here, this one is okay. Tape it back on. Who is working in Supply? Tell them to get some more dressings over here!*

I hear there's no blood bank, Susan said. *What happens when you have a lot of surgeries?*

We trade with the military, liquor for blood.

Susan smiled. *I would have thought they had a lot more liquor than you.*

The doctor laughed. *They do—a lot more liquor. But they also have more blood.*

When Susan's stomach rumbled again, the doctor said, *There's bread in the supply room. There might even be some butter, if you are very lucky.*

A baby died. She walked into a hall area where the parents were being told the news, their heads bent to their chests, their arms slack, saying nothing other than to thank the staff. The staff were always thanked, no matter the outcome. The baby was lying listless as dough in a package of pale cloth. She could not bear to see, but neither could she move her eyes from the couple.

What will happen now? she asked the doctor.

What happens all the time, was the reply.

She walked miles, it seemed, following the doctor from patient to patient, listening to the steady stream of information from the older woman, who did not take a coffee break, let alone a lunch break. Around sunset, they were corralled with a number of others into the ambulance once more, this time to the doctor's house for dinner. This was a normal practice, not a special dinner because journalists had arrived. *We're going,* Jonas said by way of invitation. He was in the same dark mood he'd been in before, a permanent condition it had to be assumed, his blond hair wagging as he moved with heavy steps toward the ambulance. He'd taken off his doctor's coat and wore a green T-shirt, same as the army wore. He had a long torso, strong legs. He might have been a soldier, except for the hair.

They took off beneath a blazing red and orange sky. The road was cratered so that the drive felt like a carnival ride. She and Son sat in the area meant for casualties, ducking their heads beneath the ambulance roof as they bumped along. In the front passenger's seat, the doctor held herself against the rocking motion of the vehicle, looking uncomfortable, exhausted. She hung her cigarette out the window and occasionally took an unsteady drag between the jarrings of the road. Something must have been paining her because she winced over the really big bumps. Susan tried to guess her age—forty-five? She had sallow skin and one of those lean faces that could be any age, a few creases that ran the length of her cheeks. Not yet fifty, Susan thought. Fifty seemed incredibly old in Vietnam.

We do need all four of these tires, the doctor told Jonas.

I can do nothing about the road, he replied. He began again to talk about all the things they needed—this was apparently a set speech for him. It was a long list and the doctor rolled her eyes. Susan caught her expression in the rear-view mirror, and it made her laugh. The doctor smiled, then looked away. Jonas said, *What? Is this so funny?*

The doctor touched him lightly on the arm in a maternal, tender way. *Right about now is shut-up time,* she said.

The doctor's house served as a canteen and supply store, a temporary home for new employees, a place for meetings and rest. It was surrounded by bougainvillea and a climbing frangipani that was so successful it threatened to invade the roof. The house appeared to have various outbuildings, one of which was missing a wall.

They were asked if they were hungry, thirsty, if they wanted to share a bed. This last question was meant to be ironic, as if they could never have wanted such a thing. The doctor spoke the words with a cunning air, tinged with disapproval. It inflamed Susan the way she said it like that, especially as the doctor knew that Son spoke English. For a moment she thought of saying yes, she did want to share a bed with Son, just to surprise the woman. She would have respected that, Susan thought. She seemed like the sort of person who held in regard those who were willing to break the rules. Who knows, she might even have thrown a polite word in Son's direction. But there was no time to reply. They were interrupted by two little girls who came running into the room, Montagnard children who it turned out the doctor had adopted after their mother was killed. Susan watched the doctor gather them up in her arms, her smile newly rekindled.

You both stink*!* she said, nuzzling her face in their necks.

There were a few nurses, an administrative assistant, some

others Susan wasn't sure about, plus Jonas, who was no more relaxed here at the doctor's house than he had been at the hospital. He was going to eat quickly and return to work, he declared, speaking to no one in particular. *That's a good boy*, said the doctor, then went to sit in a big armchair over which was draped a macramé throw, her girls crawling over her. That seemed to be a cue for the others and they all dropped into the cluttered sofas and boxes that served as seats in the main room. There was beer on a table made from a discarded crate, big jugs of water, peanut butter, some saltines in a jumbo-sized box. These things were passed around, as were a number of cigarette packs, and some photographs taken at a party. Then, suddenly, the doctor was called outside because the cook had seen a snake. The cook was terrified of snakes. The doctor watched the grass as the creature slithered slowly away from the house. *We should eat it*, she said. Everyone laughed, except the cook, who looked sullen and said nothing.

The cook was Vietnamese. Jonas told Susan that her husband was a VC province chief, but when Susan asked about her parents, where she was from, how many brothers and sisters, she wouldn't say anything at all. Either she did not understand Susan's French or she was reluctant to admit even what was for dinner that night. Clearly, there would be no answers. The cook went about performing her kitchen duties as though there was nobody else in the room.

She's always a little strange after she sees a snake, the doctor said. *And you can take it from me who her husband is. If I could find another cook, I'd hire her. But I can't. She's only a little crazy, so she stays.*

She said this in English, speaking over the cook's head. The cook was mashing spices in a bowl beside a small stack of yams with muddy roots. She didn't look up. She had a wide, low forehead, small eyes, a bewildered, piggy expression. Her appearance made her seem vacuous, like a rather dull, ugly sister destined never to leave home. She had a nervous disposition, and did everything in a flurry. On the floor and the coarse wooden table at which she worked there was evidence of many spillages; some of the fallen spices stuck to Susan's shoes. The air steamed from a pot of boiling water into which nothing, at present, had been added.

Son leaned against a wall and said, *Have you met the husband?*

The doctor glared at him. *No, of course I haven't met the damned husband.*

Son spoke in Vietnamese to the cook, who turned away from him but replied even so. He spoke again, and the girl responded in kind. She had a pretty voice, like a little bird. It contrasted with the rest of her appearance. She never once looked up but stared into the bowl in which she mashed and churned, speaking so quickly it was impossible to tell when one sentence ended and another began.

What did she say? the doctor asked.

She said she is busy, said Son.

That's not what she said. Tell me what she really said. She was talking about her husband—I got that much.

Son spoke again to the cook. This time there was a longer explanation, again spoken rapidly. Then she paused, her eyes darting from under a swatch of dark hair that had come loose from its tie, meeting Son's for a brief instant. Son nodded, indicating that he understood, and she continued in the same manner, speaking breathlessly in whispered chirpings that meant nothing to Susan. The language was confounding, the cook another example of people she could not know. Finally, the cook moved to another place in the kitchen, bringing the conversation to a close.

She says she is making dinner, Son reported.

The doctor glared at him. For a moment, she looked as though she would say something in anger, but she let it pass. *Well, praise God for that,* she said, exiting the room.

The little girls did not play with dolls but with toy helicopters, flying them around the lounge making *rat-a-tat-tat* noises. The room darkened with the sky. Dak Nhon had no electricity at night, not even for the hospital. That's why the generator had been so important. There was only one small generator that worked at present, as well as a kerosene autoclave that sterilized the surgical instruments, but night was a difficult time for them. With so many people stuffed into its wards, with no light except that of hurricane lamps and candlelight, the doctor worried there would one day be a fire.

It's just a matter of time, she said. She told her this while they moved through the house lighting candles, some of which had been made by melting together a collection of slimmer ones, with wicks that needed scraping before lighting. There were dinner candles stuck into the glass mouths of beer bottles, stubby ends of pillar candles with hollow centers that a match could barely reach, a fat oval of green that gave off a medicinal smell and was said to help guard against mosquitoes. *It doesn't appear too successful, however,* said the doctor. A few kerosene lamps and a battery-operated flashlight also helped illuminate the house. With sundown the temperature dropped so that goosebumps appeared on Susan's arms.

They ate dinner off their laps, all of them sitting in the glow of the candle flames. There were crocheted quilts and a few rough blankets draped over the furniture. The staff pulled them down on to their shoulders, over their uniforms or habits or T-shirts or smocks. A few people fell asleep on the sofas, their dinner bowls still in their laps. One of the nurses had made a pillow of a Pfizer box. Jonas wore a rainbow-colored cover and slept for half an hour or more. Susan would have liked to ask them some questions about their lives outside the hospital, but it was too late for that now.

They are like children, the doctor said, scanning the roomful of sleeping people. *Lights out, and they're off to sleep.*

When Jonas woke, he stood at once as though responding to an alarm. *I'm going back. Anyone else want to come?* he said, letting his rainbow cover slide to the floor.

Slowly, the sleeping figures came alive once more. Some left, some stayed. The house had the atmosphere of a train platform, with different people coming and going for reasons Susan could not discern.

Before the artillery begins, the doctor explained.

So that was it. When the outgoing began, everyone stayed where they were. In the hospital, or the house, or wherever they were found.

Within an hour it had started. The blasts shook the house, making its shutters rattle on their hinges. Tracers hung over the sky. They listened to the explosions, the whine that told them it was going away. Another, and another. The children went to bed late because they had been sleeping during the day. The doctor played a game with them like ring-a-ring o' roses but with different words and she and Son joined in. At some point, they were shown to a room with canvas cots (there weren't any beds in any case. The notion of sharing one had truly been a joke). The room had a sink in it, not fixed against the wall but on the floor, awaiting repair. There were piles of paper and boxes, medical supplies stacked in wood crates up along the walls. The crates wobbled with each blast, but luckily the fire was not returned and the outgoing died down.

She wrote her article by a smoking lamp that needed its wick trimmed. Son stood in the shadows, changing the film in his camera. He could do this in complete darkness, could probably do it blindfolded with one hand. In fact, she'd once seen him replace a broken part of the camera's interior with something he fashioned out of small pieces taken from the metal base of a lightbulb. But the night was not completely dark. She saw by starlight the white cotton taped over the hole on the inside of his elbow where they took blood from him that morning. She had the same. As it turned out, they shared the same blood type.

How long are you going to work?

Until this ends, she said, meaning the explosions.

It's not close—

She continued the thought for him, *Or aimed at us, or likely to fall short, but it still keeps me up.*

She fell asleep anyway. When she woke again she found herself on one of the cots, a thin blanket over her. It must have been Son who'd moved her, or maybe she'd walked sleepily to where she could lie down. She couldn't remember. She felt terribly thirsty. There was no water in the room and there was no toilet anywhere in the house. She was about to ask Son for the flashlight so that she could make her way outside when she heard a sound from across the room and realized that Son was singing. It was a quiet verse in Vietnamese; she had no idea what it meant. In another room there was a poker game going on. There was laughter, the occasional shuffling of cards, a round of betting. She could make out disparate comments: *You can tell how far south the VC have got by what strain of malaria the villagers come in with.* Or, *She named her daughter Ugly One so that the spirits wouldn't think her worth taking.* Meanwhile, Son sang on, his song interrupted only when he took a drag from his cigarette. He blew the smoke upward from where he lay on his own cot, then began the tune once more, beginning again on the exact note where he left off. He seemed to know Susan was awake. From the dark corner where he lay came his voice. He said, *The cleaner does dressings. It infuriates the nurses, though it has to be said he does a good job.*

A kind of jack-of-all-trades cleaner?

He wants to be a nurse.

Ah, well, I'm sure they can use more nurses.

Son said, *The children asked me if they can touch your hair.*

260

Susan smiled. *My hair feels like straw. Tell me, what did the cook say?*

Oh, the cook.

I heard you talking with her. After she saw the snake.

The cook says they are going to be overrun at any moment. That it has happened before, too. That she fears she will be killed.

Is she crazy? Like the doctor says?

No.

Is her husband really a VC province chief?

He was. She thinks he's dead now.

She was completely awake now. It might have been due to the thought of the Montagnard hospital being overrun by the North Vietnamese. It might have been because Son seemed to have an awful lot of information from so brief an exchange. There was something amiss. She knew there was something amiss. She told herself it was the thought of the hospital coming under attack. She did not like to think of what would happen to them all—the families, the children, the doctor and her loyal staff, the German, Jonas. Who would defend them?

She sat up. Often, in the middle of the night, she had more energy than she did the whole of the day. It was the heat, the clinging, stupefying, draining wet heat that depleted her. At night, she was free from it. The sound of the poker game made her think it could not be that late, that she ought to rise and do some work. But when she checked her watch she saw it was almost two in the morning. Even so, she would get up, she decided. She could organize her notes, fashion the first paragraph. It always helped if she framed the article before she wrote it out. She could do that now.

She crossed the room to Son, sitting on the floor next to him. She put two fingers out to ask for the cigarette, then fished out his water bottle from among his gear. They sat for a few minutes. In recent days he'd become oddly quiet, she thought. It might have been because of her own mood. Since she had stopped seeing Marc she'd been less upbeat; she'd wanted to work longer and harder. It was the one way of feeling better, she discovered, and so she stayed in the field as much as possible. She wanted to be away from Saigon—not that Marc was often there anyway, but his hotel was there, the restaurants he favored, the bar at the Rex. The whole city felt to her as though it belonged to Marc. It was hard not to think of him when she was there.

There was the gentle lifting sound of crickets pulsing their music into the night. The laughter from the card game floated around them. She could see the glow of candlelight from the area beneath the door into their room. *We might be in an English country house,* she said.

England? Son said. It made it sound far away, like Mars.

Well, not really. She was cross-legged next to him. He was sitting up now, elbows on his knees, looking toward the poker game. She swatted a mosquito, then rubbed it off her palm on to her trousers. *There are hardly any insects there. In England. Compared to here, you'd say there were none at all.*

Son smiled. *Your England,* he said, *sounds so very nice.*

It's not mine. It's only my passport that is British.

They smoked and listened to the voices next door. Through the walls she heard, *I told them bring the baby,* and then a long explanation she could not detect. She heard, *You can't persuade . . .*

They don't like me, Son said.

She nodded. *I know. I can't understand.*

Because I am Vietnamese. We are against the Montagnards.

Oh well, just— She was going to say ignore it. But hadn't that been what he'd done all day? Ignored it?

It is true, he concluded.

But not about you.

He sang his song again, then stopped. It was too dark to discern his expression. *I don't really care is the truth.*

262

That's not the same as being against.

It made her uncomfortable to hear this. It wasn't any different from how the military often spoke of villagers. They not only didn't care but seemed at times to completely loathe them. And anyone who knew the way the ARVN treated peasants knew they didn't care one way or another for their welfare. But she didn't like to hear this from Son. It surprised her. It made him seem brutal and unthinking. It made him seem like everybody else.

When they are overrun, I must remember that I don't care at all, he said.

They won't be overrun. I don't know what you're talking about. Anyway, you'd care plenty. He'd have to care. She knew he would; he was Son.

No, Susan, I won't.

If it happens—

It will—

You don't know that—

—and I won't care at all—

She found herself suddenly on her feet. There was a terrible pause and she felt awkward, standing there. It was as though she'd planned to storm out of the room and then discovered there was no place to go. She sighed. She couldn't figure out what to do with herself now. *She would be pleased to think we were arguing,* she said. *The doctor, I mean.*

Then we'll stop arguing. I am sorry. I shouldn't have said anything. It would bother you. He reached up his hand and tugged her gently down next to him. *Naturally, it would bother you,* he said.

She shook her head. She was upset and she had no idea why. *You can't care about absolutely everything around here. I don't suppose I do really—*

I hope you won't think less of me now.

Don't be silly, she said. *You're my friend, I love you—*It came

263

out so fast she could not stop it. She held her breath, waiting for his response. She wasn't sure he would even understand what she meant; the Vietnamese have four different words for love, all of which relate to stages of love affairs, and none of them were accurate in this situation. What she meant was that they had adopted one another, just as the doctor had adopted her own daughters, that she trusted him. She knew he was not perfect. He didn't have to be perfect.

He blew out a plume of smoke like a sigh. *Yêu quá,* he said, two words that translated into "so much love." She thought he was talking not only about them but about the people in the next room. About the Montagnard nurse who brushed the dust from her skirt hem and brought the gourd to each patient in turn, about the cleaner who wished to learn to change dressings and who attended a little room at the back of the hospital with a broken door and two rusted chairs, where the head nurse gave lessons to those who wished to work with patients. About the broody German, about the doctor with her new children. About all of them who came to help others and who had come to need help themselves.

The military will not necessarily defend them when they come under attack, Son said. *Not even Mike Force, or whoever they have ties with. Getting the mess officer to give you some steaks, that is one thing. That doesn't need the support of the higher-ups.*

They've probably already figured that out—

They couldn't even get a generator. He shook his head. He suddenly looked tired. *They have no idea how vulnerable they are.*

I'll write that in my piece, she said.

Son rubbed his forehead. *It won't make any difference.*

I'll write it anyway.

Time swells and diminishes in Vietnam. She might imagine that all this happened years ago, in another time, to people other than themselves. But, in fact, it was just over two weeks ago. She is sure of the date because she wrote the article, got on a chopper and cabled it the next morning from Danang. She knows when it ran and how many inches it was and which pictures they used. She knows exactly the date they sat in the doctor's house, listening to the card game in the other room, that it was a Tuesday and that earlier in the evening the sun had spread its colors out so that the room became red with its light. She had written it all down on the thin lines of her notebook, setting the notebook on to a stack of others with the date across the front.

It feels as though a decade has passed since then, that she is awake and reliving her life as though in a dream. She is hungry. The air strike scared away all the animals so that there is nothing for the soldiers to hunt for food. They walk and they look but the trees are empty except for their abundance of leaves and vines. There is some rice, but there hasn't been enough time to cook the little bit they still have and it is dark and they still haven't found the hamlet they are looking for. She has seen Anh consulting with Son about the direction they should take. It gives her a measure of reassurance to see Son involved in such decisions, because she knows him to be an excellent navigator. But so far today they've not come across anything that looks remotely like a village or a camp. No sign that people are here, were here, or will ever come here. It is a vast wilderness, more complicated than the most intricate labyrinth, and there seems no way out.

There is a pain behind her eyes. Her joints hurt: she can feel every vertebra in her back. She feels faceless, unidentifiable. It occurs to her that she may be getting ill at this most inconvenient time. What she would give now for that rusted ambulance, the lumpy sofas with their dusty coverings, the medical supplies in their boxes, the brusque discourteous doctor, the dark nurse whose fingers were the color of leaf bark.

As she thinks of it now, the hospital seemed a storehouse of abundance. She longs for their room with all the crates, the two small cots, the light of the candles, the comforting sound of laughter from next door.

"Will they be overrun, soon, do you think? The Montagnard hospital?" she asks Son. It is probably the furthest thing from his mind, but he answers without hesitation, as though he, too, has been thinking the same thing.

"Yes," he says. "They have a few months."

"You might have told them so. That would have been the decent thing."

Son squeezes her hand. "Susan," he says gently, "they *knew*."

"How could they know?"

"The cook would have told them."

"The cook?"

"Why do you think she was so scared?"

"But, then why—"

"Why do they stay? Because, I suppose, they feel they must."

The conversation takes place between stretches of silence in which it is only their footsteps they hear. Then, all at once, there is a long call from a tribe of monkeys, the scratching noise of animals scrambling through branches. Minh points his gun up to the dark trees but he cannot see and no shots are fired.

Susan says, "The doctor didn't believe her."

They walk few steps, considering this.

Son says, "That German one did."

The house, when she sees it, is so unexpected she cannot at first glean what it is. The mud walls are nothing more than darker objects against a black night. The straw roof resembles the low branches of trees. She sees the shape emerging in her vision and for all the surprise it gives her it might be an island rising up from the sea. The receding jungle, the shadows of coconut palms, the clearing to a door, all the familiar comforting geometry of four walls and the tidy results of human labor, astound her freshly as though she has never seen such things. Beside the house lies a network of narrow, shaded pathways of a small village, a pig corral fenced with low, dark wood, a boxed shelter for a chicken house. She smells kerosene, gasoline. A cooking smell, like so many smoking ovens. The village is silent, not even a dog barking, but the house is there, planted before them as though from some different, other world. All at once she craves water. Water and a chair.

They enter silently through what feels like a gap in the wall, filling the tiny house immediately. The straw roof with its peculiar smell is startling to her, and she finds herself looking up as though at the vaulted ceiling of a cathedral. Normally she would expect to be greeted by children. Always in the past when she has visited villages the children flock around her in abundance, sucking the sweet wood of sugarcane, calling out what few English words they know: *okay, coca, GI, money.* But it is late and quiet; perhaps the children are sleeping. She has seen that before, how they pile on beds made from planks, arranging themselves haphazardly like the coats of guests at a party. Older sisters, toddlers, slender boys with their bony spines, they sleep like puppies, pushed together on a bed next to an ancestral shrine.

"There are no people," she says now. "Again."

The house is so dark she cannot see the walls, nor determine where a table might be, a bed or a chair. She hears a few indeterminate noises. A creak, the thud of a footstep, something being dragged on the ground. It is Minh, his short legs uncommonly clumsy in the pitch black of the night, the sword dragging beside him against the hard earth of the floor. He arrives through the hut entrance, breathless, and speaks to the others.

"What is he saying?" she whispers.

267

Beside her, Son stands erect, his attention full on the soldiers. "That the hamlet is empty. Burnt. This is the only house standing," he says quietly.

She draws in a breath. She realizes that what she'd thought was the smell of the roof and of cooking fires was not the roof at all. It was the smell of burnt foliage, burnt houses. It is only that they happened upon the hamlet from a particular angle, so that in the blanket of night they did not see the destruction, the ruined garden plots, the sooty remnants of bamboo fences and lean-tos, the flattened remains of houses, the piles of scorched belongings. Because the razing of the hamlet has happened recently the rains have not had time to wash the remains into a muddy swell of debris. Anh gets out the penlight again, just as he did in the shelter, and casts its beam around them. This house, the one remaining house against dozens of collapsed others, is vacant, as far as she can tell. An empty shell of a room. All over the floor are candy wrappers and cans and cigarette butts and spent matches, signs of the soldiers who have been here.

She hears the word *Americans*. She looks briefly at Hien, wondering if he will blame her for this, too, wondering if they all will blame her. The three soldiers begin a fiery conversation, with Hien on one side of Anh and Minh on the other. She has no idea what they are saying. It is one of those arguments born of irritation and the fading possibility that their circumstances would now change for the better. They are all so hungry. They were always hungry—it has been almost a constant for many days—but tonight it is as though they are living at the very center of their hunger. They entered the ruined hamlet believing food would be found here—food, people, shelter—and they have discovered just as quickly that it will not. Their steps, which approached the house with energy born of hope, now slow, then stop so that now they all feel rooted to the ground like stones.

Anh is still holding the water coconut. It isn't what any of them want, that miserable fruit, still green. They want meat and vegetables, a bowl of rice with a salty broth, tea. They want the crispy skin of fried fish, some pork, especially that. They have been walking for so long. There are times when Susan has felt as though the long bones of her calves will push right through her ankles, through her heels, and down into the soft ground like stakes, that her depleted muscles and ligaments cannot hold the bones in place any longer. She is sure they all feel something similar, that the soldiers have reached a limit. She hears their voices rise up in the darkness. Hien begins yelling so that Anh speaks sharply to him. But his voice rises even more, sounding hysterical. It continues until Anh, in one awful moment, takes the water coconut and throws it on the ground so that it bursts, making a noise like an explosion, like a gun going off.

The sound makes her imagine—more than imagine, makes her *see*—a wooden sampan loaded with watermelons that blew up in the Cai Rang floating market in Can Tho. Son had been photographing the tangle of water traffic: so many boats and barges and sampans, the barefoot vendors in their conical hats, the tea women behind clouds of steam, children poking their heads from doorways of the houseboats, melon baskets, the hairy shells of coconuts, pineapples. She was writing in her notebook, her free hand shading her brow from the sun. The blast came from nowhere, a grenade that sent the harbor water raining from above. Son dropped his camera; the notebook suddenly disappeared like a bird that had flown. The noise was so loud she saw a young mother scream and it seemed as though the scream was silent. The harbor with its sampans and junks and houseboats and floating stores was now a sea of splintered wood and torn cloth, pieces of masts and hulls and baskets of fruit drifting in the water, bobbing like buoys. In the water, too, were people. They swam, yelling for one another, climbing into

269

the remaining boats. She could hear children crying. She could hear the panic and the cries and the fear. She ran for a wall, expecting another blast; she took out her camera. Two pictures: one of an old woman weeping, the other of the vendor, what was left of him.

All this comes to her in the single moment that Anh throws the melon on the ground. It is as though somehow the lid on her experience has been prised open and now floats about her so that at any moment she will be blinded by it. She thinks of Marc and his dreams and how he used to wake up in the night with that desperate desire to escape. *To escape what?* she used to ask. *The bed, the room, the hotel, the city?* No matter how hard she tried, she could not understand. Now she knows exactly. The muscles in her jaw contract and expand so that her face feels pulled. She feels her leg grow warm and has no idea why it is like that until she reaches down with her hand and understands, in a moment of slow awareness, that she has wet herself.

There is silence. Nobody dares move or speak until, at last, Son clears his throat. "There will be a pump. Or a well," he says in French.

"They will have ruined the well," Anh says.

"They forgot to destroy this house. Maybe they forgot the well, too. We're filthy. We need to bathe."

"Tôi nhìn tháy môt!" says Minh. *I saw one.* Or *I have seen one*, or *I will see one.* She isn't sure. In the darkness Minh looks like a child, his hair sticking out from all sides of his head like a hedge. In other circumstances, had he been born on the other side of the world, he'd be one of those youths who was good at many things, but whose ceaseless energy made them tiresome to adults, so that they ended up in trouble all the time. The sort of teenager who made knives out of soda cans and painted post boxes with graffiti. Here, he is no trouble at all, just a willing soldier, no doubt a volunteer. He turns toward the entrance, and is out the door instantly, asking Anh something that includes the Vietnamese word *nuoc*, meaning water.

"Go on then," replies Anh, or at least this is what Susan imagines he says. Anh searches the floor with the penlight once again, bending over to pick up the half-smoked butts of American cigarettes. When he bends down, he holds the back of his trousers at the same time so they do not slip. He has lost weight. All of them have lost weight, but especially Anh. He is the one who carries the largest pack. He is the oldest of the three and certainly the strongest. But even he is tired. His stomach looks as though it has been scooped out from beneath his rib cage and there is a weariness to his expression. He drops the pack on the ground amongst all the litter from the American troops, and unfastens one of its ties, fishing out the store of cigarettes, to which he adds new butts he picks from the ground. Susan hopes he will get out the remaining rice now, too, as they have not eaten since before the air raid and surely they cannot get through the night without food, but instead he pulls out some folded cloth. She recognizes it as her own T-shirt, which she has not seen since their capture.

"Here," says Anh. "Is there anything else you want?"

She has gotten used to the way he speaks French, to the almost shy manner in which he never meets her gaze. Like many soldiers he has reached a place where he does not look at a person directly unless through the sight of a rifle. She has no doubt he would kill her if he thought he needed to, and that the act would be conducted like any chore. But she is grateful to him now. She takes the T-shirt. It has the green smell of vegetation and moisture, a little like the rice which has become damp in the course of their march, but it is soft and clean. It feels like a pillow, like something she might lay her head against.

"Thank you," she says. The pack is still open, as though he expects she will take more. It seems that when he asked if there

271

was anything else she wanted, it was a genuine offer and not sarcasm. "There's some shorts," she says, hesitating. "And some underpants. I'd be so grateful—"

He takes out the remaining rice and then shoves the whole of the pack in her direction. She guesses he does not want to handle her things, now that he is recognizing that they are hers, or perhaps he is already regretting that he has offered them back to her when certainly the shorts—a pair of knee-length khakis—would have been useful to him. The socks, too, which the soldiers have taken to wearing at night to keep their feet warm, are in the pack, along with a few other items. She gathers her clothes, holding them away from the filthy shirt she wears so that they don't get soiled, then smiles at Anh, bowing her head as she has seen Vietnamese do for each other. It is perhaps more than she ought to do, the bow, given that these are her own clothes, but she is embarrassed by the state of her trousers, how she has wet herself. If there were any daylight, or even if the night were brighter than it is, the soldiers would see the stain and know what had happened. Perhaps Anh already knows, which is why he is making such a gesture in the first place. "Thank you," she says, backing away.

Minh arrives in the hut in a flurry of motion, speaking excitedly to Anh. He points behind him, then goes to the door and brings in a wooden bucket that he has found outside. It is a rusted pail the size of a horse's feed bucket. Anh runs his finger across the joins, inspecting it for holes, then nods at Minh and the boy disappears.

"Looks like we have water," Son tells her.

"I want a bath," she says. What she means is that she wants to sit in the broad tub in Marc's room, hearing the turbulent sound of rushing hot water, her shoulders resting on the porcelain's smooth surface. Or even a bath in her own room. That was merely a metal affair, stained where the finish had worn away. It was only ever possible to get tepid water, and of course you had to remove all of Son's photography paraphernalia to get to it. But even that would seem an extravagant luxury right now, like a display of opulence available only to very few in this world, like owning a castle. Marc's bathroom—how clearly she could see it now—had a high, white ceiling, decorative tiling, a faux marble floor. It would be heaven to be in a bath like that. She could imagine herself, her wet, pale, clean legs bent so that her knees shone with the light from a ceiling lamp, a block of white soap in her hand. Perhaps there would be music—from the radio or Marc's record player. She could hear Marc's typewriter keys, the flurry of metal wands, the pauses between in which she imagined him checking his notes, or re-reading the pages he had already typed, or drawing in smoke from his cigarette. After the bath, she would wrap herself in a towel, lying on the bed and feeling the sweep of air made by the ceiling fan against her wet hair. Marc would come and sit beside her, unfasten the towel, lay his hand on her damp skin. How often had they done this very thing and thought nothing of it? Nothing at all of the wealth of the experience: clean skin, sheets, hot water, food, the bar of soap, the sound of music. She imagines Son and her in that same bath, the two of them together. She imagines the broad, quilted bed, the sheets ironed like table linen, the boxy pillows, but this time with Son beside her. She should not do this, should not allow the thought. But it is there, a fixed image in her mind, because he is here beside her, smiling at her clean clothes, the ones she holds in front of her, away from her filthy body. He is pleased for her. That she will at least have something else to wear after so many days in the jungle. That she has been afforded the dignity of stepping out of her wet trousers.

There is a table up against one of the walls and it provides a kind of bed for Minh and Hien, who curl up next to each other like young brothers, fresh from their sponge baths and glad, she imagines, to be sleeping above ground, safe from the rats. Susan ties her hammock between two wooden struts, then goes outside to relieve herself. But when she returns she discovers that Anh has assumed the hammock, so she is left standing in the room, unsure where now to sleep. Anh is already asleep. The other soldiers may well be asleep, too. Nobody keeps watch any more. Just as they have almost forgotten how many days they've been wandering in the jungle, they seem also to have neglected the formalities of prisoners and guards. The rifles rest beside the soldiers, either next to them or across their chests, their safeties on.

It no longer feels as though she is a captive, rather that all five of them have come into a colossal bit of bad luck and are now castaways together. And though it is true that the soldiers do not speak to her often, that they in fact treat her as though she has no useful point of view, she cannot be sure they would not listen if she were to offer an opinion. The fact is, she has none. She can see that the hamlets they visit are abandoned or burnt or both, that the planes fly overhead daily, occasionally dropping their bombs. The American strategy seems to be one of random destruction, and against the incoherence of the attacks, the arbitrary, casual destruction of the rain forest, the razing of these small villages, she has little to offer.

Above her, she can already hear the scuttling of rats along the thin roof. A wedge of moonlight filters through the open window, illuminating the ruins of the village outside. The owners of the house planted herbs in cakes of earth held in shape by waxy leaves that make for a kind of pot, and it seems odd to see them there, set with care upon the ledge, while the rest of the village is in cinders.

"Susan," she hears. It is Son, of course. He is on the floor, sitting on his poncho, his knees sticking out of his torn trousers. "Sleep here."

Her eyes are move to Anh, cradled comfortably in the slope

of her hammock. She supposes it is only fair he gets it tonight as she'd been the one to have the clean clothes, but she doesn't want to sleep on the ground. She is afraid of the rats for one thing, and the hammock has taken on a kind of homey comfort for her. It was *her* hammock. But she is helpless to do anything now but lie on the ground like an animal. She tries to remind herself that at least she was given the privacy of washing by herself at the well, that she was able to remove her old clothes and rinse them. Here she is in fresh clothes while Anh and the others had the same dirty ones. But she might have been allowed her poncho liner. The liner, too, is now draped over the sleeping soldier, resting beneath Anh's dark arms and his rifle, which rises and falls gently with his breath.

Son reaches up, touching her hand, and she drops gently down next to him. She had always imagined that if a woman were to be captured, she'd be killed or raped or both. She never imagined the woman would be herself (if it happened at all) but one of the other journalists, the bolder ones whose words and photographs sometimes appeared in *Time* or *Life*, women who she imagined were much braver than she, and who took more risks. Dickey Chapelle was killed by a mine two years ago while covering a marine operation, and there is a photograph of her dying that Susan will never forget. In it, she is stretched out on the ground, her hand at her face, the metal of her earring catching the light. There is the long scabbard of her dagger across her bent hip, the blood from a throat wound pooling beneath her. It was taken by another photographer, a friend of Dickey's, and Susan often wondered how it was that he managed to frame the shot with such apparent dispassion. The mine exploded; the shrapnel entered her throat. *It was bound to happen sooner or later,* Dickey said. She'd been in so many wars by then; she expected one day to end her life in one. Her friend, the photographer, stepped back so that she felt the sun over her face. The camera shutter moved; she may even have heard it; then she was dead. It happened so fast, as you always imagine is the case in deaths on the battlefield.

But no women she knew had been captured. To be captured, well, that was a different thing. One expected—what exactly? A series of awful rapes, followed by an execution. Appalling, agonizing torment, then death. Once, a couple of ARVN soldiers tied a woman suspected of being Vietcong and submerged her in water over and over until finally she gave them the information they wanted. Susan knew this as fact because she saw it. She stood helplessly on the bank, willing the girl to speak, until she didn't think she could stand one more minute of watching her torture. *Happens all the time,* a guy from UPI told her. *Try not to be too upset.* The Vietcong butchered the bodies of anyone they considered traitors. She'd seen photographs; she'd seen remains. She'd heard the stories, and not only stories but the sad, awful confessions of villagers who watched.

But she did not know what they might do to a woman prisoner-of-war, to a Western woman, to her. So far, neither rape nor murder. Instead, she is going to grow hungrier and colder, sleep on the ground, live off unripened fruit and whatever can be caught: insects, frogs, the occasional monkey or rat. The slow assault on her body that began with her feet— which have not yet recovered, though she has been allowed again to paint them with iodine, and tonight to wash them as well—has risen now to her stomach and throat. She feels a scraping in the back of her mouth when she swallows, only a low-grade virus, she hopes, and not a streptococcus infection. She is sure they have no penicillin.

Son says, "I'll make room for you."

She cannot see his face. If she were able to see him plainly on this dark night she would understand at once the love so obviously displayed there. He holds open the poncho and guides her gently as though her legs are glass, not muscled and tough as they are, as strong as a man's. But this gesture, like so many

276

on his part, goes almost unnoticed by Susan. Perhaps she believes even now in the fictitious Han, that invention Son used to explain his frequent absences. Perhaps she finds herself so unattractive, living as she does among the soldiers, that the notion that he might love her is implausible. In any case, if she allowed herself to see what Son appears to be offering, she would be baffled by the way in which they seem to have moved from friendship into this mature, extraordinary dependency upon one another, skipping entirely the heady passions, the petty arguments, the great leaps of desire and jealousy and despair and hope that she has always associated with love. It is as though Son has come inch by inch to occupy the very core of her. If she looked into her heart she would find him there, but she is not thinking of such things.

"The rats," she says now. She is so tired her bones feel like lead in her skin. Son arranges himself next to her, then tucks the liner up under them both, providing some small protection from rat bites. She is aware of how close he is, how her head rests on his chest, his arms over her arms. Being so close to him ought to feel strange to her, yet it does not. He feels familiar and comforting. The soldiers, asleep, are invisible in the darkness. Minh snores softly above them. Anh is comfortable in the hammock.

"The Americans are destroying all the villages in this area," Son says.

She can hear his heart, his breath as it fills his lungs. For a moment she almost puts her hand on his bare stomach, that line of dark hair that begins around his waistband. His skin is softer than she is used to in a man and he is close to her height so that it feels as though she has been twinned with him here in the cocoon of the poncho liner.

"Perhaps they've had more luck than we have finding people," she says.

"They are certainly ruining all the hiding places."

277

"I don't want to hide. I want to be found." She hears the longing in her own voice and feels once again the weight of regret, how she wishes she could take back all the small steps that brought her here. But Son she does not regret. Meeting him, teaming up with him, being "taken in with him"—as surely that is what happened. She feels him near her and knows that his presence is the only thing that has made today bearable. Lying on the ground, listening to the rats above her, near her, hidden in the corners, occasionally rushing past the opening of the hut, would be impossible without him.

"You will be found, darling," he says now, the endearment sounding peculiar from his lips, as though he has never said anything of the sort before to a woman, much less to her. In all the time they have been together, the months of working side by side, not to mention the long, almost unendurable days of captivity, they have spoken of battles and strategies, of what size artillery was being fired where, who was in charge, and where they might get the best information or story. They talked about Operations that had code names like Rolling Thunder and Starlight, about press escorts, Task Forces, F-100s, divisions and regiments, people they knew and places—Happy Valley, Ia Drang, Cherry Hill—the very names of which held enormous meaning. They did not often speak softly to each other, certainly not as they are now. Neither of them had before used the word *darling*. He is not touching her in any manner other than to hold himself around her as he had to do in the circumstances, given the small space in which they were lying, but he might have; it would not have seemed extraordinary. They do not kiss; nor is there the feeling that they ought to, or ought not to. It is as if they have always ended their days in each other's arms, or, having been dependent upon one another for so long, they have become a single unit.

"You have hidden yourself all this time," she says now, "even from me."

There is a pause as he thinks about this. Everything they say, every small movement of muscle or skin, even their thoughts, feels slowed down, even deliberately, as though they know the delicacy of this moment, this intimacy that links them. Or as though the events of the past days have emptied them out completely so that all they can do is follow the simplest connection between them. No sudden declarations are required. They are Susan and Son, who might have been childhood friends, or brother and sister, or husband and wife, and are here now together.

Son says, "I am myself around you. More myself than without you."

"But to be a spy—? I guess you wouldn't call yourself a spy. What would it be?" Her voice is neutral, as though she is merely thinking aloud. She wants to understand him; she feels as though she has not been paying attention all these months and wishes she had been. "Nationalist," she sighs. "That's the way you would describe yourself, isn't it?"

His arms around her are loose, circling her in the practical arrangement of their sleep. He draws closer, tightening his hold by an ounce, no more, and in that embrace she realizes she has hurt him. His fingertips brush the inside of her elbow, his breath is upon her hair. He has laid himself upon her so completely, and while it is not what she seeks or needs now, it feels as though he will tell her anything, anything at all. He is waiting only for her to ask. He is aware of the situation they find themselves in. Until now, he hasn't been able to face it. She can sense, even in his embrace, how he longs to disentangle himself from what separates him from her. How much he loves her. He could describe the way in which he was selected for training, the classes that spoke hour by hour of the history of his country's foreign occupation and the need to liberate themselves from it. He has not seen his family for years. He doesn't know which of them are dead. He has known hunger and hard physical labor and all manner of discomfort, and he has never questioned the need for such sacrifice until now, with her. Somehow she knows this. She can no longer pretend she does not. His sleeping in her room, on her floor, the way he attached himself to her. He is probably thinking how it was a mistake, all those little steps that brought him to the place he is now, loving her. She knows all of it, all at once, as though she has swallowed his thoughts whole. The world around them has closed shut and a new one has opened in its place.

"Are you high ranking?" she asks. "Please say you are not."

"I am not."

"You are lying, aren't you?"

"Ranks don't really mean—"

"I knew it."

When she wakes he is gone, though not without having tucked the edges of the poncho liner under her. She opens her eyes and is startled first by the dawn light that washes over her, and next by the vision of Minh, lying on his stomach, his rifle raised, aimed out the door. His head is inches away from her and she can see the way his hair rises in odd tufts, the curl of his ear, the metal glint of a chain he wears round his neck. His sword, bound by a length of hairy cord to his trousers, lies at an awkward angle from his side. He is concentrating, the muscles in his shoulders taut. She hears Anh giving an order and then his footsteps as he comes closer to the house. It would appear at first that Minh is aiming at Anh, that while she slept some kind of insane coup has taken place. Anh stomps forward, still barking orders, then clamps his hand over the barrel of the gun, his foot inches from Susan's nose. He looks down at her as she stares, her eyes wide, unable to understand what on earth is going on between the soldiers and why it is that Minh would aim his gun at Anh. At that exact moment she hears the muffled squawk of a lonesome hen. It calls and coos, then calls again, looking for its flock, which has clearly been confiscated by the soldiers, the ARVN or the Americans, whoever it was who took the village.

Anh continues looking down at Susan. He still has Minh's rifle in his hands. Minh is speaking in Vietnamese but Anh ignores him altogether, addressing Susan instead. "He wants to shoot the chicken," he says in French. "Stupid."

He puts the rifle down on the table, then moves swiftly out the door. She hears the increasing chatter of the hen, some shuffling steps, flapping wings, the sounds louder and louder, the hen now squawking so loudly it might be crowing. Then, all at once, there is nothing at all. The silence is complete, as though someone has flipped a switch.

Or a wrung a neck, she realizes now.

They begin with the skin, which is seared by the flame of their fire and has the wonderful crackling texture of barbecued chicken. They sit on their heels, eating with their hands, pulling meat from bone with their teeth, moving the fat over their tongues as one might ice cream, savoring it. They eat every scrap of the chicken, even the brain and eyeballs, even the gizzard, sucking the bones afterwards, licking their fingers and lips. The bones are kept to make a soup, along with the feet and skull and beak. This bounty is packed away in a plastic bag at Minh's hip. Just before setting off to go, Minh holds up the awful contents, delighting one last time, and the five begin walking together through the ravaged village. It is past dawn, the day rising quickly as though a curtain is rising on the horizon, letting in more and more sun.

"Minh, go on, give it to me. I'll hold it!" she teases.

Minh smiles and makes to push away her fake grab for the chicken parts. The collection of bones might be pirates' loot, gold nuggets, a set of valuable coins from a Christie's auction. He will not part with them for the world.

"Aww, come on!" she insists.

Son joins in, too. "I'll be the keeper. Much better, me!"

"No chance," says Minh. "Then the woman will get a hold of it for sure!"

Now they all laugh. Minh races forward with the bones. The food has cheered them up. She feels as though her blood has grown thicker, her energy returning in a surge of new-found strength. She is still tired, of course. Her eyes itch and remain gritty no matter how often she splashes them with water, but she can walk now without feeling she may trip and fall, without feeling her legs are somehow disconnected, even failing. It is remarkable, she thinks, how at its most basic level, the body is like a machine. It works by fuel. It fails by neglect, or injury.

Hamlets like the one they now walk through are always so cleverly laid out, with shaded walkways created by woven bamboo, wide spaces for the gathering of the people, shaded by coconut palms. There is always a center area with its pump and well, the carefully fenced places for animals, the meticulously attended gardens. Susan has visited such hamlets before, marveling at how comfortable the peasants are able to make their lives simply by using the natural materials around them, and with none of the conveniences of the city.

But this hamlet looks as though it has been ransacked by animals. They pick their way around or through, dodging the walls of the former houses that lie half-burned among the heaped contents of households, laundry and baskets and hemp bags and crockery. In some areas, there really is nothing left, just charred patches on the ground, great holes in the earth where an explosive has been thrown into a shelter, or a fire has consumed whatever structure it was set to. There are torn sheaves, parts of wooden implements, coils of electrical wire, glass and pieces of gnarled metal. The trees are burnt stumps, sticking up from the ground like the ribs of some ancient half-buried monster. Further on, the fruit orchards look the same.

There are places that have somehow escaped the attack and they, too, stand, oddly pristine against the ruined landscape, a reminder of what used to be.

Susan is familiar with this kind of wreckage; it does not surprise her, and as always she finds herself searching for something human among it all. On the edges of the hamlet are signs of fighting, empty cartridge clips and shell holes. Whatever else occurred, there has been bloodshed. She has seen tree trunks against which people have been executed, the blood seeped into the bark, the darkened soil below. But that would not have happened here. Not this time. Here, it would have been the Americans who came and they did not execute people. They shot those who ran. They shot those who fired. Once in a while they shot somebody obviously innocent, but these cases were the exceptions—she still believes they are the exceptions, though she knows Marc does not. He says it's random. Whoever runs is killed, and mostly whoever hides is killed. And if you don't hide you are also in danger of being killed. So it would not surprise her, not at all, to find a body.

They no longer walk in the fashion of soldiers guarding prisoners. Anh leads the way with Son at his side. Minh pokes through the debris, using his sword. Hien looks sullenly at the surrounds, and then seems only to study his feet as he walks. The world has reduced itself to these few people: four young men with not enough food or clothes or medicine, herself among them.

They pass a low ditch around which are wet, ruined papers, plastic jugs of fluid, jagged pieces of burnt, melted plastic. She wonders if they are pieces of a bomb and asks Son about it. "No, those held chemicals. This was an area for photo processing, I suppose," he says.

"Photos?" She cannot understand. "Whose photos?"

"The LNA," he says. The Liberation News Agency, the Vietcong's press. She sees now that he may be correct. The area,

283

though now nothing more than a shelled ditch, would have been ringed by sandbagged walls, camouflaged from above by foliage and bamboo. The rudimentary darkroom with its photo dryers and processing trays has been destroyed, but she could see within the debris the sort of plastic that you would not normally find in such a small hamlet. There are broken containers of chemicals, unusual sheets of white that might be processing paper left half-buried in the ground. She sees that in appearance it was likely an area of quiet, indoor work. Yes, it could be a field unit for photography. To think that the VC had their own press corps, their own dedicated men cradling cameras as well as guns—of course, she knew this—but to see the evidence of it before her makes it seem all the more extraordinary.

"Were you trained as a soldier?" she asks Son.

Son looks at her, surprised, but not in an unpleasant way. He smiles; she thinks he looks almost pleased. "Of course," he says, and walks on.

The sun has not yet become so bright and hot that they need to preserve their energy. They walk with a leisurely, easy gait, almost strolling. Minh, holding the remains of the chicken, seems especially pleased. He pauses to inspect some small matter, then runs to catch up as a child might. From a distance, he might even be a child. It is only when you see him close up that you get a sense of the dense, compact muscles, the powerful, low shoulders, the solid, broad frame of him. He is handsome; she can see that beyond the dirt and the bad haircut and the awful clothes and the sheer menace of him with his gun and his sword, he is a handsome young man. Before they set off, she caught him looking at a set of photographs, small faded rectangles that showed a girl with blue black hair and a dimple in her cheek. "Is that your girlfriend?" she'd asked him.

"My wife," he replied, to her astonishment.

"A wife!"

"Aren't you somebody's wife?" he asked. It had been an innocent question and she found herself feeling tender toward him for asking it in the manner in which he had. First, because she imagined that the girl in the photographs was the only girl he had ever known, but also because, for all his superior knowledge as a soldier, he could not imagine the complicated explanation as to why she was not a wife and did not belong in that way to anyone.

"No," she said. "Not yet."

"Soon," he said, smiling in his fetching manner, the missing tooth showing a slice of his pink tongue. He seemed to study her face. "Soon you will be a wife, I think," he said.

Anh brings her a bit of wet newsprint, soggy, poor-quality paper as from a child's exercise book. Copies of the same page lie here and there like leaves around the hamlet. The wind has blown wads of them against tree trunks and what is left of the foundations of houses. Anh hands her the sheet and she sees it is a piece of propaganda, this time American.

"What does it say?" he asks.

The paper is written in Vietnamese. The sentences are short, but even so she cannot read it. "I wouldn't know," she tells Anh. "It's not my language."

She speaks in a tone as though Anh ought to have understood this. Anh's face darkens. He grabs the paper from her hands and she realizes in that instant that if you cannot read at all then all languages look the same. Vietnamese would look like French, which could look like Swahili for all that. Anh shoves the paper under Son's nose and Son explains carefully what the paper says, that it is a warning not to help Vietcong or else your village will look like this. He turns it over and shows Anh the picture, a crude cartoon-style drawing of bloody corpses and burning houses.

Anh balls up the notice, throws it on the ground. They head

north around the edges of the hamlet and Anh leads the way with fast, determined steps. The soldiers and Susan jog now to keep up, stepping around the remains of the trees, and then Anh suddenly turns back, his rifle off his shoulder, the sight to his eye. He aims and fires all at once, shooting a wad of balled paper, the same leaflet as before, which is lost instantly in the ash of the ground under a small canopy of smoke.

Minh raises his eyebrows at Susan.

"The boss is angry," she says in English.

"He's got reason," says Son.

V

He is asked over and again by the refugees for permission. Permission for more rice, to return to their houses, to receive more food or blankets or clothes. He constantly has to explain he has no authority. *Bao chi*, he says, but they don't seem to understand what he means. The words bounce off them unnoticed. He is not sure, himself, what he means any more. If, indeed, he is a reporter he really ought to be seen writing.

He gets out his notebook, his pens. He scratches a few words across the pages, but for some reason whenever he begins to let himself work through a thought (describing, for example, the absurd notion that by caging everyone who isn't VC in a camp the military might scourge the land of every trace of the enemy) he feels the same awful loss of Susan. He cannot understand how her disappearance re-establishes itself again and again inside him. Wasn't he prepared anyway to give her up? Wasn't she always going to leave, be reabsorbed back into the world, into the country he hopes for and longs for and cannot quite imagine himself now part of: America, a place that feels to him now like a large and distant planet? Once, in the cramped, windowless room that was given over to women reporters in Danang (a room into which he was not allowed but went anyway, crossing the small hallway with easy confidence as she was the only woman there), she lay on top of him in his arms

289

and told him she would not go back. *I cannot live in America again*, she said. *England is no better, not really, but it is perhaps easier to forget there.* The heat was terrible in that room, the air so sticky it felt like a hot flannel over his mouth, his eyes. The fan had broken and he'd hauled one from the men's quarters for her. For them.

He lay on the thin mattress with her above him, feeling her weight and the warm slick of sweat between them. The heat that rose in waves from their bodies was invisible in the darkness, though he could feel it, like the breath of a low fire pushing out into the room.

He thought she was talking about the war. He thought he understood what she meant by the need to forget. You crossed a line if you stayed long enough. A few months as a correspondent and you could probably go back home without a problem. Maybe longer, depending on where you traveled. But if you kept on, there was a danger, or something like a danger, that a kind of displacement set in. He nodded his head, agreeing with her. There were so many things he'd like to forget, but he did not think there was any place he could *go* now to forget. It was all tattooed inside him. He wanted to return to America and he kept thinking he would go back, but the months ticked by and recently he'd begun to think perhaps he never would. He said nothing, just nodded silently. If England were a place where Susan could forget all this, then she must go there. He'd been prepared for that kind of sudden exit, always ready for her to leave. It was part of it, part of the whole experience of being in country, the loss that swept through every corner of your life. You didn't concern yourself with what would happen after, not in the first instance. Just that there would *be* an after, that was everything.

Suddenly, Susan bolted up, off the cot, out of his embrace and the warm sleepy hold they'd had upon each other. She might have walked out of the room but there was nowhere to go and anyway she was not dressed. He stared at her, confused; he was suddenly brutally awake, blinking into the darkness. His first thought, of course, was that there had been some sort of emergency, an alarm he hadn't heard, a warning, the whining sound of incoming, *something,* anyway, that he had inexplicably missed. He was ready to grab his clothes, his boots, his helmet. The sweat trickled down his spine, his sideburns, into his eyes. This happened in an instant. He was even more confused when she said, *Is that what you want me to do?* in a fierce whisper. *Forget? Is that really what you want?*

He didn't know what she was talking about. He had to flip back to the conversation now, calm his ringing head. There was no sound of incoming, no shouting or the telltale noise of dozens of feet suddenly hitting the floor all at once.

He said, *Yes,* He said, *I don't know.* He said, *What is the matter?*

She hadn't been talking about the war. She'd been talking about their love affair. He realized this eventually, but it was too late: he'd already launched them here.

You're asking me what is the matter? she said, all the fury suddenly burned out, her voice deflated as though they'd been talking all night, when they had not. He wanted to reach out to her, but he wasn't sure even where she was standing. The room was dark enough to hide everything but her voice. He leaned over and got the small yellow flashlight from the floor. It flickered on, then off, and he shook it until the batteries settled and at last there was a spray of light. He saw freshly their crumpled clothing, the gray cement floor, her battered portable typewriter set up on a makeshift table constructed from old ammo boxes, a short stack of onion-skin paper on which she had already typed reams of single-spaced despatches. Earlier in the night he'd come in and picked her up off that chair, unclipped her hair so it fell against her shoulders. She'd been laughing. *Get off me! Stop, hold fire, desist!* He'd nestled

291

with her on the low mattress, kissed her throat, and put his face against her hair, breathing in the sweet smell of her shampoo. She was so important to him, a kind of tonic to the war; he'd put his hand across her back and lifted her to him. Such an easy, pleasant way they had with one another, but somehow it was slipping, had slipped, away. Now she slumped against the wall, dropping slowly to the ground, her bent knees hiding her face as she brought herself down to the dirty floor. *I love you,* she said. *That is the matter. And it sounds like you won't even miss me.*

He could not have her. Didn't she realize that? He felt unfairly glued within his marriage, almost as though he'd been drafted into it. And she didn't truly want a future with him; he didn't believe that. What he thought was that she had become temporarily mesmerized, but that just as surely as she would one day decide she'd had enough of this war, she would decide she'd had enough of him.

Oh, I'll miss you, he told her.

In the evening, the sun crosses the sky in a shroud of red, the birds in dark flocks sweeping above the trees. It is beautiful. The jungle provides a shadowed backdrop of fronds and tall, elegant trees. The sky is painted with reds and oranges, changing by the minute, by the second. On the ground, however, it is not beautiful. A child is sick and a dog eats the vomit, its tail wagging slowly back and forth like an oscillating fan. There is litter ground into the mud and bits of rope and broken boxes. He sees that the driver was wrong about the Keen: the refugees are more than happy to drink it. The mosquito nets have been taken away, the cups and stirs, the dry vats, everything, so the children climb the newly empty tables as though they are playground equipment. Out on the area between the refugee camp and the military base, stepping gingerly over a muddy road deeply grooved with tire tracks and boot prints, a string of scantily dressed girls in slit skirts and overly red lips make their way. They are the teenagers who spend their afternoons in a series of newly erected, barn-like buildings, sloppily laced with wires for electricity, with painted signs in English, reading "Paradise Club" and "Sexy Bar." Their shoes are altogether wrong for the terrain; they try to keep the mud from their clothes. Finally they stop, huddling clumsily together near a bus that will take them to Saigon to work. They are closed for business to the soldiers in the neighboring compound because the soldiers don't go out at night here. Too dangerous. So the hookers work the afternoons near the compound and then pile on the same blue bus that transports the young aid workers, those in their elegant *ao dzais*, so beautiful it is as though they've come from some other, better world. He watches the mismatch of girls, the dwindling line, and then the bus as it begins its precarious journey north to Saigon.

Halliday does not show up for days and then he appears all at once, driven into the camp in the back of a jeep by one of his advisors, and is brought into the command tent, where he stands before the press in a pair of knee-length shorts, a plaid open-necked shirt, and a straw hat around which is tied a bit of camouflage material. The hat he has brought with him all the way from Bloomfield, New Jersey, where it is not so hot, and where the strip of leather with the embossing of the hat-maker's name that makes up the band does not cause quite so much perspiration as it does here in the tropics. Halliday brushes his hand over his brow every minute or so. It is not possible for a Westerner to acclimatize fully to the heat of the Delta, but Halliday has not made a single stride in that direction. His clothes cling to him, his wet shirt rides up his middle. He is smoking a cigar, his lips pursed around the cylinder of its base, affecting the air of a man whose vacation has been interrupted by an unexpected local conflict over which he must now preside.

But he has missed a loop with his belt and his combat boots contrast the shorts in a manner that makes him look like an undressed army officer, not a holiday-maker. He begins the briefing by explaining he has been laid low these past couple of days with a medical condition which he delights in describing to his advisors and the assembled press as "a *real* pain in the ass"—a boil, dutifully lanced by the corpsman. "Size of a peach," says Halliday. "Lancing the bastard nearly sent me into orbit, so you will excuse me if I don't sit down."

There are about a dozen or more reporters present, looking uncomfortable in the hot tent. Some laugh nervously; others look completely bewildered by the lieutenant colonel's statement, by his casual clothing and the way he smokes through the briefing. Whereas a couple of days ago there appeared to be only Marc and maybe one or two other newsmen about, they are everywhere now. There had been a lot of talk about the success of these camps and then, perhaps inevitably, an outbreak of cholera that weakened the military's claim over the achievement. Finally, there was an enemy attack on one of the camps closer to Saigon. There had been no press there at the time; the story was nearly buried altogether, and so the press are here in force and likely, for a week or so anyway, to remain.

Marc has had enough of the camp, the refugees, the muddy, dug-up, stinking earth, the crying children, and the noise from yet more destruction of the surrounding jungle. If Halliday had been here—here at all, in the compound anywhere—in whatever state of health, boil or no boil, he feels he ought to have been told. Halliday catches his eye; it is clear he knows exactly who he is. No doubt he will make the same "medical" excuse for having made Marc wait for over two days. The thought that he's been duped for this long infuriates Marc. Standing in cramped quarters in the oven of the command tent, he is in no mood to hear about the man's ass.

Halliday, by contrast, seems in uncommonly high spirits.

"Are they feeding you well?" he says to the reporters up front. It's the same way the generals greet the troops, pausing on their inspection of the line. *Getting hot meals, son? Getting your mail, son?*

"Enough bunks for you all? Sleeping okay? Sorry about the noise, of course. We got to keep the perimeter safe for you. It's what we do, ya' know."

They've been sleeping in the compound, in quarters set aside for all the visiting press. Sleep has not been easy for Marc; it never is, but here in the Delta the bugs are even more persistent. Plus, he's been kept awake at night by the ARVN 5th Division firing liberally into the Free Strike Zones like a bunch of crazy cowboys. What little sleep he's managed to get has been accomplished only with effort and he often feels he is straining his body toward it, that he is asking his tired muscles for a hard thing. It isn't even the guns that bother him so much. It is only that he sometimes reaches a place where his body is like a stone, fixed, unmovable, while his mind carries on its ceaseless whirring. He is thinking about Susan and how many hours, then days, have passed without any word whatsoever about her. The constant worry seems to have settled over him like dust. He has grown used to it, so familiar with the discomfort of his thoughts that they seem normal to him, as when nightly he opens his eyes in the dark to find himself gripping his poncho so tightly his knuckles hurt, or when the blasts go out beyond the perimeter and his mind clicks off the gun and size before he has had time even to realize he is doing so. These are some of his acquired habits. He lies down with his glasses, water, and cigarettes beside him, always in the same position. A penlight, a notebook. He wears his socks; on a bad night even his boots.

His cot here in the army compound, once well away from others, is now crowded next to other journalists here to get their stories about what the military calls "the civilian half" of their operations. Even Murray is here. He sees him standing in the front of the tent now in loose, long sleeves, a pair of shorts, a cloth hat. He has a bunk near Marc's and he eats with the soldiers three times daily, walking around with a disapproving air since the cholera story broke (not his story, but his wire's story), and staying fairly clear of any interaction with the refugees. The refugees, of course, sleep without blankets, on the ground.

"This, what you're seeing here, is really the ARVN," continues Halliday. "I can't take credit for this, no sir. Our job is to get out and do the *military* half, find the Vietcong."

"And how successful have you been there?" asks one of the journalists.

"Oh, very successful, I'd say."

"You don't have a number of dead? Of detained?"

"Not an exact number."

"An estimate?" This is from Murray. He squints into his pad and prepares to write a figure, but Halliday doesn't give him one.

"It's not official yet," says Halliday. Murray nods, and makes a note.

There are questions about medical supplies, about food supplies, about how long they intend to keep the people here. The answers are vague, never quantified. The only number he hears is when someone asks how many hours the PA system is going to carry on extolling the virtues of the government. It seems to the reporter it is repeating itself, though of course he cannot understand the language. But it turns out this is exactly the case. There is a set message and it plays all the time, or near enough.

"Fourteen hours per day, every day," Halliday answers. You'd think he'd be embarrassed to admit as much.

The reporters are clustered uncomfortably in the hot tent, their boots sinking into the damp ground, breathing the gassy, hot air, their notebooks out. Some seem to have given up trying to get useful information—perhaps believing the lieutenant colonel when he says he will be sure to inform them of any "new developments" —others become angry, firing off questions about the "new area" to which the refugees are purportedly being sent, and what exactly is the strategy of the *military half* of the operation.

Halliday walks three steps one way, then three steps another in a cloud of cigar smoke, blustering on with no content whatsoever to anything he says. The advisors look almost as frustrated as the reporters. There are two of them and occasionally they whisper into the lieutenant colonel's ear some information, which he either does not report or cannot understand. Marc wonders if they have some actual information, something useful, quantifiable, that Halliday is failing to reveal. Of course, they will not interrupt their superior's monologue.

"I'm sorry, is this a *press* conference?" says Marc. It's the first thing he's said, the first time he's opened his mouth. He has no idea why it should stop everyone so suddenly, or why all eyes are on him now, as though he's just fired a pistol in the air or done something else suitably dramatic.

The lieutenant colonel says, "Yes, this *is* a press conference, Mr. Davis." His frustration is rising now; perhaps his ass has begun to hurt again. "But if you are interested in only one fact—that is, about the whereabouts of pretty young lady reporters who venture where they should not be—then I do not have any information for you *yet*. I can assure you our FAC pilots are looking. But so far, no sighting. Things may change, and I will be only too delighted when we ascertain the whereabouts of the two missing reporters. Does that help you, Mr. Davis?"

Halliday must have been waiting to say that for the last half-hour, Marc thinks. He also thinks of the times he has flown in the little FAC Cessnas, sitting with the pilots and looking out the windows at the yellowish rice fields, the villages nestled in the softer greens of coconut and banana trees, taking in the view of houses and paddies and roads and rivers. From such a height, bomb craters filled with water reflected like sequins, so that when he looked down it appeared the landscape was bejeweled. He has seen, too, black masses from napalm and the way the explosions of mines left long scars over the fields. He has even seen people, if they were wearing broad conical hats and standing in a clearing. But anywhere there was jungle, he saw jungle. Only jungle.

"Lieutenant Colonel," Marc begins, "are you telling us that currently you are *searching* for the two missing journalists?"

"We're looking for anything we can find, including the journalists."

"From fifteen hundred feet?"

"Our pilots are on the lookout."

"Fifteen hundred feet, sir? Is that what they are flying at?"

The lieutenant colonel nods. He isn't sure what Marc's point might be.

In the destroyed areas you would see ruined trees and scorched ground. If there were people in among all this, even in the open spaces where the jungle had been burned, the houses flattened, the villages bulldozed so that rainwater has left only muddy reddish patches, you would not notice them. The people would need to build a fire. They'd need to move and wave their hands to be seen.

"Are you looking for people before, say, applying the *military half* of your operation here? Before destroying the villages?" asks Marc.

"As you *know*, Mr. Davis, we only return fire. We do not initiate it."

Another reporter interjects. "Are you stating that all the people in this camp came from villages in which the US military took fire?"

"No, that's . . . uh . . . different altogether. Let's not confuse the conversation gentlemen. The people here are from villages we have had to shut down so that the enemy cannot use them to their advantage. We evacuate first. We only fire on Vietcong who are hiding in the villages."

"And how do you know they are Vietcong?"

"Because they run. Or they shoot at us. These are planned operations. We do not make a quick decision to destroy a hamlet or village just because we come across one!"

"Then what are the FAC planes looking for?" Marc asks.

"People."

"But they can't *see* people," Marc says. But the press conference is suddenly over. The lieutenant colonel has sat down.

Halliday finds him in the officers' mess, at one of the dark tables in the back. Marc has been at the table a long time, but he hasn't managed to eat, and he hasn't managed to get up and return to wherever he ought to be now—which is nowhere, he now realizes. Here in the mess there are some gas lanterns and a set of lights strung along loops of cable. The way the lights are set up, the loosely arranged tables and chairs, and the smell of smoke and beer and food make it feel as though a party has taken place recently, the guests now shuffling away or already home in a collapsed half-drunken state, with only the stragglers remaining. But there has been no party and the mood is anything but festive. Nobody wants to be here. Not the men, not him. He doesn't dare imagine the refugees in their camp, where there are only candles or spotlights, so the place is either overlit as though for a theater production, or shut up in darkness. He has a long, awful night ahead of him and, tomorrow, another day in this godforsaken place. He doesn't know what good his being here could do, but it is almost too awful to go now, returning to Saigon with no more information than he left with. When he looks up and sees Halliday, he is hardly surprised. He's probably come over to gloat. He notices also a

second man. The graying curls, the thin limbs and quick movements tell him it is Murray. He hasn't talked to Murray since
the riot in Saigon. He sees now there is still a mark on Murray's
forehead from that day, and poking out from his hand is a
white bandage, a splint, it appears, like a little boat for the
smallest finger on his left hand.

"Sorry about that," says Halliday. He slaps a beer on the table
and stands there, looking down on Marc. "Earlier. No need to
humiliate you, though you do give us a hard time, Davis. You
always give us a hard time." He shakes his head slowly back
and forth as though considering Marc, how awkward he always
was when he could have been useful.

"I wasn't humiliated," says Marc.

"It's tough," Halliday says. He has a match in his fingers that
he flicks back and forth, then sticks in his mouth, chewing one
end. He isn't a tall man but he is enjoying feeling tall, with
Marc in the chair while he looks down. "When it's a friend in
trouble, it's tough. But it happens. Any of us can get in trouble
over here."

Marc doesn't say anything. He is thinking what a waste it
was to come to the Delta, what an idiot he has been. He is
thinking the only way they might find Susan is by dropping a
bomb on her.

"It is hard. My men lose a buddy, that's hard. We all know
what it is like."

Marc takes a swig from his beer, looks down at the floor,
then up at Halliday again. "I don't need you to lecture me. You
can sit, or you can go someplace else."

Halliday smiles uncomfortably, then nods. "All right then,"
he says. "Don't mind if I do." He takes a seat, nodding to Murray,
who also sits. There is a beat of silence between the three men,
then Halliday says, "You've been around a while, Davis. How
long you been in country?"

"Twenty-three months."

Halliday says, "That's a good while."

Murray says, "We have a kind of joke among us at the bureau that the North Viets will be marching through Saigon and Davis will still be there with Locke at his shoulder filming them!"

Halliday interrupts. "You see, that's the kind of thing that just pisses me off, you know?" he says. He has an expression on his face as though someone is stepping on his foot. "I mean, thinking the North Vietnamese are going to march through Saigon."

"It's just a joke."

"Damned unfunny one." He tells Murray. To Marc, he says, "Davis, you've been here long enough to know what happens here. That sometimes things don't go as planned."

He wonders suddenly if Halliday is going to tell him that Susan is dead. It would make sense that he would approach him in exactly this way, let him have a little to drink—not too much—and then tell him the news. Suddenly, he is sure this is what is about to happen. He sits in his seat rigidly, waiting for what is coming next.

"What do you know? You've heard something?" he says. His heart is beating hard; he can feel it against his breastbone.

Halliday says, "We don't have anything new on the missing reporters, if that's what you're asking. I'm just saying that you've been around a while and you know the score."

Marc lets out a breath. He cannot hide what is happening inside him and does not even try. He looks at Murray and Halliday, the two of them sitting next to each other. They look like they could be brothers, but Murray is younger, in his late thirties. Marc will be thirty in two weeks, a fact that comes to mind suddenly, as though someone has said it out loud. "Is this a pep talk?" he asks. His voice is heavy. He is relieved, very relieved, but the ache that has remained inside him since Susan's disappearance is still there, will not go away, and he does not even want it to go away. As long as he feels this way it is because he believes she is still out there somewhere, that she has the chance of being found, so he does not want it to stop hurting. If it stops, it is because he knows she is dead. "I don't want a pep talk," he says now. Every part of him feels heavy, as though he has been asleep for hours, or as if his limbs are not attached to him or that he is drugged.

Halliday coughs, then presses a part of his body that Marc suspects harbors a boil, and says, "You know what, Davis? You need a great deal more than a damned pep talk. A great deal more."

Marc ignores him. He drinks his beer and looks toward the front of the mess, trying to make out if there is anyone he knows coming in, some other journalists, the guys he hung out with in the hut when he first arrived. Even Enright would do right now. He tries to regulate his breathing, his vision, his muscles. When did the physics of his own body become something he had to actively govern? If he focuses out across the room he feels better, more in control, so he looks there and waits to come back to himself.

Murray says, "There's a good chance they won't do much to her. She *is* a woman, after all."

Marc says, "In my experience, women blow apart just as easily as men do."

"I meant they wouldn't torture her."

"They wouldn't even know it was torture. It's interrogation for them."

"But they *won't*," Murray says. "They won't because she's a reporter. I mean, she could be traded, or . . . uh . . . she could write something about how they were kind to her—"

"You are forgetting," says Halliday, "that we are talking about the *enemy*. They are cold-blooded murderers. I'm surprised you don't know that by now, Murray."

"Even so, I don't think—"

302

Halliday interrupted: "You don't *think*? I'll tell you what, there's not a lot the VC *won't* do!"

"God, go back to the pep talk," says Marc. He's finding it difficult now to control himself. He issues himself a set of instructions: remain calm, look normal, sit in the goddamned chair. "How's your head anyway, Murray?" he says, trying to change the subject.

Murray touches his forehead lightly with his fingers, brushing the loose curls there. "Oh yeah, it's a lot better. Thanks for that. You and Locke, it was good what you did."

"Don't mention it."

"That was one hell of a day. One hell of a riot. That girl, you know, she died. I heard later."

Marc thinks of the young girl lying on the street, a college student not yet out of her teens.

"Be glad you didn't pick up the gun," he says.

"What gun?"

"The one the CIA planted next to you. You mean you didn't *see* it?"

"Planted a *what*? A *gun*?"

"This is bullshit," says Halliday. "I swear you guys make this shit up."

Marc shakes his head. "I wish."

"Well, I didn't see a gun," says Murray.

"No, you didn't," says Halliday.

"It's on film," Marc says. He thinks it is, anyway. There was so much confusion that day. Suddenly, he cannot remember what was filmed.

"Bullshit!" says Halliday. "Bullshit it's on film!"

For a minute nobody speaks. They drink their beer. They have nothing to add to or agree upon, nothing even to argue about. Then Halliday hands Marc a map and a little penlight that shoots a slim beam of white. He indicates a particular quadrant, focusing the beam on a section of territory to the

303

west. "We're moving out this way, covering this area here. I am *asking* them to look for her. How much good will that do? How the hell should I know, so don't ask."

"They won't hurt her, I don't think," says Murray. "It wouldn't do them any good to hurt her."

"Oh, shut up, Murray!" Marc says. He has taken too many of the tablets and his mind isn't where it should be. He can't focus on the map and it is bothering him. Everything is bothering him. Murray, for example. He'd like to hit him. He'd like to squash him like a bug under his shoe.

"I'm just trying to help—"

"Well, shut up! That would help."

Halliday is still talking or has begun talking again; Marc doesn't know which. He hears Halliday's voice: "—we've got some scout planes. Like you said back there at the briefing, it's fifteen hundred feet. But I'm trying anyway. Davis? Are you with me, son?"

Yes, he can hear him, but though he can see Halliday's mouth moving and hear the words, he cannot make the connections he is supposed to make or answer the lieutenant colonel. His thoughts have loosened from him. He is thinking about Susan and about the likelihood she is hurt or dead. Or dying. Then, all at once, he is thinking about last February when he sat in a chopper watching as the gunner went into an explosion of temper, unable to fire properly on the enemy troops below because they were carrying children over their heads while crossing a river. Children as shelter from American bullets, little trophies that guaranteed the Americans would not fire. It was almost a physical effort for the gunner to turn away from all those moving, targetable Vietcong, dozens of them there, treading through the river. You could see the soldiers' wet clothes, their boots splashing. The gunner could have taken them out in a matter of seconds, but for the children. All of a sudden, the gunner wheeled the gun and fired, shooting up the river banks. He was screaming and firing, strafing the water's edge. The children were screaming, the soldiers running through the water. *You getting this?* Marc had shouted at Locke. The children bounced along on the soldiers' backs. They were like pieces of equipment, shields of human flesh, crying, terrified. *Are you* getting *this?*

"Maybe she's already been let go," Murray says. "Could be at a field hospital. Could be—"

"It takes us a little time to get info back here," says Halliday. "We could hear at any time."

Marc is suddenly present once more, the images from the helicopter that day receding to the edges of his mind. "She'd get word to me," he says. "Somehow." He doesn't want to think about those children any more. Or about what might be happening to Susan. He doesn't want to think about Halliday or Murray or about this awful camp. The place was enough to make you crazy. On the way to the mess some brothers of the teenage hookers hounded him for dong, dollars, MPC. They tried to sell him beer, stolen from the base, a trained monkey on a chain. He found it all absurd and depressing. The whole time he's been in country he's kept on the move. Up in the sky in a chopper, or out on the flat plains with the open country flanking him, squinting into the brightness. He has always had the distance that a chopper or a fixed wing or even a jeep afforded him. In short, he'd been protected from the squalor and boredom and neediness created by war. He hates it. A siege would be a relief to him. An enemy attack almost welcome. He cannot imagine how the peasants hold up, why they don't just sink into the mud in which they've been dropped and give up. Perhaps they have.

Halliday sits back on his chair. "You don't have to stay," he says now. "We will be in touch if anything—and I do mean *anything*—"

He wants to scream, *Then why the hell did you bring me here!*

He wants to throw a chair across a room. Instead he says, "I keep hoping that somehow, by some miracle, she'll be found." His words are slow and strained. They hardly seem to come from him at all. He thinks he'd better stand up now. Stand up and walk the hell out of here before he says anything more. He reaches into his pocket for a tablet of diazepam and finds the foil empty. The camp, dark except where the ARVN has set up floodlights under which they construct yet more tents, puts him in mind of a prison. He wants out of here. He looks in the general direction of the jungle, which has been scalped back, so it is a good half mile away. He tells himself to stand up, but his legs don't obey. It is a dreadful time to be coming apart and he wishes it weren't happening in front of Halliday and Murray.

"They won't hold on to her," Murray is saying. "I wouldn't have thought. A woman, a non-combatant—"

"Stop it!" Marc says.

"Murray's got a point—"

"Stop it now! I can't talk about it!" He is thinking again about the children, how they were held like sacks of rice over the shoulders of the troops, their legs bobbing, their faces turned up to the choppers as the bullets sent the water into a foamy confusion around them. They were close enough for him to see which were girls and which were boys. One had put his hands over his ears. One had crawled almost completely over the back of the soldier who carried him so that his head was partly submerged in the water. There was a girl who clung piggy-back, crying into the soldier's neck. If you didn't know what was happening, you might think the troops were saving the children from drowning, or from the menace of the heli-copters above, from an invasion or fire or storm or other peril. But they were being used as shields. That was their only func-tion. Later, the children were found dead, shot by the Vietcong, and surrounded by leaflets claiming they'd been killed by Americans.

"You might think about taking a little R&R," Halliday says now. "You've been in some scraps. Now this. It's a burden. It's a big thing to carry."

"No R&R," Marc says. What he is thinking is that his wife would find out, that she'd come, meeting him in Singapore as they had done in the past, planning the dinners and the sight-seeing and the lovemaking. He couldn't bear it. "I don't want my wife to know—"

He suddenly finds it difficult to keep himself from talking about it, about all the things that are wrong. About Susan, about the barrage of intrusive thoughts that come daily now, not only when he is dreaming. Even with Halliday, a guy he doesn't like, a guy who has used him, he is ready to talk about anything the man cares to discuss. This is not how he usually behaves and it feels as though something dangerous has broken free inside him. He opens his mouth to speak. There will be no stopping him once he begins.

"A wife can be a useful thing at time like this," Murray says. "Heck, we all have wives—"

"I don't want to see anyone right now."

"I think it would be a good idea to talk to your wife," says Halliday. "Spend some time—"

"No!"

Murray looks at Halliday. "What about Locke?" he says.

Locke was the kind of man who stood up to film when everyone else was flat on the ground. No helmet because the rim got in the way of the viewfinder, and because he always claimed it wouldn't make any difference anyway. He crouched on the backs of trucks and tracks and leaned out of helicopters, balancing thirty pounds of camera on his shoulder. It was with Locke that Marc had been on every killing ground, and nearly every story. They had hidden together behind low walls and the corners of buildings, beneath the overpowering noise, the furious cacophony of bullets and blasts and thunderous explosions that made the earth shake beneath them. They had run in tandem, hearing the fizz and buzz of bullets beside them, dropped as though they were one at the low, hollow sounds of rocket-propelled grenades, climbed over dead bodies getting into Chinooks and once, evacuating a Special Forces camp, they'd carried a dying soldier in a poncho, both of them screaming to the guy to stay with them, not to pass out, not to die. That time filming the children on the backs of Vietcong soldiers, and later when they filmed them all dead—the little bodies like broken flowers on the ground, perfect except for the bullet holes—they had not been able to speak, nor look at one another afterwards. It was as though they had been part of that awful crime just by being there. Or that being in the chopper from which the soldiers had been running made them somehow complicit in what followed. He remembers, too, how once he'd been so badly hit by tear gas he spent a memorable quarter-hour in a taxi, streaming tears and spitting fiercely on to the carpeted floor with Locke pouring water from his bottle over his face. In his frenzy to escape the chemicals, Marc had rubbed his eyes along the upholstery of the back seat. He'd pulled off his shirt, which had been sprayed, and thrown it out the window. A block from the bureau, deciding he couldn't be stuck in so small a space with Marc, Locke had opened the door, got him out on the street, pushing wads of dollar bills through the taxi man's window, yelling at Marc they were going to the bureau now and asking him please not to strip off any more clothes.

"Get Locke," Marc says. Jesus, he needs to talk to someone and it had better not be these two. "If he'll come."

He waits for Locke's plane, wishing he could scrape all the mud off his boots and clothing, his pack and notebooks, but there is too much and anyway it is so hot he doesn't have the energy. The sky is relentlessly clear and bright, the sun so close it feels twice the size it should be. Locke comes off the plane wearing dark glasses and a hat. He is carrying his pack and camera, but also Marc's recording equipment, so loaded down he has to walk with a shortened gait. "I don't know why you've been down here, man. There's no story here," he says. He has a deeply lined forehead, a dark tan. His eyebrows, once black, have been sunbleached a rust color. He looks like a man who has lived a long time in the desert, as though he's just stripped off his *howli* and *guerba*, and has been put into Western clothes. He doesn't mention that he's been asked to come down here by Murray, possibly by others, but pretends it was his idea. "I'm glad I finally ran you to earth," he says.

He also doesn't mention how Marc looks in his dirty clothes, the scabs from insects up and down any part of him that has been exposed, the weight loss. More importantly, much to Marc's relief, there is no mention of Loc Ninh or the last conversation they had, in which Locke shook his fist in Marc's face, told him he was an imbecile—*a fucking moron* were his exact words. It is the only time they have argued. Their friendship is drawn in blood. Whole weeks have passed working alongside Locke, talking to him, smoking with him, hitching rides and traveling with him. Once or twice, Marc has had the curious experience of almost forgetting they are not the same person, so that when he looks in a mirror he is surprised by his own face. Perhaps a friendship like this can endure almost anything, but he would not like to test it again, and more than anything he's glad Locke has come.

They drive to the area where the ambush took place, this time as part of a convoy similar to the one that Susan rode with. They sit with the soldiers and smoke, riding the lurching track, waiting for something or nothing to happen. Marc takes some still shots of the area where the ambush took place; Locke films him as he describes the recent events on this road, the evacuation of villages, the movement of refugees. In the north, at Mang Yang Pass, they have defoliated the trees up to a half-mile from the road either side to prevent enemy attacks like the one resulting in Susan and Son's disappearance. Here, bulldozers have dug out huge boulevards through the jungle, though it seems less orderly than up north. There are haphazard chops through the jungle as though a giant lawnmower has gone awry. So much napalm has been deployed that the smell of charred wood saturates the air. They report these facts, or rather subdued versions of these facts, then pack up and thank the drivers, who have waited for them.

"The camp is a mess," Marc tells Locke. "You won't believe it."

"We're not going to the camp," Locke says. "We're getting a lift back, then getting on a plane and going the fuck back to Saigon."

"Why?"

"Take a look at yourself, man. That's why."

"Don't you want the story?"

"There *is* no story," Locke says impatiently. They drive for a mile or so in silence. Then Locks says, "We're too late."

"Who said that?"

"Your employer—you might remember a little thing called the network. I've been covering for you for almost a week now, Davis, but the 'flu I made up can only last so long." He runs a hand through his hair. He looks like a father, worn out chasing his teenage kid. "It's stressful, all this lying. I don't know how MACV keeps it up."

They laugh. They watch the sun lower itself like a hawk, level for level, in the evening sky. They do not talk about Loc Ninh. It's among the unmentionable facts, like the way Marc allowed himself to be taken in by the military, despatched on a useless voyage to the Delta. The scent of coal fire and warm urine that pervaded the camp is in his clothes and shoes, his hair. It has embedded itself into his very skin, so that he smells like one of the thousands of homeless. He feels almost as displaced.

They hitch a ride to Saigon, sitting among cargo. It's a bumpy, awful journey and they get out of the plane into a shower storm. By the time they get back into the city he is shivering from the cold and yet his face is dark with sun, looking like pottery left too long in a kiln. He needs to stay in a dark, cool room, possibly for a long time, drink lemonade with ice, not move for a while.

At the hotel room, Locke says, "Sit on the floor, not the bed, unless you want to pollute that, too."

"Am I allowed a chair?"

"No, no chair. Burn those clothes. Put them in a bag and get them incinerated, understand?"

"Affirmative," says Marc.

"I'm surprised the taxi driver didn't throw us out on the street. Honestly, Davis, what on earth did you step in?"

"I told you we should go down and look. Then you'd know what I stepped in."

Locke shakes his head, opens a window. Then he goes to the bathroom and turns on the tap, pouring shampoo from a bottle in order to make the water foam. He comes back in the room and slaps a bar of soap in Marc's hand. Marc goes into the bathroom, takes off his T-shirt, and stares into the bath in which a rising circle of foam is gathering. Then he returns again to where Locke is now sitting in the corner of the room in an imitation Queen Anne chair beside the high, shuttered window.

"Thank you," he says. Hands on his hips, chest out, as though he's making some kind of announcement. "Thank you, Don."

Locke notices the deep V of sunburn on Marc's chest, the sudden line where his tanned forearm meets the area always covered by a shirt. He is even thinner than usual, but he is in one piece. And he's not as nutty as the guys had warned him—the other reporters at the camp—including fucking Murray,

311

who told him Marc was making an ass of himself. *Heartsick as a puppy*. It still makes him burn, the way Murray said that. *Heartsick as a puppy. You better come get him out of here.*

"I'm waiting for you to scrub up so we can get something to eat," says Locke.

Later, in the bath, Marc hears Locke call out from the room.

"I didn't want to say anything until now," he says, "but Christine is on her way. I read the cable. Maybe you better pull yourself together before she gets here, huh? Meet her at the airport. Act natural."

His wife, Christine.

There is the sound of water against tile, a big *whoosh*, and then a pounding of footsteps. Marc storms into the room, dripping water everywhere, a towel around his waist, four days of beard growth, his teeth flashing as he yells, "Who the fuck thought *that* was a good idea!"

"Her," Locke replies. "The network told her you were sick. They think you should take some time. What should I have done? Suggest that you weren't sick at all, and that the last person you wanted to see was your wife?"

"You could have thought of something!"

Locke wipes his brow. "No, not this time. I've been dodging for you for a week, man. The bureau is, like, *Where the fuck is he?* I'm out of bright ideas."

His wife hates her name because it conjures in her mind the leathery face of a veteran socialite, some kind of country-club-going housewife whose children are grown, gone, and who has been left with bridge parties and ladies' golf.

Which is one reason I will never learn how to play either, she once told him. They were engaged then, the autumn of 1965, one brief month during which they planned a hurried wedding.

Both are great games, Marc said. He was stubborn even in

312

small things. He knew he was, and occasionally shocked even himself with his own inflexibility. Christine smiled, unfazed, agreeing with him. It was the simplicity with which she tossed off such appeals to argument that allowed her to defeat him, and he loved that in her company he could find himself unwittingly becoming a gracious, even friendly man. *You make me into someone I can stand*, he told her once late at night at the height of their romance. *Someone I might even like.* She raised an eyebrow; she had the most wonderful dark golden hair and it arched up away from her forehead in a crest. *Well, I like you*, she said.

He taught her honeymoon bridge, mostly because of the name. Fresh from the wedding, still finding confetti in their shoes. They played on the mattress in the mornings after making love. Two dummy hands. They'd thought she would have a baby then, too, which was why it had all happened so fast— the engagement, the marriage. She was ten weeks along, two days married. Her belly was just beginning to harden above the rim of her pubic bone. He admired her long hands as she shuffled and dealt. She had creamy skin, shapely calves. Her belly was a long expanse of naturally tanned skin. She was a beauty. He used to watch how people treated her, those incidental exchanges at stores, or news-stands, in a doctor's waiting room, or standing in line at the bank, and he'd see how differently they treated her, simply because of how lovely she was, how fine. When he pointed out how the world responds in a unique way to a beautiful woman, how *he* was never given quite the same consideration she got as a matter of course, she smiled and told him he was exaggerating, or imagining. *Rose-tinted glasses*, she said.

He told her she'd make a great bridge player. *It's a memory game,* he explained.

She sighed. *But I have a terrible memory. I can't even remember the order of suits, much less what's been played.* She dismissed herself like this all the time. He sensed that she had some kind of odd, almost clairvoyant knowledge of her life and its contents, as though each year had already been exposed to her, end to end, and that she'd peered into the vast plain of her years and found everything ahead of her a little disappointing. He felt at these times a need to cheer her up, urge her on, but he saw, too, that there was peace in having limited expectations. Christine did not want more than she had; she was hardworking without being ambitious, game without being aspiring. She was so beautiful. He touched her leg. He didn't want to upset her. If he disturbed her equilibrium he feared everything that made their lives together possible would come undone.

Bridge is a game of diplomacy as much as technical skill, he said. *That's why you will be an excellent player, while I will always be dreadful at bridge. I'm anything but diplomatic.*

She laughed. She'd witnessed his anger rise suddenly at the very start of their honeymoon, when at the airport ticket counter they were told their seat reservations had been lost. She'd seen his frustration at the taxi driver who had missed the hotel and circled around once more without turning off his meter, and his irritation that one of their bags had been damaged so that the handle was now loose. Little things bothered him—a shirt back from the cleaners missing a button—and those of larger importance, of principle, as when a piece of his own work was translated almost wholesale into a print story by someone else with not so much as a mention. She knew this about him. She shook her head, smiling, amused that he could at least admit his shortcomings. It was a beginning, she thought. Like most young wives, she believed she could change her husband, improve him.

Of course, my advantage at the moment is that I know the rules, he continued.

He'd been teaching her for days. Their honeymoon, which began in the courtyard of an elaborately decorated Lisbon hotel, had been mostly conducted inside the vast rooms in which they'd settled. The bed was situated so that when they woke they could feel the breeze from the courtyard, smell the lemon trees, the ebullient flowers, and hear the steady, soothing flow of water from a fountain statue of St. Christopher. The bathroom had a fired earth floor, intricately painted tiles, polished brass taps. She'd dropped a wineglass and it shattered into so many pieces there was barely anything left of it. The light, arriving in the mornings, was so lovely that they did not use the curtains. They enjoyed feeling the rising light across their bodies, opening their eyes to the dawn. The morning light seemed to celebrate her beauty as she lay in bed. Together like that, they were blissfully happy.

He took her dutifully to see the sights of the city. They ate in the recommended restaurants, tried *caldeirada*, a stew of shellfish scented with cloves, and *bacalhau*, prepared so many ways. They sat among the hand-painted plates, the delicate tiles. He did not ask himself if he would love her if she were not so beautiful. When Christine stood, she was as tall as the maître d' and everyone's eyes followed her as they found their table. He took her wherever she wanted to go—it was no trouble— but what he mostly wanted was to take in the landscape of her body sprawled across the ironed sheets.

In the evenings they had drinks in a parlor room with marble tables in which chessboards were embedded into the design. The dark furniture was thickly varnished, with velvet seat cushions in a rich mossy green that he had always associated with churches. They played cards and drank, though she allowed herself only the one drink as she was expecting. Here, too, her beauty was noticed. The mincing waiters approached, sometimes five in a quarter-hour, fawning above her so that they began to whittle away at his patience. In the end he scowled at them, and told them to please leave.

On the third night another guest, a tall, gray-bearded man

who wore a brimmed hat even indoors, invited them to play cards, share a box of cigarillos, drink from his bottle of old tawnies. Marc watched as the man flirted with Christine, taking in her long, bare arms, the tidy package of her hips in her cocktail dress, her pretty mouth which sipped tentatively at the port.

Oh dear, cards, she said, as though it were a slightly scandalous activity. *My husband has been teaching me bridge.*

The port was a yellowish brown color. She was drinking it but Marc could see she was unsure about the color. He wanted to explain to her that it had been aged so long it had lost its red hue, but didn't want to embarrass her. Instead, he took a long sip of his own, making sure she noticed this, and she then followed suit. The bearded man told them his name— Reynolds—and excused himself for a moment. Marc kissed Christine quickly before she could stop him. By the time Reynolds returned, Christine was wiping the lipstick from Marc's chin. Reynolds did not seem to notice. He had his hand on the arm of an elegant-looking woman with a high, coiffed hair-do who gazed down on the newlyweds as though on to baby pandas at a zoo.

My wife, Angelica, Reynolds said.

They sat north to south. Marc watched Christine take up her hand, looking suddenly unsure. He asked if she wished to declare, but she declined, absolutely, wagging her chin. He'd known she would refuse, of course. Had she not, it would have been the first time she'd surprised him.

He played boldly, making a double and a redouble. He drained his glass and received a fresh splash of the port. He found Christine adorable, how she knit her brow, following the game, how she trusted him as he gathered as much information as he could through his bids. Reynolds asked Christine questions—had she climbed up the grassy area on the Rua de Alcolena to see the Ermida de São Jerónimo? Definitely worth a visit. What about the Belém Tower? Yes, of course she'd seen that. You couldn't *not* see that. He asked these questions, paying great attention to the answers as though discussing matters of state. Reynolds was old enough to be Christine's father, but he did not seem so old. He had a fetching smile, a well-kempt beard. Though he had a paunch, his clothes were nicely tailored. He treated Christine—he treated them both—with a kind, avuncular air. Christine mentioned that she liked films and there was a conversation about whether a particular, quite famous actor was resident in the hotel right now. Marc didn't know who the guy was. He was enjoying his port when he felt his leg being caressed beneath the table, felt the familiar, high arches of Christine's feet gliding up his shin bone. He looked up, smiling at his new wife. Now she had surprised him, surprised him indeed. They were doing very well, he thought.

What I love about bridge, Reynolds was saying, *is that it is as much about how you relate to your partner as anything.*

I agree, said Marc. He felt her leg high upon his. He longed to reach across the table, lift Christine from the cushioned seat, bring her upstairs to the bedroom with its magical courtyard where he'd seen, just this morning, a little family of goldfinches. It was a kind of paradise, he thought. They'd somehow landed in Eden.

The game continued. Reynolds began to bother him a little. It might have been that he was just cranky from drinking. He tried to remain as Christine would have him: pleasant, tactful, easy within the company of others. He felt Christine's foot just above his knee, the play of her toe on the inside of his leg. He could almost sink into that one feeling alone. He was working out a detail of his game when he noticed the way Angelica was looking at him. She had long, arched eyebrows, shining blue eyes under their hoods of liner, an overly red mouth. She wasn't exactly smiling at him, but she had a distinct, cemented attention that made him uneasy. He wondered if she knew what was happening under the table. He thought he might somehow communicate to Christine that she should stop, that others had noticed. He sat up, but Christine's foot followed his movements, digging deeper up his leg. He looked rather desperately at Christine and realized, all at once, that she was turned in such a way that the foot could not possibly have been hers. She and Reynolds were engaged in a conversation about the origins of the name *Portugal*. Reynolds was clearly enjoying educating her in the complicated history of the Iberian peninsula, and now his avuncular arm was pursuing the brass tacks around the back of Christine's chair so that her hair brushed occasionally against his wrist. Meanwhile, there was Angelica, climbing like a vine up his leg.

He stood. *I'm sorry, I don't feel well,* he said.

Surely you just need another drink, said Angelica. Her mouth was open in a smile. She was younger than her husband; her hair had lost its silkiness but it was a nice shade of brown, forming a neat bowl at the nape of her neck. She held her own drink up, as though showing him something in it. Her eyes squinted at him, her teeth shone in the candlelight. He shook his head, backing a few paces, bumping into a bar waiter. He fell forward again, trying to come up with an excuse, bumbling as though he had drunk too much.

Christine looked at him, puzzled. Angelica rose from her chair and looped her elbow through his. *Let's all go outside. The night air is good for you. It will clear your head.*

Is the game over then? asked Christine.

Marc shook off Angelica rather too brusquely. She had to put her arm out to balance herself. Christine looked appalled. She took a step toward him, her cheeks flushed.

We're going now, he whispered, pulling on Christine, extracting her from the couple as though it was she who had done wrong.

Back in the room, he tried to explain. He sat her next to him on the bed, then turned so that they were catty-corner.

Imagine a tablecloth down to here, he said, slicing his hand a few inches from the floor. Then he showed her what Angelica had been doing, urging her to believe him.

I don't know, she said. *Maybe it was too much drinking. I can't believe Angelica would do that. I mean, right in front of me? That's crazy!*

You talk as though you know *them. You* don't *know them! They targeted us.*

Oh, no. I'm sure not—

Christine, don't be stupid.

I'm not stupid!

He was staring at you like he was going to have you for dessert!

We were talking!

I had to do something.

Well, fine. You've done something! Now, you've really done something!

She never believed him. Not the night the couple had tried to engage them in God knows what kind of affair, and not later, either, when he would speak of the ways in which the government was conning America into supporting the war. She did not believe him when he took up his post in Vietnam and wrote of what he'd seen firsthand, following the troops. Whenever they spoke, him barking down an unreliable telephone line, her voice small and light as though coming from the end of a long tunnel, ten thousand miles, the whole of the Pacific Ocean between them, he found himself getting more and more emphatic. *They stand there at the briefing and lie. About everything. About the outcome of every firefight or set piece or bombing or engagement. Nobody is winning. We* certainly *are not winning.* Either she didn't feel it necessary to add to the fire of his emotions—the bold accusations, the announcement of unsavory discoveries he made weekly and which he recorded, when possible, on film—or she didn't believe him. He began to suspect the latter was the case.

She suggested that perhaps he was being overdramatic; or that the things he covered made him slightly unbalanced in his view. After all, he could not know for certain the reasons for every military action; he was not privy to that information— none of them were. How much of what he reported was a result of how he'd positioned himself in the first place? He shook his head; he felt her responses had been given to her by someone else, a friend, a family member, maybe even another man, who had listened to her accounts of the strained conversations she had with her reporter husband and offered an alternative perspective, or at least an explanation.

That night in Lisbon, she'd maintained that Angelica had mistaken his leg for her own husband's, for Reynold's leg. An embarrassing, correctible mistake for which Marc had forsaken a potential friendship. She was disappointed because Reynolds had promised to take them all on a day-trip to Sintra. Reynolds had a car; they could all have gone together. No woman touches up a strange man's leg in a public place—Marc had made that up, surely. He'd misunderstood.

In the end, they'd chosen not to speak of it. There had developed a whole list of subjects they did not talk about and now here she was, arriving in Saigon just when he wishes she would not.

"I'm not sure it's a bad thing, having Christine along," says Locke now. "Strange as it might feel. And yeah, it will be strange." He is half lying on the chair now, looking like he might fall asleep, while Marc pushes his dirty clothes into the wrapping from a dry cleaner and then into a plastic trash bag. What he ends up with looks disconcertingly like a bodybag. He puts it in the corner by the door, smoothes his hands over his fresh chinos, and notices Locke shaking his head back and forth as though deciding on something. Locke continues, "What I want to know is what you got on prescription that you're out of now. You're sweating like a sonovabitch and, to my mind's eye, heading toward the DTs stage. Not that I'm an expert, but the word *withdrawal* springs to mind."

Marc gives him a brief, defiant stare. He's sweating, even through the clean clothes. He strips off his T-shirt, using it like a flannel under his arms, and then tosses it into the back of the cupboard. He gets a new one and puts it on, wondering what Christine will say if he sweats like this.

"You look sick," says Locke. "Not quite malaria sick, but getting there."

"I can't sleep."

"Symptom two. So, we've got sweating, insomnia—" He has his hand up in the air, two fingers out like a peace sign.

"You can add dizziness, if you wish."

"Dizziness," he says, popping up a third finger.

Marc hands him the box from his night table, empty now, all the little blister packs used up.

"Ah, yes, I should have known. Stop at the dispensary," Locke says. "Don't go near that lovely lady without first getting this puppy refilled."

Christine arrives at the airport in a cream pants suit, beautiful, well fed, with long golden arms, her wrists encased in silver bangles, holding a pretty suitcase with a jungle motif and shining brass buckles that look more like jewelry than something with a practical use. When she steps off the plane he feels he can barely approach her, cannot construct in his mind the fact of Christine as part of him, his wife, even. She has not changed in appearance, not much considering she is now six months along in the pregnancy. It is the way in which her muscles are smoothed by a healthy layer of fat, the generous outline of her thighs in the pants suit, her height—surrounded by petite Vietnamese. She looks regal, he thinks.

He looks as though his frame has been stretched, every tendon showing, the muscles in his face prominent, his ribs protruding so that he can see them even through a shirt. This seems perfectly normal to him now; he has spent so much time in the field, where everyone begins to look the same, with the same V of red against a white chest, the same saggy, sweat-stained uniforms, the same starved-dog look. One soldier Marc knew refused to carry the C-rations required for him to even maintain his weight, preferring the lightness of his pack and allowing his body to take what it needed from the minerals in his bones. That one was on his way to a medical discharge, he was sure.

"Christine," he says, the name coming slowly, a pit he sucks on before allowing it out of his mouth. He wants to say, *You look fat*, but he knows she will take this as an insult when what he means is that she looks lovely, healthy, glowing. He finds himself gazing at her as he's seen the village girls staring at Susan, some of them actually approaching her to touch the curve of her upper arm, the outer muscle of her shoulders, amazed at the strength. And Susan is tiny compared to Christine, a scrappy package in her fatigues, easily mistaken for a boy. Christine stands at the airport as though she's been teleported from some other world entirely. She, who blends in perfectly on a New York street, might have been a movie star at Tan Son Nhut. He hardly knows how to approach her.

"My God," she says, upon seeing him. "Your hair has gone blond—"

She puts her hand against his collarbone, into the hollow there. He reaches down to take her suitcase and accidentally brushes her belly with his hand. Even though he has been prepared for this, for the inevitable change in her shape, it is a shock to him. She lost the first pregnancy—nobody's fault, the baby stopped developing after the eighth week; even during the Lisbon honeymoon, it had already been dead—but this baby was clearly very much alive. He could feel the structure of her belly, the way her body harnessed its mass.

All at once Christine is flustered. She puts her hand on top of his, then says, "The doctor takes a measure every week. He is growing like gangbusters."

The airport is a mass of confusion. A flight is being called and people dash toward one of the terminals. In the midst of this rush, his hand rests on a hard mound of flesh, like a muscle flexed to its full, and he thinks he can feel the curve of the baby's spine beneath his palm.

"You look well with it," he says.

"I heard you were ill," she says. She has long, light eyes, strawberry-colored lips. He wants to tell her please not to wear any lipstick. The red makes him think of hookers. They all wore that particular shade. But he stops himself from speaking— thank God. "And nobody seemed to know where you were! The bureau was calling *me* to ask. I mean, *me!*"

He explains he'd been checking something out, down in the Delta.

"Can you believe it was snowing in New York when I left? I think you need a break from this place. A nice Christmas at home. What do you think? Marc?"

It is then that he realizes why she's here. To ensure he goes home, of course. She has been told to get him out of the country, to amuse him in Saigon for a few days, collect the exit visa, and leave. The executives in New York would never have guessed how transparent she would be. He wonders when the bureau was going to let him know he is being rotated out. They'd undoubtedly find some other job for him, forgetting that it wasn't clear he could do any other job.

"I think Christmas at home is a great idea? Don't you? Marc?"

At night he sleeps with her, or lies with her trying to sleep, his arm sometimes curled around her belly where the baby grows. His baby. It is this stranger whom he knew about but who he had not truly believed existed, this fluttering life inside the recesses of his wife's body, that stops him telling her about Susan. He feels he knows the baby, that they have met before, and the one thing of which he is certain is that its life is more powerful than his own. With the baby arrives a whole tide and expression of existence that is at once familiar and entirely, unimaginably new. Next to his sleeping wife, feeling the snug tightness of her womb pressing against the muscle of her belly, he senses the need not to disturb her, as one might feel when discovering by chance a wild bird nesting on a forest floor. He rises slowly, sitting at the end of the bed, his arms and legs folded like a religious man, like one of the Buddhist monks he sees on the streets and whose temples rise up in a kind of fairy-land beauty from mountains, or from stilts perched along glassy waters. He watches her, wondering what to do. What on earth.

She sleeps deeply, exhausted in pregnancy. He occasionally glances at his desk where the typewriter waits for him. Even if it were only to transcribe his notes or remember a particular event—a battle, a mission, a trip in convoy between cities, anything—he should be making a record. Nothing has been pressed upon him more strongly than the need to bear witness to that around him, to formulate some kind of history that might be read on its own one day or along with hundreds of other accounts, each one important in its own right. During the day he writes letters on Susan's behalf. *Non-combatant, politically neutral, British citizen.* But now the story is fading from interest. There's no print space available any more for the two missing reporters. They will say something more about them when they are found or when they are dead.

His typewriter remains otherwise undisturbed, the room itself feeling like a museum of some other time before now, before Susan went missing, before the baby. Instead of writing about firefights, taking care to get the names and ranks and home towns of the men whose stories he longs to transcribe, he spends his energy pushing away thoughts of Susan and those of the new baby, a little spirit housed in the elaborate garden of his wife's body. As long as she is pregnant, he will say nothing about Susan, though her life, too, holds him.

"What is troubling you?" he hears now. Christine's voice. So she had been awake. He wonders for how long.

"I'm sorry. What did you say?"

"You aren't . . . yourself."

"No."

"I don't see how anyone can be in this place. I keep seeing the most awful things in the streets here. There was a man, a full-grown man, defecating on the curb. Right in front of me, right in the middle of everything. Can you believe it?"

"That's not so disturbing," he says.

"Well, you *have* been here a long time! I think you've been here too long." She rises and sits next to him, her thigh resting beside his. She takes his arm, and says gently, "I keep thinking the war will be over soon, but—"

"Ha!" he snarls. "It will never be over."

"Marc, don't. There are some people in our government who do know what they're doing—"

"Who told you that?"

"Marc!"

He wonders briefly how she might couch Susan's capture, what reasonable, equitable explanation she would offer. Would Christine imagine the woman had been *borrowed*? Or that she had willingly tagged after the Vietcong as a reporter? He is being unfair. Of course, she'd be horrified. She'd lean into him, touch his shoulder, say, "Oh no, Marc, no. The poor girl. Someone needs to find her." She'd care. She was a caring person.

"There have been two reporters," he begins, "missing now for quite some time."

"Missing?"

"Taken prisoner."

"Friends of yours?"

"Yes."

"I'm so sorry."

He would like to tell her more, but of course he cannot. It isn't just that he can't tell her about Susan; he doesn't even feel comfortable talking about what has most likely happened to Son. That he is dead now, and has probably been dead for days.

"They'll find them," she says. "I'm sure they'll find them."

"No, they won't," Marc says. He watches the confused look on her face as he continues. He thinks she really is so naïve. "They aren't even looking."

"Well, *you* would know," she says, sounding cross now, fed up with him. Who can blame her? He doesn't blame her.

She abandons herself to sleep and he gets out another Valium and lies beside her, waiting. She seems to him something of an impostor, a woman replacing another. He no longer knows what to think, to feel. She is carrying his child, and the fact of this new life, of some part of himself, slumbering within the safety of Christine's sumptuous body, pleases him in a way he would not have expected and cannot express. At the same time, he wishes she would take herself and the baby back to America. He cannot, would never, say as much.

He can see her hair, slippery across the pillow. She had something done to it for the trip. And she is wearing a night-gown that loops around each shoulder with little fastenings made from delicate gold chains, a nightgown he has never seen before, wide enough to cover her bump. He wishes her gone and yet another part of him believes she could save him from what is around him—the exhausted soldiers, the dedicated, clueless officers, the nervy, hyped-up fatigue he inhabits. He has deepened his tendency to become overly annoyed at small matters—an obnoxious official, a critical telegram from his producers—so that now when such things occur they dig into him such that he can barely focus at all until he gets out into the field again and the war forces him once more to concentrate every thought, all his energy, stripping everything else away. At times in the field, he is grateful for the intense isolation that the soldiers loathe, the white heat that boils every thought away save that of water and shade. The long, bare hours during which they played cards or listened to the radio, the singularity of purpose that regulated their activities, their lives reduced to a kind of animal existence—eating, moving, resting, hunting—was often a relief. In some awful way, it soothed him. In the field he felt sane and whole; then he returned to Saigon and began once more to unravel, to throw his drink at someone whose remark he didn't like, to do everything possible to piss off an information officer. It was as though he was feeling his way toward a ledge, looking for a way of throwing himself off, even hoping he might get pushed. Maybe Christine would be able to save him from that, too, the excessive risk he both loathed and depended upon, his own manic ambitions, his anger. Mostly that. The anger has become a second head pinned at his shoulder, willing him this way, then that.

Look at her now, he thinks: asleep, relaxed, healthy, while he waits to be released to his own version of sleep, which is never so peaceful as hers.

He looks at the nightgown, which in moonlight takes on a glow, some kind of celestial drapery. She probably bought it specially for this visit with him. He imagines her moving carefully through the cool, perfumed air of a Manhattan department store, stepping cautiously beneath the store's vaulted ceilings, her heels making little tapping sounds over the polished wood, trailing her lovely fingers across the garments and tags. The thought of the care she has taken, the precision with which she tries to please him, has always tried, overwhelms him now. He finds himself almost tearful as she sleeps. He tries to imagine Susan in such a place, in the department store with the cool air, the wafts of perfume—but he cannot. He cannot think of her at all right now, cannot bring himself to imagine her face. She once left a card on his bed, handmade rice paper, in which she quoted a letter from General William Sherman to his friend, General Ulysses Grant. It said, *I knew wherever I was that you thought of me, and if I got in a tight place you would come—if alive*. She left it on his pillow before going north for a story about a hospital in which she had taken an interest. He didn't know where she'd found the quote, where she'd read it or heard it, but it touched him. He believed it to be true. Now he sits in a hotel room with his wife, who loves him as best she can, and he is stymied, unable to think or move. The card, which is not hidden, but rests with a stack of photographs in the top drawer of his desk, makes him terribly sad. It seems to him another fact, along with the careful purchase of a nightgown, that he finds heartbreaking.

He wakes Christine in the morning. "I'd come home with you," he says, "but you don't want to know everything that has gone on here."

His face is wet. She sits up slowly, taking in this fact, wondering why he has a wet face, then realizes he has been crying.

"Oh, darling, what? What do you mean?"

And so he tells her. He tells her about Susan, about the ambush. About where he has been, sent around like an errand boy this past week by the US military. He tells her, too, of the fighting and the dead bodies and how he was once speaking to a man who was suddenly shot dead in front of him, blood emerging on the man's tongue where there had been words. He tells her that he cannot sleep normally and that he lives hour by hour with the help of tablets. He sweats so much the room seems to fill with his smell. He gets up and splashes cold water on his face, then comes back to the bed and continues his confession. He tells her everything, laying it out the way he had once long ago laid out a bridge hand, explaining what the cards meant, and what you could do if you held such a hand.

"You should divorce me and start again," he says, then glances at her belly. "Of course, you can't. I've messed up all your choices. Everything."

But Christine has her own stories.

"It's not your baby," she says. She speaks in a measured tone. It is all very difficult for her, but she carries on. "It's . . . someone else's. I was going to tell you, I promise, but they begged me to get you home and I thought, How else can I get you to come? If I told you it was another man's, that I'd been with another man! Why would you come with me then? You'd never come!" She pauses; her hand claps over her mouth, but the words have a momentum now. They come faster, more information than she'd planned. "Ask Don! I rang him when they told me at the bureau that you were practically on a suicide mission out here. I didn't want to get on a plane. I didn't want to come to this dreadful place pregnant! I mean, really—! But I did what I was supposed to because they told me to come. I thought, It's my duty. We are all asked to do something, aren't we? For the country or for our men."

"You want me to answer that?"

"You had to know!"

An awful silence reverberates between them. The words they've spoken, made in the sweep of the moment, are too great. It is too much for Christine, who bursts out finally, the emotion rising in her throat, "Good God, don't look at me like that, Marc! You've been here for how long? For practically the whole of our marriage! And it isn't as though you were drafted— you could have come home! You could have! But you never—" she struggles now "—you never *wanted* to."

"I'm not looking at you like anything," he says. He doesn't know what he's doing. He's thinking how much he wishes he were that other man, the one who put the baby inside her. Not because he loves her, but because he would like to have been the sort of man who *could* love her. And who would be a father

329

and a husband, rise each morning and kiss the children and come home to a house of laughter and the mild, pleasant stories of the day. But he has reached some conclusions about himself of late, and he is sure he cannot be any of those things for her or for any other woman. Not even Susan.

"Does he want to marry you?" he asks.

She nods. "Yes," she says. "More than anything."

VI

She searches out a particular tree that produces a heart-shaped fruit that reminds her of a spiny pear. The leaves of the tree are glossy and dark at the top, but yellowing and a different shape altogether at the base, and they smell. The tree stinks so that it is an act of faith to eat anything that comes from it. The first time she ate one of the fruits it was Son who brought it to her, pushing his thumb into a soft end where it had begun to rot, and pulling it apart. The flesh of the fruit tears away like that of fish, and it has a bitter taste so that she grimaced the first time she ate it. But she needed no encouragement. She ate the entire thing, working her way around the dozens of pearly black seeds, the musky smell notwithstanding, the act of chewing itself a mercy.

The fruit appears on any part of the tree. At the top where they cannot reach are always the best choices, but the thin stalks at the head of the fruit can appear at the tree's base, too, growing right out of the trunk. It is a difficult thing to extract the fruit without being speared by the unfriendly outer layer, though Minh always manages to do so easily enough. Son, too, has a similar talent for denuding it, but Minh's hands are like those of a steelworker, the calluses so thick they stand out on the pads of his fingers and palms. Even at rest, Minh's hands curl at his sides as though he is holding something. In the coolness of this early morning, she sits beside him, studying his palm as he searches it for a splinter from the fruit's robust exterior. She thinks that his brown fingers, the chafed rigid skin of his palm, the blocky muscles of his thumb make his hand appear like the tool of an ancient civilization. He catches her looking, and they smile at each other. He might be the younger brother of a friend, or a schoolmate from several years below for whom she has some small affection. He thinks she is hungry so he gives her the fruit he's been peeling, then returns to the splinter. When she cannot manage to extract the rind, he lends her his knife—one of his knives. He is a bastion of weaponry, Minh, a collector of sharp objects. Nobody worries she will use the knife for some other purpose, to kill or wound, to force her way to freedom. The most freedom she could have right now is with the soldiers, which is to say there is nothing but this: the jungle, the vines.

Everything they do, they do while walking. While walking they look at the map, chat, smoke, eat, even cook, though there is no more coal for the small pot that chars insects as they travel, so they use shaved bamboo that smokes and flies up out of the fire, sometimes into the face of the one carrying it. Hien pokes his finger into the flame now, then licks it, tells the others something she cannot understand, perhaps that they had better shoot a monkey or kill one of the large jungle rats that roam the forest floor, because he is tired of living off bugs.

"What is this thing called anyway?" she asks Son, meaning the spiny fruit with the mysterious creamy flesh. The fruit is neither sweet nor refreshing, seems always to arrive rotten in places and completely unripe in others, with only a sparse area between that is even vaguely tasty. He answers in Vietnamese and she says, "No, the English word."

He shrugs; she has stumped him for the first time.

"Okay, what did the French call it?"

"They called it . . . uh . . . " He has no idea. "They didn't call it anything. The French would never have eaten it."

She laughs and now Anh wants to know what the joke is, and so Son explains it to him. But Anh is too serious to laugh and he doesn't know enough about the French to understand their particular enthusiasm when it comes to food. He looks at Susan and repeats the Vietnamese name for the fruit, and she nods.

"Say it," Anh instructs her, and she does her best. "You're among us now."

He indicates to Minh to walk in front. The person who leads must watch most carefully and this job frequently falls to Anh. But Anh wishes to talk now to Son, and she trails behind the two, unable to understand the conversation that flows easily between them. Behind her, she can hear Hien's footsteps. He no longer seems angry with her, only oddly subdued. He walks with his narrow head nodding like a horse at plow. Every once in a while he wipes his sleeve across his face and squints into the jungle. She suspects he needs eyeglasses and that part of the reason his face is full of unpleasant expressions is that he is forever trying to work out what is in front of him.

She is prodding a tree for more fruit, Son beside her, Anh waiting impatiently ahead, perhaps wondering why they all had to make so many concessions for the English girl. Minh is stabbing at an ant with his sword; Hien is drinking from a bottle, his long neck tilted back so that it shows the cartilage of his throat. Time is full of these little pockets. The night before, at the well, while washing by the monochrome light of the moon, it seemed she reached her foot only after a whole hour of wringing the swatch of cloth that had once been her shirt. She pushed it down the long planes of her thigh, the round skull shape of her knee, the tight flesh of her calf, while behind her the shadow of her body was like that of a lean Egyptian. How long had she been there? She did not know. She discovered each cave of peeling skin between her toes, the gritty ledges of calluses, the rubbery mounds of blisters, her mind completely given to the act of washing, as now it is given to that of picking fruit.

The soldiers, though impatient, are watching her now as she stretches the canopy of her clean T-shirt with found fruit. They did not watch her at the well. That had been a time carved out for her alone, a gift from them. They had even offered her the small flashlight, though she had refused it. *I'll see by starlight,* she told them. *I'll kick away the rats.* She once read that the art of survival is single-mindedness. She thinks now she would agree, though of course there is also luck.

Suddenly, she hears machine-gun fire. The sound pierces the jungle so abruptly that at first she is unsure what she is hearing. Then Son grabs at her sleeve and pulls her down. She drops the stick she was using to prise the fruit from the tree. What she has already gathered, collected in the belly of her shirt, falls like dice upon the jungle floor. She is frozen as though any movement from her, even a single breath, will break her apart like glass. As chattering bursts of machine-gun fire continue, she manages to turn her head toward Son, who is facing in the direction of the battle, as they all do now.

She whispers urgently. "Who is it? *Who is it?*"

In her mind, she has entertained a great number of rescue scenarios—stumbling upon LLRPS with their ration cans on a starry evening, finding a convoy of supply trucks going along a discovered road, seen by a medevac pilot who plucks her from the floor of the jungle like God's own hand, or saved by a paratrooper who glides gracefully toward her beneath his vault of silk. She has even entertained the improbable scenario of being found by a few roaming reporters, skirting the edge of a battle. This last way is her favorite fantasy because, of course, she does not have to figure out how to identify herself before getting fired at. She's never quite figured out how that would be done. In these scenarios, too, she is always on her own. For some inexplicable reason her daydreams do not include Son or the three soldiers; just herself, finally pulled from danger.

Now that the real prospect of discovery and rescue are at hand, however, she isn't sure what to do. The fighting continues. Son takes her hand. The soldiers have their rifles out and have assumed positions behind trees, though they are still far away from the firing. It is instinctive, the way they take cover. At Anh's signal, they run forward through the jungle. As always she finds the prospect of running toward gunfire appalling. She has to force her body forward toward the sounds and the only thing that makes this possible is the thought of being left behind, which is more frightening than the battle.

The jungle's dense network of trees and vines, of wild bamboo and low, shaggy bushes, provides some insulation for sound, but can distort it, too, so that it is difficult to tell exactly where the fighting is taking place. She can hear far in the distance the *whump-whump-whump* of helicopters. The Americans are flying in from the north, and she wonders if they are undertaking the same sort of operation that resulted in the burnt hamlets. If so, there will be no great battle. The helicopters will move in like an army of bees, each flying in the turbulent stream of the chopper ahead. They will unload their men, then zigzag into the sky once more, rising and rising again in increments as though on a pulley. There will be a loud-speaker from one, circling the hamlet or village with announcements in Vietnamese that the people must not run away or they will be shot. The village will rock with tremendous explosions and all around the periphery chopper patrols will wheel, spraying the terrain with bullets.

They reach a line of rubber trees where it is easier to see. She has become deft in her sandals so that she is able to move almost as swiftly as in boots. She fears that they are running directly into the line of fire from the choppers, but when at last they pause she can hear only one or two sets of rotors, not dozens. Ahead, filtering down into the clearing, are the shapes of Vietcong spreading out among the trees. She can see them in dark trousers and shirts, in floppy hats and bandanas, moving so low in the brush they might be pumas.

Anh and Hien are in a heated argument. Hien points to Susan as he yells at Anh. Anh pushes him, then shouts into his face as though trying to send a message straight up his nostrils. She points in their direction, signaling a question to Son, who shrugs, then listens hard.

"Why are we going *this* way?" she says, but he shakes his head for her to be quiet; he is trying to hear what Hien is now saying. The conversation had better be important. She wonders why it has to take place right *now*.

Son says, "Because they believe that's their unit. They think they've found them."

"Good God, is it?"

Son gives her a look of confusion. How would he know?

Hien and Anh may come to blows. Meanwhile, Minh is crouching behind a tree, calling back to the others. Then all at once, Hien storms over to where Susan is hunkered down at the base of a tree, grabbing her by the arm and dragging her forward. She lets out a small cry and tries to jerk away from him. But his grip is fierce, made stronger still by his determination. Son interferes and Hien brings out his dagger from a scabbard on his shoulder so fast it is as though it has jumped into his hand. When Son takes another step forward, he puts the blade to her throat. "Don't," she whispers. She thinks she can feel the presence of the blade against the skin of her neck. "Don't, please," she says, talking to them both.

They are interrupted by distant shots and now they are running again, Susan being pulled along by Hien. Son is yelling behind them and Susan repeats what she hears from Son in Vietnamese, though she has no idea what that is, of course.

She imagines Son is begging Hien to let her go. If she is unable to take cover it will only be a matter of time before she becomes the recipient of a rifleman's fire, as however far forward the shooting is, it is inevitable that they will reach the killing zone at this rate.

But it is clear the soldiers care first about getting to their unit, this more than anything else, and whatever value her life has to them pales next to the opportunity of being back with those they have trained and fought with. They progress even as the company of Vietcong are being pushed back, deeper into the rubber plantation. She can see ahead a dead Vietnamese on the ground, almost in a sitting position, his body bent as though searching for something in the leaves, the exit wound in his back large enough to put your fist through. Another just to his left is doubled over in a stream. Still she stumbles and jogs forward with Hien pulling her. Little Minh, his rifle ahead of him like a probe, slows to a walk and moves with the precision of a cat toward the other men in his unit, calling to them. They've come upon a clearing of tall elephant grass ringed by tangles of wild bamboo. The Vietcong are spread out, taking cover where they can. Minh settles among them. She can see his shining hair, the rugged thick shoulders, the sword beside him. He was always so proud of that sword. Somebody calls to him and he answers in a voice like a high school boy shouting to his friends. For one spectacular minute, he enjoys the feeling of having come home again, even if that homecoming arrives with the onslaught of American guns. He is smiling; he calls to another man, who gives him a look of such surprise that Minh bursts out laughing. And then, in a moment that seals itself in her mind, she sees his arms pull out from his sides as though he is beginning a dive, his chest forward, his neck arched. At once, he is thrown up in the air, his spine bent inward, his sword flying from his side, still held by its cord. Nobody expected the shots to come from behind. The

Americans have managed to enclose them in a vise, and now are attacking from two sides. She hears screams all around her. She is on the ground, hidden among the elephant grass, the sound of machine guns roaring in her ears. Hien seems to have forgotten all about her and he crawls in the direction of Minh. She would like to go, too; she would like to believe the boy is still alive. But she cannot bear to witness what she is certain to see, his chest blown apart, his face a bowl of blood.

She lies still in the elephant grass, containing the terror within her as one might try to contain an explosive. When Anh rushes past her, crouching low, head down, she can see the determination on his face, the pulsing artery at his neck, the effort of his moving under fire. She cannot help but admire him. He is a leader, a thinker. All those days ago, almost a week now, she wondered who it was that argued for her life. It was Anh, she is now sure of that. He understood that a reporter was a useful bargaining chip, that to deliver her back eventually to the arms of her people may mean that the Vietcong would be favorably described in the press to the people of the country, of the world. He was not simply a plain soldier, unaware of the larger political arena in which he fought; in this way, among so many other ways, he was different from Hien. She would like to think, too, that there was a deeper reason why he would not kill her, why he treated her well: because the war had not sucked out all his humanity, had not emptied him the way it did so many soldiers. He is Anh, not just a man with a gun. And when she hears the sound of Anh's body dropping into the grass not far from her, she hopes that it is only that he is taking cover. Automatically, she crawls in his direction. Inching along the sharp blades of grass, the motionless air scorching her cheeks, she thinks he is only hiding, he is only doing as she has done. She is almost certain this is the case, that he is not wounded, not dead. She sees first his sandals, his feet, his thread-bare, filthy trousers, the plain collarless shirt

340

he has worn for so long it shines with the oil of his skin. It is all right; he has no obvious injury; he is taking cover as she is.

"Anh! Anh, are you okay?" she asks. She calls out, too, for Son. But neither man answers. She moves closer to Anh and sees now that something isn't quite right with his head. The outline seems flattened, with an unnatural shape she does not recognize. Looking now, she can see he has a head wound. Leaking from a hole below his ear are the frothy rivulets of brain matter mixing with dark blood and shards of skull. She looks away, feeling her breath leave her all at once. She thinks of how he stood in the dim moonlight of the night before and handed her back the shirt she now wears, how he tried not to appear friendly and yet performed the most thoughtful of acts. The contents of his skull spill out on the dry grass. She wishes she could see him again in the moonlight of last night; she would like to say thank you once more. Not just for the shirt but for everything he did for her, that he tried to do, once he found himself saddled with her. She gulps in air, feels a wild rush of panic. His face is distorted, blown outward in a grotesque mask that she cannot recognize, his open eyes covered in dirt. She thinks, not for the first time, that life and death are too close to each other. She begins to cry and move away from him, then freezes because she is afraid even to move.

There is no sign of Son and, of course, he has no weapon. She has the awful feeling that he has not survived, that none of them will. They have come all this way only to find themselves stopped in an instant. She hears helicopters once again and now the strafing begins. The bullets will land with such density among those hidden in the grass that there is no hope. She will die among the humming insects and the flies that already gather at Anh's head. She knows she must find some way of protecting herself. She cannot sit and wait to be killed, and so she pulls herself back to where Anh lies, and in one, terrible effort, turns his body over so that he covers her, his chest toward the high white sky, the oozing of his wounds pooling at her neck. She closes her eyes and hopes the shield of his body will protect her from the bullets above.

The spray of bullets lasts only a short time, only an instant, but during that time she feels the ground being pumped with them, the sound unlike any she's heard before. Never did she imagine she would come under attack from Americans and she cannot understand how the war has carried on as long as it has, how the communists have lasted this long, if this is the manner of an American assault. By the time she pulls herself out from beneath Anh's corpse, calling out to Son, hoping by some miracle he is alive, her heart beating so hard she can feel her whole head swelling with its pulse, she thinks she would almost rather die than continue with this level of fear. She feels Anh's blood on her neck, the gray matter like a slow-moving slug. It has attracted insects which she swats away in a sudden, hysteric frenzy. Then she vomits and spits and pushes her face into the ground. As the sound of choppers recedes and still she cannot hear Son, she thinks he must be dead, and the thought of this causes her to cry out, as though struck by those same bullets that lanced the grass around her, perhaps even entering Anh's body, though she does not look. She crawls over to the body once more, finding it covered in flies, and takes the rifle she does not know how to reload. Then she wonders who on earth she thinks she is going to shoot. The Americans? Certainly not. The Vietcong? She drops the rifle and sobs, balancing on her hands and knees, moving one way then another, like some blinded, terrorized animal. She has a sudden, unaccountable image in her mind of Minh holding up the plastic bag containing the chicken parts, the beak and skull and feet and bones. He looks so triumphant, standing with the bounty, his sword curved behind him like an eighteenth-century general, his jack o'lantern smile making him so young. He is dead. Anh is dead. She believes Son must be, too. She begins to feel hazy;

342

she is going into shock. The screams and cries of dying men ring out around her, but she cannot hear any more firing.

From the corner of her vision she sees the trees send forth a shower of sparks, hears a rush of fire from napalm, and then the curling, burning grass. A minute passes and eventually there are voices. They are not far away and they sound American. She might be imagining this, but she can hear their footsteps, place their accents. She hears the rustling of elephant grass and then, all at once, a pain in her side. She thinks at last a bullet has found her. Well, it is not surprising, the same sentiment expressed by Dickey Chapelle. *It was bound to happen sooner or later.* She cries out and looks up to where the sun floats above the sharp grass. There above her is a cloud of faces, the barrel of an M16, somebody's arm pointed toward her, a .45 right in her face.

"What the *fuck*?"

"Who the fuck are *you*?"

"What the fuck are you doing out here?"

The pain in her rib is not from a bullet but from the boot of one of the soldiers. She was kicked, whether deliberately or by accident she will never know. Later she will find a bruise like a sunrise. For now, she can barely feel the pain, she is so tuned to everything outside of her, these new soldiers looking like monuments above her, moving like gods.

There is blood all down her front from Anh and it takes them a second to see that she is American and that she is a woman. One of them calls for a medic. "Where are you hit?" she is asked.

"I'm not hit."

A large lieutenant kneels beside her, the cords of his neck standing out, the sweat from his brow running down his face, the adrenaline pumping through him. "Explain to me what the fuck is going on!"

"I'm a reporter." The lieutenant says nothing and in her

confusion she thinks perhaps he doesn't understand her. "Press corps, *un correspondant, bao chi*—"

"I know what a fucking reporter is!" he says. "But we didn't come out with any reporters!"

"No, no, you didn't. We've been lost. We've been—" She digs into her pocket for her MACV card and hands it over. She begins to cry so hard she can no longer speak. She wants to tell Son that Anh is dead. That she has seen Minh fall and that she thinks he must be dead, too. She wants to ask him if Hien has survived, though she doesn't care about Hien. She just doesn't care. She puts him out of her mind, gets up, kneeling in the field of grass, the sun pressing on her skull, black smoke from the napalm billowing up to the clear pale sky. The lieutenant lifts her up and she sobs into his field jacket and feels the deep hollow of his breath when he roars to his radio operator to get a chopper down here. There are wounded and dead all over the place; and would they please get a fucking chopper down here now.

When she sees him, it is through clouds of dust and the localized hurricane that is always created by the rotor blades of incoming choppers. At first she does not recognize him. It is as though he has been disguised by those around him, the American soldiers who, even if they allowed him to get to his feet, would be almost a foot taller than he, and who have pulled his shirt off his shoulders and drawn it like a tourniquet around his elbows, holding his arms in position. His wrists, too, are tied. In the crazy wind his hair is flattened as though someone has poured water on it. He crouches in the dust with his knees by his chin, sunken beneath the tall frames of soldiers who stand over him as guards. In this way he has been made small and insignificant. She stares as though into a sudden bright light, knowing him and not knowing him, wanting nothing more than to cross the flapping leaves, the flying debris, the stones and twigs, branches and broken fronds, to come to his rescue. To untie his arms, his hands, to lift him up from the American soldiers, her own countrymen, who she is at once grateful to and terribly afraid of. More than anything, she is glad he is alive.

She watches him, unsure what to do, and then, all at once, he turns to her quite deliberately, as though he had known she was watching all along, and meets her eyes. His face is puffy. He has a cut on his cheek and someone has hit him in the mouth. It reminds her of when she first met him, first saw him in Pleiku at the 18th Surgical. He'd had a puffy lip, a hairy line of black stitches. She sees in his face a mixture of sorrow and longing, maybe even regret. He seems so sad there, helpless among the enormous Americans. The Americans are involved in some sort of radio operation, trying either to contact command operations or get the status of others searching for more wounded and dead in the bush. They hardly notice Son, squatting at their feet. And he, for his part, seems unaware of their presence except as a force that keeps him bound. He is focusing entirely on Susan now. She looks at him and she cannot think what to do or what he is asking her to do, as surely this hard, determined gaze is for a purpose. She'd asked him all that time ago: when they were captured, what would happen next? *Then what happens?* she'd said, the question posed in case, by some miracle, they were allowed to walk out of the jungle. And he'd replied, *It is up to you.* She hadn't understood then what he meant, but she does now. She must do something—that much is clear to her. But she finds herself slowly, almost imperceptibly, moving her chin back and forth, still looking at Son. She doesn't want to cross this line but she knows, even as she stands there shaking her head, that she will.

The same lieutenant who picked her out of the elephant grass and who has held on to her MACV card is still not convinced about who she is and what she was doing in the jungle. He suddenly strides over to where she stands and barks, "Who the fuck is *he*?" pointing now to Son.

She might say he is a spy. She might explain the whole matter to them, or try to. But she sees Son, the gash on his face from shrapnel making a long comma from his cheek-bone to his chin, a bruise above his eye. He is bleeding, struggling to keep up with a soldier who pulls him up and moves him out of the way of another helicopter that is landing. He stumbles in the dust, shouting in English his name, his occupation, the date and place they were ambushed. But nobody is listening. The soldier pushes him forward and tells him to shut the fuck up.

"I asked you a question!" shouts the lieutenant. He looks at Susan, then Son, then back at Susan again. She can see him making the connection.

"He's a photographer," she says.

"He's not a fucking photographer!"

"He works with me!"

"How about right quick you tell us what you know about this prisoner before we get a couple of guys to find out *for* us?"

To beat him, she realizes. Maybe to kill him.

"His name is Hoàng Van Son. He just told you that!"

"So what is he?"

"A photographer! I've told you!"

The lieutenant shakes his head, steps closer to her, and yells right into her face. "He was found with a weapon two yards away from his dead comrade! So don't tell me he's just taking snapshots for the local paper!"

So Hien is dead, too. She is not surprised.

"Get him off the ground," she says now. Her voice rises as she continues, "Get that tape off him! Turn him loose! Turn him *loose*!"

She pushes past the lieutenant, running to where Son is, but she's quickly stopped by a couple of the GIs, who hold her so that she cannot move, not an arm or a leg, not even to turn her head.

"I can prove it!" she says between clenched teeth. Then, in a moment inspired perhaps by some long-ago advice given her by her father, she tells them who her father is, his rank and standing. She shouts this information and demands they let her go. She is so convincing that for a moment it is as though her father is still alive, that she could phone him at a moment's notice.

It works. They release her all at once so that she stumbles forward, nearly falling. Then she rubs the places on her arms where the soldiers held her and goes to a stack of Vietcong bodies that have been dragged out of the field, the lieutenant following her.

"What do you want with them?" he says, nodding at the dead. "They've got nothing to say."

Some of the bodies have already been stripped of their gear—their weapons now collected and leaning against a log, their small packs in a pile. There is always so little from a Vietcong—a gun, a dagger, some rice, maybe a P38, the tool used to open American ration cans, maybe some grenades. They travel lightly while the Americans are weighed down with all manner of packs and sleeping gear, C-rations, entrenching tools, radio equipment, medical supplies. She hopes to see Anh's pack there among the captured supplies, but she does not. She scans the bodies lying near by, piled like rotting fish in the hot sun. Some are missing limbs. She can see clean bones jutting out from ragged, bloodless flesh. She can see the open mouths of chest wounds, whole sections torn away. Some are missing heads, feet, hands. Almost all of them are nearly naked, their clothes having been blown away or burnt. The napalmed bodies are the worst of the bunch. She cannot bring herself to look.

347

"One of the dead VCs has a pack on him with Son's papers inside," she says.

"Which one?"

"I don't see him. Maybe he hasn't been brought in yet."

"They're mostly here now."

This is what she must do for him, one of the things. She must work her way through the dead men, find what he needs her to find, lie for him. It is the beginning of a series of compromises she cannot at this time imagine. She holds her hand over her mouth and nose, approaching the bodies, which are already graying, no longer looking anything like the people who once occupied them. She has to kneel to see the ones at the bottom, brush the mud off the face of another. Her eyes fill, her stomach lurches. Sometimes she finds it difficult to focus, to look for the thing she needs to find, the person. Her eyes connect with a bit of scalp, the pulpy end of a severed leg. She needs to focus on the faces; she needs to find the pack. But the sight of the dead—this close up, in front of her and around her—the fluids that pool around her feet, is all too much. She pushes one body off another and the torso goes sliding to the ground so that she almost screams.

By the time she finds him, she is retching every so often between breaths. Anh's head is a hollow cave, his body attacked by red ants. She has to turn, then look again, over and over in little windows of sight through which she searches for the pack.

"There," she says, trying to get the attention of the lieutenant. "There he is."

"A dead VC. So what?"

"He has the papers. He has Son's . . . he has the other reporter's papers."

"Oh yeah?"

"They took his papers from him. From both of us."

But the lieutenant doesn't move and he doesn't ask anyone to help. What did they expect her to do? Haul out Anh's body

348

herself? The pack is beneath his left arm, pinned by his elbow. She has to remove it to get to the contents. She leans over the body, her face near his shoulder, and pulls with a clumsy inefficiency you'd never see in a soldier. The pack doesn't come away, so she has to reposition herself and try again. On the third attempt she manages to get it, the canvas blackened with blood, one of the straps missing. She steps away from the bodies with it in her hand, shaking. The pack looks like a museum piece, a bit of wreckage from some distant time. She unbuckles it and finds her arm smeared with blood from the sodden canvas. She can hardly bear to reach into it, but she does.

It must be that the lieutenant has taken pity on her because she is joined now by two soldiers. They flip Anh's body, going through his pockets without any of the difficulty she had in handling the body. They find her yellow flashlight, her plastic comb. Meanwhile, she picks through the contents of the pack, a feeling of relief flooding through her as she recognizes the last bit of rice they carried, a water bottle, the map. Everything is covered in blood. Blood on Son's cameras, her socks, on the pack straps and fastenings. At last she finds some papers, among them the documents verifying Son's status: . . . *accredited to cover the operational, advisory, and support activities of the Free World Military Assistance Forces, Vietnam.*

"There," she says, showing Son's MACV card to the lieutenant. She gives him the camera, too, and tells him he can ask Son what was on the last roll of film. The lieutenant takes the papers and camera over to his captain and they stand in a cluster discussing what to do. Suddenly, the wind is immense; everyone crouches as a chopper pivots, hopping upon the ground; the gunners fire upon take-off, terrifying her, and she wonders, Why bother shooting? The Vietcong soldiers' unit, that elusive group who they have chased through the jungle now for so many days, are either stacked here dead or long gone. Any survivors would have dispersed, evaporating like deer into the surrounding wilderness. You won't find them, she thinks, as the choppers lift into the sky. Not out there, not a chance.

What happened later stays with her, following her always like a man in the darkness with a candle and a map. That she came rushing to his side like a loyal dog. That she never stopped to consider the dead men on either side. Literally, the American dead at the other end of the temporary landing zone, not stacked as the Vietcong were stacked that day, but arranged in a neat line of three. There were Americans holding dressings over their wounds, waiting as a chopper inched its way down, its nose bowing to the left, to the right, looking like a toad might, if it had wings. Two of the GIs were on stretchers. Another sat on the ground, his legs held out uselessly. One had a lot of blood where his knee should have been. Another had passed out but was being held up by a buddy. Kids out of high school, younger even than herself; she had not considered them. Or how complicated a single lie could be.

She found the papers. She rinsed off the blood with water given to her by a private. She told them to untie Son and, remarkably, they did.

They were brought to MACV, separated, not even allowed to change their clothes until after they were debriefed. Her clothes stiffened with dried blood and sweat; her hair matted in clumps. There was salt on her skin, at the corners of her mouth, grit in her hair, dirt so deep in her skin she would have to scrub for weeks to get it off.

I'd like some clean clothes, she said. *I'd like a shower.*

She was promised both these things, but first they had some questions for her. She sat in a windowless room in her rancid blood-stained clothes. The questions were delivered without any emotion, her answers recorded by a stenographer who pointed his long nose into the keys and typed with two fingers. Did they rape you? Did they tell you where they were going?

350

Did they ask you for information about the movement of American troops? Did they take advantage of your being a woman? Did they hint at where their headquarters are? The questions came and came. She wished they'd ask her something she could answer with a yes.

They did not ask whether Son was a spy. Maybe it did not occur to them, but they did ask how it was that they'd convinced the Vietcong not to murder him.

We told them we would give them good press if they released us, she replied. *And anyway, they were too junior to kill either of us. They needed to bring us to their superiors. But they couldn't find their unit.*

Again and again this was brought up. They couldn't find their unit. They were looking for their unit. The hamlets were destroyed; there were no people. No sign of their unit.

On the field that day, just after the battle, it had seemed more complicated than that. At her insistence, they let Son go, lancing all at once the strong tape that held his arms so that he had sprung forth like a ball, tripping over his own feet before falling once more. That had been on purpose. They did not help him, but let him struggle up, then stagger forward. He was bleeding from a mouth wound and he spat fiercely on the dry ground, then marched up to the officer who held his press credentials.

My MACV card, he said, putting out his hand.

You'll get it.

You have no right to hold on to it.

I have every right. You're still a suspected Vietcong.

What grounds?

My grounds!

Do you not read the newspapers? Two missing journalists, it must have been reported—

You saying you are one of them?

I am.

Well, you're going to have to prove it!

She came forward. She told the officer who they were and that she was going to be writing the whole thing up, including the manner in which her colleague was being handled. He had shown his papers and according to the US government those papers were all the proof he needed. That was true, indeed. But there was more to it. The lieutenant glared at her.

We'll see about that, he said.

The papers were vital, but she was his proof. As they rode out on the helicopter, finally leaving after all this time, looking down at the burnt field, the husks of ruined trees, the battle and all its leftover debris that suddenly disappeared beneath them, she realized they had gotten away. Somehow, miraculously, they had lived. She looked out over the flat, water-logged earth and saw shrines between dense clusters of jungle. She saw Buddhist graves like stone bedframes, the steeples of Catholic churches. They passed a base, the sun shining off racks of gleaming cylinders, a bomb dump organized in revetments of 500-pound bombs lined up as neatly as cigarettes in their cases. She didn't dare look at Son.

Later, while waiting to be driven to MACV, she whispers, "What were you doing, then? They said you had a gun!"

"Trying to stay alive. Like you."

"You're not part of us—"

"I'm on your side. *Yours,* Susan."

"You shouldn't have asked me to lie for you."

"I *didn't* ask you!"

It was true. He had never asked her for a thing.

He glances over his shoulder, making sure nobody is listening. "Please, I need to talk to you—" he says.

"You want to know what I'll say, don't you?" Her words rush out. She doesn't know why she is talking like this and yet she feels incapable of stopping herself. "You want to know whether I'll tell—"

He interrupts her. "Do what is right," he says. He looks at her steadily and she reads in his eyes that he means it, that he is ready for whatever might happen. "That is not what I want to talk about—"

"Yes it is! Please tell me that it is. Please tell me that it is the only thing. That you want me to lie for you. Please ask me, please tell me that I have to! Or else, or else—"

She starts to cry. She has no idea why. She cries until a corporal notices and tells Son to back away. "Back right the hell up," he says.

At MACV, they are separated for the first time and it feels to her almost as though there has been a physical incision, a cutting away. It surprises her how difficult it is to be separated. In all the days in the jungle she never realized how much she would hate this moment, when things returned to how they were and she was a person on her own, without him.

It always sticks in her mind, how at MACV, in the dingy light beneath the low ceilings of a windowless corridor, he turned abruptly as though she didn't matter to him at all. And how she held on to that little bit of hallway where they parted, not wanting to go. "I may not want to see you," she had whispered to him. She didn't know what else to say. It didn't sound like the truth, and it wasn't. "I may not want to see you until this sorts itself out." And with her words he turned away as though cornering a sharp bend, and went.

What nonsense. Until *what* sorted itself out? she thinks later. His allegiances? The war? Why had she sent him away like that? Because she was going to lie. She knew it as surely as she knew her own name. She was going to lie and make sure he went free, because there was something between them she did not understand, was too young to understand. He would stay with her, would always stay with her, like a tiger stalking her from half a mile off, never near but following, so that she couldn't settle or stop or rest, or call her life her own. It angered her. That's why she said it. *I may not want to see you*, the exact opposite of what she wanted to say. She was *afraid* she would not see him, not in a few hours or a few days or a few years. He was being torn from her. It didn't matter what she said; he was going to leave and she had no choice in the matter. No choice. She could not bear it—that was the truth, but she hadn't been able to tell him. And what difference would it have made if she had?

Marc hears about it in the most sparse manner. A radio broadcast from a handheld transistor perched on a bookshelf in the bedroom, the words waking him from a drug-induced sleep: *have been found . . .*

He is at home; not the apartment he had shared with Christine in the city but at his parents' house, in a bedroom he occupied as a boy. The walls are cornflower blue. The window overlooks a small yard ringed by a chain fence. His mother's old dog is outside under the bush with a bone. His mother is in the next room watching the six o'clock news, another newscast about the war. He hears the words on the radio, the words *have been found*, and knows in an instant that Susan has reached safety or is dead.

He rushes into where his mother is, puts himself in front of the television, standing in front of it and jumping in place. He is wearing boxers and a T-shirt and his movements are like those of a marionette. "Did they say anything about the two missing journalists!" he shouts. "What did you hear?! What did you hear?!"

His mother drops her sewing. He runs to where she sits and takes her by the shoulders. He is scaring her to death, but he cannot stop himself or lower his voice or drop his hold upon her. "Did they *say* anything? Did you hear *anything*? It was on the radio but I missed it. What have they said on the TV? What have you heard?"

354

He rushes to the telephone. He wants to talk to her; he's got to talk to her. He's got to know what condition she is in, what has happened, every knowable fact.

But he finds he cannot dial the phone. He is crying and he can't move the dial all the way around; his fingers don't hold it long enough. And anyway, he can't think which number he ought to call. She is so far away from him, a day in a plane at least. He has to get on a plane. He has to go to Saigon. And then he has the terrible thought that maybe she won't want to see him. All he can think is that he's got to get a flight, and that he cannot dial the damned phone. And that the words *have been found* can refer to bodies, not people.

Outside somebody is raking leaves, somebody is driving by in a car. The dog barks, a porch light goes on. His mother stares at him, her mouth open. The television is showing footage of a demonstration in Washington. There's no mention of reporters, dead or alive.

Tonight there is no rain and the dusty air smells of pepper and fish-heads, of flowers and garbage. Neon lights break hard colors against the pavement. A sound like thunder confuses the senses, a storm of artillery. She thinks how inside her tiny room the plaster is breaking away, splattering on the floor.

It is a relief not to be squinting, or ducking beneath the pressure of the sun, but moving along a paved road, feeling the space around her instead of the close, clinging, sticky green. In these streets, she has come home grateful even for the ugliness of Saigon. She passes the charred husk of a burnt-out car, a broken bicycle, denuded of its wheels, its frame bent in a forty-five-degree angle. She passes a mound of stinking garbage, the wispy remains of an old basket.

No police, no MPs, no armored cars with their load of guns. If near by there are the usual criminal gangs, the cowboys on their Vespas, she does not hear them. Between the harbor and the airport, new tanks and cannons are banked along Hai Bai Trung. On Tu Do Street the taxis and pedicabs have collected the GIs who stream out of bars at curfew. She stands in a street that is quiet, unusually empty. The buildings are missing plaster, some have boarded windows, but the elegant, sagging balconies, the pleasant tiled roofs, the iron railings, speak of a different time, when the French tried to make their homes here and Saigon was called the Paris of the East. She admits that, at night, particularly on a pretty night like this, you do not notice the peeling paint or the bombed façades. Everything is hidden in darkness or behind the long, lazy branches of the trees lined up along the avenues, but it is a long way from Paris. The small acts of arson, the larger calamities of bombs, the constant stream of people and noise, the corrupt, inhuman police, teenage whores in run-down bars trying to be American with names like Texas and Florida, make Paris a distant dream.

She thinks of all the times she's run into other journalists arriving back into the city in their muddy fatigues, their hair standing up, the dried sweat forming wavy, concentric circles on their field jackets. They stank and they didn't care that they stank. They were drunk and didn't care they were drunk. There was a heady exhaustion that followed you back from the field, kept you moving until the film got off to the network or the cable went through. She has been swept along on that same cloud of exhaustion and spent fear, but tonight she has no story she wishes to file, no place she wishes to go. At MACV they gave her some utilities that don't fit her, a pair of shower shoes. They kept her clothes—she has no idea why. She wants to tear off her clothes and burn them. She wants to hide in a hole in the ground. Instead, she stands outside her hotel, a place she wasn't sure she'd ever see again, waiting until the time is right to step silently through the narrow set of doors, past the yellow-lit reception.

Normally, there would be Thanh in the office, doing his paperwork beneath a halo of flapping moths, or sitting quietly, as he often did, watching the tiny twelve-inch screen television that only got a military channel. On nights like this, he would wave to her, his smile like a banner across his face, speaking Vietnamese to Son, who always translated discreetly for her. *He says we look like criminals,* Son would whisper as Thanh sat on his chair, his hand opening and shutting hello, always so welcoming. *He says he could smell us from two blocks away.*

She never knew whether to believe him, or whether Son made up any old nonsense just because he didn't like Thanh. Thanh disapproved of Son, thinking of course that he was scrounging off a paying customer, which she supposed he was.

Tonight, she waits until she can see the light in Thanh's room. And then, before he returns to lock the half-dozen deadbolts he sees to every night, she skirts through the entrance. Her hurt feet make her even more careful; she kicks off the shower shoes and picks her way barefoot as though through fire. She has only minutes before he comes for the locks. The hotel at the other end of the street was half-destroyed by a bomb, deadbolts and all, and there are balconies all around the old, colonial-style building so you could climb up if you wished. Even so, Thanh attends to his locks, as much out of superstition as anything.

In the same way, perhaps for no reason at all, it is important to Susan that Thanh not see her.

In the front pocket of her fatigues is one single dry smokable cigarette. She remembers her editor telling her that smoking kept the bugs away, kept mosquitoes from flying into your mouth. On a sticky evening in Danang, when they were both getting bitten alive and had run out of DEET, Marc had put a cigarette in each ear and one between his teeth. *If this doesn't work, I'll light my head on fire,* he said. She'd have done better by lighting joss sticks, the incense that the women dried along the road in clusters that looked like spiny flowers. She had learned from such women to wear long sleeves, wide hats, and loose pants, to cook so it produced plenty of smoke. But the cigarettes were easier. Now she moves up the dark staircase, not wanting to make any noise, focusing on the fact that in a few minutes she will have the comfort of her lone smoke. She had watched the soldiers, particularly Anh, how they moved on their toes like ballerinas, twisting so as to leave even vines undisturbed. The Americans have heavy packs, seventy, eighty pounds, while the enemy has his body and his gun. She recalls the soundless, splendid economy of their movements. All three dead, she thinks, dumped into a mass grave, or doused with gasoline and set aflame. She stops her thoughts right there. No, she tells herself, and concentrates on the floor beneath her feet.

The steps turn at a small landing where a standard lamp is set on a timer. At exactly twelve, the lamp will go off and the hallway will plunge into darkness. The long-term occupants all have flashlights or kerosene lanterns (difficult to find and highly valued), or make their way down the hall by match fire. Once, she watched some sad, pathetic young American kid stumble down the hall by the light of a bong he was sucking. You could hear the water churning at the bottom, see the glow of the bowl reflected against the walls. She pointed this out to Marc, who rolled his eyes and reminded her to get a new hotel. *Anything but this*, he'd said.

There is the glow of a quarter-moon outside the window. When she hears a noise from one of the rooms, she stops. She waits until she hears only the inner workings of the hotel, the drone of the air conditioning, the buzz of Thanh's television. Until only these sounds drum in her ear, she stays still. She should have come home during the day, she decides now. She should have insisted upon it.

Finally, she makes her way down the dark hall to her door with the letter E5 on it in gold marker that is meant to look like brass. She feels a strange sensation in her chest, a kind of longing. Part of her does not want to open the door and find her clothes in their place, her books and her typewriter, her little metal pencil holder, her stack of notepaper and her stained coffee mug. She doesn't want to see Son's tidy collection of chemicals and processing trays, his clothes and bird-cages and tea-making things. The Son and Susan that occupied the room no longer exist. Until they were separated at MACV he continued his own fierce defense, angered at how the Americans detained him, while she sat dismayed at his sheer bravado, and marveling at how he knew she would not tell. The lieutenant's words keep ringing in her ears: *He was found with a weapon two yards away from his dead comrade, so don't tell me he's just taking snapshots for the local paper!*

She keeps asking herself: who was he planning to shoot?

She opens her room door, expecting to see the clutter and dust, the dead plants, the cracking paint on the window frame, a new infiltration of roaches. But inside it is tidy. The spread is smoothed out along the mattress, her clothes are in their drawers, tucked away. It appears someone has swept it, making the small space seem more expansive than it usually would be. The blind, too, has been drawn, so she knows somebody has been here. Then she notices the bird-cage is gone. Son's clothes, too, are missing from their spot under the chair. She turns immediately to her left, opening the bathroom, and discovers that it has been returned to its former self, no longer kitted out as a darkroom. Even the wire, which once held all the images Son worked so hard to process, is gone. He beat her here. How remarkable. The only thing he has forgotten is his map, the fairytale map of Vietnam that makes it look like a land of golden eggs and friendly giants. The map is still above her bed. And, too, she sees he has left a bottle of iodine on her nightstand, the same one that had been in Hien's pack. It is remarkable that it survived the battle, she thinks, and that he brought it here. He has even polished that glass. Did he think she would not be able to find her own medicine? Not look after herself at all?

She sits on the bed, then she stretches out. It feels so odd now to be lying on a mattress, to be in a room on her own.

So he's disappeared, she concludes, like all the other people she has met over the months in Vietnam. They come and go, as though through an invisible door. She should be used to it, but she's not. She will tell Marc all of this and he will help her sift through it so it makes sense, she thinks, forgetting in her sleepiness that she cannot tell him anything, not a word about Son, which means of course that she cannot see him. Not really. War is a consuming fire; it blasts through everything, every relationship. She has learned this.

But right now she is too tired to remember about secrets. She has not even noticed yet what Son has left for her. In the morning she will discover a sheet of thin paper, like the sort used to wrap pork rolls, resting beneath the iodine. The cap, which was already damaged and did not fit properly on the bottle, is so loose that when she moves it she spills some of the iodine over the white page. A word appears. She watches it emerge on the paper, unsure at first what is going on, feeling as though there is a ghost in the room. Then she gets some cotton and rubs the whole of the sheet with the iodine. A letter unclothes itself, sentence by sentence, until it reveals itself fully in her hand. Of course, it is from Son.

She reads the letter in the quiet of her room, suddenly missing him so much that it feels like a wound opening across her chest, making it hard to breathe. She has so much she wants to ask him, but also to say to him. She thinks of how they curled up together that last night and how it felt—it really did feel—as though they were one.

You can do anything with rice, the letter says, *even write a secret message to a loved one! I have left for the place on the map (go look).* She glances up at Son's map and sees a tiny circle with two dashes for eyes and a smiling face, located just beside the city of Hanoi. *I have much to thank you for, dear Susan. One day, when our countries are not at war, I hope you will come back to be with me, or that you will consider letting me come to you! Yes, a proposal*

of marriage, written with rice starch, a first! For I will always love
you, and have always loved you. If you do not hear from me, it is
not because I have forgotten, but because where I am I cannot write
to you, though always I am writing to you in my thoughts, telling
you what happens each day until a time, I hope, when we can once
more have our days together. You must promise me to leave the
country now. Yes, leave Vietnam! If I had paper enough and rice, I
would explain more. Believe me, please, you must go. Leave before
Tet. Tell Marc to leave, too. And Locke. Yours always, Son.

The message waits for her all night as she sleeps. It stays with her, hidden in the lining of a hat box when she packs for home, remains part of her for ever, like a tattoo or a scar. As the year ends, and she indeed departs for America once more, she wonders at times if he pretended everything—their friendship, his love for her—all for the purposes of the war. Always the war. He is smart enough to know that, if he stayed in Saigon, she would eventually have to let someone know, even after everything they had been through, and everything he had saved her from. She would not tell in anger, but because she was someone who yearned for truth, who did not feel comfortable with that which is hidden. And because, too, they kept sending her countrymen home in boxes. He is smart enough to understand all that, and therefore to slip away, not to write to her again. With time, the urgency to reveal him diminishes. It almost becomes irrelevant. There are moments, however, when she swears she will find someone who will listen to her and she will tell who he is, for surely it must be told. After all the stories of battles and deaths, of torture and loss and hatred, someone should tell this one, too, about a man who moved among them, who seemed to love them. But he has left her little to say that matters or is newsworthy. The facts seem to erase themselves, like footprints in snow. The clever man. Such a clever man. She cannot, with certainty, even remember what he ever confessed to have been.

ACKNOWLEDGEMENTS

Although I have taken liberties where it suited the storyline of *The Man from Saigon*, I have tried to remain faithful to the general history of America's war in Vietnam. I am indebted to those whose books, photographs, websites, films, documentaries, and stories described for me the extraordinary events that took place during the war and its impact on people across many nations.

The characters in this novel are fictional portraits with a few notable exceptions. Georgette Meyer "Dickey" Chapelle was a famous war correspondent and one of the pioneering women in this field. She died from a shrapnel wound while traveling with Marines and her last words have been recorded in many places, including my novel.

Kate Webb, whose work is mentioned in the novel, was a respected journalist working in Vietnam and other war zones throughout her lengthy career. I am grateful for her account of her capture, along with several other journalists, in "Three Week Captivity", which makes up a chapter in *Women War Correspondents 1961–1965* by Virginia Elwood-Akers (NJ and London: The Scarecrow Press Metuchen, 1988), and also appearing in *War Torn: Stories of War from the Women Reporters Who Covered Vietnam* (NY: Random House, 2002). Ms Webb's captors took her shoes as well as the shoes of the other journalists and herded them barefoot through the jungle for nine days before, eventually, releasing them unharmed.

Cathy Leroy was one of the most famous photojournalists working in Vietnam. Her essay, "A Tense Interlude", which appeared in *Life Magazine*, February 16, 1968, details her own day with the Vietcong during the Battle of Hue and helped me deliver a more historically accurate portrayal of such circumstances.

Several newswomen were, in fact, taken captive by the North

Vietnamese at various times during America's war in Vietnam, though none of them in the same manner as my fictional character Susan Gifford. In addition to Kate Webb and Cathy Leroy, there was also a brave young woman named Michele Ray whose vibrant account of her own three-week experience as a captive of the Vietcong in her memoir, *The Two Shores of Hell* (London: John Murray, 1967) makes for extraordinary reading. I was delighted to embrace Michele Ray's opinion of Saigon restaurants and am grateful for her description of setting off booby-traps in military training grounds, which introduced me to such an idea so that I could put my character through the same type of experience. Her account of being in underground bomb shelters during American air raids also helped me evoke some of the terror of such an experience.

I am indebted to Hugh Lunn's insightful and moving memoir, *Vietnam: A Reporter's War*. Mr Lunn covered the October 1967 battle of Loc Ninh and I drew from his account of the battle and its effects on those whose homes were destroyed. His portrayal of the press conferences in Saigon and the military's excessive use of an acronyms influenced my own portrayal of such events.

I drew from Jonathan Schell's beautifully written book, *The Village of Ben Suc*, in describing the conditions for refugees in Vietnam during the conflict. Descriptions of the squalor and food shortages, the bewildered people who had lost their homes, the ever-present public address system, the endless erection of tents and the way prostitutes boarded buses for Saigon in the evening are all drawn from facts observed by Mr. Schell, whose writing forms a rich history of the entire conflict. *The Village of Ben Suc* is part of a three-book collection called *The Real War* (NY: Pantheon Books, 1987).

I am very grateful to Keith Walker's *A Piece of My Heart: The Stories of Twenty-Six American Women Who Served in Vietnam*, a striking book from which I was able to draw material for the scenes that take place at the 18th Surgical Hospital in Pleiku. I am indebted to the accounts of daily life portrayed by the extraordinary and admirable women interviewed in Mr Walker's book. I have incorporated into my novel some of the facts of working in a military a hospital as they describe them. However, it is important to say that I have taken some creative liberties and invented practices when it suited the storyline of my book. For example, to my knowledge no patient in real life was ever handcuffed as described in my novel.

I am deeply appreciative of Hilary Smith's astonishing memoir, *Lighting Candles: Hospital Memories of Vietnam's Montagnards.* Though my novel's portrayal of a hospital serving the Montagnards as well as the portraits of characters within it are a product of my imagination, I have drawn from Hilary Smith's real life experience as a nurse in a hospital that served the needs of the Montagnard people during the war and am indebted to her in this regard. I have based some of the nursing procedures on real procedures as described in her book and some of the conversations between the staff in my novel were inspired by reported conversations as described by Ms Smith.

I have been inspired by Tim O'Brien's work and am especially grateful for his excellent memoir, *If I Die In A Combat Zone* (NY: Broadway Books, 1975) for what it taught me about mines, particularly Bouncing Bettys, as well as being out on night patrols.

My thanks to Joe Galloway for his advice on cameras and his permission to use facts about film from his work, *A Reporter's Journey from Hell.*

Thank you to Mr Twining, whose purchase of a character name for the benefit of the charity Autism Speaks enabled me to give a character the same name as his wife, Tracy Flower.

Many thanks to James Robison who offered his advice and support early in the project as he has done so often during my writing career, and to Whitney Otto whose insights and suggestions transformed my approach to the early chapters.

As always I am indebted to my editors, Nan Talese and Clare Reihill, who have guided the novel so brilliantly.

And finally, for all of those whose work has enabled me to write such a novel, who lived or fought or worked in Vietnam during the war and who have recorded their experiences so faithfully, I am full of admiration and gratitude for everything you have taught me.

Marti Leimbach
February 2009